"Hey, Billy. Can you come? Margaret needs a ride home."

"Yeah, sure. You guys done for the day?"

"Yep. Happy Friday, huh?" He nodded to Margaret. She was a good friend, a good boss, a neat person, and he liked being helpful.

"Oh, it is, isn't it?" Billy chuckled. "I was pretty lost in this article. You want to do something? Go out to lunch? Down to the waterfront? Or the market?"

"Sure, but Margaret says that there's a bad storm coming, so we need to plan for that."

"Bad enough we don't want to get caught out in it?" He could hear Billy moving around, getting ready.

"She's hurting real bad, Billy." Too bad.

"She needs to be less stubborn about taking stuff when it gets bad. I'm just locking up now. I'll be there in two shakes."

"Thank you, Billy." His lover was like his hero, really.

"Anytime, love." Billy made a kissing noise and then the phone clicked off.

"He's on the way, huh? We'll take you home."

"Thanks, Tanny. You two are good eggs."

He flapped his arms playfully. "Bawk, bawk, bawk. Let me clean up and you wait."

She patted his hand. "I'll tell Billy you deserve a reward."

He grinned, kissed her temple, then got to work. He loved his job, his life, where he was. It made him happy.

This is a work of fiction. Names, characters, places, and incidents either are the product of the author's imagination or are used fictitiously. Any resemblance to actual events, locales, organizations, or persons, living or dead, is entirely coincidental and beyond the intent of either the author or the publisher.

Snared
TOP SHELF
An imprint of Torquere Press Publishers
PO Box 2545
Round Rock, TX 78680
Copyright © 2009 by Sean Michael
Cover illustration by S. Squires
Published with permission
ISBN: 978-1-60370-874-6, 1-60370-874-X
www.torquerepress.com

First Torquere Press Printing: December 2009
Printed in the USA

The Hammer Novels

Bent

Forged

Spoken

Found

Snared

Snared

Snared
by Sean Michael

www.torquerepress.com

Snared

Chapter One

"Tanny?" Margaret's voice always filled up the room when she talked. Always.

"Yeah, boss?"

"Don't forget that Sunny's book needs to be done today before you leave."

"It's already done and wrapped up, Mags." God, it felt good to say that.

"No shit?" Margaret came over, limping a little; her arthritis was getting worse.

"Swear to God. Are you okay? Is there going to be a storm?" The spring had been brutally stormy, with mud slides and everything.

"Yeah, there is—I'd bet the house on it. And look at you, finishing up so quickly." She patted his arm. "You're not going to need me much longer."

"Bullshit. You're the expert..." He still needed her.

"And you're sucking up to the boss. I like it." She gave him a wink and settled down onto a stool with a sigh. "It's going to be a bad one. You should get home before it hits."

"Yeah? Do you need help getting home? I could call Billy."

She took a deep breath and then nodded. "If it won't

be too much trouble, I think I just might take you up on that."

"I'll call now. You sit." Poor love. He hated that she hurt so bad. He grabbed the little cell phone Billy'd given him and called home.

Billy's voice was warm, soft when he answered. "Hey, love."

"Hey, Billy. Can you come? Margaret needs a ride home."

"Yeah, sure. You guys done for the day?"

"Yep. Happy Friday, huh?" He nodded to Margaret. She was a good friend, a good boss, a neat person, and he liked being helpful.

"Oh, it is, isn't it?" Billy chuckled. "I was pretty lost in this article. You want to do something? Go out to lunch? Down to the waterfront? Or the market?"

"Sure, but Margaret says that there's a bad storm coming, so we need to plan for that."

"Bad enough we don't want to get caught out in it?" He could hear Billy moving around, getting ready.

"She's hurting real bad, Billy." Too bad.

"She needs to be less stubborn about taking stuff when it gets bad. I'm just locking up now. I'll be there in two shakes."

"Thank you, Billy." His lover was like his hero, really.

"Anytime, love." Billy made a kissing noise and then the phone clicked off.

"He's on the way, huh? We'll take you home."

"Thanks, Tanny. You two are good eggs."

He flapped his arms playfully. "Bawk, bawk, bawk. Let me clean up and you wait."

She patted his hand. "I'll tell Billy you deserve a reward."

He grinned, kissed her temple, then got to work. He loved his job, his life, where he was. It made him happy.

He'd just finished up when Billy came into Rainbow Artists, saying hi to Catherine, who was working the register, and then coming on back. "Hey Margaret." She got a kiss on the hand and then Billy was coming toward him.

Tanny had a smile for his lover—a real, honest smile—and Billy was hugging him.

His chin was tilted, Billy taking a warm kiss. "Hey."

"Happy Friday." So good.

"Yeah. You, too." There was a gleam in Billy's eyes, a certain tone in his voice.

Margaret chuckled. "You two have fun indoor plans for the weekend? The weather's not going to be fit for anything outside."

"Uh-huh. We do." A wicked grin settled on Billy's lips. Uh-oh.

Tanny felt his cheeks heat and he ducked his head, his bangs falling forward. "You ready to go?"

Billy pushed his bangs back, half of them getting tucked behind his right ear as the rest fell forward again. "I am. Margaret?"

"Yeah, just give me a minute to get moving. Once I'm started I'm good."

"I parked right out front."

He offered Billy another smile and gave Margaret his hand.

"Oh, thank you, honey." She leaned on him to get up off the stool, and it was slow going the first few steps before she evened out.

He waved to everyone and out they went, Margaret heading right for the car. The sky sure looked clear.

Once Billy got them into traffic he looked over at Margaret. "You sure about this storm? This is about the nicest day we've had in a dog's age."

"I bet you a million dollars." She shook her head. "The joints don't lie."

"That would be a sucker bet. I haven't known you to be wrong yet."

"Well, then." She winked at him in the mirror, then poked Billy in the arm. "What're your plans for the weekend?"

This time it was Billy who met his eyes in the mirror. "Stuff."

"Oh, excellent. It'll be a good weekend for it."

Chuckling, Billy nodded. "Yeah. If it's really bad, we'll be able to have a fire. It looks so pretty glinting off Montana's skin."

"Billy! God."

Margaret just laughed.

Billy glanced back, smiled at him, eyes still twinkling.

Tanny just... He. Well, shit. "I'm not nervous."

Billy glanced at Margaret and winked. "Does that mean I'm doing something wrong?"

"Absolutely. You need to work harder."

Billy chuckled. "When it comes to Montana, I'll work as hard as I need to."

They both laughed and Tanny shook his head, turning to look out the window. They just... God.

Billy pulled up in front of the house where Margaret lived in with her lover. "You need help going in, Margaret?"

"No. No, I'm good. Get home, the rain's coming."

"You sure?"

"Thank you, but I can do it."

"All right, Margaret." Billy leaned over and gave her cheek a kiss. "Have a good weekend."

Tanny nodded, got out of the car, and helped Margaret out. She patted his cheek. "You're a good boy, thank you. Have fun this weekend."

"You call me if you need anything."

"Oh, I'm not going to interrupt your weekend with Billy." She chuckled, patted his arm, and headed up the walkway.

He watched her make her way to the door, before trotting to the car.

Billy smiled as he came into the car. "You off the clock now, love?"

"I am. You?" He leaned close, offered Billy a kiss.

"I am." Billy closed the distance between their mouths, lips warm and smooth against his own.

"Mmm..." He licked at Billy's lips, humming softly.

"God, I'd love to do you right here."

"Mmm. You'd make Margaret gag."

"Somehow I don't think so." Chuckling, Billy sat back and started up the car.

"Uh-huh. She's a dear old lady." He let his hand rest on Billy's leg.

"She's as kinky as they come."

"No way." That was so a lie. Billy gave him a look, one eyebrow raised. "What? There's no way!"

"Think about it, Tanny. About the questions she's asked, the things she's commented on."

"Nope. No way. Uh-uh."

Billy just laughed and patted his knee.

He chuckled, leaned a little. "Where are we going?"

"I thought we'd hit the Taco Bell drive-through, go eat on the beach if Margaret's storm holds off." Billy's voice dropped an octave. "Then go home and start our weekend."

Tanny couldn't stop his shiver.

"Yeah, that's right, I want you to be thinking about what we're going to be doing this weekend."

"Billy..." He moaned a little, ducked his chin.

"Of course, if that storm takes its time, we could stop at the tattoo shop on the way home."

"The what? Why?"

"I think it's about time I do what I've been threatening ever since I learned how sensitive those little nubs of yours are."

"But..." Oh, God. His nipples. He. Uh. Wow.

"No, not your butt, your nipples." Billy gave him a wink, turning into the drive-through.

"I..." He sort of blinked.

Billy grinned over at him before turning his attention to the speaker box and ordering their lunch. He loved how Billy knew what he liked, what he needed to eat. In short order, they had their lunch and were headed for the beach, the sun still shining brightly.

"It's pretty. Do you think she's right?"

"About the storm? I don't know. Looking at the sky, I'd say no, but the alternative is that she's getting worse, so I hope she's right." Billy handed him his tacos.

"Oh." God. Right.

"So how was your day?"

"Busy. Busy and good. I finished all my work." He had finally found his stride.

Billy's slow smile was the best reward. "Good for you."

"Yeah. Yeah, it is. Means I'm off until Monday."

Billy got that glint in his eyes again. "I know. I have plans."

"So you said." His nipples actually went tight.

Billy's smile was evil. He could feel that dull, desperate ache just beginning to build in the pit of his stomach.

"Eat, love. You're going to need your strength."

"Tacos, right." He couldn't really settle, though. Not with Billy looking at him like that. Billy didn't seem inclined to chow down very hard, either, and they were soon tossing the balance of their meal into the garbage. "Did... did you want to take a walk?"

"No, let's go get this done because you can't think of anything else."

"But..." Oh, God. Oh, God.

"No buts, love." Billy held a hand out to him.

His body went—hand sliding into Billy's without hesitating—but his mind skittered.

Billy held his hand all the way to the car and once they were in it he was given a smile. "What are you thinking?"

"Nothing. Everything. Stuff." Those types of questions were hard.

"Go on," murmured Billy.

"I don't want to talk about it."

"No? I think you should tell me what's on your mind, though."

"Why?"

"Because we're in this together. Because I'm going to pierce your nipples." Billy gave him a long look. "Because I said so."

"I..." This sort of thing made his heart slam in his chest, made him not be able to breathe.

Billy's hand slid over his thigh, squeezed. "Breathe, love."

"I..." He looked over at Billy. "This is hard sometimes."

"I know it is. But we're in it together and we go

through it together. And that means that sometimes you have to talk to me, even if you don't want to."

"I don't know what to say. I never know what's right."

"There isn't any wrong answer in this, Tanny. It's our life."

"I'm scared." He didn't even know that was what he was going to say.

Billy didn't blink or try to talk him out of being scared. "Okay. What's making you scared?"

"How much I want from you. How much I want you to..." He stopped, chewed on his bottom lip.

"Do things to you?"

Tanny nodded.

"Does it scare you because you think it's wrong or you think I'm going to take it away from you?"

"Because I think I could need it." Oh. Oh, he needed out of the car. Now. He opened the door and stepped out.

"Montana!" Billy got out of the car and came after him.

"I just needed to breathe."

"You always take off, or try to, after revealing something of yourself." Billy fell into step with him. "Maybe we should only have serious talks when you're cuffed to the bed."

He reached out, took Billy's hand. "I just have to breathe, huh?"

Billy squeezed his hand. "I know. I get scared, too, though, sometimes."

"Really? Of me?"

"Of you leaving. That one day you might take off to breathe and not come back. Not often, but sometimes. I worry."

He stopped and stared, looking at Billy. "I promise

you, with all my heart, I'll always come back after. If nothing else, to say goodbye. I promise."

Billy smiled, eyes serious. "Thank you, love. That means a lot."

"I love you. I don't want to hurt you."

"I love you, too." Billy didn't even glance around, just leaned forward and brushed their lips together gently. He leaned in, let himself rest against Billy, just for a minute. "Come on, let's go back to the car and get moving. I think Margaret's joints were right." Billy nodded toward the east where storm clouds were starting to grow in the sky.

"Wow. Look at that." That was going to be... big.

Billy nodded, hurrying them back to the car.

"Are we still going to the shop?"

"Yes. It's only five minutes away, and it's early enough in the day they shouldn't be busy yet."

"I... but... what if I don't want to?" Did he want to?

"Then you'll safeword."

"Just because I don't want to?"

"It has to be important enough to you that you'll safeword. Because, really, they don't have to be permanent." Billy smiled as he started up the car. "Besides. I know that you want to."

"I don't know..." He didn't know at all.

"You love it when I bite and play with them. It makes you wild when they're all swollen and sensitive." Billy reached out and slid a hand over his chest, grazing his nipple through his shirt. "Makes me wild, too."

"I... Help me?"

"I'll be right there with you, love. Right at your side."

He didn't know what to do, so he just held on.

Billy was right, it didn't take any time at all to get to the tattoo parlor and the storm was still only just threatening. They bypassed the tattoo side, heading for the piercer's door. Billy had his hand, fingers squeezing and releasing. There was almost a bounce to his step.

"I don't want to do this." He was worried.

"Why not?" Billy asked as they went in.

"I don't know."

Billy squeezed his hand and waved to the man behind the counter. Tanny nodded, chewed his bottom lip.

"Hey there, Billy. How can I help you?" asked the man behind the counter.

"Treat! Good to see you. You haven't met my lover yet, have you? This is Montana. Montana, this is Treat, he's Killian's partner."

"Hi." God, Billy knew a lot of people.

Treat held out his hand, shook Tanny's. "Nice to meet you, Montana. Killian mentioned you had someone new, Billy."

Tanny was slowly learning about Billy's friends. They all got together at a club, a lot, but Billy didn't go anymore, not as far as Tanny understood.

"I have someone special now." Billy wrapped an arm around his waist. "We'd like to have Montana's nipples pierced."

"Do you know what kind of ring you'd like?"

"I was thinking one ring, one barbell, actually."

"That's different...what kind of metal?"

Tanny stood there, a little frozen.

"I think gold will look best against his skin." Both men wandered over to a display case and started talking like he wasn't even really there. "Yes, that's perfect." Billy nodded and held out a hand. "Come see, love."

He wasn't sure he wanted to, but he did. Something in him had to. Billy's hand wrapped around his and he was drawn to the case where a small velvet box sat. There was a small, gold barbell there, along with a ring, a single cobalt-blue captive bead on it.

"You don't want them to match?"

Billy shook his head. "No. They never do when I play with them—one's always more swollen than the other."

"Billy!" His cheeks were on fire.

Billy bumped their shoulders together. "It's true."

"But..."

"But what?"

"But that's not, like, common fucking knowledge."

Billy tilted his head, frowned. "I'm not proposing we take out an advertisement."

"I. I. Fuck this. I can't. I..." He couldn't do this right now.

"Treat, could you give us a moment, please?"

"Sure. Come on to the back room. More private."

Billy slipped an arm around his waist and led him into the back room.

"I need to walk." He needed out.

"I have something different in mind." Billy led him through the door into a small room.

The moment the door closed, Billy had him up against it, mouth hard on his. His eyes went wide, the kiss stealing his breath away. One of Billy's hands slid beneath his T-shirt, found his nipple, and pinched. His cry pushed into Billy's lips, his nipple tender and sensitive and hot.

Billy's mouth dragged away from his. "This is going to be amazing, love."

He stared a little, stunned. "Uh-huh." Amazing.

Then Billy's mouth was on his again, taking total control. Something inside him relaxed, and he could open up, their tongues sliding together. Billy pushed against him, cock hard against his hip. Then the strong body backed away and Billy tugged him toward the chair. He found himself in the chair, shirt off, Billy's hands keeping him there.

Billy called out to the piercer. "We're ready, Treat." His lover's eyes never left his.

The door opened and Treat snapped on a pair of gloves. "Killian has paperwork on file, yeah?"

Billy nodded, fingers sliding over the name on his belly. "He does."

"Do you want explanations, Billy? Or just do it?"

"Just do it. I know how to care for it—Montana will, too, soon enough."

"I don't..." Billy's fingers pushed into his lips and he started sucking instinctively. Billy's eyes went dark, and a low noise growled out of his throat.

"He's lovely. You must be so proud." Something cold brushed his nipple.

"I am. Proud and in love."

"Congratulations, my friend. Ring or barbell in this one?"

"Barbell on the left." Billy was still looking into his eyes.

"You got it."

Something grabbed his nipple and pulled and he whimpered, sucking harder on Billy's fingers.

"That's right, love. You keep your focus right here." Billy's voice was gruff, like speaking was too much of an effort.

The needle burned and Tanny whimpered, pulling harder, trying to keep from crying out. Billy groaned, and he could see how aroused his lover was. He started gasping, hands reaching for Billy, wanting to touch his nipple, to ease the burn.

"Shh, shh. Breathe through it, love. Just keep sucking my fingers and breathe through it." Billy's free hand grabbed one of his, holding on tight.

"Jesus, Billy. He's a firecracker." The piercer chuckled softly, and something tugged and pulled his nipple.

"He's mine." Billy growled softly.

"That's obvious."

He moaned, closing his eyes, then opening them.

Billy beamed. "Yeah, I'd hope it is. You're doing a lovely job decorating my boy."

He couldn't quite breathe, he couldn't think of what to do, and he couldn't figure out how to let Billy's fingers go. Not that Billy seemed to be worried about his fingers.

"One more," Billy told him, gaze still holding his.

He groaned, shook his head a little.

"Yes, love." Billy grinned. "Just keep sucking."

But, he...

The clamp caught his right nipple and he bit a little, shaking.

"Almost there, love. You're doing well. I know more than one man who'd be screaming at this point."

He squeezed his eyes tight as the needle pushed in. No. No more. No.

Billy's moan sounded loud. "Look at that. God. So hot."

There was a pull and a burn and a tug and then something cold and wet brushed both of his nipples, cleaning them, making them ache.

"Perfect." Billy sounded like he was about to come. "How long until we can play with them, Treat?"

"I'd be gentle for a couple of weeks. No mouth play for three days, huh?"

Billy pouted, but then gave him a wink. "Got it. Nice work, Treat, thank you."

"You're welcome. You know about basic care?"

"Yep. We'll pick up a bottle of the antiseptic stuff, though, before we go."

"Good deal. You... want a few minutes?"

Billy looked at him and then grinned, nodded. "I think that would be wise."

"I'll be in with Kill. Let yourself out."

"Thank you, Treat." Billy's fingers were still in his mouth.

His heart was slamming in his chest, his mind screaming.

The door clicked shut and Billy smiled at him. "Now we're alone."

Billy's fingers slipped out of his lips so he could talk. "I want to go home."

"We have privacy if you need anything else first."

"I can't think. My heart's pounding."

Billy pressed their foreheads together. "Breathe, love."

"I don't know how." He gasped, took a deep breath.

"Just like that." Billy's fingers slid down his breastbone, leaving a damp trail.

"This was weird." He wasn't going to look.

"Weird?" Billy shook his head. "Toe-piercing? That would have been weird."

That made him chuckle, and those chuckles turned into laughter. Toe-piercing. Billy grinned at him, fingers idly tracing the ink on his belly. Billy's name, spelled out for anyone to see.

"Yours." He knew that.

Billy nodded. "You are. Come on. Let's get home before that storm strands us."

"I... Do you like them?" Were they okay?

Billy took a long, slow look. "They're perfect, love. They're sexy and hot."

He couldn't look. He couldn't.

"Montana, look at me." Billy waited until he looked up into his lover's eyes. "They're on your body. Look, because you're certainly going to feel them."

"I can't."

"You will." Billy took his hand and tugged him up.

His chest ached, but he grabbed his shirt, pulled it on, abs going tight as the material touched his nipples.

"They're going to be tender." Billy got a bottle from behind the counter as they went out.

"Uh-huh." He nodded to the piercer standing in the doorway to the tattoo side of the shop, whose name he'd forgotten. "Thank you."

"You're welcome." The man gave him a grin. "Enjoy."

What was he supposed to say to that?

"We will!" Billy gave a little wave and they went out.

The wind whipped around them the minute they walked out. Tanny shivered, headed for the car, feeling a bit undone. By the time they were buckled in and heading home, the rain had started, huge drops that made a racket as they landed on the car.

"It's raining." He was freaking right the fuck out.

"It is. We'll be home in a few minutes, though, and it's not like we melt or anything." Billy reached out and laid a hand on his thigh. "Are you okay?"

"I'm a little wigged. I... I could use a red right now." In fact, Tanny thought he could use two. It'd been months since he'd used. Months since Billy'd taken him in, but sometimes...

Billy squeezed his leg. "I know what to do when you

need a red, don't I?"

He nodded, bouncing a little. "Still, it's weird."

"That you're not using?"

"No." He didn't like to talk about what they did.

"What then? That I know how to make you fly higher than any pill?" Billy, on the other hand, seemed to get off on talking about it. Tanny groaned, chewed on his bottom lip, and refused to answer. Billy chuckled. "I'm taking that as a yes."

"Don't talk about it."

"Don't talk about how I'm going to tie you to the bed, spank your ass rosy, and then come inside you?"

"Billy!" God. God.

"And then I'm going to plug your ass, keep my come inside you. I think we'll use the cock ring on you today, too. Keep you from coming until Sunday night."

He shook his head, swallowing hard. At least it wasn't the cage. The cage made him a little crazed.

"We're going to fuck all weekend long."

"Stop it..." He reached down, rubbed his cock.

"In the bedroom. In the kitchen. In the living room. I'm going to fuck you all over and everywhere."

"Billy." He cupped his balls, the motion making his shirt rub his sore nipples.

"You're touching yourself. Better do it now—when we get home, you're not allowed to touch yourself without my say-so."

"It's my cock," he challenged.

"And you're mine."

Tanny groaned, pushing his hand into his pants, jacking hard.

"I can smell you. It's hot. Like sex."

God, it felt like he hadn't jacked himself off in weeks.

It was so hot.

Billy turned off on the wrong street. "We'll take the long way 'round."

"Uh. Uh-huh." He pulled harder.

"Enjoy this, Montana. Because when we're home, I'm calling the shots again."

"I... I can't not jack off for three days." His thumb worked the tip.

"Oh, I'm sure you can. That's why you're not going to be allowed to jack off until Monday next week."

"No way." Oh, it felt good.

"Yes, way. Maybe even longer, but we'll start with Monday." Billy breathed in, the sound audible. "Take it out."

"Huh?" He was sort of stupid with pleasure.

"Undo your zipper and take your cock out." The words were like little growls.

"We're outside." He did it, though; the tip was red and swollen and wet.

"We're driving. And you're beautiful. Now spread that pre-come over the head." God, Billy's voice was strained, he sounded so needy.

He nodded, fingers moving over the spongy, slick skin, teasing his sensitive slit.

"Yeah, that's it. Now work the shaft."

He groaned, protesting a little. He got off faster working the tip.

"Tell me how it feels."

"Good. Hot. Sorta... bad, in that good way, huh?"

"Mmm, yes. Very naughty." Billy looked over and winked.

His cheeks heated, his chin ducked. God.

"Don't stop."

"Billy..." His belly went tight.

"I'm watching you. I'm smelling you. Don't stop."

"You're...you're supposed to be watching the road." He bucked up, driving into his touch.

"I am. Mostly." They were crawling along one road after another, Billy wandering around the neighborhood.

"I'm going to come. I want you. Real bad."

"So come. We're almost home and you'll have me. All weekend long."

Tanny grunted, bit his bottom lip once, and let his arm nudge one sore nipple. Thunder crashed as he shot.

"Fuck." Billy reached and squeezed his thigh again, then swiped a finger through the mess on his cock. Billy licked his finger clean.

"I... Never did that before. In the rain, in a car, with someone watching."

"You were great, love. Amazing."

They turned onto their street. "Zip up, love."

He nodded, cleaned himself up with a napkin from the glove compartment, and zipped up. The rain was bashing down now, visibility almost zero.

Billy pulled up in front of the house and cut the engine. He peered out. "Man, we're going to get soaked. I vote we go in and head straight for the shower." Billy smiled at him. "You can hold your hands over your nipples and I'll wash you."

He didn't want to think about his poor, throbbing nipples. Not at all. "Okay" was all he said, though.

"On three," Billy suggested, hand going to his door handle. "One. Two. Three." Billy threw open his door and launched himself out of the car.

They hurried, the rain plastering their clothes to them almost immediately. They were soaked right through by the time they were inside, Billy laughing as the water streamed down his face.

"God. Margaret was so right."

"She was. We shouldn't doubt her next time, no matter how beautiful a day it is." Billy chuckled again and leaned in, licking at his lips. He pushed close, then jerked away as his nipples touched Billy. "Those are going to be tender for awhile."

"Uh-huh." No shit.

Billy grabbed his hand and tugged him toward the bathroom. They left puddles as they went.

They both stripped down, shivering. He squeaked as the lights went out, then flashed back on. "Wow."

"Yeah, we should light a fire so it doesn't matter if the power goes out and stays out. Shower first, though. I don't want you getting sick."

"I won't." He hadn't in all the time he'd lived on the street.

"Good. This will help." Billy began stripping him.

His nipples ached a little as he stretched his arms up, but he still didn't look.

Billy made a low, growly noise as the T-shirt went over his head. "Beautiful."

"They burn a little." Not looking.

"Uh-huh. It'll ease over the next few days." Billy touched the barbell.

"Don't touch them." He stepped back.

"Do they hurt badly?" Billy's fingers circled them.

"I... No. I mean, they ache."

"That's not a bad thing, love." Billy smiled and touched, a barely there touch, to the tip of his ringed nipple. He whimpered, his breath caught in the back of his throat. "Mmm... we're going to have so much fun with these."

"We shouldn't touch them."

"No, that's not what Treat said. He said no mouth-play for three days. This isn't my mouth." Billy touched his ringed nipple again.

He stepped back, cock jerking a little. "Let's get in the shower." Billy followed him, stripping quickly.

His nipples were pierced.

His nipples were pierced.

It was raining and thundering and his fucking nipples were pierced.

Billy turned on the shower and tugged him into it, turning him so the water hit his head and back, protecting his nipples. His pierced nipples. Tanny shuddered, looking up at the ceiling in the shower stall. Billy kissed his back and began to wash him.

"I... I feel all weird."

"You're going to faint weird, or there's metal in my nipples and it's all I can think of weird?"

Tanny chuckled softly. "There's metal in my nipples weird."

"You'll get used to it." Another kiss landed on his back, Billy's soapy fingers sliding over his ass and into his crack.

"Sometimes I don't think I'll ever get used to this."

"Then it'll always be exciting and fresh. That's not a bad thing." His balls were washed from behind, then Billy's hand slid down the insides of his thighs.

"No. No, we're not a bad thing, Billy. I promise." It was unnerving, Billy cleaning him.

"I know." Open-mouthed kisses landed on each ass cheek, the backs of his thighs and his calves.

"You'll get stuck down there."

Billy laughed and slapped his ass. "Are you saying I'm too old to bend over like this?"

He groaned, spread, his hips arching instinctively. A moan answered his groan and Billy gave him another slap, mouth nuzzling at his hole. Tanny braced himself on the tile, spread, body begging.

"You need so beautifully." Billy gave him two more swats and then licked his hole.

"Only you." He'd only ever needed the drugs like he needed Billy.

Billy growled. "Good."

"Yeah?" His eyes closed, the water slamming around them.

"Yes. Only me. Mine. My Montana." Each word came with a spank.

"Y...yours. Yours."

"Mine." One of Billy's hands slid around and stroked his belly, fingers tracing the tattoo of Billy's name on his belly.

"I promise."

"I promise, too." Billy's fingers drifted upward, heading for his nipples.

"Don't touch." He went up on tiptoe.

Billy chuckled. "Just a little nudge."

"No touching." God, his mouth was dry.

Billy's fingers found the outer edge of his areole and began to slowly trace it. Tanny set his lips. He wouldn't look. He wouldn't. The tantalizing touches continued, Billy's fingers threatening but never actually touching the nipples.

"Billy... We should. We could get out."

"Continue this in bed, you mean."

"I don't know what I mean."

Billy's chuckle was warm along his back. "I like that. I like knowing my touch has you not knowing if you're coming or going."

"You make me a little stupid."

"I addle your brains, do I?" One of Billy's fingers touched the barbell.

"Yes." His cock jerked at the touch.

"Good." He thought he could hear laughter in Billy's voice. "I like the thought of being able to do that to you."

"I'm not sure how I feel about it. Part of me likes it, part of me doesn't."

"Let's go with the part of you that likes it." Billy's hand slid down and wrapped around his cock.

"Oh..." He arched up, hips thrusting into Billy's hand, body immediately and unquestioningly eager.

"Yeah, I knew you'd like that." Billy's fingers were too loose, but they were moving up and down on his flesh.

"Who... who doesn't?"

Billy's chuckle licked at the back of his neck. He started thrusting faster, cock going from interested to diamond-hard. Billy's other hand swatted his ass every time he pushed back toward it. The blows weren't too bad, the sting was almost gentle, but they warmed him. And Billy's hand tightened on his cock, making the pleasure bigger. His sounds got louder, fighting the falling water, the thunder outside.

"More," growled Billy, smacking him harder.

"M...more? More what?"

"Sounds." Billy swatted him harder.

"Oh." He cried out and went up on tiptoe.

"That's right. More like that."

Another blow hit his ass, this one stinging. "Please!"

"Please what, love? This?" Billy smacked him again,

the sound loud. He nodded, swallowed his groan. "I can do that." And Billy did, one swat after another.

He rested his forehead on his folded arms, butt shaking as he rode out the pleasure. He moved between Billy's hands, each one bringing its own brand of pleasure. His balls drew up, his climax slowly building inside him.

"You get to come once, love. Make it good."

His laugh was incredulous, husky. "You always make it good."

"I try." Billy kissed one of his ass cheeks and then started spanking again.

"I..." He wanted. Oh, God. He wanted to be over Billy's lap, plugged and hard, aching for it.

"You get to come once, love, and then we're going to have so much fun."

"This... this is fun." He wasn't going to come. He wasn't.

"It is. So is not letting you come for days. So is plugging you and spanking you and making you scream."

"Oh, God..." He bit his bottom lip, trying to control himself.

"No, just me." Billy laughed and bit into one stinging ass cheek.

"Fuck..." He jerked away, swallowed hard.

"Yeah, we're going to do that, too." One of Billy's fingers pushed into his hole.

He couldn't stop his groan, his ache of desperate need. "Yes." A second finger followed the first, the stretch burning a little. "More?" God, he needed.

Billy's fingers disappeared altogether, but then they came back right away, three, large and slick, pushing in. This sound left him, something more than a gasp, but less than a scream. Billy twisted and scissored his fingers, spreading him open and then pegging his gland.

"Billy!" He arched, spunk pouring out of him in waves, his entire body shuddering.

"That's it, love. God, I love that smell."

He was too far gone to answer, too busy riding out his aftershocks. Billy kept fingering him, mouth on his shoulder. His cock flagged, but the heat, the pleasure was still right there.

"I think we're clean and warm enough, don't you?" He could hear the need in Billy's voice.

"Uh-huh." He would have agreed to anything. Billy's chuckle said he knew.

The water was turned off, a towel wrapped around his shoulders, and Billy dried him off before leading him back to the bedroom. "Making love, cock-ringing, and ass-plugging first. Then we'll relax in front of the fire and see how long Margaret's storm lasts."

"She says all weekend."

"That's right. And that's just fine because all our plans are indoors." Billy's hand slid along his ass. That touch made his hips arch, even if his ass was sore. "I'm going to make love to you and you're going to feel every thrust against your ass."

His moan echoed a little bit. Billy turned him and brought their mouths together. He moaned into the kiss, tongue fucking Billy's lips, loving on his man the best he could. Billy's cock poked him in the belly, left wet drops on his skin. He wrapped his fingers around it, stroking slowly, petting the long column of flesh.

Groaning for him, Billy touched his shoulders, pressed against them. "Suck me?"

"Anytime." He loved the way Billy loved his mouth, loved being blown.

"Now would be good. Really good." Tanny laughed as he knelt, his tongue already out to slide over the tip of Billy's cock. "Sexy," muttered Billy. "You're so damn sexy."

"Yours. All yours." Then he took Billy in, all the way, loving him.

Billy's hands slid into his hair, fingers wrapping around the strands. "So good."

He nodded, tongue slapping the heavy shaft, moving on Billy's flesh. Billy made a noise that told him it was really good, and the hands in his hair tightened a little. It felt good and Tanny swallowed, head bobbing over the hard, thick flesh.

"Yeah. Good, that's good." Billy was vocal about what he liked, about how good Tanny was doing.

He offered Billy everything, sucking hard, eyes closed. More words of praise rained down on him even as Billy's cock started leaking, one drop after another. Hot. So good. So hot. He moaned around the flesh in his mouth. Billy began to move, pushing the hot prick deep into his throat again and again.

He reached up, fingers wrapping around Billy's hips, dragging him deeper. Moaning, Billy moved faster, shoved harder. Come for me. Come on. Love. God, he loved.

"Oh! Montana!" Billy cried his name out and then whispered it. His lover's hips jerked and then punched, pushing deep. Salty heat filled his throat.

Tanny groaned, drank deep, pulling Billy into him. Shuddering, Billy kept moving, stroking slowly into him. Cleaning Billy's cock with his tongue, Tanny let himself float. Billy's fingers slid over his head, a low, happy rumble sounding in Billy's chest. He grinned up, kissed the tip of Billy's cock.

Chuckling, Billy stroked his scalp again. "Come to bed, love."

He nodded, slowly getting to his feet. The storm was raging outside.

Billy pulled him into bed, eyes dancing wickedly. "Are you ready to have the weekend of your life?"

"Uh-huh." Maybe.

"Good. We'll start with the binding. Cuffs and cock ring."

He moaned, lips open, nodding.

"I bought new cuffs. Heavy leather."

"Why?" Heavy leather. God, that sounded perverse.

"I wanted you to be able to feel them around your wrists, even when you're not pulling or tugging." Billy gave him random kisses. "I might make you wear them even when we're not playing."

"Make me?" He still didn't know about that part.

"Uh-huh." Billy met his gaze, held it. He shuddered, arms wrapping around his waist. Billy chuckled and bit at his earlobe. "Get me the cuffs, love. They're in the box on the dresser. There's a new cock ring there, too. Same leather."

"I love you." He needed to say it.

Billy dragged him in closer and kissed him hard. "I love you, too."

He nodded, took a deep breath. He knew.

He went to get the cuffs. He could feel Billy's eyes on him, watching him. He grabbed the box, jumping as the lightning flashed.

"Wow. I wonder if we're going to lose power." The rain was still pouring, lashing down and slamming against the windows.

"I hope not." Thank God he was in here, not sleeping

under the boardwalk.

"We have the fireplace if it does." Billy tugged him back down onto the bed. "It's not like we need electricity for what we're doing, anyway."

"Glad we're here, though, not outside."

"Yes." Billy held him close. "We're inside and warm and we have each other."

He nodded, twining his legs with his lover's. Inside. Warm. Together. That right there guaranteed it was going to be a great weekend.

Chapter Two

The power had gone out around five and still hadn't come back on. It didn't matter, though. They had the blankets spread in front of the fireplace, where a fire blazed hotly. Montana lay spread out on the blankets, body glimmering in the dancing light. The cuffs were still wrapped around Montana's wrists, and the cock ring was still around Montana's cock; his lover was also plugged.

Billy's cock was valiantly trying to come back. The view was certainly inspiring enough. Montana was beautiful—skin limned with the firelight as he dozed. Billy slid his fingers along Montana's arm, that skin like silk. Montana offered him a smile, even dozing. That made something in the pit of his belly go tight and warm.

Groaning in response, he leaned in and kissed Montana softly on the lips. Montana reached for him, the heavy cuffs making his lover blink awake.

He took Montana's hand and twined their fingers together. "Hey there, sleeping beauty."

"Hey... lights still out?" Montana rolled closer, warm and lazy against him.

"Yeah, I think so." He hadn't actually tried them recently, but the rain hadn't let up any and the street lights were still out, as far as he could tell without getting up. He stroked Montana's belly with his free hand.

"Mmm. It's cozy here."

His fingers traced his signature. "It is. Our own little world in the middle of the storm." He slid his hand up, fingers unable to stay completely away from the nipple piercings.

He loved how they looked—one ringed, one with the barbell. They made his cock ache, just knowing Montana had let him do it. He couldn't wait to taste them, to feel how they moved on his tongue.

"Don't touch..." Montana's voice was a soft groan.

"I have to. I can't not touch." He slid his fingers gently across the barbell and Montana's nipple.

"Billy..." Montana's eyelids fluttered.

God, he loved that. "Yes, love?"

"I... Please. I. They ache."

"This aches, too, I bet." He slid his hand down and rubbed the tip of Montana's bound cock.

"Yes..." Montana arched for him, cock sliding on his palm. It was so hot and felt like silk. Groaning, he played with the tip, pushing his thumb into it. "Billy. Billy, I need..."

Billy smiled, touching more. He knew that Montana needed. He also knew that need didn't have to be focused on Montana's pretty, bound cock. Bending, he took a long kiss that started easy and slowly increased in intensity. He kissed Montana until he was sure that his lover's focus was entirely on his mouth. He loved the look in Montana's dark eyes—dizzy and caught, happy and horny.

He didn't break the kiss, but he slowed it down again— not the intensity, no, he made slow licking and sucking as intense as a deep tongue-fucking. Montana's moan pushed into his lips; the sound was fucking amazing and made him shiver. He slid his fingers along Montana's side, not going near nipples or cock or ass—he was going to show Montana that you didn't have to hit those hot spots at all. That earned him another, soft moan.

"I love that," he murmured. "I love all the sounds that come out of you."

"I make weird ones, sometimes."

He grinned down at Montana. "I love all of them."

He got a smile, a wink, and a stretch. "The cuffs are heavy." He didn't think that was a complaint.

"They look good on you." His fingers found them automatically, the leather warm from Montana's skin.

"Do they?" Montana's fingers curled.

"They do. Sexy. Hot." Leaning in, he kissed one, and then uncurled Montana's fingers and kissed his lover's palm.

"Billy." Montana's fingertips brushed his cheek.

"That's me." He traced the lines in Montana's hand with his tongue.

"Love you." It was warm here, cozy, quiet. Perfect.

He continued to explore Montana's hand with his tongue. He traced each line on the palm, licked Montana's knuckles, teased his tongue in between each finger.

"Oh. Oh, Billy. I. That's so big." Yes, such a little thing, but so big. Smiling, he kept doing it. Montana rolled, trying to move against him.

He chuckled and moved backward. "No, we're not doing that at the moment."

"Billy?" Sweet, confused lover.

"We're playing the how wild can I get you without touching your cock, ass or nipples game."

"Oh. That's a good game." He did love that laugh.

He chuckled himself, bending to nuzzle Montana's wrist with his cheek. "It is."

"The storm's raging." Montana's fingers brushed his cheek.

"Yeah. The one in here is, too." He rubbed against Montana's thigh.

Montana spread and arched, balls wrinkling up and going tight. That was so hot. So sexy. Groaning, he made himself focus on following the vein in Montana's arm from his wrist on up with his tongue. Montana's hips began to move, to slowly fuck the air.

God. Billy groaned and kept licking and sucking the soft skin. And he watched. His sub was glowing, ass working the heavy plug, cock leaking. Montana was lost in it, moans filling the air. He worked his way up to Montana's neck, lips closing over the throbbing pulse point.

"Please. I can't think. It's so good."

He laughed. "No thinking allowed."

Montana groaned, licked his lips. "Are you sure?"

"Absolutely." He blew on one of Montana's nipples. The newly-pierced flesh went tight, Montana's hips jerking up into the air. "I didn't even touch you." He blew on the other one.

"N...no touching."

"I'm not touching," he pointed out and then blew again, hard enough for his breath to glide over both nipples this time.

"Fuck..." Montana rolled away, cuffed hands coming down.

"Uh-uh-uh. Get back here." He hauled Montana back into the middle of the blanket, put his lover on his back again. "I'm not finished with you yet."

"Billy. It's too much."

No. No, Montana was awake, aware, hard, right there with him. "I don't think so." Billy trailed his fingers down Montana's breastbone and played them through Montana's navel.

"I want you."

He knew that.

"When I've finished exploring every inch, I'm going to take your mouth. Slide my cock into your throat..."

Montana's entire body shuddered. He moved to Montana's legs, nibbling and licking, searching out every sweet spot. Montana's motions became more and more restless, cock leaking on the pretty, inked belly. He found a particularly sensitive spot behind Montana's right knee and he tongued it, breathed over it.

"Fuck. Fuck, Billy." Montana rolled, trying to get away.

"No, not fucking. Kissing. Licking. Loving." He stopped Montana as soon as his lover was on his stomach, and began to tease the crease where thigh and ass met with his tongue.

"Loving. Okay. Okay, Billy. That works."

"Loving takes all night long. I won't even let you come at the end of it, and it's still loving." He licked and licked, loving the taste of Montana's sweat right there.

"Are you really making me wait 'til Monday to come?"

"Yes."

"Billy." Montana was beautiful like this.

"Yes, love?" He licked along the red ass, finding fingerprints here and there.

"I don't know what to do. I can't think."

"You don't need to think."

"I do." Fuck, he loved that gaspy, husky sound.

He chuckled. "No. No, you don't."

"I do. This is all so big."

"No, I'm pretty sure that, big as it is, you don't need to think about it at all. You can think about it on Monday."

"I don't know how." He smiled where he knew Montana couldn't see. This was how it worked—fighting the submission, struggling through each new phase. Montana was meant for this life.

"You'll learn. You'll be overwhelmed. Let it happen."

"That doesn't make sense."

"It doesn't have to." He licked along Montana's scars, traced them.

"I hate them, except when you touch them."

"They're a badge of your strength and courage." He continued to lick and trace them.

"They mean I lived and my sister died."

"Yes, they mean you lived. That you did and your sister didn't doesn't mean it's your fault."

"I want to believe that." That was progress.

He found a small patch on Montana's shoulder that wasn't scarred and began to suck up a mark. Montana whimpered softly, scooted forward. He wrapped his arm around Montana's waist and tugged him back again. "Where are you going?"

"I don't know..." Sweet man.

"You're staying right here with me. And I'm going to blow your mind."

"I'm a little wigged, just a little."

"I'm not going to stop because you're a little wigged." He sucked out another mark on the top of Montana's arm. Montana moaned, shifting under him.

He continued to lick and to suck and to touch until he was lost in the way Montana smelled and the way

Montana felt under his tongue and fingers. Montana was quiet now, moving under his fingers, almost lazily. He got to Montana's feet and kissed the sole, testing how ticklish his love was today. Montana's toes curled, but he didn't pull away. Billy kissed a little harder and then licked before biting gently at his lover's heel.

"Love you." The words were barely breathed out.

"You, too." He spelled the word out with his tongue on Montana's calf.

He was going to get out the little flogger he'd picked up once he had Montana's skin all sensitized. All warmed up. Montana eased onto the floor completely, giving himself up. Billy spent another half hour sensitizing Montana's skin. He could feel his lover beginning to get restless again, to move from bonelessness to tension.

"Time for a more intense connection."

"Hmm?" He felt Montana try to rise up, look at him.

"Shh. Stay where you are." He kissed the back of Montana's neck and stood. It made him proud, that Montana stayed.

He made short work of grabbing the flogger, making a pit stop in the kitchen on his way back to collect a bottle of water. Montana was curled up, looking at the fire, almost asleep. "Mmm... beautiful." He went over and slid the leather along Montana's arm.

"What's that?" Montana's eyes were on his.

"It's called a flogger. I'm going to work your skin with it."

"Why?"

"Because it's going to make you fly. Better than any drug ever did."

"Is it going to hurt?"

"A little. It's going to burn, ache. This is a lightweight one."

"I don't want to get all stressed out again, Billy, but I'm going to." The honesty made him nod, pleased him that Montana could offer it to him.

"You're allowed. As long as your reaction is honest, it's the right one."

"I don't understand that."

"I don't want you to freak out because that's what you think you should do. I want you to freak out because that's your honest reaction." He continued to let the leather slide over Montana's skin.

"I don't want to freak out at all, you know?" Montana breathed, nice and slow.

"You don't have to." He kissed the tip of Montana's cock and then slid the leather over it. The heavy flesh bobbed at the touch, and Montana moaned. "My sexy lover."

"Yours. Undo my hands?"

"Nope. You're not actually tied to anything, remember?"

"I know, still. It's... big."

"I know. That's why I chose them. Because they're heavy. Because you can't forget them."

"I can't." Montana shifted, tried to sit up.

"On, your stomach, love." He stopped Montana shifting, helped turn him over.

"Billy." He put pillows under Montana's thighs, the flat belly, making sure there wasn't friction on the needy cock.

"I'm here, love. Right here."

Montana's breath was coming faster now, the scarred back tense. He wouldn't use the flogger on Montana's back, but that ass and the backs of his lover's legs called out for the harsh kiss. "I'm going to start now." He wouldn't leave Montana in this space alone; he would talk and make sure his lover knew he was right there with Montana.

He didn't put much force behind it, not yet, he simply let the leather strips fall across Montana's ass. Montana tensed, shuddered, then relaxed as the second blow fell, just as easily. Billy spread out the blows all along Montana's legs and ass. He knew that they would slowly build, that he didn't need to use any more strength or force for Montana to slowly feel more and more sensation. The heat kept Montana relaxed and easy, kept him still.

"The flogger is making your skin glow. It'll get darker as I keep going."

Montana's moan was perfect, made him smile.

He focused on the backs of Montana's thighs for several strokes, hitting the same place over and over again. Montana tried to roll away from the next blow, tried to avoid it. "No. You have to lie there and take what I give."

"Billy..." Montana shook his head, fighting him.

He put his hand in the small of Montana's back and leaned in to whisper into Montana's ear. "I'm right here, love. Right here with you."

"Help me. I'm scared."

"I have you and I'm right here and I won't leave you alone."

"This is so stupid, how I feel."

"No." He bit the word out fiercely. "No, how you feel is never stupid."

"I just... I don't know how to do this."

"You just do it, love." He kissed Montana's ear and then began flogging his lover's legs again.

Montana started shifting and moving with the blows,

the tension ratcheting higher. Soon it would break again, leave Montana relaxed. He flicked the leather across Montana's soles.

"No. No, don't!" Montana curled his legs up under him.

"I think I should." The more Montana protested, the more it was important to push.

"No!" There was an edge of panic.

"I have you, Montana." He pressed his hand against the small of Montana's back again, putting pressure there as he hit Montana's feet a couple more times with the flogger.

"Stop it. Stop it. I want to get up. I need to move. Let me go."

"You're doing so well." He flicked the flogger over Montana's feet one more time, and then moved it slowly back up again, hitting ankles, then calves, then the backs of Montana's knees.

"I don't... I'm not. I... Please."

"Tell me, Montana. Don't be afraid to tell me anything. Everything." He focused on the backs of Montana's knees for several hits, and then did the soles of Montana's feet again.

"I don't want to do this. I don't want this. I..." The flogger hit Montana's ass, the sound sharp.

He slapped that sweet ass again, a little harder this time. Montana needed to sink into the pain, not try to fight it. He hit again, focusing now on the twin mounds, the pale rose turning darker.

"Why do you want to do this?" Montana screamed the words out, the action seeming to release something inside.

"To make you beautiful." He hit Montana's ass again.

"To make you fly."

"I'm scared. I'm scared of this."

"You're scared you'll need it too much."

Montana nodded, sweat sheening the tanned skin.

"I'll always be here to give it to you. Always. I promise."

"And we don't lie to each other."

"I don't lie to you, love." He never had and he wasn't about to start.

"I don't lie." Montana seemed to relax a little more.

"I know." He kissed one asscheek and then began again with the flogger. He kept the blows light, working Montana gently. "You're beautiful." He spoke between each blow, keeping them connected. "I love you."

"Love. Please, it aches."

"When I'm done, I'm going to take out the plug and I'm going to make love to you."

"Promise? I need you."

"I swear." He punctuated the words with a hard swat to Montana's ass.

Montana bucked, almost coming off the pillows. Billy groaned and set four more hard flogs in a row, utterly entranced. Those lean hips fucked the air, jerking and moving furiously.

"Yes. Yes, Montana. Feel it. Feel me."

"I do." The words came out in sobs.

"Yes. Yes."

Two more strong hits and he put down the flogger, panting. Montana curled into himself, rocking slowly, panting too. Billy ran his hands down Montana's back to the hot ass and squeezed, bent and kissed one rosy ass cheek. Montana curled up tighter, protecting himself, trying to control it.

Sean Michael

He teased out the plug and then curled his body around Montana's, his arms coming around to hold Montana tight. Montana's skin was warm, muscles tight as the man rocked. He worked his own ass until he was in just the right place so that each of Montana's movements back toward him took his cock into Montana's amazing ass. He needed Montana to understand, to know neither of them was alone in this.

"I'm right here, love." He pushed in deep. He felt Montana's moan, all along his cock. "Mmm..." He began to move, long slow motions. In and out and in and out, he did it smoothly, fluidly.

"Please."

He never changed his rhythm, driving in and out and in and out. "Love. Can you feel it?"

"Feel what?"

"The burning. The love. The two of us."

Montana nodded, the low groan filling the air.

Billy latched onto Montana's neck and began to suck in time with his thrusts. Montana moaned for him, both of them rocking together. Billy let himself get lost in Montana's body, in the way it felt wrapped around his cock and the way it smelled in his nose. They moved, nice and easy, Montana beginning to relax for him, to breathe, to submit.

He could feel the heat pouring off Montana's ass and legs from the flogging. It made him moan and shift slightly, his cock finding Montana's gland.

"Oh. Oh, Billy."

"I know, love." He kept nailing that spot, low groans beginning to come from him every time he pushed into Montana's heat.

"I need to come." Oh, he didn't think so.

"You can. On Monday."

Montana's ass clenched around him, almost stealing his breath.

"Fuck, that's good." He kept moving, pushing his way into that tight heat over and over.

"Please."

"I'm going to come soon." He could feel it, building in his balls as they drew up against his body.

"No fair..." Montana chuckled, the sound soft.

"All's fair in love." He kissed the back of Montana's neck, his eyes closing as he felt it coming.

He thrust twice more and moaned, his body going stiff as he shot. Montana's hips kept working him all through his orgasm. It felt like it went on and on and then finally it was over, little shivers seeming to still chase their way across his spine.

"Billy. Billy..." Montana was still moving, driving back against him.

He pushed forward, staying buried inside his lover. His hand drifted down, found Montana's cock and held it. Not to make Montana need to come more, but to hold that connection between them. He didn't squeeze or rub, he just held on.

"I love you," he said softly, feeling warm and good and right with his lover, his sub. His Montana.

Chapter Three

Every muscle in his body ached and he shifted, trying to find a comfortable position, trying to rest. Finally he slid out of bed, going to the little guest room where his work was set up. He started moving around, cleaning.

A half an hour or so later Billy wandered in, naked and easy in his skin. "Mmm... don't you look sexy."

"I don't feel sexy. I ache. I can't settle. I can't rest."

"Come on. Let's go get a shower."

"Okay." He held his hands out to Billy, almost ready to beg for help.

Billy took his hands and kissed them, then began walking backward, leading him to the bathroom. The cuffs felt heavier somehow with Billy holding his hands.

"You'll take the cuffs off for the shower, right?"

"No, I'm thinking I'll cuff your hands around the showerhead."

"But, they can't get wet..."

"I'll hook you up before I turn on the water."

He groaned, not sure what to do. This was all so fucking big.

Once they were in the bathroom, Billy pulled him in,

kissed him. "I'm here, Montana. You can always turn to me."

"I'm just... I can't rest."

"You have to let go." Billy led him into the shower and raised his hands up to the showerhead, clicking the cuffs together.

"You say that like it's simple. I'm trying to do what you want."

"I know, love. I know. And you're doing a good job. But you have to let go. Like when you take the pills and they change everything—you give in to that, right? This is the same, just give in to the way your body feels, to your needs. I'll be here to catch you if you fall."

He was fucking horrified to feel his eyes fill with tears. "I don't know how to do it. I keep trying, but I don't understand!"

Billy kissed his cheek and licked at the tear that escaped. "You think you're supposed to react a certain way or feel a certain thing, and you're fighting to get there." Billy shook his head. "Stop doing that. Just feel what you feel and react how you react. Stop thinking so hard."

"I just want to do this right for you." He just didn't want to fuck up so bad that Billy made him leave.

"Love. Don't you understand yet? Whatever you do is the right thing for you."

"My head hurts, Billy." None of this made sense.

"Then close your eyes and enjoy the shower, hmm?"

The shower came on, warm water pouring down over him. He had to close his eyes, had to focus on breathing carefully, because the water was on his face. Just doing that made it a little easier to relax. Billy's hands dug into the muscles near his shoulders.

"Will..." He shook his head, sputtered. "Will the

nozzle hold?"

"The nozzle will hold, love. Stop thinking and worrying about things." A slap hit his already aching ass.

"Don't. Please." He was so tired.

"I'll stop when you do. No more worrying, just give in to your body—feel."

He lifted his face back up into the spray and let the tears come, knowing Billy couldn't see. The massage continued. Billy's hands moved over him, touching him everywhere. Sometimes the touches were hard, sometimes gentle, but they came and came. Billy touched him everywhere—there was nowhere to hide. The silent tears became hard sobs that wracked his body in a quick, furious storm, then dissipated and left him boneless and swaying.

"There you go. Better, hmm?"

Billy's prick pushed at his hole and then slipped in. Billy's solid hands wrapped around his hips as Billy began to rock into him. He didn't really feel aroused—he was being touched and loved, filled, and he let it happen, let Billy make things happen. Billy didn't seem upset that he wasn't aroused, the man just continued to love on him.

His muscles stopped holding him up, Billy supporting him, keeping him upright. He felt Billy's come, slow heat filling inside him. They stood there like that for a long time, Billy holding him, the water flowing over them. All Tanny thought about was breathing while the water fell. In. Out. In.

"That's it," whispered Billy. "Just be, love."

He didn't even have the energy to nod; he just felt, trusted that Billy was there.

He had no idea how long they stayed like that, but eventually Billy turned off the water with one foot and then took his hands down. He let Billy take him out of the shower, move them into the bedroom, like it was nothing. The bed felt cool and soft against his skin, almost like he was floating on a cloud.

Tanny thought maybe he cried again, or maybe he laughed, he didn't know. Billy held him through it all, was right there.

Then, somehow, he was asleep.

The storm finally broke late Sunday, and Billy woke his sleeping lover with a kiss, his hand moving to take off the cock ring that had bound Tanny to his will all weekend. His lips found one of the marks he'd left on Montana's neck, his tongue tracing the dark bruise. Montana murmured softly, muttering at him. There had been tears and panic, interspersed with much rest, many long naps.

He murmured back, not actual words, just sounds and nuzzling. He was going to call Marge in the morning, tell her Tanny needed a day to recover, to come out of this subspace. Tonight, though, he was going to luxuriate in it. In Montana. He continued to nuzzle, to trace the lines of Montana's body with his tongue. He found each mark, each spot where he'd bitten, and he played with the sensitive flesh.

"Mmm. Billy." Montana's eyes fluttered open. "Lights are on."

"So they are." He chuckled. He hadn't even noticed, all his focus on his lover.

"Mmm." Montana leaned in, begging a kiss.

He granted it, lips sliding on Montana's, tongue

slipping into his lover's mouth. God, Montana tasted good. Montana's body snuggled into his, staying warm and close. He loved how loose Montana was, how relaxed in his skin his lover had become once they'd found Montana's subspace together. His lover needed so much of his focus, so much attention. Lucky for them both he had it to give, needed to give it.

"Love you." He got another slow blink, and then Montana smiled.

He chuckled, rubbing their noses together. "God, you're beautiful."

"Yours." Montana stretched, rubbing all along his body.

"Yes, every inch." He let his fingers creep up and touch the ringed nipple. This time, Montana didn't flinch, didn't do anything but moan. "Can't wait to play with these with my tongue." He touched the other one, too, just gently. Montana moaned again, fingers sliding on his stomach.

He let his own fingers drift down, caress the now bared and free cock. Montana's skin was heated silk, so soft. His lover shuddered, looking up at him, questioning.

"It's Sunday night—almost Monday. This time you'll be allowed to come. On my command."

"I'm nervous about it."

He kissed Montana for the honesty. "It'll feel good."

"Most things with you feel good."

He nodded. "That's the way it should be."

Montana nodded, leaned in to kiss his throat. He loosely stroked Montana's cock, enjoying the way it slowly filled in his hand. Those swollen lips caught his skin, sucking rhythmically. Groaning, he shifted, rubbing his own cock along Montana's skin.

"I want to suck you. Please."

He nodded. He wasn't going to say no. "Yes. Do it."

Montana slipped down, licking and sucking on his skin, heading for his cock. He groaned, spreading his legs and shifting closer, giving himself up to the pleasure.

"I love you." Montana's lips were swollen, soft, hot around the tip of his prick.

He made a noise that was meant to be a reply, but he had to clear his throat before he could make actual words come out. "You, too."

Montana's tongue dragged across the tip of his cock, tugging a little at the slit.

"Love!" Damn, Montana was getting so good at that. Billy was fairly sure the top of his head was going to come off, the pleasure was that perfect, that hot. His fingers found Montana's hair, the black fall like heavy silk.

Montana wasn't hurrying, wasn't pushing, but was adoring him, mouth surrounding him.

"So good, love." He chuckled softly as Montana nodded around his prick, head bobbing. He continued to touch and stroke Montana's skin, staying connected. He was almost breathless with pleasure, the waves pouring over him. "Soon," he whispered.

Those lips sank down to the base of his cock, the suction slow and sweet. He whimpered, the sound torn out of him. Huge, warm brown eyes stared up at him, smiling for him.

"Montana..." He breathed out his lover's name as he came.

His sweet lover drank him down, swallowing around his cock. It sent more shivers of pleasure down his spine and he groaned again. He cupped Montana's head, stroked the long hair, the soft cheeks. Montana's eyes dropped closed, that soft tongue cleaning him.

"I love the pleasure you take in that." He also loved the way compliments made his lover blush. "Come give me a kiss, beautiful, and let me taste myself in your mouth."

Montana wiggled up along his body, face lifted for a kiss. He dropped his lips over his lover's, moaning as he tasted himself there. Shudders rocked Montana's body and that pretty cock was full, heavy, leaking against his belly. He loved that Montana got aroused when sucking him off. He met Montana's rocking with movements of his own, giving the sweet cock a little friction.

Those dark eyes rolled, fastened on him. "Please."

"You need so beautifully, love."

"Just you. Please. It aches so bad."

He slid his hand over Montana's belly, feeling up the pretty muscles before finding the long cock and wrapping his hand around it. "How long has it been since I last let you come?"

"Friday."

"Mmm... two whole days. That's nothing. I should make you last until next Friday." He stroked Montana, though, keeping him hard.

"I can't. I can't, Billy. You promised."

Billy chuckled. "I'll let you come, but eventually, you'll be able to go weeks, months."

"M...m...months?"

"That's right." He increased the pace of his strokes slightly and played with Montana's slit every time his thumb went by it

"That's impossible." Montana's eyes crossed, hips moving faster.

"No. And one day I'll prove it to you. But not today." He bent to lick at Montana's mouth, tongue tracing his lover's lips.

Montana moaned, opening for him, soft cries filling his mouth. He tightened his hand and stroked faster. He wanted to see if Montana would wait for permission. He was given a desperate look, then Montana's eyes rolled, need clear on the flushed face. Leaning in, he licked the sweat from Montana's neck, moaning at the taste of salt.

Then he smiled against the warm skin before drawing back so he could watch. "Come now."

"God, yes." Montana whimpered, then bucked, riding his hand for only a few more strokes before coming.

The smell of it was wonderful and, after giving Montana a few more gentle strokes, he brought his hand up to his mouth and began licking his fingers clean. Montana tasted as good as he smelled.

Billy looked down, chuckled softly. Montana was sound asleep already. So beautiful and such a natural sub. Billy didn't know how he'd gotten so lucky, but he loved Montana and wasn't letting go.

Chapter Four

Montana woke up, stumbling through the routine of coffee and toast and God, he was tired and sore, but happy, so happy, even if the weekend was over. His ass felt odd, empty, and his hands felt light without the cuffs. Hell, his cock felt weird without the bindings.

Billy came in as he was finishing up his breakfast, looking happy and pleased. "I'm going to call Margaret, tell her you need a day and will be in tomorrow."

"Yeah? You think that'll be okay?" That sounded like heaven.

"Oh, she'll understand. In fact, I imagine she'll be pretty pleased about it." Billy came over for a kiss.

He gave one happily, their lips moving together easily. "Coffee and juice?"

"I think maybe just juice this morning. I'm going to take the day off, too." Not that Billy had to call in and clear it with anyone—there were advantages to being your own boss.

"Okay." He smiled and nodded, heading to pour Billy some juice.

"Sir."

"Huh?" He grabbed a glass.

"Okay, sir."

"What?" He was damned tired. He poured Billy's juice.

Billy's hand slid over his back, warm and good. "What, sir. You're my sub, I'd like it if you'd call me sir, especially during a weekend like the one we just had."

His eyes closed at the touch; it felt so good against his scars. "I'll try to remember." That wasn't too much to do for his Billy.

"I'd like that." Billy gave him another gentle kiss.

He hummed, kissing Billy back, letting things just go where they would. One kiss flowed into another, and then Billy rubbed their noses together, smiling at him.

"Love you." He smiled back, fingers sliding up Billy's shoulders.

Billy straddled his hips, arms looping around his shoulders. "And I love you."

"I know." He was so fucking happy.

Billy chuckled, one hand coming to trace his face, warm and gentle. Tanny couldn't help his happy, quiet hum.

"This is a good look on you."

"Sleepy on a Monday morning?" He winked.

Billy chuckled, but shook his head. "Happy, satisfied."

He kissed the corner of Billy's mouth, tongue slipping out to taste, just the tiniest bit.

"Mmm." Billy turned his head, tongue touching Tanny's. The kiss took forever, the touches long and slow and lazy. "Could do this all day."

"Okay." He was melted, boneless.

Billy laughed softly. "Okay. I need to call Margaret and you need to go sit in the living room so we're comfortable when we start this up again."

"Yes... yes, sir." He tried out the words.

The smile he got from Billy made it more than worth the effort. "Thank you." Billy dropped another kiss on his lips and then got up and grabbed the phone.

Tanny wandered into the living room, grabbing a couple of pillows and a quilt on the way.

Billy chuckled as he came into the living room, still on the phone. "Thanks, Maggie. He will. Bye now." Billy hung up the phone and prowled over to where he was sitting.

"She okay?"

"Yeah, she was pleased, actually, that she didn't have to go in. She's in what she's calling recovery mode from the storm playing up her arthritis."

"Oh." Tanny hated that she hurt so much.

"Yeah, these storms hit her hard." Billy sat down next to him, fingers reaching for him.

He lifted the blankets, let Billy in. Billy pressed close, muscled body warm and solid against him. "Morning." He nuzzled into Billy's lips.

"Good morning, my love." Billy's kiss stayed soft and warm, tongue licking at his mouth. He rested against Billy, their legs tangling together. Billy chuckled. "We're going to have to do that more often."

"Hmm? What part?"

"All of it. It makes you shine from the inside."

He blushed, but he couldn't argue. The whole weekend had left him feeling high.

"I told you." Billy gave him a smug grin. "I told you I had something better than drugs."

"I... Are you sure it's better?" he teased.

Billy laughed. "I am. I can tell just by looking at you."

"Can you? For real?" He stayed close, warm.

"I can. I told you that you were shining. I meant it literally."

"I... I don't know how... I don't know how to tell you what I feel." He didn't know how to do this the right way.

"You don't have to tell me."

Oh. Something inside him relaxed, something that had been tense without him even knowing it had been there.

Billy rolled over on top of him, fingers sliding along his arms and bringing them up over his head. "You could tell me something, though. Tell me a fantasy."

"A fantasy? Like a sex one?"

"Yeah, a sex one." Billy's fingers slid to his belly, tracing his tattoo.

"Mostly, when I get myself off, I think about things we've done." He hummed, toes curling. "About how it feels."

Billy's nose slid along the skin of his neck. "What do you think about the most?"

"I think about your hands. I think about when you put one inside me, when you spanked me. I think I'll think about this weekend a lot, too." There. Honest.

"I promise there will be many more memories like this weekend." Billy chuckled. "There will also be times when you're not allowed to touch yourself, not allowed to have any release."

"I don't know how I feel about that. About you saying I'm not allowed."

"You'll do it, though." Billy sounded so sure.

"What if I don't?" He wasn't being belligerent; he was curious.

"I'll have to bind your cock and balls again." Billy licked his ear.

He shivered a little bit and wrapped around Billy,

looking for comfort, connection.

"You look so pretty like that. No, that's not the right word. Stunning." Billy's fingers slid over his skin, touching him everywhere.

"Like what?" He moaned—he couldn't help it. He wanted that rush again.

"With your cock and balls bound in black leather. And then there's the cage." Billy groaned and rocked hard against him.

"I don't like the cage." He scooted down, lips finding Billy's nipples.

"Are you trying to distract me?"

"No. I just wanted to taste." He found it comforting to have his mouth busy.

"Okay, I'm not complaining." Billy's hand wrapped around the back of his head, held him close.

He closed his eyes, sucking slowly, hiding a little from all the feelings, all the newness. He could feel Billy's cock, solid and hot against his belly. Tanny kept sucking, using his teeth every so often. Billy began to rock against him, the thick cock leaking at the tip and leaving a trail along his belly.

"Tell me your fantasy?" He moaned the words around one nipple.

"I'm looking at it."

He looked up into those warm, happy eyes. "For real?"

Billy's fingers slid over his lips, his cheek. "For real."

"You should still tell me something."

"It's very naughty."

He looked up, intrigued. "Is it about me?"

"Oh, yes. I hope to make it come true someday. Are you sure you still want to hear it?"

Tanny nodded. As long as he was in it.

"You're wearing the cock cage and you're plugged." Billy's gaze held his. His cock jerked a little, shifted on Billy's thigh. "Your hands are cuffed and you're over my lap. I begin with a spanking—I tan your hide good and red."

He nodded, shifting a little, hips just barely rolling.

"And then I fuck you with the plug." Billy groaned, cock moving on his belly, leaking all over his skin.

Tanny headed south, lips parted as he went toward that heavy cock. "Don't stop."

He could hear Billy swallow, could feel the hands sliding into his hair stutter and then still. "I wouldn't let you come, of course. You couldn't, not with the cage. But I'd keep that plug moving—get your gland. You'd scream for me."

He groaned, moving to suck his lover, needing to hear more even as he worked Billy's prick.

"In my fantasies, I rub my cock against your belly, getting closer and closer as I fuck you with the plug."

His hand slid down, cupped his own balls.

"You're so sexy when you need to come, but can't."

Tanny groaned, sucking harder, needing desperately to shoot.

"Come on, love, suck me."

He nodded, pulling hard, hips driving in rhythm. He wanted to hear more, to know more.

"I'd fuck you until I came. And then I'd hold you, listen to you beg me to let you come."

Tanny groaned around Billy's cock, swallowing hard, hips pushing against the sofa.

"That's it. Gonna come soon. I am."

Tanny groaned, working his own cock along with

Billy's, knowing he shouldn't. Wait. Shouldn't he? Fuck.

"Don't stop, love. Don't stop."

No. No, he wouldn't. He wouldn't stop. Oh, God... Billy's hips began to push, to thrust the long cock into him. He had to stop jacking himself, to brace himself for the fucking Billy was giving his mouth.

"Love your mouth. Love you." Faster, harder, Billy moved into him. Love. He swallowed around the tip of Billy's cock. "Montana!" Billy shouted his name and come poured down his throat.

He stroked Billy's thighs, swallowed his lover down. Moaning, Billy relaxed back against the couch, fingers stroking his scalp. He hummed, reaching for his cock as he cleaned the salty spunk from Billy's prick.

"No, that's mine. Bring it here." That growl in Billy's voice was sexy.

"Yes. Yes, sir." He glanced up to check Billy's reaction.

Billy groaned and looked like he wanted to come all over again. Tanny scrambled up into Billy's lap, pressed close. Billy's lips took his as one of Billy's thick, square hands wrapped around his cock. He kissed Billy desperately, fingers digging into the strong shoulders. Billy jacked him, hand tight around him.

"I can come, right?" His eyes were rolling.

"Yes, love. Today you can come." Billy's thumbnail flicked across the tip of his cockhead.

"Fuck. Please. Again." He wouldn't need much.

"Needy love." Billy gave him what he'd asked for, though, thumb back and dragging over his most sensitive skin.

Tanny groaned, shot hard, driving into Billy's fingers over and over. Billy's kisses swallowed his groan and any other noise he cared to make, the hand around his cock staying nice and tight, giving him all the friction he needed. He shuddered through the aftershocks, clinging to Billy's shoulders.

Billy's hand finally slid away from his cock and Billy brought it to his own lips, licking the come from them.

"W...wow."

"I love that look on your face."

He grinned. "Dazed?"

"Dazed and amazingly sated."

Tanny nodded. That sounded about right.

"You know what I love more? That I'm the one who put it there." There was a wealth of satisfaction in Billy's voice.

"You're good to me, Billy." Billy was his life.

"Well, you make me very, very happy, so I guess we're a good match."

He looked up, nipped at Billy's chin. "You guess?"

Laughing, Billy nodded. "Yes."

"Butthead."

Billy bit at his lower lip. That made him laugh, made him shiver a little. "I could lose myself in you. Dive in and never come out again."

"Is that bad?"

"No. Not at all. Except we might get hungry." Billy gave him a wink.

"Uh-huh. Munch, munch, munch." Tanny relaxed, leaned into his lover.

Billy chuckled, hand sliding on his arm, his side, drifting back to idly trace some of his scars. "I do enjoy days like these. Lazy and sweet."

"I love this. I feel... whole." The words made him blush, but they were true.

Billy beamed at him, though. "I know that feeling. I

feel it, too."

"Yeah? Cool."

"Yeah, it is." Billy kissed him and then settled him close.

He tucked the blankets all around them, cuddling.

"Perfect," murmured Billy, patting his back. "Just perfect."

"No. Just yours."

Chapter Five

Billy headed into the Hammer, taking off his sunglasses and making a happy sound as the air hit him. It had been too long since he'd come in for lunch with Oliver. He looked around, finding his friend at the usual table. Waving, Billy headed over.

Oliver smiled, hailing him. "William, my friend. You have been a stranger."

He smiled back and settled in a chair across the table from his old friend. "I've been a little busy." Preoccupied. In love.

"How's Montana doing? Still working with Maggie?"

"He is. And he's doing wonderfully. Both on the job and off." He knew his smile was somewhat goofy, but he wouldn't apologize for it.

"Excellent news, my friend. You should come to the house or out for an evening. We miss you."

"I'd like that. I haven't been avoiding it, exactly, but Tanny found Christmas at your place rather... intense."

"I hope he wasn't offended."

"Oh, no. It was just a lot for him. He's not used to the lifestyle yet." Billy couldn't keep from smiling. His Tanny was learning, though.

"You look happy." Oliver patted his hand. "I'm so glad."

"I am. Tanny is amazing, and he's really coming into his own."

"No... issues with the addiction?"

"Nope." He grinned at Oliver. "I found him something much, much better than any high the pills can give him."

Oliver's smile answered his, slow and naughty, those eyes twinkling.

"How are you doing, Oliver? How is your Jack?"

"Busy, as always. He's on assignment right now, so I miss him."

"How long has he been gone?"

"Almost a month. He'll be home in March."

"Oh, that's a long time. You should come have supper with us one night this week." He'd been neglecting his friends, wrapped up as he'd been in Montana.

"I'd love to, if you think your Montana won't mind."

"I think he'll be just fine with it."

Oliver beamed at him. "I would love the company, my friend. That house is... huge."

"You should have called, Oliver. If I'd known, I would have invited you sooner."

Oliver shrugged. "You've been busy, my friend."

"I have, but a good busy." He smiled at the little waiter who came over to take their orders. "I shall have the meatloaf, please. Gravy on my mashed and a glass of milk to wash it all down." He gave Oliver a grin. "Sometimes the classics are the best."

"That they are. I'll have the chicken, please, with a coffee."

He waited until the waiter had left and then turned his full attention back to Oliver. "So what have I been missing the last few months?"

"Nothing mind-shattering. Marcus is in quite a bit, sharing his wares and his expertise."

"Excellent. I must admit, I do miss the Dom nights." He hadn't been to one since he'd met Montana.

"You should come. Montana could visit with the boys."

Billy started to chuckle. "Would that be safe?" he teased.

"If any of them are in heavy submission? Not at all."

He spent a moment enjoying the idea of Montana also in heavy submission. "We are lucky men."

Oliver nodded happily. "We are."

Their lunch came and they both spent a few minutes simply eating the food.

Finally Oliver leaned back, smiled at him again. "So, we've dispensed with the pleasantries. How is your boy's training coming?"

"Very well. We recently had a full submission weekend." He smiled, remembering how well Montana had responded, how happy he'd been.

"Indeed? How fabulous! He responded well?"

"He responded beautifully." Billy sat forward, unable to contain his smile. "He was blissed out by the end of it."

"William, how wonderful! I'm so pleased for you."

He nodded, laughing happily. "Thank you. He's really beginning to come into his own."

"I'm tickled." Oliver looked like he meant it.

"Me, too." He gave Oliver a wink and then laughed.

Oliver's laugh joined his and two more Doms wandered over to join them. Billy shook hands with them, and they chatted about their subs for awhile. All in all, it was a lovely lunch. He needed to remember to come more often, to stop being so isolated.

"Is anyone planning anything wonderful for summer?"

Rick nodded, rolling his shoulders. "We're going to a private campground of like-minded guys. Woods, campfire, leather, being bound to trees..."

Billy made a face. "Mosquitoes, black flies, Deep Woods Off..." He winked.

Rick's eyes danced. "Whipping with switches, having your lover act as your table."

"Sleeping on the ground, running into unfriendly and smelly wildlife."

"No way. I'm renting a cabin."

"Ah. So you're not really roughing it." Billy couldn't keep back his grin.

"Nope. Well... Timothy might be..."

He put his head back and laughed. God, he was having a ball. "What about you, Ollie? You and Jack going to go native out in the woods?"

"Are you quite insane, William?" Oliver looked almost affronted.

That had him laughing again. "How about your backyard—going native out there?"

Oliver had the best backyard with a huge pool. Best of all, it was very private.

"Every chance we get, my dear boy. Every chance we get."

He liked that, liked knowing that things were still hot between Oliver and Jack even after all their time together. He hoped, with every fiber of his being, that the same was going to be the case with him and Montana. He glanced at his watch. "I'm afraid I'm going to have to go, gentlemen—I promised I'd pick Tanny up from work."

"Oh, lucky lad! Getting chauffer service!" As if they all hadn't done that.

"On occasion." He stood and shook everyone's hands. "It's been great."

"Call me about supper at your place?" Oliver asked.

He nodded. "I will—it'll likely be tomorrow evening."

"I'm free."

"I'll call to confirm."

He gave Oliver's hand an extra squeeze and nodded to the others before heading out to pick up his boy.

"I'm going home, Margaret. Do you need anything?" He cleaned and swept, smiling at his boss.

"No, I'm good, honey. Is Bill picking you up today?"

"He is." Tanny nodded happily. They were going grocery shopping, and he was hoping to convince Billy to stop for a fancy coffee first.

"Excellent." She gave him a warm smile and patted his cheek. "I must say, you've been really happy, steady since that big storm. It's nice to see."

"It was a good weekend, even with the lights out." It had been... different. Very. He was possibly, maybe interested in trying it again. Maybe.

Margaret chuckled, and there was a twinkle in her eye like she somehow knew what he and Billy had been up to.

The bell on the door at the front rang as it was opened, and Billy's voice followed it. "Hi there, Teresa. How's business?"

"Not bad, Billy. Tanny and Margaret are still in the back."

"Thanks."

He bounced on his toes a little, unable to hide his excitement.

Billy came back, looking happy, a big smile on his face. "Hey, love. Are you all done yet?"

"I am. How was your day?"

"Good. I went to visit some old friends at the Hammer today."

"Oh, very nice." Billy had kept his friends. What few friends Tanny had had before Billy had... faded away.

"Nice to see you, Margaret." Billy gave her a kiss on the cheek, and then Tanny's hand was taken and he was led out. "Oliver's at loose ends at the moment—his Jack is off on assignment. I thought it might be nice to have him over for supper tomorrow night."

"Okay, Billy." Oliver didn't like him, but they'd come to be nice to each other. Mostly. "We could order pizza."

"Or we could go to the market and find something fresh to make..."

"Okay." He was easy, and he liked working with Billy in the kitchen. Together they invented interesting things.

"Cool. We need to do groceries anyway, right?"

"Yes." The urge to say 'yes, sir' hit him and he bit his bottom lip. That was weird.

Billy reached over and pulled his lip out from between his teeth. "Was there anything else, or are we good with just the market?"

"I... Would you like a coffee?"

"Sure. Your treat?"

He nodded. He made good money, even with rent and all. "My treat."

"Then where would you like to go?" Billy opened the car door for him.

"Huh? Thank you." That 'sir' wanted to pop out

again. Damn it.

"For coffee? I guess I assumed you had someplace in mind. And you're welcome." Billy leaned in to give him a quick kiss as he slid into his seat.

"Oh! Oh, sorry. I... Distracted. Stupid. Jo-Jo's?"

"Don't apologize—I'm happy to be distracting to you. Jo-Jo's it is."

Billy came around to the other side of the car and got them moving into traffic.

"How was your day?"

"I went to the Hammer for lunch. You really are distracted—what's up?"

"It's nothing." It really wasn't. It was just... he needed to think.

"You sure?"

Tanny sighed, then chuckled a little. "I'm sure. I just... I got thoughts that I gotta try to understand."

"Well, I'm always happy to talk things through with you." Billy's hand slid over his thigh in a soft caress. "Not that I'm pushing."

"It's silly, huh, really." He leaned a little, fingers on the back of Billy's hand.

"There's nothing I would consider too silly to share with me. But like I said—I'm not pushing. This time." Billy shot him a quick glance, eyes twinkling merrily.

"I just... Have you ever wanted to do something— nothing bad or anything—but you don't get it?"

"Sure, I think everyone has moments like that."

"Well, that's what's up with me. I want to do something and I don't get why."

Billy gave him another look and smiled. "Something kinky?"

"No. Well, I mean. No." No. Maybe the wanting to

have time like their weekend was, but the sir thing wasn't. Was it?

Billy found a spot close to Jo-Jo's and pulled in. "We can talk about it over our coffee if you want."

"Okay." He wasn't sure if he wanted to. "What do you want?"

"A double-foam latte with a shot of cinnamon."

"Yes, sir." He hurried in before thinking too hard about how fucking good that felt to say.

Billy made a noise that sounded rather pleased, though, just a quiet hum, and one warm hand slid along his back. That little touch settled him, and he went to order, getting himself a mint mocha with whipped cream.

Billy went and found them a table next to one of the large windows. It was open, letting in a lovely breeze. Tanny paid, chatting a little, easy in his skin.

Billy had a bright smile for him as he brought the coffees over. "I always feel very decadent when I have one of these."

"I love them. I used to spoil myself with them before."

"Coffee and uppers, huh? You sure did like to go."

"Yeah. I do. Did. I mean, it's a rush."

"It would have killed you sooner than later." Billy touched his hand, squeezed it. "And I'm very glad that didn't happen."

"I know. Me, too. I just... I like the mint." He squeezed back. "Want a taste?"

"Sure. If you'll try mine."

They traded cups and Billy took a deep sip, holding the coffee in his mouth a moment before swallowing. "That is nice. Sort of feels like I've brushed my teeth."

He chuckled. "Yeah. Chocolate, coffee, and mint. Yours is good, too." Not as good as his.

"I like it." Billy took another sip and then caught his gaze. "So, what's on your mind, love?"

He started to shake his head; he opened his mouth to tell Billy not to worry about it. "I keep wanting to... to do things. Ask you for things. Call you sir. I mean, I don't get it and I don't mind it, if you ask me to, but it doesn't make sense. It's just dumb." Well, that wasn't what he'd intended to say.

"It isn't dumb at all. I'd be very pleased if you called me sir. What is it you don't get? Why you want to do it?"

Tanny nodded, hid in his coffee cup.

"You enjoyed our weekend together very much, didn't you?" At his second nod, Billy continued. "By the end of it, I asked you to call me 'sir.' I imagine, in your mind, calling me sir is associated with how good you felt after our weekend. And a part of you understands how it's all a part of being my sub."

He thought about what Billy said and it worked. It sounded like logic, and he felt less ridiculous. "I just don't know how to feel about all this. I want to do it right. I want it to make sense, you know?"

"You're doing great, love. I'm very proud of you and very happy with our life together."

"Yeah? You think?"

"I don't think—I know."

"I'm happy, too. Scary happy."

"Try and enjoy it instead of worrying about it."

"I am, honest. I told you, it wasn't a big deal. I just needed to work it out."

"Okay, okay. We can change the subject." Billy chuckled. "How's work going?"

"Good!" He laughed, nodded, happy to talk about his day, his books, the stacks of paper and the things he learned.

"That's great. Margaret seems really happy with your progress."

"I hope so. I really do. I like making things."

Billy took his hand and turned it over a few times, tracing his fingers. "You've got an artisan's hands."

"Thank you, sir." His fingers curled, the sensation sliding up his arms.

"Mmm, you're welcome." Billy continued to stroke his fingers, the touches gentle but compelling.

Tanny let himself relax, let the quiet coffee shop and Billy and the warm coffee make him smile.

"What do you want to do after we've shopped?"

"I want to go home and..." He blushed, met Billy's eyes. "I want you, huh? I mean, not just fucking, but I want you."

Billy's eyes went dark, intimate. "You want your sir."

He nodded, his belly aching and tight. "Is that okay?" He needed to know this was good, right.

Billy nodded. "More than. It's us." Billy's hand wrapped around his. "You're mine and I'm yours."

"Yes, sir. You're mine."

Billy looked very pleased at that. "I am."

Their hands stayed linked together as Billy took another sip of his latte. Tanny finished his coffee and it was nice, to sit. Be together. He thought he could get used to it.

The place started filling up with afternoon patrons and Billy glanced at his watch. "We should head out to the market before the nicest stuff is gone."

"Sounds good." He stood up, took their cups to the bin.

Yeah. Yeah, he could get used to this.

Chapter Six

Billy hummed as he went through the drawer where they kept their 'toys.' They were going to need a chest soon; the drawer just wasn't cutting it. Not to mention he wanted to make choosing the things they'd use a part of the ritual.

He grabbed the cock cage. He'd suck Montana and then put it on, make his lover wear it until just before Oliver came over tomorrow. He also took the heavy leather cuffs—Montana had really gotten off on the weight of them, and he'd gotten off on how they looked. Next, he pulled out a fat little plug so he could come in Montana's ass and keep his seed inside.

Once he had everything out that he wanted, he stripped. Montana was in the shower, washing away the day's work, but Billy didn't figure he'd be too long. He carried everything in a blanket out into the living room, where he'd already started a fire.

His Montana had asked for this, for him. The look in those dark eyes... It made him hard, made him ache. He said a little prayer to whatever gods looked out for Doms and subs and brought them together. He'd found his match, and it felt very good.

He laid the blanket out in front of the fire and the toys

out on the coffee table so Montana would see them.

Montana came padding out to him, wrapped in an old blue robe. "I didn't know.... whether I should get dressed."

"I like undressing you, but it's not necessary today. Come stand by me." Montana walked over, stepped close. "Mmm." He slipped his hands into the robe, fingers stroking over his lover's belly before slipping down to wrap around the lean hips. Montana's prick was half-hard, the dark pubes above them glossy, shiny. "I have the things we're going to use this evening out on the coffee table."

Montana looked, chewed his bottom lip.

He leaned in to nibble on Montana's neck. "I'm going to suck you off, first. Then it's cage time."

"I hate the cage, sir."

"A part of you enjoys it. A part of you loves it." He dropped his hand down and began to stroke the long cock.

Montana's moan filled the air as he shook his head. "I don't think so."

Billy started to go down to his knees. He licked Montana's neck on the way and whispered, "Liar."

"Am not."

Billy's chuckles wafted over Montana's nipples. Those pretty bits of flesh went rock-hard for him, tightening around the piercings. He flicked the ring with his tongue and twisted the barbell with his fingers.

"Billy." Montana groaned, went up on tiptoe.

"I love how sensitive these are." He flipped the ring with his tongue again, caught the tip and tugged. He could smell Montana's need now, feel the heat of the heavy cock. He went the rest of the way down onto his knees and rubbed his cheek along the thick heat. He groaned.

"So good. That feels so good."

"From this end, too, love." He rubbed a little longer and then turned his head, tongue sliding along the same path his cheek had taken.

"Love..." Montana's fingers stroked through his hair, petting him.

He nodded and took in the tip of Montana's cock, lips sliding over the sensitive flesh.

"Oh. Oh, please. Your mouth is..."

He pulled off and smiled up at Montana, winked. "All yours." Then he went back down onto the hot prick, taking it all in.

"Mine. Please, sir." Montana's head fell back, throat working as that hard cock pushed into his mouth, over and over.

He rumbled around Montana's cock, adding vibrations to his suction. The little sounds got louder and louder, Montana's hips moving faster. He slid a hand behind Montana, working one finger slowly into his lover's ass.

"I want... I want you. I like your hands."

He knew. His hands liked Montana, too. His head bobbed faster. Montana's eyes closed, his sweet lover losing himself to the sensations. Billy pushed his finger in and out of Montana as he sucked, his tongue slapping at whatever part of Montana's cock it could.

"More? More, please?"

He pushed a second finger in with the first, Montana yielding to him beautifully.

"Yes.... Thank you, sir. Thank you. So good."

He nodded, then took Montana deep, swallowing around the tip of his lover's cock. Montana's hips rolled, driving in deep once more before hot spunk splashed on his tongue. Billy swallowed it all down, his fingers pushing deeper and pressing against Montana's gland. Sharp sounds pushed out of Montana, that pretty cock not flagging. He nipped on the tip, his teeth scraping a little.

"Fuck." Montana jerked away, pushing his fingers deeper.

"Mmm... yes. I do think that's on the agenda. Eventually." He wriggled his fingers, sliding against that sweet gland again.

"Oh, Billy. Please. More..."

He pushed against it a few more times and then let his fingers slide away. "We'll come back to it." Montana groaned, but didn't argue. "Grab the cage," he ordered, still on his knees in front of Montana.

"Billy. I won't fit." Montana reached for the cage, fingers trembling.

"We'll wait until you do." He knew how to relax Montana, make him melt. The metal was cold on his fingers, but warmed quickly. He moved to sit, his legs spread. "Come sit here." He patted the space in front of him.

Montana sat with him, back cuddling up against his chest. He dropped soft kisses along Montana's shoulders and neck, his fingers reaching around to massage his lover's thighs. Montana hummed, thighs parting for him easily.

"I want you to go soft so we can put on the cage." He kissed Montana's earlobe.

"Why?" Montana moaned, pressed back against him.

"Because you're not going to come until I say you can." He was trying to decide if that would be tomorrow morning, or if he'd make Montana wear it during work.

Montana was breathing with him, beginning to relax. "There will come a time when you'll go soft because I ask it of you."

"That's impossible..."

Billy chuckled and shook his head. "No, love. It's not."

"Just being near you makes me hard."

"Mmm, flattery might get you a hand job." He slid his fingers along Montana's prick.

"Not flattery. Truth." Montana moaned, hips moving slowly. "Your hands."

"You love them touching you." He kept touching.

"Yes." Montana loved being touched, spread, made to feel.

He traced Montana's cock over and over, loving it with his fingers. He nudged the heavy balls, giving them the same treatment. Such things they could explore together, such pleasures. He rubbed one finger over Montana's slit. Then drew it back again, this time pressing in over it.

"Oh..." Montana's entire body arched.

"I saw a special cage the other day. I want to get it for you." He kept mixing it up—hard and soft touches, pinches and caresses.

"Special?" Montana's ass rubbed against his cock, over and over.

"Uh-huh." His voice had gone thick. "It had a middle piece that filled you here." He pressed his finger into Montana's slit again.

"I... I... That's not real, is it?"

Chuckling, he shifted Montana slightly, that sweet ass rubbing in just the right spot. "I shall have to buy it so you believe me."

"Oh, God. Billy."

"Uh-huh." He licked Montana's skin, his hand finally circling the hard cock and stroking it.

"Your hand feels better than mine."

"Your own hand is simply business, hmm?"

"Uh-huh. Just a way to start the day."

Billy tilted his head. "Do you masturbate every weekday morning?" He knew Montana didn't on the weekends—they woke together, then, and often got each other off, too. And of course, Montana didn't when he asked his lover not to.

"In the shower, to wake up."

"I want you to stop." It struck him as funny, him telling Montana to stop masturbating while he masturbated Montana.

"What? Why?"

The temptation to say "Because I said so" was huge. "Because when and how you come is a part of what we have together. I get to say when you can come, when you can't, and how."

"But..." Montana frowned. "That's not really... I mean... I sorta need that."

"No, you don't. You need me to be your sir, and part of that is I control the orgasms. All of them."

Montana whimpered softly, head ducking. Billy kept kissing, kept jacking.

"Sir. Want you."

"I know, love. You'll have me. After the cage is on." He loved those needy, deep cries. "We have to deal with this first, though, hmm?" He teased the tip of Montana's cock with his thumb on every upstroke.

"S...sensitive. It aches." Montana twisted for him, pushed into his touch.

"So hard for me."

"Yes. For you." The little drops were falling faster.

"Show me, Montana. Come for me." Come on his command.

"Love." Montana's belly went rock-hard, eyes unfocused and wide, as seed sprayed.

"Yes!" He buried his nose in Montana's neck, taking in the smell of his lover's skin and come mixing together.

Montana slowly relaxed, leaned into him. He grabbed the cage and slipped the rings over Montana's prick while it was softening. The steel framed the sweet cock, compressed it, contained it, and he slipped the tiny gold padlock in to close it.

"There you go. So beautiful." It made him so hard to see Montana wearing the cage.

"Billy..." Montana groaned, fingers sliding over the cage.

"Now you can obey me when I say 'no coming.'"

"Yes. Yes, sir."

"I do like the way that sounds."

"How long will you keep the cage on me?"

"Until tomorrow night." No one would know Montana was wearing it. No one but him and Montana.

"But... but, Billy. I work tomorrow."

"You'll be wearing pants, won't you?"

"Yes!" Oh, that was a horrified look.

Billy chuckled. "Then no one will know."

"Billy..." Montana pushed into his arms, seeking comfort. He ran his hands over Montana's skin, top to bottom, touching the skin he loved. "Why do you like the cage?"

"Aside from the fact that it looks sexy as hell? I love the way it makes you yield to my demands."

"But I don't say no..." Montana leaned into him, the

steel of the cage warming.

"If you weren't caged, would you be able to not come for days?" Weeks. Months. They were going to explore Montana not coming. Explore it a lot.

"I don't know."

"With the cage, we can be sure. Plus it has the added bonus of being very sexy." It made him so very hard.

Montana pressed closer, hiding in him.

"I brought out the cuffs. I won't make you wear them to work." Although the idea had his heart thudding hard—he could feel each beat in his cock. "This time."

"Billy! Billy, I'll get fired for being a pervert. Please, I love my job."

Billy had to laugh at that, he just couldn't help it. "First of all, the leather cuffs look like heavy-duty bracelets and only people into the lifestyle would probably know differently. Second, rather than thinking you were a pervert, I imagine Margaret would approve."

"You keep saying that. That's just weird."

"Why? Margaret's a bigger, badder top than I'll ever be."

"Margaret is a sweet old lady, Billy."

"Yes. She's also a Dom. The two are not mutually exclusive, love."

"Like, as in leather and whips and stuff? Margaret?"

"Like bondage and submission and anything that includes. Like leather and whips."

"That's just weird."

Billy chuckled. "Why? Because she's old? Or because she's your teacher?"

"Yes. Mostly because she's like my gramma."

"In that case, I can see where you'd want to see her as a sweet old lady."

Montana chuckled, face nuzzling in his throat. "I love you, huh?"

"I know, I count on it." He slid his hands down to cup Montana's ass, one of his fingers finding that sweet hole. Montana's cheeks squeezed, tightening for him. Groaning, he pushed his finger deeper. "So tight. So hot." All his.

Montana's lips were on his throat—soft, heated, gentle. He lay back onto the covers, bringing Montana down with him. Tilting his head back, he encouraged the soft movements of Montana's lips. Montana loved him easily, tongue tracing the lines of his throat, making him gasp and swallow hard. He moved his finger in and out of Montana's body, going slowly as well, making it about the sensations rather than getting off. Montana made him need, made him ache, more than a little.

"Gonna have your ass, love. Gonna spank it and lick it and fuck it." He felt the little, desperate moan. "And then I'm going to put the plug in and hold me inside you all night long."

"All night?" Montana liked that; he could tell.

"Yes. I won't make you wear the plug to work. Not tomorrow, anyway." One day, he'd send Montana off entirely done up: plugged, caged, the cuffs. He'd know that Montana was desperate for him, for relief, for sensation. Moaning at the thought, he rolled them, putting Montana beneath him. Arms and legs wrapped around him, held him close. "Hungry, greedy, beautiful love." Billy interspersed each word with a kiss.

"I just want to be right for you, to be enough."

"You are, love. Through and through."

"You're sure?"

"Very sure." He pushed a finger back into Montana's ass.

Montana moaned. "Do you remember when you put your hand inside me?"

"How could I forget something like that?" He flicked Montana's nipple ring. "You want me to do it again?"

"I don't know. I just... I think about it, sometimes."

"Tell me your thoughts."

"I remember it, that's all. I remember how it felt, how it was."

"You like remembering it." After all, Montana had confessed to jacking off to that memory. He pushed a second finger in; Montana took it easily.

"I do. It was special."

"It all feels special with you." He knew it sounded like hyperbole, but it was the truth.

Montana nodded, beginning to ride his touch again, up and down, up and down. "Can we do it again? When the cage comes off?"

"Tomorrow night. Your ass and my hand have a date."

Montana's laugh rang out, so sweet, filling the air.

He let his fingers slip out and lubed them up before pushing three into Montana's ass. He felt Montana's moan all around his fingers. Smiling against Montana's skin, he wriggled his fingers and found that little gland. That earned him a groan, and Montana jerked away.

"So sensitive now." He nudged it again.

"Yes..." He watched Montana blush.

He played with Montana's ass for a while, enjoying the sensation of that tight little ass squeezing around his fingers. He could see the effect of the sensations, the feelings clear on Montana's face. His free hand drifted over Montana's body from neck to the pierced nipples and on down to the caged cock. Montana's skin was hot and so soft compared to the hard steel of the cage. Montana whimpered, ass muscles clenching on his fingers.

"My beautiful lover." He touched the tip of Montana's cock through the cage and then reached for the sweet balls, rolling them easily.

"Yours..." He watched Montana twist and arch.

While Montana was distracted, he slid his fingers away and pushed right into Montana's heat. His lover's cry filled the air, deep and needy. Groaning, he held himself there for as long as possible. When he couldn't possibly stay still for a moment longer, he pulled out almost all the way before pushing back in again. He wanted to scream with it, with the pure pleasure of it. Instead, he repeated his lover's name over and over. "Montana. Montana."

"Yes. Love. Yours."

"Mine!" He called it out and kept pounding into Montana's body.

"Yours." Montana's bound hands stroked his chest.

Groaning, he held on as long as he could, pushing into Montana's body like it was the pathway to heaven. At last he couldn't hold back any longer and he cried out, filling Montana with his come. He held Montana's hips, kept that ass tight around his cock. Panting for each breath, he lay over Montana's body, enjoying their closeness for a moment.

"Love you." Montana sighed, smiled, fingers stroking his skin.

He smiled back. "Yes. Love you." The spell broken, he reached for the plug and got it ready. A little lube and he settled in place, ready to push it in as soon as his prick came out. Montana's body clenched, squeezed his cock. He groaned. "Love. I need to come out eventually."

"Why?" Montana teased.

That had him laughing and he nearly slipped out

before he was ready. He ran one hand down Montana's ass, squeezed. "Now, love. I'm going to come out now." He gently began to pull out.

Montana panted, body fighting him for every inch. He watched Montana's face as he withdrew and then pushed the plug in. Montana groaned, lips parted, cheeks flushed. He twisted the plug, playing with it, with Montana, before settling it in.

"S...so mean." Montana's heart wasn't in the complaint, not at all.

He chuckled. "That's me. Mr. Mean."

"Mr. Meanypants." Montana was beginning to laugh.

"Meanypants." He shook his head and his chuckles turned into outright laughter.

"Meanybutt?"

"If I'm Meanybutt, then you're Pluggybutt." Billy couldn't remember a time he'd been so silly or laughed so hard. It was rather fun.

"Pluggybutt!" Montana howled for him, both of them gasping for air.

It took awhile from them to come down. He'd stop laughing and Montana's giggles would set him off again, and vice versa. Montana ended up in his lap, warm and relaxed, still chuckling every now and again. He nuzzled into Montana's neck, breathing in sweat and musk and love.

"Mmm. It's been a good day."

"Yeah." He kissed Montana again. "They're all good with you." It was sappy and cheesy, but also the truth. Montana's smile let him know that he wasn't alone in that, not at all. "Love," he murmured, holding Montana close.

Love and peace and happiness. It was all good.

Chapter Seven

Okay. Okay. He'd chopped vegetables and cut meat and cleaned the house. The floors. He'd been to the bedroom and had seen the lube. The towels. Tubing attached to the short, wide, cock-shaped nozzle which didn't even belong in the bedroom and how was he supposed to entertain Oliver knowing that it was there and his cock was in the cage?

Then there were two plugs—a big one and a really big one. Why did Billy need two? Why were they out? What was he going to do?

Billy came in with his closed laptop and stowed it next to the dresser. "Hey, love. What do you need help with?"

"Everything's ready to stir fry. The house is clean. Should we... put this away?"

"We have an hour before Oliver should be here."

"Uh-huh." He looked at Billy, just a little panicked. Surely Billy wouldn't ask him to do something as huge as taking his lover's hand and then entertain.

"Let's go shower together, clean you out, and put in the plug. I love the way you move with it in."

"I. I. I." It was like the single word was stuck in his throat.

"Love." Billy took his chin in hand and tilted his face.

Then Billy kissed him. Hard.

Oh. Better. He stepped closer, letting Billy make his head swim. Billy hummed and rumbled into the kiss, filling his mouth with love noises. The knot in his stomach relaxed, released. Billy's fingers traced over the scars on his back, right on down to his ass. He hummed, leaned toward that touch. Fingers digging in, Billy pulled him close. One finger strayed, finding his hole and teasing it. That touch he understood. Hell, that touch he needed.

"Come shower with me," Billy whispered, fingertip pushing into him.

Tanny nodded, lips clinging to Billy's, that slow, gentle touch mesmerizing. Billy reached for something, lips staying with his the whole time. As Billy started walking backward out of the bedroom, Tanny could feel something in Billy's hand, something cold. When he opened his mouth to ask, he got another kiss, Billy's lips hot, hard against his. Billy kissed him all the way to the bathroom, making a meal of his mouth, his lips and teeth and tongue. He held onto his lover's shoulders, cock trapped and aching, throbbing in its cage.

Billy didn't bother turning on the light in the bathroom and still didn't let him go as he turned on the shower. Tanny leaned, letting Billy breathe into him, the act making him dizzy. Billy was there to hold him up, though, strong and sure. He rested against Billy's chest, blinking so slowly. His clothes disappeared under Billy's fingers and before he knew it, they were in the shower, the water warm and good on his skin. It was dark and intimate, quiet, both of them in the steam.

Billy washed him with soap and then rinsed him; Billy's hands knew him so well. His lips were on Billy's throat, tongue flicking out to taste the water and salt of Billy's skin.

"I'm going to clean you inside now."

He moaned and stepped closer, needing Billy's love, strength.

"I have you."

"Okay. Don't let me go."

"Never. You're mine, remember." Billy's fingers slid over his name tattooed on Tanny's belly.

Tanny smiled. Yes. Yes, he knew.

"Turn around for me, love. I need to lube this thing up and work it into you." This thing was the cock-shaped nozzle that he'd seen on the bed earlier.

He turned, groaning a little. He wasn't sure about this. He wasn't sure at all. Two of Billy's fingers, slick and familiar, pushed into him. The water and the darkness surrounded him, made it easier to breathe. Soft kisses slid over his shoulders, Billy drinking the water from his skin. It was easy, here, not to think. Not to worry. Those fingers spread him, opened him up and got him wet and slick inside. Tanny rested his arms against the tile, his cheek on his arm.

"Love you, Montana. Love you so much." A third finger joined the first two, stretching him wider.

"Love." He propped one foot on the side of the tub, spreading.

"I think you're ready now." Billy's fingers disappeared.

"Are you sure?"

"Yes." The heat of Billy's cock was suddenly pushing inside him.

"Billy!" It surprised him, thrilled him, and he pushed back, eager.

"Yeah." Billy's hips met his ass and then his lover began to rock into him with long, slow strokes.

He met each stroke, grunting as Billy filled him. Billy's

hands slid over his chest, played with his nipple piercings and then stroked his belly.

"Love." They found a solid, forceful rhythm, one that left him shivering, aching.

Billy's hand grabbed for his cock, fingers warm where he could feel them through the cage. Then Billy groaned against his neck and came deep inside him. He sobbed softly, wanting so badly, needing help, needing his sir.

Billy came out of him and the hard, cock-shaped nozzle slipped in. Then Billy came around in front of him to press soft kisses over his face. He reached for his lover, moaning softly.

"Love you." Billy's arms wrapped around him.

"This is hard."

"Sometimes good things are hard." Billy fiddled with something and suddenly liquid began to slide into him from the nozzle.

"Oh, God. Oh, God. Billy."

"It's okay, love. I have you." One of Billy's hands stayed on his ass, the other snuck back around to stroke his belly.

"I don't like this." He was shaking, his heart beating so hard.

"You're almost done, love. Just a few more moments."

"Love you, huh?"

"Good. You, too."

He was going to cry, maybe, or something. Billy's mouth found his, tongue pushing in and bringing the flavor of his lover with it. He sobbed, latching onto the kiss, onto the promises it made. By the time Billy stopped kissing him, the water had stopped flowing into him.

"I... I... What do I do?"

"Just hold it in while I take out the nozzle."

"Oh, God. Please, don't. Please don't make me." He got another kiss that stopped his panic.

"You're fine, love. Just fine."

"I'm scared." He wasn't fine.

"I'm right here, love. Right here, and I'm not going anywhere."

He chuckled and tried to breathe. "I'm not sure that's better. I'm about to explode."

"Just hold on a moment longer and we'll get you to the can."

"This is embarrassing."

"I've had my hand right inside you, Montana. There's no reason for this to be embarrassing."

"I know, but... it is. That's private."

"All of you is mine, Montana. All of you."

He sobbed once, his heart slamming in his chest. Billy kept rubbing his belly, now leading him to the toilet. He was devastated, panicky, hand clinging to Billy's.

"I have you, Montana. It's fine. You're good."

He sat, head in his hands. "Please go."

"You don't have to be embarrassed, love." Billy's fingers slid through his hair, massaged his scalp.

His body couldn't hold the water and he groaned as it left him. "I'm sorry."

"Sorry? For what?"

"I don't know."

"Then you don't need to apologize." Billy tilted his head and kissed him, lips soft and sweet on his.

Tears leaked from him, wetting his cheeks, and he didn't understand why. Billy simply kissed them away, murmuring softly, loving on him. His trembling hands slid up Billy's arms.

"You've done very well, Montana, and I'm so happy."

"I don't know what to do."

"There isn't anything to do, love. We'll go back into the shower to rinse you off, and then, before you get dressed, we can put one of the plugs in."

"I won't be able to eat. I feel all shaky."

"Fifteen minutes together in bed and I bet you'll be feeling much better." Billy stroked and petted him.

"You think so?" He could trust Billy. He knew he could.

"I do. You and me and some quiet time kissing and necking? I bet it settles you right out." Billy gave him a wink and encouraged him back into the shower. His legs were like rubber bands, all bouncy and loose. "I've got you," Billy reminded him, arm around his waist, guiding him.

"I know. I think I know that."

Billy kissed his shoulder. "I like saying it. I like knowing you know it. It's important."

"Will you always? Have me?"

"I will. I love you, Montana."

"I love you." The water was still warm, still good.

Billy gently sponged him down to get him soapy again, and then rinsed him off. Then they were out of the tub, heading for the bed, his body wrapped in a huge, soft towel. Billy laid him down on the bed, set the alarm for twenty minutes, and crawled in with him. He hid, eyes closed, surrounding himself in the warmth and smell of Billy.

Those strong hands moved over him, stroking and touching, keeping him warm, safe. Keeping them there and together and whole. It stayed unhurried and loving until the alarm went off. Billy switched it off and then continued to touch him, two slick fingers gliding into his ass like they still had all the time in the world.

"It's okay? Your friend." He couldn't even remember the man's name.

"We have plenty of time, love. And Oliver will be exactly on time."

Oliver. That was it. God, Billy made him stupid, fuzzy in the head.

"My cock aches." The cage was coming off after their supper. Billy had promised.

"I know. Think of how amazing it's going to feel when I take it off later tonight."

"I'm trying to."

Billy's fingers stretched him wide, and then the head of a plug pushed against his hole.

"B...Billy." It was big. So big.

"Right here, love." Billy's mouth slid along his throat.

"It's big." The plug stretched him and spread him.

"You need to know it's there or there's no point."

"I... I'll know. I'll know."

"You definitely will." Billy twisted the plug, pushing it a little deeper.

He whimpered softly, hips moving in random jerks. Billy played with his ass and the plug for a few minutes, and then pushed it deep, seated it. He crawled up Billy's body, almost desperate now.

"After supper, when Oliver's gone, I'll take the cage off, let you come."

He nodded. "And the rest?"

"We'll move you up to the next-sized plug after that."

He shuddered. "Then what?" He knew. Then more water, more pressure, and Billy's hand.

"Then I'll give you what you really want." Billy's hand slid over his ass, fingers spread wide.

He closed his eyes, muscles going taut.

"I love how even just talking about it makes you glow."

"I don't know what to say, Billy."

"You don't have to say anything. Your body is glowing, your eyes are shining. I don't need more than that." Billy kissed him softly and then stroked his arm "We should get up and get dressed. Oliver will be here soon."

He nodded, trying to not let the worry back in. "I don't want to embarrass you in front of him."

"You won't, love. You've never embarrassed me in front of Oliver. Not that time we went out for supper, not at Christmas, and you won't tonight."

"Promise? I'm not... all together."

"I promise, Montana. No matter how 'together' you think you are. You're mine and I love you. You."

"Yours." He nodded, tried to take a deep breath. "I wish Jack was coming, too."

"You like Jack, hmmm? If you'd like, we can ask Oliver to have him give you a call when he's back from assignment. The subs tend to get together a few times a month for movies and dinners and whatnot."

"Maybe. Maybe just him. I'm not good at making friends."

"Maybe you just make them a little slower than most, hmm?" Billy patted his hip and gave him a soft kiss.

"Maybe. Are we friends?"

"Friends, yes. And lovers. We can be both."

"That's good for me."

"Mmm, for me, too." Billy got out of bed and held a hand to him, pulled him up.

Moving slowly, the plug inside him pressing, heavy, he made his way across the room toward his dresser. He glanced over at Billy, who was watching him, eyes on his ass.

"What?" He reached down, covering his crack.

"Don't do that. I love the way you look, the way you walk with that big a plug in you."

He moaned. He had to. He didn't have a choice.

Billy nodded and chuckled, the sound so husky. "Yeah, that's how I feel."

"You make me a little crazy."

"Just a little?"

He carefully bent and grabbed some soft, loose slacks. "Uh-huh."

"I'll have to work harder at it, then." Billy's voice sounded closer and suddenly a warm hand slid over his ass.

"Billy!" He jerked forward, hips pumping, ass working the plug.

"Shh, shh. I'm just touching, love." He turned and pushed into Billy's arms. Billy's arms wrapped around him, a soft kiss dropping on his head. "You are jumpy. I think I know how to help you relax." Billy slid down onto his knees and began working open the cage.

"Oh. Oh, God. Please." Please.

As soon as the cage was off, Billy's mouth slid over his cock. His cock went immediately, desperately hard. Billy didn't waste any time, he simply went up and down on him, suction strong. It only took seconds before he was coming, shooting so hard he screamed.

Billy swallowed him down and sucked a moment longer, pulling off slowly. His hip was patted. "Better, hmm?"

"Uh-huh." He blinked, nodded. "Thank you."

Chuckling, Billy stood and handed him a pair of

underwear and the soft pants he'd already chosen. He thought he might survive dinner. At least the stir-frying part. Maybe.

Billy dressed nicely but casually, and by the time they were back in the kitchen, checking they had everything ready to fry, there was a knock on the door.

"Ah, he's perfectly on time. As always."

"I'll stay in here and start." Oliver didn't like him; Tanny knew that.

"No, come with me to greet our guest." Billy's arm slid around his waist.

Every step moved the plug inside him and made the pit of his belly ache. Billy's hand was hot on his hip. Hot and huge. Full of promise.

Oliver smiled as the door opened. "William. Montana. So nice of you to invite me over." A bottle of wine and a huge chocolate cake were handed over.

Billy rescued the bottle and let him take the cake before moving in to give Oliver a hug. "If we'd known you were all on your own, we would have invited you sooner."

"Well, I don't like to impose. I do love the new paint, William. Beautiful color."

"Thank you. Montana did a great job." Billy closed the door and they all wandered back toward the kitchen. "We usually eat in here, and I didn't think you'd mind if we didn't stand on ceremony while you were with us this evening."

"Not at all."

He could feel Oliver's eyes on him.

"Tanny, why don't you start the stir fry and I'll set the table."

"Sure. Would... would you like a drink, Oliver? Sir. Uh. Billy, I mean. Uh."

Billy came over and touched him lightly, hand on his shoulder. "You can call me whatever you're comfortable with, Montana. Oliver won't balk if you call me 'sir.'"

"Of course not and I would adore something to drink, thank you."

Tanny nodded, still jittery. "What about you?" he asked Billy.

"I'll have some of that lemonade you made with the fresh lemons."

"Oh, that sounds luscious." Oliver nodded. "That sounds perfect."

Oliver sat and Billy started setting the table, both of them chatting away. Every now and then Billy would ask him a question, draw him into the conversation. Oliver was surprisingly funny, making him laugh again and again with his little jokes.

The stir fry didn't take long to make and soon they were all sitting down to eat, which brought the plug he was wearing right back to the front of his mind. He tried not to wiggle, not to move, but it was hard. It was getting hard, too.

After they'd cleaned their plates, Billy brought out Oliver's cake, cutting them each big slices. His was passed over with a knowing smile and a brush of Billy's fingers against his. He nibbled, not really hungry anymore, more anticipating.

"Would you like an after-dinner drink, Ollie?"

"I'd better not—I'm driving tonight and Jack will kick my ass if he comes home and finds out I drove under the influence."

Billy chuckled, then nodded, and Tanny started cleaning up.

"Thank you for having me, my friend. I admit, I was

beginning to feel quite lonely. You and your boy have reminded me what I have to look forward to."

Was he Billy's boy? Was it okay if he was?

"We should have you over again when Jack's back."

"Jack and I would love that. We could play cards."

"Sounds good. Give me a call when Jack's back and we'll work something out."

"I think I should head home, my friend. Jack is supposed to call later for a little chat."

Billy patted Oliver on the back. "We don't want to keep you from that." Billy winked and laughed.

"No. No, they come too few and far between, my friend." Oliver stood, held a hand out to Tanny. "Thank you for dinner."

He shook, nodded. "You're welcome."

"If he's going to be longer than a couple more weeks, you let me know, Ollie. We'll have you over again." Billy gave Oliver a warm hug.

Oliver nodded. "Enjoy your evening, lads. Thank you again."

"You're welcome." Billy waved as Oliver started down the stairs and closed the door behind him. Locked it.

Tanny's hands were shaking and he stared at Billy, locked in place.

Billy turned around and gave him a smile. "That was a good dinner, don't you think?"

"Uh-huh." He stared at Billy.

"What are you thinking, love?"

"I need you."

"Good thoughts." Billy opened his arms, just like that.

He nodded and headed over, pressed into Billy's embrace. Billy's mouth found his, the kiss hard and sweet at the same time. One hand slid down to tap at the plug filling him up. He whimpered, tongue fucking Billy's lips. Billy started walking them down the hall to the bedroom, hands roaming his back and his ass, fingers playing with the plug as they continued to kiss. He stayed wrapped around his lover, groaning, moving with Billy.

"I'm going to put in the other plug," Billy told him, speaking against his lips. "Going to stretch you."

Tanny couldn't stop his moan, his little cry.

"Get you ready for my hand."

"Billy. I love you." He thought he'd just say it, over and over, until he thought of something else.

"Good. Good." Billy's mouth covered his for another hard kiss. "I love you, too."

"I don't know what to do. I need help."

"What you have to do is what you always have to do. Feel. Let it happen." Billy's fingers slid beneath his shirt and started skimming it off.

"Are you going to put more water in me tonight?" His pierced nipples ached, throbbed.

"You'd like that, wouldn't you? Like to be filled in this new way." Billy's fingers moved to his piercings, flicking and tugging, playing.

"I don't... No. No, I don't..."

"No? That's what you always say." His pants were undone, left to fall onto the floor.

"It is not." Except that was another no...

Billy chuckled, fingers slipping around to slide along his crack, moving toward his hole and the plug. He let himself relax, let himself trust Billy, follow. Billy's fingers grabbed the end of the plug, twisted it. His body went tight and he stumbled forward a few steps.

Billy's hands caught him, kept him from falling. "Let's get you bent over the bed, love."

"Oh. Okay. Okay." Bent over sounded more stable, absolutely.

"Mmm... love this ass." Billy's hand smacked his right butt cheek.

"No spanking!" His toes curled.

"You're asking me to resist this beautiful ass?"

"I'm not beautiful."

Billy chuckled. "Are we going to start this old argument again?"

"Yep." He relaxed a little, laughing himself. Oh, that was better. Much.

Billy's fingers dug into his ass, two tugging at the plug, slowly working it out. His body held onto it, muscles staying tight. Billy's hand swatted his ass again. "Come on, love. I won't leave you empty."

"I'm... I'm trying. I'm sorry."

Billy's tongue was suddenly on his ass, licking around the plug. This sound jerked out of him, lost and rough and raw. Billy's hands moved over his back, over his scars as that tongue continued to lick and wet him. His hips began to move, to ride the pleasure.

Thick fingers reached between his legs and rolled his balls, then rubbed the skin between his balls and his stretched hole. He spread wider, offered every inch of himself. Billy kept pushing at the end of the plug as he licked, sending it across his gland over and over.

"I'll come," he warned, as his toes curled.

"Don't." Billy disappeared for a moment and then came back and slipped a leather band around the base of his cock. His spine arched, cock throbbing. "There. Now we can have some fun."

"F...fun?" He leaned forward more.

"Yes. Bigger plug, sucking, nipple tweaking..."

"So mean." So good.

"Yeah, I think we already covered that. Mr. Meanypants, wasn't it?"

"I think so." He chuckled, went up on his toes. "Thank God I'm off work tomorrow."

"Are you? I might have to change my plans somewhat."

"Uh-huh." He'd be sore tomorrow, needing Billy's strength.

"Yeah. I think I'm going to start with this." Billy's hand landed on his ass.

He jerked forward, surprised, the sting shocking him.

"I love seeing my handprint on your ass."

He groaned, eyes closing. "Why?"

"It's sexy. Beautiful. It means you're mine." Another smack landed on his right cheek. He went up on tiptoe, his cock starting to drip. "Look at you." Billy's hand kept smacking him, working both his cheeks, nudging the plug.

"I don't want to." He wanted to watch Billy, to feel.

"I do, though. So beautiful." Billy's tongue dragged along his ass cheek, hot and stinging.

He crawled up on the bed, hips jerking.

"Where are you going?" Billy tugged him back down, fingers beginning to work with the plug again.

This time, his body let the plug go, and his cry echoed through the air. Billy hardly let any air hit his hole before the thick, hot cock pushed into him.

"Billy!" He hadn't expected that. Not at all.

"That's right. It's me." Billy chuckled, hands hard on his hips as the thick cock thrust into him again.

"I didn't... I didn't think... Oh, fuck."

"You didn't think I'd want to be buried inside you?"

"I. I don't know. I mean... Billy." He couldn't think.

"Shh. You don't have to talk, love. Just feel." Billy changed angles and found that spot inside him, cock hitting it over and over again. He rocked back, squeezing and moaning, trying to make Billy as hard as he was. "Gonna leave my come inside you." Billy's words were husky, harsh, like he was speaking around rocks.

"Yes. Yes, sir. Yours. Please."

"Yes!" Billy pushed harder, faster. "Almost there."

"Almost." He jerked, squeezed Billy as hard as he could.

"Montana!" Billy slammed into him, and come pulsed deep inside him.

His arms gave way, his ass working Billy's cock. Billy collapsed onto him, pushing his torso into the mattress. Tanny took a deep breath, his heart slamming in his rib cage.

"Mmm... my love." Billy's fingers moved over him, the cock inside him shifting.

"Uh-huh." Billy's. He was.

"Reach me the plug, love."

He moaned but stretched, his entire body shifting as his fingers found the plug. Billy groaned, fingers sliding along his sides. He handed the plug back, dropping it twice on the trip. Billy chuckled, the motion jiggling the cock inside him again.

"S...sorry. I'm a little clumsy."

"I like to think I'm responsible for that." Billy's hands kept touching and stroking him.

"Uh-huh." More than a little, he thought.

Billy's kisses slid along his back, warm lips on his skin regardless of whether it was scarred or smooth. He relaxed, melting into the mattress. The thick cock inside him slid out slowly, but as soon as it did, Billy pushed the tip of the plug in. This plug was wide and heavy and the pressure was huge as Billy worked the rest of it in. He crawled up onto the bed, thighs spread wide.

"Sexy. Mine." Billy growled softly and kept working in the plug.

"Uh. Uh-huh. Please." It was finally in, pushing against his gland as it was seated. This deep, raw sound left him, pushed out of him.

"That's it, love. Give me everything." Billy's tongue slid along his ass.

He was going to shake apart. He couldn't help it.

"Climb higher," murmured Billy, body moving to cover his.

"Wh...what?"

"Hands up near the headboard, love." Billy moved to the dresser and came back, smacked his ass. "Move it."

"S...sorry." He scrambled to the top of the bed, a little confused.

Billy climbed up onto the bed and slid over him, body warm and solid. His hands were taken, drawn up over his head. It was soft and sensuous. He let himself relax again, let his heart rate slow. Billy rubbed against him like some great big cat, hands sliding up to cuff his wrists to the headboard. He didn't resist; he didn't even want to.

Billy continued to lie on him once his wrists were attached to the headboard. It was so warm, and Billy's weight pressing him into the mattress felt good. Tanny's eyes closed and another sound left him, low and husky. Billy touched him everywhere, hand soft and warm.

"Love." He stretched a little longer.

"Mmm..." He could hear it in Billy's voice, how much Billy was enjoying himself, being lazy and sensual.

"Did Oliver enjoy dinner?"

"You know he did. He enjoyed spending time with you, too."

"Uh-uh." He knew better.

"He did, Montana. You have to give him time to get to know you, to be friendly with you. And if he truly didn't like you, he wouldn't be okay with you and Jack hanging out together."

"No? I like Jack."

"I think Jack likes you, too. Very much." Billy pressed a kiss to the back of his neck. "I love being with you like this. Quiet and peaceful, the smell of sex all around us."

"It's good. I never would have thought this could be real."

"That love and sex would be like this?"

"Yes. Yes, exactly. I'm happy, Billy."

"That, my love, makes me happier than you could know."

He sighed, relaxed into the covers more fully. Billy stayed right there on top of him, the peace shared between them.

Chapter Eight

B illy let them rest about a half hour, and then he climbed off Montana and undid the cuffs. He kissed Montana's ear. "Time to shower again, love."

"Again?" His sweet, strong man took a deep breath.

"We'll clean you again and then I'll hold you in my hand." Tanny had been wanting this, hinting at it for ages.

"I don't like that part," Montana said.

"We didn't clean you with the nozzle the first time you had my hand in you." That didn't mean Montana wouldn't grow to love the ritualization of it.

"I know." Montana pressed closer. "It's hard. Embarrassing. It's so private."

Billy wrapped his arms around his lover. "I've held you in my hand, Montana—there is nothing so private between us that it can't be shared." Instead of pulling away, Montana pushed closer. "You have nothing to be embarrassed about, love."

"That doesn't change that I am."

"Possibly familiarity will help."

"You think so?"

"I do." It was a good reason to do it, anyway. He brought their mouths together, slipping his tongue between Montana's lips. They had the rest of the evening; there was no reason to hurry. Montana had tomorrow off, even. They had hours. He took a moment to tweak Montana's nipple ring. Montana groaned, shifted under his touch. He loved how extra sensitive the metal made Montana. He turned the barbell in place.

"Billy. Sir. Stings."

"Yes. It makes your nipples ache, doesn't it?" That was the point.

"It makes everything ache."

"Good." He slipped his hand down the slender belly and wrapped it around Montana's bound cock. He stroked a few times. That got him a soft, almost desperate little cry. "God, you're sexy. Special." He licked his tongue across Montana's lips. "Okay. Let's go clean you."

"Okay. Do we have to?"

Billy chuckled. "Yes, I think we do."

Montana sighed but nodded. Billy gave his lover another kiss and then got out of bed, holding his hand out for Montana's. Montana moved, slowly, reluctantly, but moved, following him.

"Start the shower, love, while I give the nozzle a wash and get everything ready."

"Will the water hurt this?" Montana motioned to the cock ring.

"We can switch to a metal ring."

Montana nodded. "I don't want to ruin it."

"You start the shower. I'll go get the metal ring."

"Yes, sir." The words left Montana's lips and his lover blushed, but turned to start the shower.

Billy took a moment to admire Montana's ass as his lover bent. Then he made short work of getting another cock ring, this one shiny and metal. Montana was removing the leather ring when he came back in.

"Tsk, tsk. That's mine to free."

"I was trying to help."

Perhaps, but that was his to touch. "I don't need your help to free your beautiful cock. Nor to bind it again." He took the leather from Montana and then stroked the hard cock a few times. Montana's legs spread, hips rolling. "So lovely." He slipped the metal ring around Montana's cock and pushed it down to the base. Montana groaned, then spread as he slowly, carefully worked one testicle through, then the other. "Beautiful." He gently petted the stretched balls, the long prick.

"I..." Montana groaned, hands sliding down his belly.

He grabbed Montana's hands, twined their fingers together. "You are. I won't hear you denying it."

"Okay." His name was scrawled, inked permanently on that fine belly. It was hot, arousing.

He kissed Montana and tugged him over to the shower. It was time to do this again, to let Montana begin to be more familiar with it. The fine tremors were starting again, Montana almost clinging to him. "Concentrate on what I'm doing now, not on what's coming." He had to take out the plug, use his fingers to make sure Montana was slick enough to push the penis-shaped nozzle in.

"That's easy for you to say."

"It's easy for you to do as well. I know you like this part." He began playing with the plug, twisting it, pulling it partway out before pushing it back in again.

"It's so big." Montana's body was like a vise.

"You need to relax, love. Let the pleasure have you, enjoy it." He stroked the small of Montana's back.

Montana moaned, his entire body arching slowly. "Yes..."

Billy nudged the plug forward so it would hit Montana's gland; he would make this a pleasure, at least the part leading up to filling Montana with water. Montana bent, hands landing on the edge of the tub. There, it was working. He bent and kissed the small of Montana's back, worked the uber-sensitive skin with his tongue as he continued to nudge the plug into Montana's gland over and over.

"So good." Montana was beginning to shift, to rock, to move back against him.

That's what he wanted. He began to twist the plug, began to put some force into sliding it in and out.

"Fuck..." Montana went up on tiptoe, then back down.

He slid his free hand up over Montana's belly, tweaked the barbell.

"Billy. Fuck. Aches."

"You can feel this in your balls, can't you?" He flicked the nipple ring as he said it.

"Yes. So bad."

"I think you mean so good." He flicked the ring again and tugged the plug right out.

Montana's knees buckled, his lover landing in the bottom of the tub. Billy rubbed Montana's shoulders, working the tight muscles.

"Love you." Montana slowly relaxed, tension easing for him.

"I know. It makes me very happy." He gave Montana a long, slow kiss and then got him standing again, leaning against the tile.

"I feel empty."

"You won't for very long, I promise."

Montana's laugh was husky, rough, a little wry.

He washed his lover, using the soap that smelled of leather and lingering, fingers slick and sliding on Montana's skin. Montana spread for him, arched for him, moved against him. He loved touching Montana. He loved how responsive his lover was, how alive and sensual and—Billy pressed their lips together and stopped thinking, let himself feel.

Those clever, wonderful fingers found his arms, his shoulders, stroking his skin. Groaning into Montana's mouth, he slid his tongue along Montana's, thrilling at the interplay between them. Montana began to wash him, to focus on him in a way that left him breathless. He hadn't expected to get hard again during this portion of their evening, but Montana had him groaning for more.

He wasn't going to come, not for a long while, but the sweet touches were perfect. It brought them back in it together. They spent a long, long time in the dark bathroom, touching each other through the water. Montana licked the water from his nipples, from his shoulders, both of them laughing softly. They touched and explored thoroughly. He thought he'd managed to touch every inch of Montana's skin, and his lover had returned the favor.

Finally, he slicked his fingers and began to play with Montana's ass. It was time. His lover didn't tense; Montana propped his leg up on the bathtub edge for him. "Mmm... hot. Mine." Billy slipped a finger inside.

"Yes, sir." Montana's body accepted him easily.

His cock jerked at the 'sir.' It meant so much to have Montana say it. He added a second finger, spreading the tiny ring of muscles. There was nothing like the feeling of the soft walls that squeezed his fingers. He pushed them deep. Montana gasped for him, the sound tickling his shoulder.

He got a third finger in and kept them moving. It wasn't necessary, Montana hardly needed to be stretched after wearing the plug, but Billy enjoyed doing this. He knew Montana did, too. Montana gripped his fingers, squeezed him, muscles jerking.

"Love." He groaned and began finger-fucking Montana's ass.

"Yes." Montana rode harder, faster.

He slowed them down, added more lube to his fingers, and spread them inside Montana's body.

"Yours." Montana's spine arched.

"That's right. Through and through." He let his fingers slide away and reached for the nozzle. This time, Montana didn't tense, simply waited for him. He slipped the tip in, pushed gently. Montana whimpered, pushed back against the nozzle. Good man. "That's right, take it in."

A blush climbed up Montana's spine at the praise, and Montana pushed back more.

"So sexy." He helped the last little bit, pushing the cock-shaped nozzle right in. He ran his finger around the sweet, stretched hole, smiling as Montana shivered. "Beautiful. Mine."

Bending, he licked the stretched skin, and then he began to fill Montana's ass. Montana sobbed once, shivers turning to shudders. He moved to stand in front of Montana and hold on to his lover. Montana leaned into him, arms wrapped tight around him.

"I have you. I have you."

"I don't like this." Montana was easier this time, more familiar.

"I know. But it's important. It's something you'll learn to love."

Montana's chuckle was husky. "I don't think so."

"We'll do it often enough and long enough that you won't have a choice." He gave Montana a wink and stopped the flow of water.

"I..." Montana groaned, clinging to him, eyes huge as they searched his face.

"I'm so proud of you."

"Yeah?" Those dark eyes held his.

"Yes. So very proud. And I love you." Billy smiled, stroking Montana's belly. "It's a happy combination."

Montana's eyes closed, his breath coming shallow and fast.

"I'm going to take the nozzle out now, love. All you need to do is hold on."

Montana nodded. "Okay. Okay."

He worked the nozzle out, not jerking or yanking, but giving Montana a chance to be able to hold the liquid in once the nozzle was out.

"Oh, God. Sir. Billy. Love."

"I'm right here, love. I have you." He kissed Montana's face.

"I need to... I have to get out."

"You can hold it a moment longer."

"Billy..."

"You can." He kissed Montana before another protest could be lodged.

Montana's kiss was fucking wild, tongue pushing into his lips, over and over. He sucked on it, let Montana focus on the pleasure between them. Montana groaned, breath panting from his lover.

"Okay, love. Let's get you over to the toilet."

Montana moved carefully, shaking and crying out, trying so hard.

"You're doing great, love. Just great." He helped Montana over and sitting down.

Montana hid his face in his hands, refusing to look at Billy. He kept touching, hands sliding on Montana's shoulders, through the straight, dark hair. "I hate this." Montana was fighting it, body struggling.

"It isn't dirty, it isn't bad, it's a part of you, a part of what we do together."

"It's not right. Damn it, Billy, it's not right." Montana looked at him, eyes wet with tears.

He met Montana's gaze, fingers wiping away the tears. "What's not right about it?"

"It's private."

"There's nothing so private between us that we can't share it." Montana would not hide from him.

"That's not..." Montana's legs drew up, eyes closing.

"Shh. Shh." He rubbed Montana's scalp. "Just let go, love. And we'll go back to the shower."

"I love you. I can't." He did, though. It had to happen.

"Sure you can. It's nothing to be embarrassed about, love."

"I am." Montana fought it hard, but his body finally submitted.

Billy took a kiss, offering his love. Montana groaned softly, arms wrapped around him. Yeah, he had his lover, would never let go. Not for anything.

"I'm sorry."

"For what? You have nothing to be sorry for."

They moved to the shower, Montana pressing close. He grabbed the soap and began once again to wash Montana. Like the first time, he spent his time on it, letting Montana feel the pleasure in the simple act of being cleaned, albeit very slowly and sensually. Montana moved for him, gentle and easy, relaxing.

He cleaned every inch, letting the anticipation for what they were about to do build. Montana whimpered, entire body shifting, back and forth.

"You need so beautifully." He had to let Montana know.

"I need you."

"Then it's a good thing you have me."

He brought their mouths back in another kiss, putting everything he felt into it. His lover was right there, bending for him, yielding to him. The kiss lasted for a long time, and then he turned off the water and drew Montana out of the tub.

"Are you happy?" Montana sounded dazed.

"I am, my love." He toweled his lover off. "Are you?"

"God, yes. Even when I'm scared."

He beamed at Montana. "Good." Then he took Montana's hand and led him back to the bedroom.

They curled together in the covers for a moment, warming up, breathing each other's air. The lube was under the pillows, easy to access, but Billy waited. He let the tension and anticipation build.

"The water worries me. The things we do, sometimes I can't think of anything else."

"The things we do are meant to take up all your thoughts. Sometimes."

Montana ducked his head, blushed dark. "I know. What do you want? I'm an addict."

"I rather like the thought of you being addicted to me, love. That's certainly how I feel about you. I never can get enough."

"Never is a long time."

"Possibly long enough." He planned to grow old with Montana.

"Mmm. Maybe. If we're lucky."

"Yes."

He kissed Montana again and then grabbed the lube. He slicked up his fingers, the routine of it settling him. He'd start with a single finger. Montana's body was well-stretched, opening to him easily. He fucked Montana slowly with that one finger, and then slid in another.

"Love when you touch me, sir."

And he loved it when Montana called him sir. "It's my favorite thing in the world to do."

Montana grinned at him. "Flattery will get you... Oh!"

He pinched one nipple, twisting the ring. He chuckled softly, pinched again.

"Oh, more..."

Pushing a third finger in, he tapped the barbell in Montana's other nipple.

"For you. Whenever I feel them, I know that."

"And I imagine you feel them a lot." He played with barbell and ring some more, wanting Montana to feel them forever.

"Yes. Yes, I do." Montana moaned low. "I touch them in the shower."

That made him growl. His. They were his. Montana shivered, ass gripping his fingers. He spread them, twisted them, the heat making him moan. Montana shifted, pushed down against him with a husky cry.

"We need to move. You can't take my hand like this."

"How do you want me?"

"On your back, love." He wanted to see, to watch Montana's face.

Montana nodded, shifted to lie beside him.

"Yes, like that." Leaning in, he kissed each nipple and then Montana's lips.

He watched the long, lean body stretch, arch under him, easy as could be. He got more slick on his fingers, on his hand, and curled his four fingers together, working them slowly into Montana's ass. Montana moved like he was swimming, rocking on his hand. It was fucking beautiful. He slid his fingers in and out a few times, stretching the little hole.

Montana's eyes went heavy-lidded, lips parting.

"Yeah, you're almost there." He twisted his fingers.

"I'm full."

"Not quite yet, you're not."

He let his fingers slide away, put more lube on his hand, and then tucked his thumb in with his fingers and began to push. Montana cried out, eyes wide open, staring at him. He stared back, his hand pushing in slowly, but surely.

"Sir..."

He could scream, just from the look on Montana's face. "Right here, Montana. I'm about to hold you in my hand." He was coming to the hardest part, the part where his hand was the thickest.

"It's so big." Montana twisted, panted, beginning to sweat.

"It is." He wouldn't deny that, not for a moment.

"I don't know. I'm fucking scared, Billy."

"No, I have you. I won't hurt you, you know that."

"I know. I'm still wigged."

He stopped moving his hand, leaned in and pressed their lips together. Montana groaned, tongue sliding against his. He kept the kiss going until he felt Montana beginning to relax into it. He pressed forward and, this time, Montana bore down, accepting him, welcoming him inside.

"That's it, love. Almost there. Almost..." His hand suddenly sank in, swallowed up by Montana's body.

"Sir!" The word was wild, almost screamed out.

"Yes, Montana. Yes!"

Montana arched, then those knees drew up and back, spreading wide.

"So beautiful." This was... this was prayer and praise and the best thing they could do together. "Love you," he murmured, curling his fingers into a fist.

"Love. Love. Sir. Please."

"You're in my hand, love. I have you."

"Yours. I'm all yours." Montana's eyes were open, wild.

"That's right, love. Mine." The words were fierce in his mouth and he began to move his hand inside Montana's body.

Montana panted, watching him constantly. He held that gaze as his hand continued to move.

"Full." That one word seemed to say so very much.

"Yes. Yes." He nodded, his knuckles brushing across Montana's gland.

Montana screamed, hands shooting up to wrap around the headboard. Groaning, he kept nudging that spot.

"Billy. Billy!"

"Right here, love."

"I can't breathe!"

"Yes, you can." He pressed his mouth to Montana's again, breathing into his lover's lips.

Montana cried out, body clenching around his wrist, heels thrumming on the mattress. He kept kissing, kept moving his hand, pushing Montana hard. Montana's cock was dripping, his lover wide around him, beneath him.

"I love you," he told Montana.

"I know. I know. Please."

"What do you need, love?"

"I don't know. More?"

"Good. Yes." He nodded, gave Montana another deep, hard kiss, and began to move his hand again. He kept it slow and made sure he continue to brush against Montana's gland as often as possible.

Things seemed to slow impossibly, their connection unbreakable. It was like there was nothing else in the world but the two of them and this moment. He met Montana's eyes and held the gaze.

"Love." Montana's lips were open, swollen and damp.

"Yes. Love." He looked from Montana's mouth down to his cock, the tip dark red and leaking, the ring at the base looking almost too tight.

His gaze continued downward to where his hand, his whole hand, had disappeared into Montana's hole, the skin tight around his wrist. It made him groan, made him swallow as a wave of heat and need swept through him.

"I need to come. Please, sir. Please."

"I like the way you beg." He didn't say that Montana could come, though. Not yet.

Montana flushed, hands sliding down his belly.

"No touching." He growled it out, feeling very fiercely that the long, hard cock was his.

"Oh, fuck." Montana's eyes held his. "No?"

"No. No touching. No coming unless I say so. You're mine."

Montana whimpered, that hole clenching around his arm.

"Beautiful. So beautiful." Montana's need made him shine.

"And yours."

"Mine. All mine. Every fucking inch."

"Every inch." Montana's groan was so sweet. "Please."

"Say it again."

"Yours. Yours. All of me, I promise. Please."

"Good. You can come." He tapped the gland inside Montana, hard, and spunk spilled from the hard cock, spreading over his name inked on that flat belly.

"Yes. Mine." Bending, he licked at Montana's come, taking the flavor in.

Montana was still, quiet, resting hard. He pressed kisses to Montana's lips, the pierced nipples, the tip of the sweet cock. He left his hand still inside his lover's body.

"Love you." The whisper was barely audible.

He nodded. "Yes. Love. So much love." He licked the tip of Montana's cock again and began the slow process of pulling out.

His lover didn't even move, didn't protest. Montana was melted. With soft strokes of his lover's belly and warm kisses, Billy managed it. His Montana sighed, once. Softly. He petted Montana's belly and then leaned over his lover, taking his own cock in hand.

Those dark eyes opened, dazed, unfocused. "You need?"

"I'm good." Jacking off over Montana would do him just fine.

"Yeah?" Montana's eyes closed again, throat working.

"Yeah, love. I'm good. So good." He watched Montana breathe, remembered what it was like to have his hand inside Montana's body. He came with a shout.

His spunk sprayed across Montana's body, painting his lover. Groaning, he let himself go and began to rub his come into Montana's skin.

"Love you. Yours." He didn't think Montana was even awake.

"That's right, love. Mine." He nodded and curled up around his lover, joining Montana's peace.

Chapter Nine

He woke slowly, dazed and sore, aching and... bound. Bound? Montana's eyes popped open. Billy lay curled up next to him, eyelashes casting shadows on the tops of his cheeks.

"Billy?" He stretched, tried to move.

Billy's eyes popped open and his lover smiled at him. "Hey, love."

"Uh. I'm tied up?"

"You are." Billy grinned, one finger sliding along his chest, heading toward his right nipple.

"Why?" His nipple perked up, trying to get Billy's attention.

"To keep you in your subspace." Billy skirted the nipple, but then came back toward it from another angle.

"Wh...what does that mean?" He arched a bit, let his muscles stretch.

"You know the feeling you get when I've fisted you? That far away, melted, everything is peaceful and perfect for a moment place?"

Tanny nodded. It was like the best part of being high.

"That's what I call your subspace. I know it's good there and I wanted to keep you there, here, as long as possible. So I cuffed you to the bed."

That teasing finger finally found his nipple and flicked across the tip, ignoring the metal piercing it. For now. Tanny gasped, tried to roll toward the touch. Billy's finger slipped away, though, and his lover chuckled softly.

"Billy!" The urge inside him was to call Billy sir.

"Yes?" There was a happy, evil glint in Billy's eyes.

He smiled—he couldn't not. "You're being a meanypants again."

Billy threw back his head and laughed. "I'm going to get that tattooed on your ass. 'Property of Mr. Meanypants.'"

"No!" They were laughing together, now, both of them.

As Billy's laughter faded, he twisted the barbell in Tanny's nipple.

"Oh." He jerked, his ass cheeks clenched, and he moaned at the ache. That had Billy groaning, and the ring on his other nipple got flicked. "Sir, they're tender." Not sore, but tender.

"Good." Billy flicked the one with the ring again. He groaned, eyes closing a little. "Mmm..." Billy went back to sliding that finger on his skin. It traveled down to trace the tattoo on his belly. It circled his cock and then touched his hips, one and then the other.

He took one deep breath, then another.

"That's right, love. Find your subspace, ride the pleasure."

Tanny let his breath go all the way out, remembering how he'd ride the high. This was better.

Billy's tongue slid across his barbelled nipple. Then Billy's teeth scraped the tip. His breath caught in his chest and he gasped. Billy's tongue came back, flicking back and forth across the tip over and over.

"Oh." He shuddered, his toes curled.

"God, I love that sound." Billy moved to play with his other nipple.

"I feel you, everywhere."

"Can you still feel my hand inside you?" Billy breathed across his nipple, making him shiver. Tanny whimpered, nodded. "Good. I can still feel the heat and tightness of your body around it."

Oh, fuck. Oh, fuck, that was... so hot. Billy's tongue slid down to his navel and circled it, fucked it. "Billy..." He didn't know if that was hot or icky or what.

Then Billy blew against his belly, raspberrying him. His laughter rang out, shocked and surprised. Billy's joined his, and then his right hip bone was nipped, the base of his cock kissed. It was only when Billy kissed him there that he realized he wasn't wearing the ring anymore. His cock jerked happily, swelling even more.

"Mmm... knees up, love."

He drew his knees up, stretching his lower back.

"Yes, like that." Billy bent again, this time his tongue playing over the skin behind Tanny's balls. And then lower. He groaned, his eyes rolling back in his head. "So sensitive." Billy licked and then blew and then licked again. The alternating hot and cold and hot was enough to drive him crazy.

His hole was so sensitive, so tender, tingling. Billy's tongue felt like a brand. It also felt huge. His eyes rolled, his body was on fire. Billy blew again, then took one of his balls into that hot, hot mouth.

"Billy..." His body went tight.

His only answer was a humming, the vibrations around his ball unbelievable. Tanny started panting, breathing shallowly, his head swimming. Billy let that ball go, only to take the other one in. He was spinning, dizzy and lightheaded, yet not ready to orgasm, at all. That hot mouth kept tasting him, moving to his cock, back to his hips, and then his nipples again. Billy didn't let up for a moment.

"Help me." He wasn't sure what he needed help for.

Billy's mouth closed over his, tongue sliding into his mouth as his lover's compact, muscled body pushed him into the mattress. He opened to the kiss, accepting with all he was. Billy's tongue slid back and forth between his lips, fucking his mouth. Oh, God. So warm. So good. The pace was fast and then it slowed and finally Billy pulled away to look down at him.

"H...hey."

"Hey." Billy smiled, eyes hot.

"Love, huh?"

"Yeah." Billy nodded and pressed a soft, almost chaste kiss on him. "Love."

He couldn't stop smiling. He didn't want to. Billy smiled back at him, the two of them just lying there, grinning like fools. It felt good, though, not like they had to say anything or do anything; they could just lie there and smile at each other.

He chuckled softly. "This is a little weird, hmm?"

"Weird?"

"Just lying here, me tied up."

"You think so? I think it's sexy."

"It is, but it's also odd. It's good."

"Oddly sexy?" He could hear the teasing note in Billy's voice.

He laughed. "That's it. Oddly Sexy and Mr. Meanypants." God, they were dorks.

Billy snickered. They might be dorks, but they were

happy dorks. Happy and together and...

"You're going to have to let me loose." He had to pee.

"Why's that?"

"I have to go to the bathroom."

"Ah. I guess I do have to let you go for that." Billy chuckled, kissed him, and then rolled off. He grinned, jangling his cuffs. Billy undid him from the bed, but then attached the cuffs together in front of him. "I'll help you."

"Billy?" That was unexpected.

"Yes, love?" Billy hauled him up off the bed.

"I have to pee."

"Yes, I'll help you with that as your hands are cuffed together." Billy put an arm around his waist and started walking him toward the bathroom.

"I don't..." Oh, he didn't know about that.

"You don't have a choice, love."

He shuddered, his breath coming quickly.

"It'll be just fine." Billy stood him in front of the toilet.

"Billy..." This was like last night, like Billy was touching all of him.

Standing close behind him, Billy reached around and took his penis, aimed it. Billy's cheek rested against his back between his shoulder blades. "Relieve yourself, love. I'm not even watching."

He tried to catch his breath, tried to relax.

"You can do this, love."

"It's hard, huh?"

Billy squeezed him gently. "No, it's fairly soft, actually."

"Billy!" He shook his head, but finally—finally—he could go.

Soft chuckles wafted across his skin, and when he was done, Billy shook him off and then turned him, took a kiss.

"I don't know about that, Billy." He pressed close. "It makes me uncomfortable."

"A number of things do. I'm glad you tell me when we come across one."

"Does that mean we'll stop?"

Billy chuckled. "It'll depend on what it is. Probably not, most of the time."

"Why not?" It wasn't a bitchy question. He needed to know.

"Because part of the point is pushing, expanding your boundaries."

"What do you get out of it?"

"I get to push. And I get to watch you."

Tanny leaned into Billy's warmth. "Watch me what?"

"Fly, love. I like to watch you fly. I love knowing I did that to you."

"Do you think you'll get tired of me?"

Billy snorted. "Not a fucking chance."

They washed up—him with Billy's help—and headed back toward the bedroom. "What about your other lovers? What happened with them?"

"I don't know if I've ever really had 'lovers.' Not now that I know what the word really means. I've had friends with benefits, I've had subs. I've cared about the men I was with, but..." Billy shrugged and then looked right at him, let him see Billy was serious. "I have never felt about anyone the way I feel about you."

"It's shitty and selfish of me, but I'm glad."

"Why is that shitty and selfish of you? It's only natural to want to be the most important person in your lover's life."

"Yeah, I guess, but a good guy would want you to have been, like, perfectly happy all along."

Billy snorted. "A saint, maybe."

"Yeah. Saintly I'm not."

"Nobody is, that was my point."

"No? I think Oliver is." He chuckled as he teased.

That had Billy laughing. "Oliver, a saint? No, no, I've seen him behaving in a distinctly unsaintly manner."

"Have you?" They didn't stop at the bedroom, but went to the kitchen.

"I have." Billy's eyes twinkled. "What are you hungry for?"

"We could have Pop Tarts."

"Yeah? I guess we could."

"We could have waffles. Or cereal."

Billy shook his head. "Yes, we could. But I asked what you were hungry for."

"Really? I want sausage and biscuits." The words surprised him, sort of. Those were old comfort foods.

"Yeah? I might have frozen stuff in the fridge." Billy started poking through the freezer.

"I haven't had those in a long time."

"Then I'm glad you said someth—Bingo!"

"Did you find something?"

"Frozen biscuits and a package of sausage." Billy gave him a grin.

"Oh, cool!" He stood up, going to look.

Billy did indeed have biscuits and Jimmy Dean sausage. And a kiss for him.

"Yum. This is what I used to have when I was a teenager."

"Yeah? That's cool. And now I know, I can make sure we have it on hand."

"It's like comfort food, or something."

Billy nodded. "Like tomato soup and cheese sandwiches."

"Yeah. Or fry bread."

"Do you know how to make fry bread?" Billy put a pan on the stove and took out a cookie tray.

"No. I mean, a little, but I'd fuck it up."

"So we'll keep practicing until you get it right. I bet it doesn't take as long as you think." There went Billy again, doing that believing in him thing.

"You know I'm a screw up by nature, huh?"

"No, you're a screw up by nurture—someone tells you that you can't often enough, then you begin to believe it yourself, and once you believe it..." Billy shrugged. "I believe in you, though."

"You always have. Weirdo."

"I thought I was Meanypants?"

Tanny chuckled, shook his head. "Right, I forgot."

Billy grinned and kissed the top of his head. Then the biscuits were put in the oven, the sausages into the pan. "You want to eat in the living room? We could watch some I Love Lucy, or talk."

"Sure." He held out his hand. "You going to uncuff me?"

"Oh, no. I'll feed you." Billy looked pleased about it.

They went to the living room, and Billy turned on the TV. He glanced at the time. "Fifteen minutes I should go back for the food, until then we can snuggle." Billy sat and opened his arms. He climbed right in, snuggling happily, so at home it hurt. Billy found some old movie on the TV and they cuddled. "You have anything you want to talk about?"

"Like what?"

Billy shrugged. "Like the accident." Every now and then Billy brought it up, tried to convince him it wasn't his fault.

"It was dark, I fucked up, and my sister died. Period."

"Do you remember what happened yet or are you still going by what you were told?"

"I don't remember anything. I don't remember that day, really. I ain't talking about it."

Billy stroked his arm all the way down to the cuff. "It's going to keep haunting you until you do figure out what really happened."

"I don't want to talk. You can't make me."

"No, I can't. I'm hoping that you'll eventually let me in."

"Let you in to what? I did a terrible thing." His heart was beating harder. Let Billy in? He'd let Billy in deeper than anyone.

"It was an accident."

"I killed her!"

Billy stayed calm but wouldn't let him look away. "You didn't do it on purpose."

"I know that. It doesn't make it right." He wasn't calm. He was angry. Why the fuck was he so angry?

"You're angry." Billy squeezed him tight.

"I am. I'm fucking pissed off."

"About what?"

"I don't know. I don't want to be, but I am."

"Are you mad at me for pushing?"

"A little bit. I'm mad because you won't leave it alone; you keep touching me there."

"I don't believe leaving it alone is going to help you get over it."

"Why should I get over it? I deserve to feel bad about it."

"No, I don't think you do. I think between yourself and your family, you've been punished enough for what happened."

He shook his head. "I don't what to talk about it." He had the sneaking suspicion Billy was going to make him, though.

"That's not good enough. Tell me one thing that you remember—not that you've been told about that day, but that you remember."

"I don't remember anything about that day. There's a week that's gone."

"How can you beat yourself up for something you can't even remember?"

He looked at Billy. "She's dead."

"And you don't know how that happened!"

He was going to scream. "What does it matter? I was driving! I was the adult! I was the one who LIVED!"

"How do you know you were driving?" The words were spoken so quietly.

"What?"

"You've said your sister is reckless, that she wasn't wearing a helmet—how do you know she didn't talk you into letting her drive?"

"Don't say that." He tried to stand up, pull away. "The biscuits'll burn."

"Then they burn." Billy held him close. "You can't have it both ways. If you can't remember what happened, you don't actually know what happened, and any scenario could be true."

"No. I was driving. I had to be driving. Don't say that."

"You don't know that you were driving. I'll say it as often as I need to."

"Don't say that." He was going to shake apart. He had to have been driving. Had to have.

"You don't know that you were driving."

"Don't say that." Billy had to stop saying that.

"I will keep saying it until you consider that it might be true or remember that it isn't." Billy looked into his eyes and said it again, "Maybe you weren't driving."

"STOP IT!" He jerked away, falling off Billy's lap. He needed a hit. Needed it. Now.

Billy dragged him back up and put him over Billy's lap. The swat was hard, shocking as it rang out. "I won't stop."

"Stop it! Stop it! Let me go! You fucker!"

"Admit it's a possibility." Billy swatted him again and again, the words punctuating the swats.

"NO!" He struggled, screamed, kicking furiously. Billy was too strong, holding him down and spanking him over and over, saying it again and again.

He let himself simply... lose it. The room went away, everything did but the pure fury and pain and fear and rage pouring out of him in wave after wave. Through it all, there was an anchor. Billy. Billy was there. Finally it had to ease, had to run out, and he slumped over Billy's thighs. The swats slowed, stopped and Billy's hand rubbed over his ass.

His breath hitched and he shivered. Billy gave his ass one last soft tap and then pulled him up into his lover's arms. "I have you, Montana. And I love you."

"Sorry." He wasn't crying. Damn it.

"You don't need to apologize, love."

"Okay." He let his eyes close.

Billy just held him, breathing with him.

Eventually Billy put him down, disappeared into the kitchen, but not before wrapping him in a blanket. He didn't know how long it was, but when Billy came back, he had two glasses of milk and two grilled cheese sandwiches.

"Th...thank you." He was shaking as Billy pulled him close again.

"I have you," Billy told him. A kiss was dropped onto his head.

"I'm really tired."

"I'm not surprised." Billy kissed his forehead again and picked up the sandwich, offered it to him.

His hands were cuffed and trapped in the blankets, so he opened his mouth, took a bite. It was good. It was quiet and warm and he could feel how much Billy loved him, cared for him. They ate the sandwiches, drank all the milk, then Billy settled him on Billy's lap, keeping him still and quiet. It felt good.

He leaned his head against Billy's shoulder, eyes closed. He just might lie like this forever.

Chapter Ten

They ate, they dozed; he held Montana close. Billy thought they had maybe made a breakthrough. He really wished Tanny could remember what happened that day, that week. Montana needed to confront what had happened when his sister died. He kissed the top of Montana's head and kept holding, kept touching. Montana's eyes opened every now and then, then dropped closed again.

After a good, long while, he broke the silence. "You want to talk about it?"

Montana shook his head, pressed closer back into the curve of his body.

"Now why doesn't that surprise me, hmm?"

Montana shrugged.

"Tell me how you're feeling."

"My head hurts. My butt hurts a little. I just want to hide from everything."

"You can't hide from yourself." Although it certainly seemed like Montana had done a good job at exactly that so far.

"I can, too."

"I won't let you."

"You can't stop me..."

"I can, too." He chuckled softly and took a kiss. "I'm not going to stop bringing it up."

Montana sighed, wrapped around him. "I don't want to."

"Sometimes we have to do things we don't want to do. You need to deal with this."

"Why?" Montana didn't sound like he was being an asshole. It sounded like he genuinely wanted to know.

"Because it's eating you up inside."

"I'm getting better, though."

"You let some of your anger out; that was very good."

"I don't want to."

"No, you'd rather keep it all inside you, eating you up?"

"God, I want a hit. So bad." Montana wrapped tighter in the blankets.

He held his lover close. "That's your reaction when you're faced with stuff you don't want to deal with."

"No shit."

He chuckled and tilted Montana's head up, took a soft kiss. When they were done, he had to ask, "Would you consider seeing someone who could help you to remember what happened?"

"What? Why?" Montana wrapped around him, held on.

"Because you don't really know what happened, and the things we make up in our mind are usually much worse than reality."

"Why do you care so much? What if you find out I'm right? That I did it?" Montana was so focused on that wreck, on all the blame that his family had spread.

"Then we'll know for sure." He wasn't doing this for him, he was doing it for Montana.

"And what then?" Montana looked at him, eyes red and worried.

"I will not love you any less. You've told me you killed her already, and it didn't chase me away."

"I miss her." That was new. Montana hadn't ever talked about his sister, not really.

"I bet. Was she like you?"

"She looked like me. She was smart."

"Older or younger?"

"Younger, by ten months."

"Did you have any other brothers or sisters?"

Montana nodded. "We had an older brother. He died in the Marines."

"I'm sorry."

"I didn't know him very well." Montana shrugged. "We were Mom's attempt to save her second marriage."

"That's a hell of a thing to tell a child."

Montana looked at him, obviously confused. "Why? It was the truth." No wonder Montana thought he was good for nothing.

"Because telling your children things like that destroys their self-confidence."

"I thought you were always, always supposed to tell the truth."

"There are some truths you don't have to share."

Montana nodded. "I think so, too."

"And then, when your sister died..."

"Then they made me leave. Everyone hated me. They took me to the road, showed me where she hit. There was a stain."

"Jesus Christ."

Montana shrugged, crumpled into himself.

"They weren't there, love. They don't know what

actually happened. They needed someone to blame." Still, no matter the excuses, he couldn't believe Montana's mother had done that to her only remaining son.

"Yeah. Me."

"Yeah. You were hurt, too, and mourning your sister, and they threw you under the bus."

"I deserved it. I lived. All those good kids, and I lived."

"That's a load of bull. You already told me your sister was a wild one, that she refused to wear a helmet."

"Yes, but..."

"But what?"

"I'm the fucked-up one." That panic was there again, right under the surface.

"Because that's what you've been told."

"Just stop, please."

"I'll stop when you're willing to cut yourself just the smallest break and admit that, even if you were fully at fault, you never meant it to happen. It was an accident."

"I didn't mean for it to happen. I loved her. She was my best friend."

He hugged Montana tight. "I'm so sorry for your loss."

"I need a hit, Billy, so bad. It hurts inside."

"I can give you what you need, love." He took Montana's mouth, kissing him hard.

Montana kissed him back, then pulled away. "I want to hurt myself. I have to go."

"No, if you need to be hurt, I can do it. Where it's controlled, where it's done without anger. You know I can make you fly higher than any pill."

Montana shook his head. "I can't do this. I can't fucking cope, man."

"You can. You are."

"How? I let you hit me. I want it! I can't fucking deal!"

"It's been months—months—and you've coped just fine. I am not going to let you lose it now."

"You can't stop me. I'm a fuck up!"

There was that anger again, and Billy was so fucking proud that Montana trusted him enough to show it.

"You're not a fuck up just because people tell you that you are."

"I have to get up." Montana struggled to kick free of the blankets.

"No, you don't. You have to stay here with me." He wrapped Montana in the blankets, holding him close.

"Let me go." Montana groaned, struggles easing a bit.

"No, I'm not letting you go." He held Montana closer still, began rocking his lover. "I'll never let you go."

Montana groaned. "I can't handle this."

"You don't have to. You just have to let me hold you."

"I can't HANDLE this!"

"You can yell as loudly as you want, you can be as angry as you need to be. I have you and I'm not letting go."

"Stop it! Stop it. I can't fucking COPE!"

He pressed his head against Montana's neck, holding on even tighter. He kept whispering, "I have you," over and over again.

Montana began to sob, deep, wracking sounds that hurt him. A hard, painful lump in his own throat, Billy simply held on and let Montana let it out. Had his lover even cried for his loss before now? Or had he been kicked to the curb and turned to the drugs before he'd had the chance?

The storm passed, leaving Montana quiet, still in his arms, breath hitching. He didn't break the silence. He figured Montana had to have a monster of a headache after that. When the peace began to fade, he'd take his lover in for a nice, warm, soothing shower.

Montana didn't say a word when he stood them up, walked them to the bathroom. He started the water before removing the cuffs and gently rubbing Montana's wrists. Then he kissed the corner of his lover's mouth and helped him into the lukewarm shower.

The tears started again, slow and silent this time, and Billy didn't try to stop them. He washed his lover, hands moving slick and easy over Montana's skin. Montana began to relax again, leaning into his touch. He rubbed Montana's shoulders, massaging them. He dragged his fingers up to slide along Montana's neck. Montana's head fell against his chest.

"Love you, Montana."

"Why?"

"Because you're beautiful and strong and something inside me reaches for you whenever I see you or think of you."

"Okay."

Billy couldn't help but smile at that.

He slid one hand down and cupped Montana's ass. God, he loved it. Montana pressed closer, cheek on his shoulder. He started to rock, just moving gently from side to side.

"Love you." Montana sighed the words.

He gave a little squeeze. "Me, too."

"My head hurts."

"Yeah, I imagine it does. I've got some aspirin in the cabinet. You can have some, along with a big glass of water, when we get out."

"Okay. I'm sorry."

"For what? Being human?"

"Yeah." Montana nodded, leaned into him.

"You haven't done anything to apologize for, love." He kept holding, pressed small kisses over Montana's face.

Montana let him take care, let Billy guide his lover out of the water, into a soft towel. He dried Montana off and then filled the bathroom glass with water, handing it over along with a couple of aspirin for his lover's head. The pills taken, Billy led Montana into the bedroom, into the bed.

He pulled the covers up over them, making a cocoon for them both, warm and cozy and dark. A place for them to hold each other and keep the world away.

He slept for hours, it felt like. Every time he woke up, the tears started again, and Billy eased him into sleep. It was like detox. Sometimes Billy would feed him water or juice, sometimes it was just sweet words and gentle touches. Billy was always there, though, with a touch and a word and gentleness. Once he woke and it was pitch black; the next time, the sun was out. It felt like work, somehow, what he was doing. Billy was snoring the one time he woke up, noisy sounds. He managed to fall back asleep regardless.

Finally, he woke up fully, stumbling to the bathroom on weak knees. Billy came in while he was relieving himself, filling a glass of water and then handing it over once he was done.

"How are you feeling, love?"

"Like I've been in a fight." He reached out, stroked

Billy's arm in greeting.

Billy stepped close and made a happy little noise at the touch. "You have been, really. Only with yourself. Do you need more aspirin?"

"I don't know yet. Maybe in a few minutes?"

Chuckling, Billy nodded. "Not awake yet. Come on; let's get some food into you."

"I'm sorry for all this, you know." He went and put on a pair of soft shorts, the fabric tickling his still-warmed ass.

"You don't have to apologize. I encouraged this to happen. I think you needed to go through it." Billy pulled on a robe, not bothering to tie it up.

He didn't understand why, but he didn't suppose he had to.

Billy poked through the fridge. "Hmmm... we need to do groceries. How about we get something delivered?"

"Pizza?" He arched, stretching. "I can buy, I think."

"Sure. You choose what toppings." Billy gave him a wink. "I'm easy."

"Pepperoni and olive. Please."

"Sure." Billy tossed him the phone. "Get some of those garlic sticks, too."

"Okay." He nodded, then stared at the phone. A year ago, he was on the street. A year ago, he couldn't have done this.

"You need the number?" Billy asked a few moments later.

"Huh?"

"For the pizza place. Do you need the number? You were staring at the phone like you'd never seen it before."

"I just." He stopped, shook his head. "No. No, I got it."

"All right." Billy came and rubbed his lower back.

"I'm fucked up." The words came out of him.

"No, you aren't at all."

"No?" He leaned back into Billy's touch. "I feel like it."

"No. You've got your issues, but don't we all?"

"Most people aren't as special as I am."

"No, you are special, but I mean it in a good way." Billy popped his ass.

"Ow!" He jerked away, butt stinging.

"No denigrating yourself."

"You can't stop me from admitting I'm a fuck up."

"But you aren't!"

"I am, too!"

"You absolutely are not."

"I am. A big fucking fucker fuck up."

Billy took the phone from him and put it on the counter and then got right up into his space, eyes on his. "You've made mistakes—we all have. But you are not a fuck up."

"I am, too. When are you going to figure that out?"

"There's nothing to figure out. When are you going to figure out that you don't have to judge yourself by what others say to you, call you? You can be anyone you want."

"I want to be smart. I want to be yours."

"You are already mine and I know how smart you are. How long did it take you to pick up the reading?"

"I should have known how..." He wanted this. He wanted Billy to insist, to fight for him.

Billy snorted. "No one had taught you before, of course you didn't know how to read. People told you that you weren't smart so you believed them and lived up to that. I know better. You're sharp as a tack and we both know it."

"I'm still a fuck up."

"Don't make me beat you—we both know that isn't true."

"What if I fucking want you to?" He stopped, shocked at himself. Then he turned and ran. He'd lost his fucking mind.

Billy followed, calling after him. "Montana! Stop right there."

Oh, God. Oh, God. He was crazy. Really.

Billy grabbed his arms and held on, turned him. "You know I'll give you what you want, what you need. And there is no shame in telling me what that is."

"I can't do this. I can't fucking believe this. I'm going crazy, Billy. I swear to God, I'm losing my fucking mind and I was FINE yesterday!"

"You're fine today, too, love. And you know you're not going crazy."

"I..." He stepped in closer, trying not to freak out more. "What's wrong with me?"

"Absolutely nothing." Billy kissed him hard. "What we do is beautiful and necessary."

"I feel like something's wrong with me."

"Really? You're not on drugs anymore. You're holding down a job. You have a lover. Tell me what's wrong about any of that?"

"I." He shook his head. "I don't... Shit, I don't know."

"You need to eat. You'll feel better with food in you." Billy linked their arms and led him into the living room, sitting him down. Then Billy grabbed the phone and called the pizza place.

He stood up, headed for his wallet. Billy ordered the pepperoni and olive pizza, along with the garlic sticks and some drinks. He could feel Billy's eyes on him, though, watching him. He pulled out two twenties, set them down, then just stood, breathing in and out. Billy hung up the phone and then held open his arms.

Tanny looked over, then ran. Ran right into that embrace, ran right to his lover.

Billy's arms wrapped around him. "This is where you belong. This is where everything is right."

He pressed close. "Okay."

"You can say anything to me. Anything." Billy held him tight. "I won't think you're weird or crazy or wrong."

"I'm tired, Billy. I'm tired of trying so hard to be good. I'm tired of worrying."

"Then don't worry, love. Don't stress it. Because you're doing so well."

"Help me."

"Always."

His eyes closed, and he let Billy hold him. They stayed like that until the doorbell rang.

"I'll get it." Tanny grabbed the money, went to the door, handing over the cash.

The pimply-faced kid passed over the pizza boxes and said, "Thanks, Mister."

"Yeah. Have a good night." Mister. Huh.

"It smells good." Billy took the bag with the drinks and carried it over to the coffee table.

"It does." He followed along, feeling... dazed.

Billy must have seen it, because his lover took his hand and tugged him down onto the couch. It wasn't long at all before a slice of pizza was handed over. "Eat. Before you fall down."

"I. Okay?" He took a piece, hands a little shaky.

"Go on," murmured Billy, all but bringing his hands

141

up to his mouth for him.

"I'm sorry." He ate, the first bite making him queasy, the second bite going down better.

"So am I. I should have been more aware of the time and how long it had been since we last ate."

He ate his first piece, then took another. Billy ate more slowly, but patted him on the knee, looking pleased. "Good job. I bet you feel better already."

He nodded. "Yeah. Yeah, I do."

"Everything looks bleak when your blood sugar takes a dip."

"I just..." Tanny sighed, curled his legs underneath him. "I just get to a place that's even and things dip and change again."

"That's because every time things even out, your mind knows it's safe to open up a part of yourself."

He took a bread stick, thinking about that. "Yeah? You think so?" Was it normal?

"Yes, I do. I think that's why you don't remember what happened, either. Your mind is protecting you from the truth."

"The doctors said that it was normal, to lose memory."

Billy nodded. "Did they say it would probably come back over time?"

"Some of it. Maybe never the accident itself."

"Maybe no and maybe yes, hmm?" Billy's hand slid over his shoulder, squeezed his arm.

He nodded. "I guess."

Billy leaned in and licked some grease off the side of his mouth. "I love you, no matter what, okay?"

"I love you." He leaned in, took another kiss.

Humming, Billy deepened the kiss. It was a little easier to scoot closer, touch Billy. Billy leaned back, legs spreading to give him room. Tanny crawled up, moving against Billy. Billy's mouth opened wide, letting him taste. He lapped at Billy's lips, holding his lover's gaze. No one had ever looked at him like Billy did, like he was good and right and special.

He took a deep breath, let himself start to relax. Billy continued to sprawl beneath him, letting him touch and kiss and explore.

"When did you find out about being a top?"

"I was a sub first, did you know that?"

"Were you?" He settled, interested. "Honestly?"

"I was. I knew that wasn't where I'd wind up, but I went to the Hammer, intrigued, wanting to know more, sure I was a top and ready to wade in." Billy chuckled. "Despite the fact that I was cynical and tough, I was incredibly naive when it came to the lifestyle. I was told I'd have to learn from the ground up, which meant bottoming first."

"Did you hate it?"

Billy wriggled. "I didn't hate it."

Tanny tilted his head. "No? You didn't like it."

"No, I didn't like it. It wasn't who I was. But without the experiences... I wouldn't be a good Dom."

"Do you think it's who I am?" The question was serious. He needed to know that he was doing what he was meant to.

"I do." Billy stroked his cheek. "You call to me. I know that you're a sub. My sub."

He beamed. He couldn't help it. Tanny rested close, cheek on Billy's chest. "Is there anything we haven't done that you want to?"

"You mean literally the physical acts, or the emotional impetuses behind them?"

He wasn't sure he knew exactly what impetuses were. "Yes."

Billy chuckled. "Everything we do is about trust and love and flying higher than you ever dreamed possible. It's about connection. It's about wanting to crawl into your body and stay there where it's quiet and perfect."

"Did that answer my question?"

"I don't think that it did, really. Yes. There are things we haven't done that I want to."

He chuckled, fingers sliding over Billy's belly. "Like what?"

"I want to put a sound in you."

"That's the metal thing, huh?" He was less wigged out than he'd thought he'd be. Of course, it wasn't right in front of him at the moment, was it?

"Yes. It is." Man, Billy's eyes could be wicked. "And then there's that beating you mentioned wanting."

"I wasn't in my right mind."

Billy threw his head back and laughed. "No? I imagine you were very much speaking from deep in your mind."

"Yeah, yeah. I was freaking out."

"And that's when the truth can come out, hmm?"

"You think so?" He kept his eyes closed.

"I do. I heard the truth in your request."

His cheeks heated. "How does that make you feel?"

"Pleased. I am more than ready and willing to give you whatever you need."

"Yeah? You don't think I'm a pussy?"

Billy snorted. "That's the last thing I think you are. You have strength, Montana. I know you think you're weak, but I know better. I've seen your back. I've held you in my hand. I know how strong you are."

He took a deep breath, so deep it hurt, almost. "This

is hard."

Billy met his eyes. "It isn't often easy looking inside yourself, discovering who you really are."

"Do you ever? I mean, do you ever discover anything?"

"Sure. You get old and crotchety if you don't keep learning."

"Sometimes it feels like you don't get anything but trouble from me."

"Is that how you see it? I don't see it like that at all. I get to watch you grow, watch you blossom into a beautiful man who's learning all about himself, about his subspace, about his smarts, his abilities."

He asked one of the questions that worried him. "What about when I've learned so much? Will you get tired of me?"

Billy's eyes narrowed and he didn't answer right away, obviously considering the question seriously before answering. "No. To start with, I don't believe we'll ever stop learning, either of us."

"No? Because... I don't want to bore you."

The look Billy gave him said he'd finally said something crazy. "You never will, love."

"I worry about that, you know? You're the best thing I've ever known."

"Same here."

"I can't believe that."

"Why not?"

"Because..." He squeezed his eyes shut. "Because I've met some of your friends and they think I'm trash even when they pretend not to and you had all this life at that club and you haven't taken me and whenever someone has to give up stuff like that, it comes back."

"Oh, Montana." Billy stroked his belly. "Love, the

only reason I haven't taken you to the club yet is because I thought it might be a bit overwhelming for you. I'll take you on Saturday—we'll have dinner and watch the show and you can bombard me with questions after. And my life before you came into it was very boring, very ordinary. I wasn't unhappy, but it certainly can't compare to what we have together."

"Are you sure you're not ashamed? I would be."

Billy shook his head. "I am not in the least bit ashamed of you. If I was, would I have invited Oliver here? Would we have gone to Oliver's place for Christmas?" Billy grabbed his hands and held on. "I have not shared you on many occasions because I am a very selfish man and have wanted you all to myself. I'm sorry that it's made you think I was ashamed of you."

"Oh." He opened his eyes, stared at his lover. "I want to be your good thing."

"You are. You're my very good thing, and you make my life whole, complete." There wasn't anything but need and love in Billy's eyes.

"Good." He pulled Billy down into a hard, hungry kiss.

Billy's mouth opened, sucked his tongue in. He moaned, rubbed a little, his heart pounding. Billy's hands found his ass, squeezing. He wanted so much. Needed. He didn't complain at all when Billy's fingers began undressing him. In fact, he returned the favor.

"I want you to suck me."

"I want you... I want to call you sir." He wanted Billy to need that, too.

"God, yes. I love it when you do that." Billy's eyes met his. "I want you to do it all the time. Even when we're in public."

"Billy..." His cock jerked, eyelids actually getting heavy.

"You heard me. Now suck my cock."

He shuddered, looked at Billy, then scooted down and licked up along Billy's shaft. Right before he took the fat prick in like he needed to, he whispered. "I almost said make me, just to see what you'd do." Then he sucked Billy in, sucking hard.

Billy groaned, but then one hand landed in his hair and tilted his head slightly upward until their eyes met. "I would have made you."

He whimpered, suddenly so turned on he hurt, and he sucked harder, cock sliding on the blanket. Hands staying his hair, Billy got his head moving, bobbing up and down on the thick heat. He reached down, free hand wrapping around his cock, tugging in time.

"No!" The order was barked out, Billy's voice rough with his pleasure. "That's mine." Tanny moaned around Billy's cock, eyes flashing up to Billy's. "No coming until I say so. No touching until I say so. If I say so."

He let Billy's cock out until he was teasing the tip. "Until when?"

Billy growled. "That's up to me."

Fuck. Fuck, that was hot. "Or what?"

"Or you'll wear the cage for a month."

"Billy!" He groaned, took Billy's cock in, sucking hard. His cock was harder than ever. What was happening to him?

Billy started thrusting, pushing the thick cock in deep, over and over. He took every inch, begging for more. Soon, Billy's hand twisted in his hair and the thrusts became hard, unforgiving. He looked up, worried, needing to know Billy was pleased, with him. Billy's eyes stared right at him, full of love and lust. He opened farther and let Billy take everything.

"Mine," growled Billy, the thrusts losing their rhythm.

Two more thrusts and Billy's eyes went wide, let him right in as Billy shot down his throat. Tanny swallowed hard, took in every drop, his entire body alight. Billy's hand stayed in his hair, even as Billy relaxed back against the couch. He kissed Billy's stomach, tongue cleaning the sweet cock.

"Mmm... so good."

He nodded, kissed the tip of Billy's cock. Billy's fingers slid over his chest, heading for one of his nipples. He arched up, pushing toward the touch. Billy's fingers grabbed the ring and tugged, twisted.

"Billy!" He pushed against Billy's thigh, rubbing off.

"No coming," Billy reminded him.

"Why?" He climbed up Billy's body, burning up.

"Because that's mine. Everything is mine."

"Fuck, that's hot. I want you."

"You get me up again and you can ride me."

He reached down, fingers careful, sliding on Billy's shaft, stroking from base to tip. Groaning, Billy spread his legs, giving him room to work.

Tanny chuckled. "You look like the cat that got the milk."

"No, you're the one who got the cream." Billy gave him a wink.

That made him laugh, deep and hard.

"God, I love that sound."

"I love you. You're so damn funny."

Billy grinned and took a kiss, drawing him close.

"That was hot, before." He traced Billy's lips, hand still moving, nice and slow.

"It's always hot."

"Yeah, but..." He shrugged. That had been... wild.

Billy nudged him. "Remember that I want to hear everything you have to say, hmm?"

"I just. It was." God, this part was hard.

"Hot?"

"Yeah. Really."

"Groan and complain as you might, you like me being in control of your orgasms."

"I like you being... You."

Billy smiled and nodded, hands sliding over his cheek and through his hair. "I like being me, as well."

He arched into the touch, toes curling. "Cool..."

"Uh-huh. Now make me hard, Montana. I plan to fuck you until you scream."

"Yeah?" He started stroking again, good and hard.

"Yeah, spread you open and stretch you wide. Maybe I'll even let you come."

"I...I'm already stretched, Bi... sir."

Billy made a happy, rumbling noise. "Not by my cock, though."

"You stretch me more than anyone." Ever.

"I try." Billy's hips began moving, pushing the thick cock through his fingers. Tanny focused on touching, refusing to think about how hot Billy had made him. "Good," murmured Billy.

His mouth was taken suddenly, power and strength in the kiss. It made him shake again, his breath coming in short, sharp gasps. Two of Billy's fingers pushed into his body. Tanny bore down, riding hard. "God, you're sensual. I love that." Two fingers became three, Billy letting him ride.

He was flying, the world hot and close and good all

around him.

"Me now," growled Billy as those fingers disappeared.

"Yeah. Yeah, Billy. You."

"That's right." He felt the heat first, Billy's cock on fire as it pressed against his hole.

He bore down, spreading easily, feeling every inch. Billy's gaze held his as the thick cock pushed in and in, not stopping until he could feel Billy's balls against his ass. He squeezed tight, not looking away.

"Love you," Billy groaned, hips starting to move.

He nodded, shoulders twisting as he moaned. Billy kept moving, thrusting into him. The speed built slowly, harder, faster, more. "I need you. This."

"I know. Me, too."

"Good." He nodded, mind sliding back to that growl, that intensity from before. Just the memory made his body creak.

Billy didn't answer him with words; instead, the thick cock pushed in even harder. Wrapping his legs around Billy's waist, he encouraged his love in deeper. The sound that came out of Billy was close to that growl, the thrusts become short, sharp as Billy's cock moved inside him.

"Yours." His head tossed and he whimpered, balls tight, aching.

"That's right. Mine. Mine." Billy began to repeat it with each and every thrust.

He arched, fingers clenching into fists. Billy shifted slightly, cock banging into his sweet spot.

"Oh!" His eyes flew open, entire body aching.

"Yeah, right there." Billy's cock stayed on that spot, making his body sing.

"Fuck. Fuck. Billy..."

"I am." Billy's eyes looked wicked and happy.

His laughter bubbled out of him. Billy's joined him, those hard strokes not stopping or slowing down for an instant. The chuckles slowly faded, becoming gasps and groans. Billy's hips kept punching, pushing into him.

"Billy..." Fuck, he needed.

"Mine," Billy growled, hand wrapping around his cock.

"Oh..." He was going to shoot.

"No coming 'til I say so." That growl was back.

He shook. "I have to."

"Not. Until. I. Say. So."

"Or what?" He had to know. Had to.

Billy stopped, stared at him, and then answered. "The cage. A month. I'm serious, Montana."

His body shuddered, stomach tight. "Shh. Okay. Okay. I hear you." Fuck. Fuck him.

"You want it," growled Billy.

"I want you." Needed him.

"You got me." As if to prove it, Billy started slamming into him, hard and fast and so good.

He whimpered, eyes squeezed tight, teeth sinking into his bottom lip as he fought not to come. Billy's hand tightened on his cock, holding him now instead of stroking. He wasn't going to come. He wasn't. Damn it.

Billy finally came, mouth opening, shout filling the air as long pulses of heat filled him. Tanny whimpered and twisted, his entire body hard and aching.

Groaning, Billy pressed a kiss on him. The hand around his cock remained still, tight. "You want to come."

"Fuck, yes."

Billy chuckled, kissed his neck. "Okay, love. Give it up for me."

"Really?" He could barely focus, barely believe it.

"Yes, love. Do it now." Billy fisted him, hard and fast.

"Fuck. Fuck. Fuck..." He squeezed Billy tight, body arching in a bow.

Billy groaned, hips pushing the thick cock inside him some.

"Yes..." He bore down harder, demanding a little more and then a little more, his balls so tight they hurt.

"Come," growled Billy.

"Yes..." He shot so hard it burned, heart slamming in his chest.

Billy moaned for him and brought a hand up, licking his come from it.

"Fuck, you... We... Wow."

Billy chuckled, the sound deep, happy. "Yes, we did."

"Uh-huh."

Billy kissed him hard and then suddenly got up. "Don't go anywhere."

"Huh?" He watched Billy walk away. Weirdo. Nice ass, though.

A moment later Billy came back. The view was just as nice from the front, Billy's cock still half-hard, swaying against a muscled thigh.

"Pretty."

"What?" Billy looked behind himself.

"You. You're pretty."

"Me?" Billy chuckled, gave him a wink. "You're biased."

"Well, yeah. I love you."

That had Billy beaming, strutting a little for him. He watched, licked his lips, and moaned.

"I've got something for you," Billy told him, coming closer.

"What?" He blinked, shifting, moving closer.

Billy brought his right hand forward, offering over the cage, the metal gleaming in the light.

He shook his head. "I waited."

"Which means it doesn't go on for a month."

He shuddered at the thought. "I was good..."

"You were. Three days." Billy pushed the cage into his hand. "You put it on yourself."

"But... why?" He'd done what Billy'd asked.

"Because I told you to."

"Are you pissed at me?"

"What? No." Billy sat next to him, hand warm on his skin. "I'm not pissed at you. I don't do this when I'm pissed." He arched into the touch, needing it, needing Billy close. Billy drew him in closer, so their bodies were together. "This isn't about anger. It's about pushing boundaries. It's about flying high."

He snuggled in, the comfort an addiction. Billy's fingers slid along his tattoo, tracing the letters in a familiar move.

Tanny hummed, his worry easing, melting away. "Yours."

"That's right, love. Mine." Billy always said that word like it was the most important one ever.

He took the cage in trembling fingers. "You'll have to help."

"With whatever you need, love."

He slid his prick in the cage, shaking hard, feeling suddenly angry, then sick, then shaken.

Billy's fingers slid over his, stilling them. "Talk to me, Montana."

"I'm mad. I'm really mad." It wigged him out a little bit.

"Tell me why."

"Because I'm doing this. Because I'm doing this on purpose!"

"Why does doing it on purpose make you mad?" Billy looked genuinely confused.

"I don't know." He shrugged. "I don't understand, but I am. I'm mad at myself."

Billy cupped his cheeks and made him look into his lover's eyes. "Because you've been told this kind of thing is wrong. Kinky isn't bad, Montana. It's just kinky. And what we do together is nobody's business but ours."

"I know, but... I want it. That's heavy-duty fucked up. I mean, I really want it." His eyes actually got wet.

"It is not fucked up. Taking drugs, that's fucked up. Taking control of your life, of what you need—that's not fucked up at all."

"No?" He scooted closer. "Billy, I'm putting a thing on my cock."

"I know. And I'm telling you there's nothing wrong with that." Billy's hand dropped to his cock, pushing the bottom link down over the base of his prick.

He groaned, eyes closing. "Then why is it so hard?"

"Because it's different. Because it's looking into yourself and admitting what you want. Self-examination isn't high on your list of things you like to do." There was a slight twinkle in Billy's eyes, his words teasing.

"Don't make me beat you." His own laughter felt good.

"No, that's my job." Billy winked at him this time.

"I'm sorry for freaking. Sometimes all this fucks with me."

"I don't mind you freaking at all. I'd rather that than you not saying anything and internalizing it."

"What does that mean?"

"That means I like that you told me."

"Oh." He nodded. "I feel better."

"See? Talking about things can be good."

Tanny's eyes rolled. "Hush."

Billy laughed and planted another kiss on him. Together they got the cage on before his cock could consider filling again. "It's beautiful," murmured Billy, fingers stroking the cage, his cock through the metal.

"Don't touch..."

Billy gave him a look and stroked again.

"Billy!"

He was beginning to feel that heat again, that raw need.

"Yes, love?" As if Billy could be anywhere near as innocent as he was trying to look.

"No touching." He pushed, not sure why he wanted to.

"That's not up to you."

"It's my body." He kept watching Billy, captured, caught.

"So? You're mine." Billy's voice growled over that last word.

Tanny moaned, lips parting. "Am I?"

"Absolutely. Top to bottom."

"I want to push; is that normal?"

Billy grinned. "It is. It means you want my attention. You want to be punished, for me to prove that I see you."

"But... I'm not a kid." That was something children did.

"God, no."

"Grownups aren't so... stupid, are they?"

"Plenty of grownups are plenty stupid. You aren't, though, and I don't want to hear you saying that you are."

"But I am. I'm not smart."

"You are, too!" Billy made that little growling noise at the back of his throat again.

"No, I'm not!"

"Are we going to have this argument on a regular basis?"

"Until you give in."

"I'm not going to give in until you admit that you're smart."

"Then we're going to argue."

"I don't want to argue with you, love. Not about this."

"I just want to be the best for you."

"You are. You're just what I want. What I need."

He nodded, reached out for Billy again, and held on.

Billy held him close and kissed the top of his head. "I'm not letting you go, love."

"Promise?"

"I promise. We don't have any plans tomorrow night, do we?"

"No." He took a blanket, covered them both up.

"Then I'd definitely like to take you to the Hammer. We can have dinner, watch the show. I don't know who's doing what onstage, but there's usually something interesting going on."

"You don't have to, Billy. Honestly." He knew that it would be hard, to introduce him around.

"I want to, love. I haven't yet because I was worried it might be too much for you. Some of the members are very free with their sexuality, with their kinks."

"Like Oliver?"

"Like Oliver, and more so. You remember Christmas at his house? The Hammer will be much more in your face."

"You don't have to do this. You don't have to introduce me."

"I want to—I want you to meet everyone. I want them all to know how lucky I am."

"I'm the lucky one."

"We both are, then."

"Okay." That was acceptable.

Billy chuckled and drew him in for a kiss. "Love you."

"Good. I need you to, huh?" More than anything.

"Well, I do." Billy kissed him again and then just held him, keeping him close.

That was what he needed. More than anything. Now.

Chapter Eleven

Billy showed the doorman his membership card and he and Montana walked through the door and into the club. It was busy—he maybe should have made sure to reserve a table, but he'd been hoping he'd be able to share a table with someone, let Montana get to know some of his friends better.

He looked around for familiar faces. He saw Rick and Rob, Ben and Mic, then Gordon and the twins. He smiled and waved, drawing Montana closer so anyone looking couldn't mistake that they were together. Montana stayed close, that worried, belligerent, stubborn look coming out.

He squeezed Montana's hand and headed for the closest table with people he knew. Pretty little Ben was in Mic's lap, newly shaved—no hair, no eyebrows, just smooth, bared skin—blindfolded and quiet.

"Mic, so good to see you and your boy."

Mic smiled slowly, the near-ebony skin making Ben look all the paler.

Montana nodded, pressed closer to him.

"I'd like to introduce you to my lover. This is Montana. Montana, this is my friend Mic and his sub Ben."

"Montana. That's a beautiful name. Ben's silent today,

but I'm sure he's pleased to meet you."

"He's positively glowing, Mic. I can see things are going well for you both."

"He's beautiful, my boy. Come, have a seat. We've missed you."

"Thank you." Billy pulled out a chair for Montana first, and then sat himself. "I've been a little preoccupied."

"Preoccupied? The beginnings are always so good."

"They are. Ours has been, hasn't it, Montana?" He wanted to include his lover without Montana feeling like he was being put on the spot.

"Yes." Montana stayed close, eyes watching everything.

"Have you eaten yet?" he asked Mic. He wondered what Montana would make of watching Mic feeding his lover.

"No, we were waiting to see who would join us."

Billy chuckled. "Wonderful! I have to admit, I'm starving. Do you know what tonight's specials are?"

"Finger foods."

The perfect thing to feed one's lover. "Oh, how wonderful for you!"

Mic's smile was almost wolfish. "And you, hmm?"

He looked over at Montana. "It could be, yes."

Montana's cheeks blazed a bright pink, but he didn't bolt, settling in beside Billy.

"Maybe we'll feed each other." He could suck Montana's fingers clean after every mouthful.

"I could do that." Montana didn't look at Ben, was careful not to meet anyone's eyes.

He reached and put a hand on Montana's thigh, wordlessly offering comfort and reassurance. "So, what have you been up to, Mic?"

"Working, mostly. Ben has been at a meet." Mic met Montana's eyes. "He's a speed skater."

"Oh."

"How'd he do? Is he Olympics bound?" Ben was that good. He'd nearly made the team the previous Olympics.

"He did well, but he's having some issues. We're working through them, with the help of his coach."

Billy imagined that was what the shaving and blindfold were all about. "Is everything all right?"

Mic nodded. "Sometimes competitive spirit is counterproductive."

"It looks like you have everything well in hand."

"It's my pleasure."

He actually thought Mic looked worried, but this wasn't the place to ask or push about that. "Give me a call if you want to talk. Mornings work well." Not that he wanted to hide it from Montana, but it would offer Mic more privacy if his lover wasn't home.

Mic nodded, reached one hand out and squeezed his. "Thank you, friend."

"You're very welcome."

A sweet-faced young man came to their table to ask if he could take their orders. Billy turned to Montana. "Would you like to share the finger foods with me, love?"

Montana beamed at the endearment, nodded. "That sounds perfect."

He caressed Montana's thigh, squeezed it a moment. "Cool. And a Coke to drink?"

"Mmm. Yes, please. I love the bubbles."

He chuckled and ordered the finger foods for two and two Cokes from the little waiter, who bobbed and asked for Mic's order, and then bobbed again before scurrying off.

Mic smiled at Montana, then at him. "There's a show tonight, I think. Marcus has new whips."

"Oh, wonderful! Has he brought someone, or will he be asking for volunteers?"

"I'm not sure, honestly. I've been focused elsewhere."

Billy chuckled. "Of course."

Mic winked. "I do know he's selling his wares after, though. Club discount."

"Smart man." He looked at Montana. "Maybe you'll be interested in something more than a paddle or that little flogger we have."

Montana's cheeks went dark. "Billy!"

"What?" He did love to push his lover.

"We're at a restaurant!" Montana hissed.

Mic chuckled softly.

"Love—look around you. This isn't a restaurant, it's a private club where you and I are very tame." He'd taken the cage off Montana for this outing. He wanted his lover to get hard, to realize he was affected by what was going on.

Montana pressed closer. "It's really nice in here. Quiet. Private."

He nodded. "It's a safe place for us."

Montana smiled for him, leaned into his side. "Like you."

It always melted him when Montana said things like that. "Thank you, love."

Montana cuddled in. "So, is there a chef here who changes the menu every day?"

"Yeah. He has free rein, from what I've seen. There's some stuff that stays the same—for instance, you can always get a steak—but the specials are at his whim."

"That must be a lot of work. Does he have helpers?"

Look at his lover, asking questions, being curious instead of running away.

"You know, I've never asked. We could invite Xavier over—he manages the club. I'm betting he'd be thrilled to answer your questions."

"Oh, don't bother him."

"I doubt it would be a bother, love. He's very proud of the club."

Montana shook his head, fingers twining with his. The music started and a few couples began dancing, swaying together.

"Would you like to dance?"

"Oh, yes. Very much." Montana's eyes actually twinkled.

Chuckling, delighted by Montana's response, he stood and held out his hand.

"Have fun, boys." Mic was stroking Ben's bald head, murmuring softly as they walked away.

"Is he okay?" Montana asked.

"He's going to be just fine. You know how I do things to you, to make you feel better, to make you fly? Mic and Ben have different things, but they're working toward similar goals."

They turned toward each other as they got to the dance floor. Montana reached up for him, eager and ready, relaxed for him. Billy slipped his hands around Montana's waist and tugged him in close. They danced in the kitchen often, and Montana moved with him like a dream. It felt nice, being out in public and sharing their love.

Montana's cheek rested against his chest, eyes closed. It was a sweet moment and he hoped they had many more like it. Montana was a natural, moving with the rhythm, hips swaying side to side. "We should do this more often." There wasn't always dancing at the Hammer, but there were other gay bars in town that did have regular dancing.

"Mmmhmm. It's nice."

He kept a half an eye on their table, not wanting to miss the food when it came, but aside from that, he let everything else but the music and Montana wash over him.

He should have done this earlier, should have introduced Montana to this part of his life. He'd been so worried Montana would freak that he never considered his lover thought he was ashamed. He was mad at himself—he should have trusted his lover.

They turned as they danced and he noticed the food was being brought to the table. "You ready to eat, love?"

"I could dance forever, but yeah. Hungry."

Chuckling, Billy took Montana's hand and led him back to the table. Mic was already feeding Ben, fingers gentle, careful.

"Look at that," he murmured quietly. "You can see the love in the way he feeds his sub."

Montana ducked his head. "Isn't it rude to watch?"

"If they wanted privacy, they wouldn't have come out."

"Oh." Montana picked up a stuffed mushroom. "You like these. Open up."

He did, letting Montana feed him and making sure his lips closed over his lover's fingers.

"Careful." Montana winked, actually playing with him. "No biting."

"No? But your fingers are so tempting." He snapped his teeth.

Montana pinched his nose. "No. Biting."

He laughed and grabbed Montana's fingers. "And no pinching."

"No?" Montana looked so happy.

"No. No pinching." He winked and picked up an empanada, holding it up for his lover.

Montana snapped the empanada up, moaning happily. He slid his hand along Montana's cheek, admiring.

"It's good."

"Yeah, it is." He stroked again and then looked to see what to choose next.

Montana took some cheese before he could decide and fed him.

"Mmm..." It melted in his mouth. "Nice choice."

"Yeah?" Montana took another piece, offered it to him.

"You try it." He took Montana's hand and turned it back to his own mouth.

Montana's lips parted, eating easily, lips soft and swollen. Groaning, he leaned in and pressed their lips together, kissing and stealing a bit of cheese. His lover went tense, but only for a moment, then Montana pressed closer and opened to him. He kept kissing, staying right there for a long while. Montana stayed close, cuddling into him.

He broke the kiss and smiled, then reached for a prawn, handing it over.

"Do I like those?"

"I bet you will."

"Okay."

Mic chuckled as Montana opened up for him.

He grinned at Mic, winked, and then fed the end of the prawn into Montana's mouth. He leaned in to bite off the tail end. Montana's laughter tickled his lips. He licked them, smiling back.

"What do you want next?"

"I don't suppose you're on the menu?"

"Billy!" Montana's laughter rang out.

"It's a valid question!"

"Do you see me on the table?"

"Oh." The visual that gave him stopped him for a moment. He could see it, see Montana stripped naked and spread out. Everyone would admire, would want, but nobody could have except him.

"Have a bite of fruit, hmm?" Montana had no idea, did he?

"Only if you're feeding me."

"Okay. It's a little bite of something." One tiny bite was offered to him. He opened his mouth and pulled in the food as well as Montana's fingers. "No biting."

He raised an eyebrow, but he didn't bite. Instead, he sucked. Montana's eyelids went heavy. "Mmm..." He licked Montana's fingertips and then slowly let them go.

"S... Billy."

"You should trust your instincts, love." That 'sir' would have been perfect here of all places.

"Yeah? Even if I'm wrong?"

"I bet most of the time you won't be. Not when you trust your gut."

"I want to..." Montana leaned close, lips on his ear. "I want to call you sir."

"This isn't the first time you've said that, love. Just do it." He wanted it as much as Montana did.

"Yes, sir. It scares me that I want to."

"Trust me and trust yourself, love."

Montana nodded. "I can trust you."

"That'll do as a start."

Montana's cheek settled on his shoulders. He grabbed a slice of apple with cheese melted over it and offered his lover a bite. Montana opened to him, nibbling delicately. He licked his own lips, tasting the food and the hint of Montana there.

"I like that."

"You want another one?" He grabbed another cheese-covered apple slice and took a bite first before handing the rest over. It was good, almost as good as Montana's face as his lover ate.

They continued to feed each other, one little bite of food after another. It was both delicious and sensuous. He was definitely turned on by the time he was getting full.

The dessert tray came then, chocolate and fruits and tiny cakes. Montana clapped, eager and happy. "Dude. Look!"

Billy chuckled. "Will you be able to choose?"

"Uh-huh." A strawberry was dipped into chocolate sauce and popped into his mouth.

He chewed, his eyes closing to enjoy the flavors.

"Mmm. You're so hot." Montana's fingers, sticky and sweet with chocolate, trailed over his lips.

Groaning, he grabbed Montana's fingers and sucked them in.

"Sir..." Montana was almost in his lap.

He patted his thighs, encouraging his lover toward him.

"Yeah?" Montana slipped onto his lap, moaning happily. "Thank you."

"You're very welcome. Now feed me some more of that sweet stuff."

"Bossy." Montana found a chocolate-dipped cherry and dangled it by the stem.

He thought he heard Mic laughing. "I'm supposed to be." He leaned up and made a grab for the cherry with his tongue.

"You want to see something neat?" Montana asked, after feeding him the fruit.

"Of course I do."

Montana grinned and took a cherry, holding the stem between his teeth. A few seconds passed and Montana stuck his tongue out, the stem tied in a knot.

Billy crowed. "I thought that was an urban legend."

"Nope. I can do it."

"So I see." He leaned in and slid his tongue into Montana's mouth.

Montana's tongue stroked his, the flavor there sweet and tart. His hands slid along Montana's back, heading steadily downward. The soft moan vibrated his tongue. His fingers curled around Montana's ass.

"Billy... You want another bite?"

"Mmmhmm. I do." Maybe not of food...

"Strawberry? Cake?"

"You." It wasn't a question this time. He leaned in and nipped at Montana's neck.

"Billy!" Montana's chuckle was delicious.

He did love the way Montana said his name like that. Slightly scandalized, partly turned on. He licked at the spot he'd bitten.

"Yours." That word was soft, sweet.

"That's right, love. Through and through, you're mine." He gave one last kiss to that spot and smiled up into Montana's eyes, thrilled with how their night out at the Hammer was going. That Montana had been comfortable enough to sit in his lap was a great sign.

Of course, Montana trusted him, loved him, and wasn't terribly (outwardly) worried about what others thought about him. He was about to ask Montana to dance again when the music faded away and the lights came up on the stage.

"I think the show's about to start."

"Okay." Montana took a petit four and nibbled on it, cheek on his shoulder.

Billy turned his attention to the stage, where big, bald Marcus was grinning out at them. The whip master pulled out a few pieces and started showing off, the whips snapping at the air.

"Are there any volunteers this evening?" Marcus called out.

Montana shrank in, pressed close to him.

A tall, thin man stepped up, wearing a simple pair of jeans, a T-shirt. "I'll help you out."

"Excellent! I have a beautiful little whip here that I'd like to demonstrate. If you'll all give us a few moments while my new assistant and I work out a few details..." Marcus bowed and stepped out of the light, the man in the jeans following.

"Who's that? Why would he just volunteer?"

Billy chuckled. "I'm not sure who he is—Mic?" He turned to ask their dining companions.

"Tucker Davis. He's a carpenter."

"He's new." Billy watched the man speaking with Marcus for a moment and then smiled at Montana. "He's volunteered because he wants to be whipped and I imagine he doesn't have a Master. Or if he does, his Master maybe doesn't do whippings and has allowed him to volunteer with Marcus."

"He wants to be..." Montana frowned. "Will it fuck him up bad?"

"Not at all. I imagine he's going to enjoy it very much."

"I don't know, Billy. That seems extreme, huh?"

"You think so? You like to be spanked. You like the cage. Some people would say that's extreme. We've already established that that isn't bad or wrong."

"I'm not saying it's wrong, just scary."

He held Montana close. "Watch the man's face while Marcus whips him."

"Do I have to?"

"You do."

Montana sighed, just barely keeping his eyes open.

"Worried you might like to try it?"

"No!" Montana jerked, pulled away a little.

"Shh. I was just teasing." Montana's reaction was very interesting, though. They'd worked with a flogger before, but never a whip; the sensations would be quite different. If they did do whip work, he'd need to make sure he was adept enough at it that he didn't catch his lover's back by accident.

He took it as a good thing that Montana trusted him immediately, relaxed into him. He found that bundle of nerves just above Montana's ass, where the skin was still smooth and unharmed. He slowly stroked it as Marcus and Tucker stepped back into the circle of light. Tucker was stripped down bare, proud and unashamed as Marcus bound him to a St. Andrew's Cross.

"Look how beautiful he is in his submission." He nibbled at Montana's earlobe. "He doesn't glow like you do, though."

"He doesn't look happy."

Billy tilted his head. "He doesn't look unhappy,

though. And the whipping hasn't started yet."

"Still." Montana shrugged, fingers playing with his, restless.

"Let's wait and see, hmm?" He grabbed Montana's hand and wrapped their fingers tightly together.

Marcus wielded the whip with ease, the leather snapping, slowly warming the tall sub's skin.

"It's a beautiful thing, watching a Master wield a whip."

"I don't like the noise."

"It's a lovely rhythm. It will be even better when the sub begins to vocalize."

Montana frowned. "Is that your fancy-top way of saying he's going to scream?"

He chuckled. "He might scream. I was thinking more of moans and groans."

"Uh-huh." Montana's wink made him grin. God, he loved this man.

He held onto his lover, sharing the experience of watching the whipping. The sub moved into the blows, obviously trying to find Marcus' rhythm. He found himself holding his breath, waiting for the two men to really mesh. Marcus was talking, the words slow, too soft to hear, and it was painful, watching the sub fight, try so hard. He found himself stroking Montana, petting him soothingly.

The club was quiet, all eyes on the stage, watching. All of a sudden the sub let out a low, wanton moan.

"Yes." Mic nodded, eyes focused on the stage, breathing hard. "Good boy."

Billy nodded, finally taking a breath of his own. "Yes."

The tension in the room dissipated, Marcus making the man fly.

Billy chuckled and nodded. "Oh, yes. Nice."

"Is it better now?" Montana whispered.

"Can't you feel it?"

Montana nodded. "It's like the balloon popped."

"Yes, good comparison." He bit at Montana's earlobe.

Montana gasped, ass pushing against him. He licked at the lobe he'd bitten, a deep, aroused chuckle coming out of him. He wanted to push Montana over the table and take him, make his pretty lover scream. "I want you," he growled into Montana's ear.

Montana shivered, moaned so softly.

"Right here, right now, I want you."

"Billy... We can't. The police." Montana scooted closer.

"This is a private club, love. There's a naked man on stage tied to a St. Andrew's Cross, being whipped by another man."

"But..." Montana's hips were moving, rocking against him, steady, hungry.

"But we wouldn't be the only ones. Look around." The club was alight tonight, sex everywhere. He slid his hands to Montana's jeans, tugging open the top button.

"This is a bad idea..." Montana was hard, leaking, aching for him.

"No, I don't think so." He undid Montana's zipper, careful not to catch the beautiful cock in the teeth.

"We can't do this..." Montana's lips were on his ear.

"Why not? I'm willing. You're willing." He slid his fingers across the wet tip of Montana's prick.

Montana arched, pushed toward his touch. He slid his hand down around the shaft and began to stroke, using the sound of the whip falling to guide his strokes.

"Sir. Sir, please." Montana groaned, dark eyes wide.

"Your hands."

"I have you, love." He kept stroking Montana, his free hand slipping up under his lover's T-shirt so he could tug on Montana's nipple ring.

"I don't..." Montana leaned closer, tongue lapping at his lips.

He touched his tongue to Montana's. "Don't what?"

He got a soft chuckle. "I don't know. It feels so good. You feel so good."

"Then just enjoy it, love." The movements Montana made were driving him crazy, his lover's ass rubbing against his cock. Montana nodded, beginning to move harder, body rippling. "Beautiful," he murmured. He wasn't watching the stage anymore.

Montana's lips were open, hips bucking. He squeezed the head of Montana's cock and then ran his thumb across it.

"Sir..." Montana jerked, knees knocking the table.

"Less moving," he ordered.

"Sorry. Sorry, I..."

"Shh. Shh. Just focus on the feelings, hmm?"

"Uh-huh." Montana's eyes closed, head falling back against him.

He latched onto Montana's neck, lips tight, tongue working the skin. Montana's prick dripped for him, hot and wet, perfect, the flesh swollen. "God, you're sexy."

"I want you, sir."

"How do you want it, love?"

"I... I don't know. I don't know what's right here."

"Anything goes, love. I can take you right here, like this." He pushed up and had his cock slide against Montana's ass. "All we need to do is shift a few clothes."

"Oh, fuck." Montana's spine arched.

He pushed at Montana's pants, tugging them down past his lover's hips.

"Promise me we won't get arrested."

"I swear it, love." He bit at Montana's earlobe again. "We're not the only ones taking advantage of the low lighting."

"Okay. Okay. I trust you. "

"Good." He got his own pants undone, his cock pushing out eagerly. He put his fingers to Montana's lips. "Suck, love."

Montana's lips wrapped around his fingers and the suction hit him hard. Groaning, he humped up against Montana's crack. There were soft moans in the air, hidden under the thump and thrum of the music, the sounds of the whip hitting flesh. He pulled his fingers out, needing to get Montana stretched and wet before it was too late. Montana moaned, shivered just slightly.

"Two," he muttered, pushing both in. He didn't have the patience for a long, slow preparation. He'd bet Montana didn't, either. Montana pushed back against him, riding him hard. "Wait for me, love. No coming yet."

Montana's nod was sure, immediate.

He managed to find Montana's gland, pegging it hard with his fingertips. The hot flesh that held him squeezed. He wanted inside Montana. Now.

"Please. Please, sir."

He pulled his fingers out and let go of Montana's cock so he could use both hands to hold Montana's ass. He raised his lover up, lined up his cock, and let Montana sit back in his lap. Montana went still, ass tight as a fist around him. He growled and bit at Montana's neck. "Let me in, love. It's what we both want."

"Yes..." Montana moaned for him, back arching.

He held onto Montana's hips and slowly lowered and raised Montana. Each time Montana sank down, it took him in deep and made him groan.

Things hadn't been so wild, so heated in the Hammer in months. The whole place smelled like sex, heat and musk and male. It was heady. As were the sounds coming from the stage, the whip hitting flesh, the moans and groans of the sub. Most of all, though, the heat of Montana around him and his lover's cries made him fly.

His boy. His sub. His lover. His.

He wrapped his hand around Montana's cock and began jacking it in time with his pushes into Montana's ass.

"Sir. Sir. Sir." The words were just breaths, simply whispered.

"Yes, love. Yours." Faster and faster he moved them.

"Mine!" That wasn't as quiet.

"What was that?" He squeezed Montana's cock tighter.

"Mine. You're mine. My lover. My sir."

"Yes." He pushed in hard. "Come for me now."

"Yes, sir. Yes. Please." Heat spread over his fingers.

Moaning, he let himself go as well, coming into Montana's willing body. Montana shuddered and shook, body working his cock. He held on tight to Montana, a shudder moving through him. Montana's breath slowed, his lover relaxing.

He nuzzled Montana's neck, and then nibbled at Montana's earlobe again. "Love." He whispered the word.

Montana nodded. "Yes."

He didn't want to pull out, but they were at the

Hammer. "Pass me a napkin, love."

The cloth was passed back. "You're not going to get in trouble, are you?"

Billy snickered. "I already told you we weren't the only ones. Look around, love." He cleaned up Montana's cock, and then pulled out, using the same napkin to make sure they didn't wind up with come all over their pants. He cleaned Montana's ass, making a mental note to bring a plug next time.

They wriggled and together got Montana's pants done back up, and then his own. "There. All tidy."

"Tidy is a weird word, huh?"

Billy grinned, dumping the napkin in the little garbage can subtly placed beneath the table. "Is it?"

"I think so, yeah. It's like finicky."

"I like persnickety myself."

Montana grinned. "That one's good."

He chuckled. "You do have a way with pillow talk, love."

That laughter rang out, and Mic grinned over at them. "He's cute, Billy."

"He is. He's mine." He knew Mic had no designs on Montana, but the words had popped out anyway; he'd laid his claim.

"I can tell. Congratulations." One hand pinched Ben's chest. "This one is mine."

Billy grinned and nodded. "Sorry. Kind of a knee jerk reaction."

"It's fun, though, needing them."

"Fun and... satisfying."

Montana ducked his head, swallowed, smiled.

Billy finally turned his attention back to the stage, only to realize the demonstration was over, Marcus helping the sub down off the cross. Montana wasn't watching, but it didn't matter. He'd done so well, performed beautifully.

He turned Montana's head enough to kiss him. Montana moaned, tongue fucking his lips gently. He sucked on it, fingers sliding beneath Montana's T-shirt to tug at the nipple ring. Montana moaned, body stretching, reaching for him.

"So sexy."

"Only for you, Billy."

"That works for me."

Montana offered him a warm, wonderful smile.

The music started up again and he smiled, rubbed their noses together. "You want to dance?"

"I'd love to dance."

"Good." He patted Montana's ass to get him to move off his lap, and then stood as well, taking his lover's hand.

For the second time, Montana moved into his arms. Just like that, everything else faded away and it was just him and Montana again, moving together.

Like it should be.

Chapter Twelve

I gotta go, Margaret." He grinned. "I'm going to stop at the store and get light bulbs for Billy on the way."

"Be careful, Tanny. I'll see you tomorrow. I'll be late. I'm getting a haircut."

He nodded, smiled, and grabbed his backpack. Store, a quick stop at the 7-Eleven for a Dr. Pepper and a Snickers bar, then home. He needed a shower and a nap. Billy had an article and...

A hand landed on his arm. "Where do you think you're going?"

"Home." He pulled away, shivering as he met cold, hard eyes in a red face. Fucking pigs, and this one was the worst, always looking at him, always watching him. "What do you want?"

"To search your bag. A customer at that shop you came out of said you were dealing in there."

"Fuck you. I haven't. I was at work."

"Dealing."

He stepped backward. "No. No, I didn't. I never did that." Never. Shit, he used to use, not deal.

"Then give me the backpack."

"No." No way.

"Then I'll arrest you. Right here. You think your

boss'll like that?"

Fuck. Fuck. "Can't you fucking bother a real criminal?"

That hand shot out, grabbing his arm hard enough that his muscle ground against his bone. "You are a criminal, Tanny. You've been in, what, four times for possession? Five? Once we got you on a big deal—you had plenty on you."

"What do you want?" He wanted to go home. Please.

"And then there's your pimp, huh? Is he helping you?" He almost nodded at the words, but the cop kept talking and he was glad he hadn't. "I bet he's cooking your shit up for you. God knows you're not fucking smart enough to do it. Idiot."

"He doesn't use. I don't either. What the fuck do you want?" Why was this guy fucking with him? He didn't understand. He didn't.

The ugly, smarmy fucker grinned at him. "I want your help, asshole. And if you don't want me to skull fuck your world, you'll give it to me."

"Fuck you. You can't prove anything. I haven't done anything."

He yanked his arm away and started jogging, moving fast. He wasn't even paying attention to where he was going, just heading home by the shortest route possible. He had to get home, get away from that jerk hassling him. Why couldn't they just leave him alone?

He'd only just crossed the street to turn into the nice neighborhood where Billy lived when the cop car pulled up in front of him on the sidewalk, cutting him off. The same asshole stepped out, the sound of his laughter nasty.

"I've got you now, boy. You crossed on the red light—that's called jaywalking. And, oh. Oh. Look at this." A little baggie of rock was held up, dangled. "Add that to your record, your use, and the fact that we know you're dealing, maybe even whoring, and your ass is mine. I'll pull your pimp in, too. Maybe they'll let you share a cell."

Chapter Thirteen

Billy hummed as he chopped salad for fajitas. He had all the fixings spread out on the kitchen table, the tortillas ready to warm in the microwave, the meat cooked and waiting in the oven. The other night at the Hammer had been amazing; he was still humming from it. They'd have to go back again soon.

He glanced at the clock and frowned. Montana should have been back over an hour ago; had they made lunch plans that he'd forgotten about?

As if his thoughts had conjured up his lover, Montana came in through the front door, heading straight for the bedroom. "Stinky. Going to shower. Be right out." The bathroom door closed behind Montana. Now, that wasn't quite right.

Billy finished up with the lettuce, made sure there was soda pop in the fridge, and then slowly made his way toward the bathroom. He could hear the shower running, hear Montana splashing. He went into the bathroom, picking up Montana's clothes and popping them in the hamper. "Everything okay, love?"

"Yeah. Just dirty. I needed to get clean."

"Margaret working you hard?" He debated joining Montana, but figured they should maybe eat first. If he got into the shower they'd get... distracted.

"Always. Today was hard, long. A long day." Montana started scrubbing his hair.

"Do you need some help with that?" It wasn't like the food wouldn't keep, and so what if he'd just talked himself out of getting into the shower with his lover? He could change his mind.

Montana didn't answer right away, but then he got a "Sure, if you want to." Well, that wasn't like his lover.

He stripped quickly and climbed in, grabbing the soap. Montana pushed into his arms, hands sliding around his middle.

"Hey, love." He wrapped his arms around Montana, pulling him in close and holding on.

"Mmm. You feel good."

"Yeah? You always do." He brought their mouths together for a long kiss.

Montana felt tense to him, but only for a minute. He lost himself in the kiss, then, opening Montana's mouth to slide their tongues against each other. They rocked, nice and slow, steady. His hands drifted down to grab Montana's ass, to pull his lover closer. Montana nodded, one leg wrapping around his hip. He pushed his lover against the wall, humping.

"More. More." Suddenly it wasn't slow anymore.

He bit at Montana's lips, hips working, bringing them together hard.

"Yes." Montana moaned, nodded.

He stared into Montana's eyes. "I've got you."

"I need you."

"I've got you," he repeated. He kept humping against Montana.

"Yes." Montana grunted, rocking against him

He leaned in to suck a mark up on Montana's neck, and then he whispered, "You're allowed to come."

"Yes. Yes, sir." Montana didn't, though; he simply kept bucking and moving. Reaching around, Billy grabbed Montana's ass, squeezed it. "Please." Montana arched back into the touch.

He turned Montana, pushing his lover up against the tile. He grabbed the lube and slicked up his fingers, pushed two into Montana's tight little hole. Montana's ass bucked, taking him in deep. He hit that little gland and stayed there, fingertips working it.

"Oh. Oh. Fuck. Fuck yes. Right there."

"I know." He knew. He could feel it in the way Montana's body rippled around his fingers. Montana arched and nodded.

He tugged his fingers away and slicked up his prick with the lube they kept in the shower. It took only seconds to slide into that amazing heat. Montana started riding him immediately, fucking himself almost violently. Growling, he grabbed Montana's hips and slowed his lover down; he took charge.

"Billy..." Montana groaned, trying to push him.

"I set the pace." He pushed in slowly.

"I need you."

"I'm right here. Right here." He changed his angle and found Montana's gland.

"Oh..." Montana arched, groaned, riding him harder. Stubborn boy. His fingers tightened on Montana's hips, digging in as he forced his lover to follow his pace. "Billy. Billy, please. Please."

"When you're focused. When you're here with me." He kept pushing in, each movement deliberate, careful.

Montana whimpered. "How the fuck do you know?"

"Because I know you, love."

"I'm here. I am."

He chuckled. "I know. I can feel you. Can you feel me?" He pushed in a little harder, nailing the sweet little gland.

"Uh. Uh-huh."

"Good." He wrapped one hand around Montana's cock, the other still holding on tightly. He was still running the show, setting the pace.

"Love you. It was a bad day. I need you to make it right again."

"That's what I'm doing." Taking control. Being the Master. Giving Montana what he needed. He began rocking, his thrusts hard, his pace still not fast.

"Yes. Yes, thank you."

"Just let go and feel, love. I have you. I do."

He began to stroke, letting each push into Montana's ass shove his lover's cock along his palm. Montana nodded, finally relaxing, opening for him and letting him in. He fell into the rhythm of their bodies, of their heartbeats. They could love like this for hours, it seemed, moving and moaning, rocking together. The water would eventually run out, though, so he moved faster, tugged harder on the sweet cock in his hand. Montana's groan split the air, that tight ass squeezing his cock.

"You're allowed to come."

"Yes. Yes, thank you." Montana arched, body moving faster.

Billy controlled it, using his hand to guide Montana back onto his cock over and over. He could feel Montana's orgasm shuddering all around him, that sweet body going tight. He kept pushing through it, extending it as his prick hit Montana's gland. He kept tugging and pulling

Montana's prick, keeping it hard so he could bind it, control it.

There was a metal ring in the soap dish, and he grabbed it, sliding it around Montana's prick even as he kept burying his cock into his lover's body.

"So mean." Montana pushed back, squeezing him tight.

He laughed. "That's me. Mr. Meanypants." He looked around for a plug so he could come and keep it inside his lover.

He felt Montana's laughter all around his cock. It made him chuckle as well, and he licked the back of Montana's neck, lips lingering after his tongue.

"Where's a damn plug when you want one?" He muttered the words against Montana's skin.

"Plugs don't belong in the bathroom."

"There ought to be one in here. We make love in the shower often enough." After all, that's why there was a cock ring in here.

Montana chuckled. "Then leave one in here, turkey."

Laughing, too, he smacked Montana's ass. "It's Meanypants, not turkey. And I do believe I shall from now on. For now, we can go to the bedroom and I can make love to you there."

He let himself slide from Montana's ass, still hard and needy. Montana chuckled and turned to push into his arms and give him a kiss that melted him.

"I think we'd better get to the bedroom fast or I'm going to make the floor in here all sticky."

"As long as you clean up after yourself..." Montana laughed for him, and he swatted that fine ass.

He chased Montana all the way back to the bedroom, tackling his lover down onto the bed, laughing away.

Montana chuckled, bounced on the bed, snuggling into him. He found Montana's lips, kissing as he rubbed his hard on against Montana's belly. Montana's fingers wrapped around his prick, petting and stroking. Moaning, he pushed into those touches, beginning to get revved up again.

"You feel good." Montana was focused, touch sure, exploring him.

"I do. You're making me feel even better." He couldn't wait to sink back into Montana's body, fill his lover with his need.

"You want me to ride you?"

"I do." He rolled onto his back, one hand lingering on Montana's skin.

His prick was ready, hard, wet-tipped. Needy. Montana groaned and straddled him, taking him in deep. Calling out to his lover, he bucked up, his cock pushing in deep. Montana's hands landed on his chest, and they started slamming together. It was rough and good, their bodies coming together again and again.

"Love you." Montana bit his bottom lip, hard.

He jerked and pushed up, slamming in. "You, too."

"Again." Demanding boy.

He wrapped his hands around Montana's hips and pulled him down hard to meet his thrust. A sharp cry pushed into his lips. He kept bringing Montana down as he thrust up, primal sounds filling the room. Montana's ass was tight and hot around him, gripping him fiercely.

"Soon, love." He shifted one hand from Montana's hip, searching for a plug.

"Soon." Montana couldn't come yet, not with the ring on, but his lover was doing everything to get him off.

He nodded his agreement. He was almost there. He

found the plug to hold himself inside Montana, and that's when he let go. He came, the world sparkling for a moment. Montana kept moving, kept riding him through his orgasm. It felt like it went on and on and he gasped, bucked, body going limp by the time he was done.

Montana smoothed his hair from his forehead.

"Mmm…" He nuzzled into the touch. "I do love you."

"I know." Montana kissed his temple.

He brought the plug up, rubbing it along Montana's ringed cock. His cock was squeezed, Montana's hole jerking. "Oh, you like that." He rubbed fake and real cock together some more.

"I like most of the things you teach me."

"That's because you're a beautiful, sexy, sensual man."

Montana chuckled. "It's because I want you."

"That, too." He gave Montana a wink and bucked a little, pushing deeper inside Montana.

Montana squeezed again, laughed breathlessly.

"We could do this all afternoon." He could, too, Montana's tight heat keeping him hard for now.

"We'd both get sore."

That had him laughing and reaching to tweak Montana's barbelled nipple. "So practical."

"I am." Montana grinned at him, eyes laughing.

"Let's get this plug into you." He so got off on leaving his come inside Montana. Montana moaned and Billy grinned. He wasn't the only one.

He'd become good at this, at pulling his prick out and pushing the plug in so that none of his seed escaped. He loved how Montana moaned, how those dark eyes went wide at the stretch. He played with it a moment or two, twisting and turning the plub.

"I think that's cheating."

"No such thing."

"Sure there is!"

"Not in this." He twisted Montana's barbell again.

"Uh. Uh-huh. Cheating!" Montana's ass was working the plug.

"Not at all." He watched Montana move, loving the sensuality. Montana's legs went tense, knees drawing up. "Look at you. So damn beautiful."

"You make me happy, you know that, huh?"

"Entirely mutual, my love."

Montana gave him a quiet, wistful-seeming smile. He cupped Montana's face and brought it down for a kiss.

"Love you, huh?"

"Yes. I know. I love you, too." Another kiss followed his words, gentle and good. Every day, he was thankful that he'd found Montana and brought him home.

"I know." They settled then, eased into the heat and the softness of the bed, the pleasure of each other.

"There's lunch all made up when you're hungry."

"'Kay." Montana nodded.

He smiled and kissed Montana's forehead. He imagined it might be awhile before Montana was hungry. He could live with that.

Chapter Fourteen

Tanny stood in the rain, looking into Billy's house, shivering. He'd been running for two hours, feet sore and soaked, blistered.

He was cold and tired. Filthy. Ashamed.

He'd gone to Carrerra down on Mission and bought horse.

Horse. Him.

Shit.

He'd bought it and given it to Tom the Dick as soon as he'd gotten out of the neighborhood, gotten out of sight. The fucker was sitting and watching from a sedan, and he'd bent over to talk to him through the passenger's window, knowing that everyone watching thought he was a whore.

"You'll do the same thing tomorrow, asshole. Next week, you'll start going twice a day, then you'll wear a wire. I'd stop eating so damned much, too. You need to lose some fucking weight, junkie."

Right. Right. Oh, God. Please. Help him. What was he going to do if he got caught? What if they hit him where it showed? What if they followed him home? What if they made him use it? God, what if they made him use again?

Billy's face appeared at the window and Tanny shrank

back into the shadows. Hiding.

He needed to hide.

"You back again, little brother?"

"Si. Si, I need it." Tanny could feel the cold sweat sliding down the back of his neck. He hadn't ever worn a wire, hadn't ever gone into a deal with something taped to his ribs and shit.

God, he wanted to run. He needed to. He was so damned scared.

Dark eyes and a scarred, pitted face seemed to gleam in the lamplight, and that smile was pure evil. "Oh, little brother. Everybody needs. I got needs, eh?"

"What?" He stumbled back a step, running into one of Chico's enforcers, who shoved him forward again. "I got cash. I can pay."

One thick, brutal finger pushed into his lips, dragged against them, pushed them against his teeth, and Tanny tasted blood. "Oh, you gonna pay little brother. Everybody gotta pay."

Billy. Billy, please. I love you. I'm so sorry. I... Please.

"I can't do this no more, Tom." He was starving, scared, and ashamed. Not only that, but they wanted him to prove his loyalty. Shoot up. If he did that, even once, it would be all over. The need was already on him, chewing like a rat at his spine. He wanted it so bad, but he'd promised, he'd sworn to Billy that he wouldn't and he hadn't ever lied to his Billy. His best friend. His lover.

"I can't. They want me to... I won't do what they tell me to."

"You have to, Tanny. You can't stop now. Man, we almost have enough to put this fucker and his supplier away." Somewhere along the line, the fucking cop had stopped treating him like a junkie and started treating him like a person. Started pretending they were friends. Like they could ever be friends. It didn't matter that the asshole wasn't being evil. It was still wrong. Still.

This wasn't right.

"I can't sleep no more. Billy's starting to ask questions, man. For real." Billy wasn't stupid and shit was starting to show. The tape was tearing up his skin, the bruises were sticking, and he'd lost all the weight he'd put on. Billy wasn't dumb.

"Three more days, that's all. That's all we need. We need him to give up his supplier on the big drop."

"I... What if they follow me home?" That was his biggest fear. They were watching him all the time now. Really hard.

"I'll protect you. I will. Three days, man, and you're home free. No record, no worries. 'Kay?"

Tanny nodded, the sick feeling in his belly grinding and grinding. "Okay. Three more days, but that's it. No matter what. That's it."

He couldn't risk Billy any more. He just couldn't.

He couldn't risk what they had together. Damn it.

Chapter Fifteen

B illy washed his dishes and put them away. He tried not to look at the clock again, but he couldn't help himself. Montana was late. Again. It was happening more and more often over the last few weeks, and Billy couldn't figure out what was going on. There was something big, he knew it. He could see it in the way Montana was pulling away, losing weight, looking haunted.

He had to trust Montana, though. He had to trust that the man wouldn't start using again. Montana would tell him what was up. Eventually. Of course, it wouldn't hurt anything if he reminded Montana that he was there for anything Montana needed to say. Not that he could do that until Montana showed up.

A knock came to the front door, sharp, demanding. Frowning, Billy went to the door.

There was a short, tattooed guy there, frowning at him, bouncing. "Hey, man."

"Can I help you?"

"Yeah. Yeah, I got a message for your boy."

Billy's frown got deeper and he stood up straighter. "I beg your pardon?"

"I got a message for him. Tell him Chico don't like snitches."

He saw the gun come up, heard the report of the shot long before the burn spread in his chest. His eyes went wide, and he clutched at his chest, stunned. He'd been shot?

"You tell him. No snitches." The guy turned and ran, even as his downstairs neighbor's voice sounded, calling for him.

"911," he shouted, but he couldn't hear the sound of his own voice. The world was slowly tilting.

"Billy! Billy, Jesus." Barb's hand seemed so hot and she was screaming into a phone. God, she needed to shut up; his poor head was pounding. His chest hurt, too. God.

"Mon..." He tried to catch his breath and call out to his lover, but he couldn't quite make it before everything started going black.

Chapter Sixteen

He ran all the way to the hospital from the police station. He'd heard the fuss, heard the cops talking, then Tom had looked at him with this horrified, panicked, sick look, and he'd known.

Shooting. Assault. Billy's address. Oh, God.

He'd taken off, knowing that he'd been made, somehow. Knowing that they'd found Billy, their house. He went in through the emergency doors, looking for Billy as if he'd be right there. He wasn't, though. No Billy. It had been at least half an hour, maybe forty-five minutes, since he'd heard. Billy had to be somewhere, right?

His eyes fell on Oliver, on Barb from downstairs, and he headed over. "Where's Billy?"

They both turned, looked at him.

"What? Where is he? How bad is it?" Oh, God. Oh, God, please.

"Billy said it was somebody there for you. I saw him; he was one of those horrible drug dealers. He shot Billy." Barb's voice was icy cold.

He ignored her, looking up at Oliver. "Where is he?"

"That's none of your business." Oliver's hand whipped out, caught him across the face, and he stumbled back, shocked.

"Wh... Oliver? I need to see Billy."

That hand shot out again, this time catching him in the cheekbone, hard enough that the room spun. "Don't you even speak his name, you filthy, foul little bastard."

"What? What are you doing?"

Oliver grabbed his arm, started hauling him out. "I told him. I told him you'd go back to that shit. I told him you were worthless, and look what you've done. We opened our lives to you and you've gotten him shot."

"But I didn't..." He hadn't. He hadn't had a choice. He'd been working for the police. He'd been trying to do the right thing.

"Fucking liar. Give me the keys to his house."

"What?"

Oliver hit him again and he fumbled in his pockets, handing over the keys.

"You get out. If I catch you near him, I will flay your skin from your worthless body, do you understand?"

He stood there, frozen, completely, utterly, fucking freaked.

Oliver's hand dug into his arm, the muscles screaming. "Do you understand me? Answer me, you fucking junkie."

"I get it. I get it. I'm gone. Tell him..." I love him.

But Oliver had shoved him and he was careening down the stairs toward the street.

Okay. Okay, right. Right. He knew this would end. He'd known. He needed... He just needed... Tanny picked himself off the concrete and headed toward the studio. Margaret would pay him so that he could do...

Something. Right. Do something, even if it was wrong.

Chapter Seventeen

Oh, God, he hurt. Billy wasn't sure what hurt more, and frankly, he didn't feel much like examining any of it too closely.

"Mon...Montana?"

"Master Billy. It's Jack. You're in the hospital, okay? You're going to be fine."

The hospital? Jack? Where was Montana? Where was his love? "Montana?"

"No, Master Billy. It's Jack. There's a nurse coming, okay? You're just a little out of it."

No, he wasn't out of it, he wanted Montana. If Montana wasn't here, something must have happened to him, too.

"Jack. Hush. Montana."

"I... I don't... Oliver. Let me get Ollie. He's talking to the police."

Oh, God. Jack wouldn't tell him. Something had happened to Montana. He forced his eyes open, wincing against the bright lights.

"William. William, how are you feeling, my friend? The bullet has been removed; you'll be up and around in no time." Oliver was there, looking down at him.

"What hap—" He coughed, his throat was so dry. He

finally settled on another "Montana?" Please, Oliver. He had to know.

"He's a problem for the authorities now. You don't have to worry about him." A straw was pressed to his lips.

A what? He pushed at the straw with his tongue to get it out of his mouth and tried to get up.

"Shh. Shh. You're only just down from recovery. I don't imagine you remember much, but we're here. Marcus is coming to sit with you later. He arranged to have the floor cleaned at your place after the police were finished there. Don't worry; it's all been taken care of. Everything's been taken care of for you."

He whimpered as his body refused to let him get up. Everything hurt. Everything. Damn it. Oliver was handling him and he didn't like it. "Montana," he repeated stubbornly. He shot Oliver a glare, putting all his hurt into it.

"Is gone, Billy. He's in trouble with the law, again. The police say he was most likely involved with the drug dealer who shot you."

"No." No, he didn't believe that. Not his Montana.

"I'm sorry, my friend. I truly am."

He turned his face away. He didn't believe it. He wouldn't. Montana would have told him if he was using again.

A pretty young nurse came in, checked him over. "You look great. Young, healthy. You'll be home in a couple of days, max."

"It hurts a lot when I try to get up." He needed to get up, to go find Montana, find out what the hell was going on. He only had a vague recollection of some tattooed punk at the door.

"It will, for a day or two. I'm going to have you up and walking around before lunchtime, though, mark my words." Lunchtime? What?

"I don't understand." Montana had been late for lunch. He was worried and then the doorbell had rung. How could it be before lunchtime now?

"You had surgery last night. You've been in and out of consciousness and have slept hard. Try to think—do you remember the recovery room, maybe?"

"No. No, I don't fucking remember the recovery room. Where the hell is Montana? Somebody'd better tell me what's going on right now." He didn't care anymore that it hurt trying to get up, he struggled to do so anyway. There was something very wrong, because, if he was in the hospital, Montana should be here with him, watching over his bed.

"The police would like to speak with you, William." Oliver was right there, looking miserable, furious.

He didn't care how angry Oliver was, he was rapidly becoming extremely pissed off himself. "Where the hell is my boy, Oliver?"

"I told you, he's gone. He was involved with this nonsense, the police are trying to find him in connection with it. He is an addict and not worthy of your trust."

"He's not, Oliver. He isn't here because he can't be here. I can't think of anything that would keep him from my side." He had faith in Montana, no matter what Oliver said.

"I made him give me his keys. I told him to go. He had no right to be here, after his activities almost killed you."

"Oliver!" He felt a stab in his heart that hurt more than anything else. "Who the hell do you think you are?" Montana was his. HIS.

"Your friend. Someone who cares about you. Someone who isn't blinded by love."

"You took his home away from him! Where will he go? God damn you, Oliver, that's my and Montana's home, not yours. I don't... I can't..." He couldn't believe it. He'd thought Oliver had come around, had come to accept Montana. He felt tears come to his eyes and he swiped them away angrily. "Help me get up." He had to go find his lover.

"He is an addict, at best a weak man who puts his lover at risk. At worst, he's dangerous."

The door opened, two policemen standing there. "We need to ask you a few questions, Mr. Davern."

Billy shot a glare at Oliver before nodding to the police. "I don't remember exactly what happened, but I'll do my best." And then, by God, he was getting up and going to find his lover.

"Excellent. If we can start with the basics. What do you remember?"

"There was a knock at the door, and when I opened it there was a strange man standing there. He was..." Billy closed his eyes, trying to focus on the flashes of memory. "Scrawny, tattooed. He said... something about a message."

"A message?"

"Yes." Billy frowned and closed his eyes again. Damn it, he was going to remember; it was important. "He mentioned a Chico, said Chico didn't like snitches. Then there was a gun in his hand. Oh, fuck." His hand went to his chest as he remembered the shot, the feeling of burning in his chest that slowly expanded. It left him gasping, sweating.

The nurse was right there. "Breathe. Breathe, please?

It's over. You made it."

As she was speaking, he saw the officers talking furiously to each other, then one left. "Sir, can you tell us where Tanny—aka Montana is?"

"No, damn it—he should be here with me. I'm worried about him."

He needed out of this bed; he needed to be out there looking for Montana. His poor love. He was going to kill Oliver. Kill him.

"So are we."

Everyone stopped, looked over at the police officer.

"I beg your pardon?" Billy said softly, his heart in his throat now. "What? Why?"

"Tanny's been working with our Vice department to get information from Chico Donados. Chico has been a growing threat in the area. Obviously, Chico made him, and we need to find him."

Billy snarled at Oliver. "I told you!"

Then he started struggling to get out of the bed again. "Help me get up, damn it! I need to find him before something awful happens to him." Something else awful. He couldn't imagine how Montana had felt when Oliver had stolen his house keys from him and told him to go.

"Stop. Stop, you'll pull your stitches. Don't make me call security." That little nurse was strong.

"I'll go look." Oliver headed for the door.

"I don't want you anywhere near him!" he shouted at Oliver, near tears as he fell back against the bed, panting. Damn it. Damn it.

"Do you have any idea where he'd go, sir? Any idea at all?"

"The beach. Under the pier." He supposed Montana going and breaking into the condo to stay because it was his home, damn it, was too much to hope for. "Try our place, too. Just in case."

"All right. You rest. We'll have a guard at the door. We're going to pick up a few suspects; there will be pictures soon for you to look at."

He nodded. "Anything I can do. Now go. Find him before someone else does."

Montana should have been here with him, safe at his side. He'd worry later about how his sub could keep something so huge from him, could hide something so dangerous.

Chapter Eighteen

Trust to her word, the little nurse had had him up and about that first day and that had made a good start to getting his ass well enough to be checked out. It didn't hurt that Billy was well motivated. He needed to be well enough to leave the hospital so he could find Montana. The police had not had any luck so far, and Billy's only relief was that they hadn't found Montana's body, either. But what if the drug dealer had taken him and hidden him somewhere? What if the man was busy torturing Montana? No matter where Montana was, he had to be scared and hurt.

Billy wasn't sure he was ever going to forgive Oliver for what he'd done.

He got into the wheelchair and the orderly wheeled him down the hall. Marcus had said he'd be there to help get him home. Billy had a few places he wanted to check out, first.

"Hey, man. You ready to re-enter the land of the living?" Marcus was there, solid as a rock. Billy hadn't seen hide nor hair of Oliver.

"Absolutely." He found a smile for Marcus and let the big, bald man help him up out of the wheelchair.

"Okay. So, I have strict instructions to take you home

and make sure you rest." Marcus loaded him into the sleek sedan, leaned over him to buckle him up. "So, where are we looking first?"

"The beach, down near the pier where the homeless stay out of the rain." He hated to think that Montana was out there by himself, miserable, maybe high, but it beat quite a few of the alternatives.

"Okay." Marcus was a decent man—a good friend.

They headed down toward the pier, but the place was deserted, construction going on.

"Let's walk along the bea..." His voice faded away at the look Marcus shot him. He had to admit, just the thought of trudging through the sand had him tired, and he was still in the car. "Rainbow Artists," he directed instead. "Hopefully, he's still going to work."

"You think? That would be good if he was." Marcus headed in, pulled up in front of the place. "You go in; I'll find a parking space."

"Okay. Try to find one close by." He'd been lying down for days, you'd think he wouldn't be this tired.

He hauled himself out of the car and walked slowly into the store. He nodded at Teresa, who was working the cash register, and continued on back to the studio. His lips moved in a silent prayer.

Margaret's eyes met his as soon as he walked in. "You lived."

He had no problem dispensing with the pleasantries— he only had one thing on his mind, after all. "I'm fine. Have you seen Montana?"

"Yep."

Relief surged through him, making him stagger until he grabbed hold of one of the work benches. "Thank God. Where is he?"

"That's none of your business."

"Of course it is! He's my boy."

She snorted, shook her head. "He's a scared, sick kid who didn't know where to go or what to do after he got the shit knocked out of him."

"Sick? Sick? What's wrong with him? Please, Margaret, I'm not the one who sent him away and I got here as soon as they let me out." Surely she wasn't blaming him for this?

"He'd been beaten up. Hit. He's scared, Billy. He's been doing that undercover shit for the police, trying to clear his record, and this has just destroyed him."

"Damn it, why didn't he tell me?" Why hadn't he pushed? He'd known something was up; he'd been hoping Montana would start opening up to him instead of him having to drag every last detail out of his lover. "Where is he, Margaret? I need to see him. I need to bring him home."

"He was scared. He was trying so hard to close that shit up." Margaret nodded to the bench. "Sit down, would you? He's not here."

Billy sat down; he was panting now. "Where is he, Margaret? Is he safe?" That was the most important thing.

"Yes. Yes." She walked across the room, got him a bottle of water. "I sent him to my sister's on a Greyhound. He's been there a couple of days. He's sleeping a lot."

Billy buried his face in his hands. Montana was okay, safe. He was out of the city. "Where?"

"Up north. Oregon State. He needed to rest, to be safe."

"Oregon State!" Jesus. "Give me his number, I'll send him some money for a plane ticket home."

"He doesn't have an ID, Billy. Remember?"

"Damn it." He knew that. He'd just managed to forget. "I can't go get him yet. There's no way I can do that kind of driving right now. But you give me his number and I'll talk to him. I need to make sure he's okay—that we're okay."

"If you upset him, I'll tell Heather to refuse your calls, you understand? Tanny is a good boy."

"I know he's a good boy, Margaret—he's my boy." Even as he growled at her, he was so pleased that Montana had someone else in his life, besides Billy, who cared for him this much.

"Then fucking involve yourself." She looked at him, eyes flashing. "Give him what he needs. Jesus, Billy, the kid screams lifestyle sub. Quit pussyfooting around and make him yours."

"What do you think I've been doing these last months?" He shouted the words back. It felt good to let go, all his worry and upset going into the words.

"Playing house." Margaret stood up to him, the toughest, strongest bitch he'd ever known. "You're so scared to lose him, you don't push him. He's yours. He's fierce and strong and totally committed to being your boy. Take him." Then Margaret sniffed. "And tell your friends that I'll commit murder if they hit him again."

"The line for that starts behind me. Give me his fucking number already, Margaret. I need to make things right."

She scribbled down a phone number, handed it over. "Do you have someone to take you home?"

"Right here." Marcus slipped into the room like magic and gave him a sheepish shrug. "You two seemed... deep in conversation, and I didn't want to interrupt."

He clutched the number in his hand and let Marcus

help him stand. "Thanks. Can you take me home now, please?"

"I can. Hey, Megs."

"Goodfellow. Take our friend home, please? He looks like shit."

"And is standing right here," he grumbled. He hated it when people talked around him. There'd been a lot of that at the hospital, and he was done.

He turned and began to shuffle off, feeling suddenly far older than he was. This being shot business sucked.

Being without Montana sucked worse.

Chapter Nineteen

Heather's house was like a... florist's fairy had exploded in it. There were flowers on the carpet. Flowers on the wallpaper. Flowers on the furniture, the towels, the sheets, the dishes. It was weird. The bed was soft, though, and Heather was just like Margaret, but gentle. She fed him when he woke up, hugged him whenever she could, and let him sleep a lot.

He'd called Margaret twice, just to make sure this was okay, that he could just stay for a few days. Margaret always chuckled, called it a 'retreat,' and told him everything would work out. Like things could work out now. Like things would ever work out. He cuddled into the pillows and closed his eyes again.

Heather's soft knock sounded at the bedroom door. "Honey? There's a call for you."

"Margaret?" He crawled out of bed, took the portable with a smile of thanks. "Margaret? Is everything okay? Have you heard about Billy yet? I need to know he's gonna be okay."

"I'm fine, Montana." Oh, God. Oh, God, that was Billy.

His knees buckled and he landed on the floor with a thump. "Billy."

"Oh, love. It's so good to hear your voice."

Heather's head popped back around the door. "Are you okay?" she mouthed.

He nodded, tried to smile. "He's okay. He's alive." Alive.

She gave him a smile and came in to pat his head. "Do you want me to stay?"

"Montana? Are you still there?"

"I am, yeah. Just a second." He took her soft hand, kissed it. "I'm cool. I just need to talk to him for a minute."

She squeezed his hand. "I'm just down the hall if you need me." Then she headed out to the flowery hall.

"Sorry. Are you out of the hospital? Are you okay? It is bad? I'm so sorry."

"I'm fine, love. They let me out of the hospital this afternoon. And I'm sorry, too. I'm sorry Oliver said those things to you, and I'm even sorrier that you felt you had to leave your home just on his say-so."

"I got you shot. I know that. I didn't use, though. Not once."

"I don't care what you did, Montana, Oliver did not have the right to treat you like he did, nor did he have the right to demand your key back. You are my lover, my sub. He had no right to treat you like that." There was a fierce, angry note in Billy's voice.

"I'm sorry." He sighed, fingers tangling in his hair. "Are you feeling better?" He didn't know what to do.

"Yeah, yeah, I'm fine. How about you? Are you okay?"

"Yeah. I'm having a... a retreat. Sleeping a lot." Like a loser.

"As soon as I'm up to the drive, I'm coming up there and bringing you home."

"I... You are?" That sounded... definite.

"I am. I'm hoping it'll be in a few days. I'll hire a driver if I have to. You belong here with me."

"I didn't use. I was trying to do the right thing."

"I wish you'd told me, love. But you have to know I'd never have asked you to leave like that."

"I couldn't tell. You wouldn't have liked it. There was... ugliness." Hitting. Cussing. Threats. But he hadn't used.

"I hate that you went through it alone. We'll be talking about that when you come back. We'll be talking about a lot of things."

"Are you sure you want me?" This would be Billy's chance to get free.

"Absolutely. I love you and you are mine." That sounded very sure.

"I... I'm sorry you got hurt. I've been thinking about you, every second."

"I've been thinking about you, too, love. I miss you so much."

"I miss you. I ran all the way from the police station when I heard. I came to be with you."

"I looked for you when I woke up—I couldn't understand why you weren't with me, and I thought it must be because you'd been hurt, too."

"No. I mean, yes, but not from Chico or his guys. I just... I didn't know what to do next, so I went to Margaret."

"I'm glad she was there for you, love." Billy sighed. "I want to hold you."

He nodded, his heart aching. "How bad are you hurt?"

"Not so badly. They took out the bullet, sewed me back up, and sent me on my way. I'm going to be just fine.

I swear."

"I wish it'd been me." This was his fault.

"I don't. I'm glad you weren't home, that you didn't get shot. They might have killed you." He could hear the shudder in Billy's voice. "I love you, Montana. I need you and you need me. We belong together."

"I love you. I'm so sorry, about everything."

"Shh, shh. It's okay, love. I'm going to arrange for a driver. I'm coming up right away. We need to do this face to face."

"No. No, you should rest. I'm okay. I took a bus here. I'll take the bus back." That hadn't been too bad.

"No, I'm coming for you. It'll be faster. I can sit in a car and relax, sleep. You make sure you're ready for me, hmm?"

"You shouldn't stress yourself, love..." His heart was beating so fast, so hard.

"It's decided, Montana. I'm coming. I should be there sometime tomorrow."

"Please..." His voice dropped. "Don't bring Oliver. Please."

Billy snorted. "I'm not letting him anywhere near you. I'm not letting him anywhere near me, either, not without some heavy-duty apologizing to you."

"He hit me, which, okay, he thought I hurt you, but he called me a liar, and I'm not."

"We can press charges if you want, love."

"No. No. I won't do that. He did it because he's your friend."

"I don't care why he did it, it still wasn't right."

"No. I should have been there to take care of you."

"Yeah. You should have." Billy sighed. "It won't happen again, love. I swear to you, you'll never feel like you have to let someone else kick you out of your own home. Never."

"I love you." He did, no matter what.

"Good. I love you, too. I wish I was there, already. Or you here."

He nodded, crawled up on the bed. "You shouldn't stress yourself out."

"I'm not stressed out now."

"You probably shouldn't drive." He could just listen to Billy's voice forever.

"I won't. I'll hire a car and driver." He could hear the smile in Billy's voice. "A limousine. I'll bring you home in style."

"I'm not worth that, Billy."

"You're worth that and more."

He shook his head. "I..." What was he supposed to say?

"I know, I know. You don't like it when I compliment you. Tough. Get used to it."

He chuckled, just a little unnerved.

"Things are going to be more intense, better. And you'll know you belong with me, no matter what anyone else ever says."

"I don't. I don't know what to say, Billy."

"Tell me you love me again, and that you can't wait to see me."

"I love you, very much, and I wish you were already here." That was easy.

"There, that wasn't so hard, was it?"

"No. No, please take care of yourself. If you change your mind, love, I'll take the bus."

"I won't." Billy voice dropped suddenly, became sexy. "I miss you."

"I miss you. I'll come home, take care of you. I promise." He wanted to come home.

"I can't wait. I could take care of you now."

"No. No, that's not right, Billy. You're hurt and it's all my fault."

"Stop that. I'm fine. You didn't shoot me—you were trying to do the right thing. If I want to make you come over the phone, that's exactly what I'm going to do."

"No. I can't. I'm not hot or anything. I'm just tired."

"I didn't say I was giving you a choice."

"What?"

"I'm the Master, you're the sub, remember?"

"You're. This is the phone. I don't even think I can think about sex." Billy had lost his mind.

"I control your orgasms, Montana. I get to choose when you come and when you don't come. A nice, mind-clearing orgasm is just what you need right now."

"You're hurt." And he was confused.

"That doesn't mean I'm not still your Master. Are you alone?"

"Yes... but..." He shook his head. This was ridiculous. Wrong. Weird.

"Open your pants." Billy's voice had dropped, the timbre deep and low.

"Billy..." This was nuts.

"Yes, love. I want you to reach in and take out your cock. I want you to imagine that it's my hand around it."

"I'm not hard, Billy."

"Not yet."

He didn't deserve to feel good. He didn't.

Billy's voice came through the line. "Touch yourself, Montana. Touch yourself and imagine it's my hand on your body. Tweak your nipple barbell and then tug on the ring. Can you feel my breath against your skin?"

He sat there, blinking. "He shot you. Can we still do this?"

"Forget about him. Forget about everyone. It's just you and me now, Montana. And we are doing this."

"I don't want to hurt you. I want to love you." He pulled the blankets up over his head, hiding in the darkness.

"Mmm, I know, love." He could hear Billy's breathing pick up some. "Wrap your hand around your prick, love. That's me hold you, touching you." Billy moaned softly. "You fit perfectly in my palm."

"I..." He rubbed his palm against his cock, the pajama bottoms soft.

"I love the way you feel, all hot and silky. And the way you taste... Montana."

"Billy, we shouldn't. I... When can I... Did the doctor say how long before I could make you happy?"

"Hush, Montana. Trust me, you want to enjoy this—when we get you home again you're going to be wearing the cage for a long, long time."

"I..." He shook his head, but his cock jerked, filled.

"No, not you. I get to decide. I was being too easy on you before. You didn't realize your place with me was solid, inviolate. You didn't realize that not Oliver, not anyone could tear us apart. So jack your beautiful cock, my love, and enjoy every second of this."

"I miss you." His heart was beating so hard. "I was so scared."

"I'm with you now, love. And I'm never letting go." He heard Billy licking his lips. "I love how you taste, how that soft skin feels stretched tight over your hard cock."

He closed his eyes, finally relaxing enough to touch

himself, to slide his hand into his pants.

"When you get excited, the tip of your cock gets slick. Shiny little drops that come from your slit. You smell so sweet and taste so good."

He moaned, spread his legs a little bit.

"Oh yeah, I love your noises. I love the way you let me know how much you're enjoying something, even when you don't always want me to know."

Tanny's cheeks heated, but he loved the praise.

"Those little moans and your swallowed words. Mmm..." Billy's groan sounded like he was aroused.

"Don't hurt yourself." He spread, toes curling as he arched.

"I'm not. I won't come tonight, but talking about how you taste and smell and feel makes me hot. I can't help it."

"Love you. Love you so much. Want to come home."

"You are, love. You're coming home with me. But we do this first. Come on, stroke yourself. Be a little rough around the tip."

He nodded, touching himself, jerking the tip of his cock.

"Use your other hand to touch your nipples. The ringed one first. Nice and gentle. Then the barbell one. I want you to tweak that one." His moan tugged out of him, low and raw. So good. "Yes." Billy groaned, too. "That's it, love. Keep touching, keep stroking. Keep pretending it's me."

He nodded, hips bucking into his hand.

"Suck on one of your fingers, love. I want to hear it."

"Billy. Billy..." This was driving him crazy.

"I'm right here, love." Billy's voice sounded like he was so needy, breathing into his ear.

Tanny sucked his fingers, pulling hard. In his head, it was Billy's cock,

The way Billy started moaning let him keep the illusion working. "That's it, love. Suck it."

He needed. He needed so bad.

"You ready, love? You close? I know you are—I can hear it in the desperate way you're sucking."

"Uh-huh. Want you." Now. He wanted things to be right again,

"Then come for me, love. Right now. Let me hear you."

"Billy..." He sobbed, shaking, fingers jerking himself off.

"Right here, lover. Come on. Come."

Seed poured out of him, his balls aching and tender as they emptied.

"Mmm... I know what that sound smells like."

He whimpered softly, shivering as he came down. Billy's voice was still in his ear, whispering soft endearments.

"We're gonna be okay?"

"We're going to be just fine, love. Just fine."

He heard Billy blow him a kiss. "No more coming now, though, until I give you permission."

He nodded. "Okay. Okay. Do you have to go already?"

"No, I can stay on the line for awhile."

"Okay. Cool." He would take it for as long as he could.

Chapter Twenty

Billy'd arranged for a car and driver to get him up to Oregon. It wasn't quite a stretch limo, but there was plenty of room for him to lie down and basically sleep the entire way. It would bring him and Montana back in style, as well. He'd actually managed to sleep most of the way, and by the time the driver informed him that they were arriving, he was feeling pretty good compared to yesterday.

He looked out the window. The house looked like something out of a fairy tale—little and well-kept, covered in flowers and surrounded by trees. A smaller, slightly younger version of Margaret was in the front, pruning roses. He let the driver help him out and looked eagerly for Montana.

"Are you Bill?" She smiled at him but stepped toward the door.

"Billy, yes. You must be Heather, Margaret's sister. I wanted to thank you for taking care of Montana." He went toward her and held out his hand.

"He's been a huge help. He's dressing, I think. We went and bought a few shirts and such for him."

Montana had been left with only the clothes on his back. It made Billy angry all over again. "Thank you, again. How much do we owe you?"

"You don't." She smiled for him again, shook her head. "Tanny makes Margaret so happy, Bill. He's a huge light in her life."

"He's a wonderful man." He beamed at her. He loved the people who really saw Montana.

"He is. Thank you for sharing him with me." Her voice dropped. "His face is still quite bruised and his palms cut from his fall."

He growled a little bit, unable to stop the noise. "I haven't heard the full story of what happened to him." He looked around again; he needed to see his boy.

"I haven't, either. Would you like tea?"

Montana appeared in the doorway, dark eyes meeting his. "Billy? You're here."

He nodded and moved carefully up the porch stairs. He held open his arms. "I am."

"It's okay? To hug you? It won't hurt you?"

It had been nearly a week. A week since he'd held his boy. "Come here." Montana was obviously going to be careful, and frankly, he didn't care. He ached to hold his lover.

Montana pressed close, cheek on his shoulder. "Billy."

He closed his eyes and wrapped his arms around Montana. "Mine."

"Missed you. How do you feel? Are you sore?"

"I'm pretty good—the car's almost as smooth as our bed. And how are you? Look at your poor face." He was going to kill Oliver.

"It's just bruises."

He didn't say anything, just stroked his fingers over Montana's face.

Montana's eyes closed. "I didn't use. I didn't."

"I'm very proud of you for that."

"Thank you." Montana's shoulders started to shake.

"Heather, is there a quiet place we can sit?" He couldn't do this standing, not at the moment.

"Absolutely. The house is yours. I told Tanny I need to go to the bakery in town." She smiled at Montana. "Come kiss me goodbye, sweet lad, in case you're gone before I come home."

Montana headed down the porch steps, hugging Heather tight. Margaret's sister was a real sweetheart. Billy sent up another little prayer of thanks that Montana had Margaret in his life.

Montana came back up, took his arm. "Come on. Let's sit down."

"Yes. Then you can kiss me hello properly."

Heather's house was... insane. Flowers decorated every surface. Billy felt his eyes widen. "How on earth did you get to sleep in here?"

"I was really tired." Montana chuckled softly. "It's crazy, huh?"

"Just a little." He chuckled and settled with a sigh. He was ready to be healthy again. The couch was comfortable, at least, even if it did look like a garden gnome had vomited all over it.

"Can I get you something? Make it better?" Those dark eyes searched his, so worried.

"I need a kiss." He slid his hand into Montana's hair, tugged him closer.

Montana leaned in. "You look good."

Those lips brushed his. His fingers fisted in Montana's hair and he pressed their lips together in a real kiss. He felt Montana's soft sob, the breath pushing into his lips. Moaning, he deepened the kiss. He pushed his tongue between Montana's lips. His boy. His sweet boy. Montana leaned closer, the kiss tasting like tears.

"I'm never letting go."

"Never?"

"Never. This whole week we've been apart has sucked rocks."

"Well, it started with you getting shot."

"Yeah, that's never a good sign, hmm?"

"No. No, I'd say that's just bad."

He chuckled. "We made it through, though." He stroked Montana's cheeks and stared into those dark eyes.

Then he slammed their mouths back together again. Montana cried out, fingers curling over his arms. He devoured Montana's mouth like he was starving. Which he was; starving for this, for more of his lover, his sub. His boy.

Montana sank into the kiss for a long moment, then pulled away. "You'll hurt yourself."

"I'm fine. And your kisses do me more good than harm." He didn't let go of Montana. Not at all.

"Where are you hurt?"

"They got me just below the collarbone on the right side. Doc said I was lucky." He shook his head. "I'm not sure I'd describe it as lucky."

"I'm so sorry..." Montana looked at him, obviously devastated.

He cupped Montana's face and looked into those dark eyes. "Tell me what you're sorry for." Montana hadn't shot him, but Montana had hidden something huge from him.

"I'm sorry you got hurt. I'm sorry they found your house. I'm sorry that I'm a junkie. I'm sorry that I couldn't tell you about the police."

"That last one is the apology I want. And I want an explanation. How could you not tell me about this huge thing going on in your life?" It wouldn't happen again.

"I couldn't. I had to do it or they were going to always be there, at work, outside, always watching everything. This way, I did what they wanted."

"That still doesn't explain why you couldn't tell me." He would have gone to the cops and not allowed them to blackmail his lover into helping them.

"Because. There's lots of reasons."

"Let's hear them." He wasn't letting Montana off the hook on this. He needed to understand why, and then he needed to impress upon Montana that this kind of thing would not happen again.

"Because you would have said no and then things would have gotten worse. Because you'd worry about the... bad parts. Because I have to make that part of things right by myself. I'm not a liar. I'm not, but I've been in a lot of trouble." Montana pulled away, started pacing. "You don't understand how hard it is to do this. It took all of my goodness, every motherfucking drop, to not use. I didn't have anything left."

Billy thought about that for a long time. He thought about how he'd just been thinking that he would have gone to the cops to deal with them if Montana had told him. He thought about how he might not have allowed Montana to do this, even after his lover had explained that he needed to do it to make things right.

"All right. I think I understand why you didn't tell me. But you can't keep stuff like this from me anymore. I promise to listen, to not just jump in and come up with a solution for you. But I will try to help, try to make things easier for you—I'm your lover, and more, your Master, so some of these things are built in. Still, I'll try. But you have to promise to not hide things from me anymore. Nothing gets kept back, no matter how you think I'll react."

"Those are two separate things. The Master thing and everyday just sort of life."

Billy shook his head. "No. Not in our life, they're not."

Montana looked at him. "I don't get it. That's about sex and stuff."

"No, love." He held out his hands, pulling Montana down onto his knees in front of him. "No, that's about us. It's our life together."

Montana, his beautiful, dear boy, looked completely confused.

"Tell me this, love. You know how you want to call me 'sir'? Is that only when we're having sex?" He knew well it wasn't.

Montana swallowed hard, but shook his head.

"It would be easier for you if you could keep believing it was just about sex, I know that. But the truth is that you won't truly believe you belong with me until we bring it into all of our life." He stroked Montana's cheek. "Will you be my submissive, Montana? Will you share your life with me?"

"I don't understand, Billy. I thought I was sharing my life with you." Montana leaned into his hand, eyes closing.

"I mean full-time, all the time, no matter what happens, share it with me. I mean if Oliver tells you to go away and demands your keys, you tell him to get lost share your life with me. I mean if we could legally get married, that's what I'd be asking you share your life with me."

Montana smiled, cheeks warming. "Oh. You mean like a real person?"

"Oh, love. You are a real person."

"Only sometimes, man. Lots of times, I'm just... trying to be one."

"No. You're real. And mine." Margaret had been right, he'd just been playing house. He'd been so worried he'd scare Montana away that he hadn't seen how much Montana needed him to grab hold and take what was his.

"You remember your safeword, hmm?"

"Armpit?"

"That's the one."

He slid his hands over Montana's shoulders. "I think we should go home now, don't you?" The flower explosion was not conducive to topping.

"I could come home."

"Excellent. Let's make sure our driver can make the return trip, and we can go." He just wanted to get Montana back where his lover belonged.

"I'll get my backpack."

"Okay. I'll wait here." Frankly, he was a little scared of what the rest of the place might look like.

Montana headed off, and he watched. It was time to take his boy home and stop playing games.

Chapter Twenty-One

He'd been dreaming about making books—about the feel of the paper in his fingers, the smell of the glue, the way the colors matched. He dreamed about Margaret, walking him through each step, each piece. Then they hit a bump and his eyes flew open.

A car. He was in a car. "Billy?"

Billy's hand slid over his thigh, patted him.

"Sorry." He let his eyes close again, let his heart rate slow.

"What's the matter?"

"Nothing. Was dreaming."

"Yeah? What about." Billy tugged Tanny into the curve of his side.

"Work, mostly. This doesn't hurt you, right?"

"No, I was shot on the other side." Billy kissed the top of his head. "You were dreaming of work? Was this a good thing?"

"Uh-huh. It was just so real and the bump startled me. Work is a good place."

"I'm glad. Not surprised, either. Margaret's a good woman."

He nodded. She was. She was always so sure. "She reminds me of you sometimes. I like her. She's my friend."

Billy chuckled at that. "I'm not surprised she reminds you of me. And she is—she's a true friend. I'm so glad she was there for you."

"Me, too. I was scared and pissed off and she helped me." He brought his hand to his face, shook his head.

"From now on, you don't take orders from anyone but me. And Margaret for work stuff."

"I didn't know what to do and he was so angry. I didn't expect him to hurt me, and I never got to explain."

"It was inexcusable. A Master doesn't hit his own boy in anger, let alone anyone else's." Billy shook his head; he looked sad.

"He thought you were dying and that it was my fault." Tanny pulled away, arms wrapping around his middle. Of course, it was his fault. There was no arguing about that. He was the one with the record. He was the one who had to do what the police said. He was the one who had led Chico to the house. To the house. Where they knew he lived.

Jesus. What was wrong with him? What had he been thinking? He couldn't go back there. They'd come back, hurt Billy again. Oh, God. Oh, God.

"Love?" Billy grabbed him and tugged him back into the solid body.

"I..." He closed his eyes, trying to figure out what to do. If he ran when they stopped, Billy couldn't catch him, but Billy might hurt himself trying.

"What's going through that head of yours?"

"It doesn't matter." Maybe Billy would understand if he just stayed somewhere else.

Billy growled. "It does matter. You matter."

"I'm just thinking."

"About what?"

About what a worthless piece of shit he was. "I made a mistake."

"We all make mistakes. Go on."

"Huh? Where?" Okay. Where was he going to go? Maybe he'd just stay... Jesus. Where. Where was safe?

"I meant continue. Tell me about this mistake."

"I can't go home."

"What are you talking about? Of course you can."

"They'll come back. They'll hurt you. This is already my fault; I'll make it worse."

"Now wait a second. You've said two very different things. I hadn't considered that they might come back, but you could be right. We'll stay at a hotel when we get in and then call the police, see what's happened." Billy kissed him hard then. "But this isn't your fault."

"A hotel. Oh." Oh, okay. Yes.

"You see what happens when you tell me things?"

"I just was worried." He took a deep breath.

"I know. But you told me and you were right—I hadn't thought of it at all. And now with both of us in the know, we came up with a solution."

Tanny moved back over, hand on Billy's arm. "I don't want you hurt. Ever again."

"No, I'd rather not experience being shot again. And that goes for you, too, hmm? My heart ached for you when I found out what happened. I was so scared for you—I never wanted you to feel homeless again."

"I was so ashamed." The words made him duck his head, hide behind his hair.

"I'm so sorry, love." Billy squeezed him, stroked his back. "You have no reason to be ashamed."

"It's my fault."

"The only thing you did wrong was not tell me about

it. If you'd known helping the police out would get me shot—would you have done it?"

"No." No, he would have... done... something.

"Well, then. You were doing the right thing. Don't be trying to assume guilt where there isn't any. I know that's one of your things, but it has to stop."

He didn't understand, really, so he didn't respond. What was he supposed to say to that?

Billy held him quietly for a moment or two, and then his lover shifted, one hand landing high on his thigh. "I brought along something special."

"You brought you."

Billy beamed at him. "Me, plus something else."

"Thank you." He hummed, leaning into Billy happily.

Billy chuckled. "Are you still going to be happy when you hear it's the cage?"

"That you're here, yeah, but... I... Why did you bring it?"

"Because you're mine, and it's the best way to show you."

"You say stuff that doesn't make a lot of sense sometimes."

"You don't think that made sense?" Billy nodded toward the bag that lay on the floor. It was the laptop bag he'd made for Billy. "Reach that for me, love?"

He nodded, reached down, and handed it over. Billy opened up the bag and pulled out the cage before pushing the bag back onto the floor.

"Billy, we can't put that on here, man."

"The privacy shield is up." Billy took one of his hands and kissed the palm. "Undo your pants for me and then put it on."

"But..." He looked at the window dealie. "I. He can't

see, right?"

"That's right. I'm not into sharing. You're mine."

Tanny shivered, bit his bottom lip. Yeah. Yeah, he was. He liked hearing it, though. Liked knowing it.

"Now, fish out your cock and cage it."

"Shh..." Billy was going to make him hard, then he couldn't.

The low, deep chuckle said Billy knew. "Do it, and I will hush."

"You'll make me hard. Quiet."

"If you had it on already, it wouldn't matter. I said I'd stop telling you to do it when you actually started doing it."

He turned the cage over and over in his hands, mind spinning.

"Montana." There was a warning note in Billy's voice now.

"What?"

"Put on the cage."

"I'm a little wigged out."

"You still need to put the cage on."

"I... here?" He searched Billy's eyes, caught up inside.

"Right here. Right now. Because I said so." Billy's fingers reached out and touched his cheek, reminding him they were in this together.

"For you..." He fumbled, trying to make sure the driver couldn't possibly see, but he managed to force the cage on.

"For us," murmured Billy, and he could hear the pride in his lover's—Master's?—voice.

He got his jeans done up, but it was uncomfortable, too tight, the metal pushing into his groin.

Billy reached into them and shifted his cock to the

right, the pressure easing as room was found. "You may come again when I do."

He nodded. That was fair. Billy not being able to was his fault.

Billy pulled him back close and then pulled out a cell phone. "Call Margaret and let her know you're okay, that you're coming home with me. She'll want to know."

"Okay." He dialed Margaret's number, waiting. When she answered, he smiled. "Margaret."

"Son. Heather called. He came?"

"Uh-huh."

"Good. You okay?"

"Yeah."

"The police were at the shop today, looking for you for questioning, son. They made some arrests."

His heart started racing. "Oh, God. I'm sorry, Margaret. Did they bother you?"

"I'm just fine. I told them you were out of harm's way and that was good enough for me. It isn't right, the way they used you." Her voice had gone all hard and he could just see her, standing up to the cops and giving them what for.

"I... Thank you, lady. You're so good to me. We're going to go to a hotel tonight, just in case."

"That's smart. Let me talk to Billy for a minute, son."

He handed over the phone.

"Margaret, hello... That's good... Okay. Okay. Yes. Oh." Billy's eyes shot to him. "We will. Thank you. Yes, hopefully that'll be soon. Talk to you later."

Billy handed him the phone and he took it. "Is everything okay?"

"Everything is going to be fine, Tanny. I'll see you at work Monday, yes?"

"It's only Wednesday." He wasn't lazy.

"I know." She chuckled. "But Billy needs some care taken, yes?"

"Right."

"Take care of yourself, honey. And of Billy. Night."

The phone went dead and Billy's arm slid over his shoulder, pulling him close once again.

"Is everything okay?"

"Yeah, it's fine." Billy kissed the top of his head. "Tell me how you came to be helping the cops against these drug dealers?"

"There's one that... he's always been on my ass. You met him once, I think. He was at the studio, over and over. Waiting for me, waiting for me to get out of work, following me home, waiting for me to fuck up. One day, I did."

Billy growled. "You should have told me he was still harassing you." His lover cleared his throat. "Sorry, go on. What do you mean by one day you fucked up?"

"I didn't wait for the light to change. I didn't see it was red, really, I was in a hurry trying to get home to you, and he fucking pegged me for jaywalking and then he had rock and..."

"Son of a bitch. Nobody charges anyone with jaywalking." Billy hugged him in together.

"Yeah, but I have a record." A record, and he wanted to make things better.

"He only pegged you on that, though, because he's an asshole." Billy took a deep breath. "I'd like to sue him for harassment, I really would."

"He told me, if I helped them, it would stop. They'd let us be, let me work, not always be there, waiting." And if he didn't, they'd be there for every single breath and maybe they'd get Billy involved in his mess.

Billy nodded. "He used you. And then he didn't bother to take care of you."

"It's not his job to take care of people like me."

"If he puts you in danger while you're doing a favor for him, then it's his job to make sure the people you're informing on don't come after you!" Billy growled, hand curled into a fist.

"Do you think they cared about that? Really? If they'd killed me, it would have been a fast conviction and then one less queer junkie to worry about."

"They should care about that. Their job is to take care of people. Nobody is pure as snow. You are a reformed drug addict. If you were good enough to use for information, you were good enough to protect."

He didn't know what to say to that.

Billy held him close and then kissed the top of his head. "So what exactly did they ask you to do?"

"They wanted me to be with Chico—pretend to buy and stuff. I wore a wire." It had been... awful.

"Oh, love."

"I was lucky. They didn't hit me. It was still in that whole 'seduce the guy into the club' thing." He'd been heading toward trouble, too, because he was going to have to use to stay in, and then it would have been over.

Billy hugged him hard. "I'm so sorry they sent you back into that world."

"Me, too. I was scared, Billy. I was scared and worried and... man, I gotta tell you, it's bad when you're high, but when you're clean? It's hell."

"Never again, Montana. I don't care what anyone threatens you with I don't want you forced into that world ever again. I'll take you away, first."

"I just wanted things to be better, so that I could be with you for a little while longer." Never was a long time.

"Now you don't need to worry about that. We're committed to each other for the long haul. Through the good and the bad."

He wanted to believe that. "What do we do, when we get back? Chico's going to want to kill me."

"Like I said, we take a hotel room for the night and then we call the police. See where things stand and what kind of protection we'll need."

"Protection?" He shook his head. "God, I've made things so fucked up."

"You had a little help there. The police have a responsibility in this, too." Billy looked him in the eyes. "And we'll figure it out. As long as we're together."

"Aren't you mad at me?"

"What am I supposed to be mad at you about?"

"Bringing all this trouble into your life."

Billy shook his head. "I'm not happy that you didn't tell me what was going on, but you've promised me you'll talk to me in the future. And I still don't see how this is all your fault and not the cops'."

"Because if I hadn't ever been a junkie..."

"But you were. And I knew that when I met you." Billy kissed the top of his head. "Not everything bad that happens to the people you love is your fault."

"No, but some of it is."

"Okay. I forgive you for the parts that are your fault."

Tanny chuckled, rolled his eyes. "Even the getting you shot parts?"

"Yep. I know for sure you didn't pull the trigger. Or send the guy to shoot me. So we're good, you and I."

"I just... you make it sound easy." Sometimes Billy

could be so... trusting.

"I love you, Montana. That makes it easy."

"I love you, Billy."

Right this second, it was enough.

Chapter Twenty-Two

Billy was worn out. Perhaps it hadn't been the best course to go back home right after going all the way up to get Montana, but he was pretty sure staying in the house of flowers would have given him nightmares. And honestly, he wanted to be alone with Montana. He wanted to hold his lover and not feel like he had to be quiet or up at a certain time for breakfast or anything.

They checked in, took the elevator up, and he let them in. He went straight to the chair next to the window and sat, unable to keep his groan from sounding.

"How can I help?" Montana was right there, looking worried.

"Oh, I'm just tired. This day feels like it's been going on forever." Of course, it kind of had been. He wasn't even sure what time it was. His wound was aching, too, but he was sure he'd be fine after he got some sleep, and he didn't want Montana to worry any more than he already was.

"You want me to run you a bath or something?"

"I'm not supposed to get the dressing wet. Why don't we order some room service and then hit the hay once we've eaten?" He just needed to rest for a bit.

"Okay. What do you want?" His boy was so nervous.

"I want you to come here and kneel between my legs."
He spread them, giving Montana room.

"I can't get you food then..."

"This first. Some things are more important than
food."

Montana came over, looking at him. "Are you sure?"

Good grief, his boy was ornery sometimes. "Kneel.
Now."

Those dark eyes blinked, went wide. He stared back.
Montana was lost, he could tell, but they had to do this.
They needed to settle this. Montana pushed between his
legs.

"Hands together behind your back, love." His hands
twitched, aching to soothe with a touch.

"Why?" Montana put his hands back.

"First of all, because I said so. I'm the Master, you're
the sub. Secondly, this is 'the position.' If I say 'assume
the position,' you kneel, your hands linked behind your
back, your head bowed. I'd like to see that now."

"What? I don't. I mean. Wait. This..." Montana closed
his eyes, took a deep breath.

"Assume the position and then we can talk about the
things you need to talk about."

Montana whimpered, started to shiver, looked down.

"Very good." He slid his hands through Montana's hair
and kissed the top of his head. Then he tilted Montana's
chin up. "I love you. Now, we talk about this."

Montana's eyes were wild; not scared, really, but
unnerved.

"Tell me why you're freaked out by this."

"Because... because... you're different. This is
different."

"No, this is just more. All the time instead of just some

of the time." And it was what Montana craved, needed, wanted.

"I don't understand what you want."

"I want to be your Master twenty-four seven. Full time. You and me in the life."

"Why?"

"Because we both need it."

"I don't know if I can do this... this thing, all the time, man."

"You won't be kneeling non-stop, I can promise you that."

Montana chuckled softly, shook his head. "This is weird."

"It won't always be. Soon enough, this will be the quickest way for you to find your subspace, your peace." He smiled and then brought their foreheads together "Close your eyes, love." He closed his own.

"You say stuff that doesn't make sense." He felt Montana's eyes close.

"Shh. Just breathe with me. In." He breathed in slowly. "And out." He let his breath out just as slowly. He repeated the words, the breaths.

Montana began to breathe, focusing on him.

"There we go," he murmured.

Then they just breathed together, in and out. He could almost fall asleep like this, but he didn't; he enjoyed the quiet, the togetherness. He could hear Montana's heart, the beat steady, sure.

"I love you." He let the quiet last a little longer "Whenever you kneel like this, I want you to know that, to feel it deep inside you, no matter what else is going on."

"Love you, too, Billy." Montana took a deep, shuddery breath.

"Good. I'll know that, too, when you do this." He brushed his lips gently against Montana's and then sat back in the chair again.

Montana's eyes opened. "You want me to get you food now?"

He shook his head. "When I tell you. Close your eyes again. Get back to the quiet."

Montana frowned but closed his eyes. "Okay."

"Good." He closed his own eyes again, let the quiet it settle over him.

Some time later, he opened his eyes and smiled. "All right, love. Now you can order us some food."

Montana didn't answer, though. His sweet boy was kneeling there, sound asleep. Billy burst out laughing. Well, at least he knew Montana could find peace in it.

Those pretty dark eyes flew open, Montana falling backward. "Shit!"

"Shh, easy now." He moved forward automatically, reaching out to catch his lover. He cried out as pain flared in his right shoulder.

"Oh, God! Fuck!" Montana jerked himself up, eased him back into the chair. "Oh, God. Okay. You sit. I'll get ice."

He didn't say anything, not trusting his voice just yet as his shoulder throbbed painfully. Montana ran from the room, disappearing into the bathroom to grab the ice bucket before running out the door. Damn it, he hoped this didn't affect Montana's ability to find his subspace next time they did this. He was beginning to worry that his boy was cursed.

The pain had backed off a little by the time Montana got back, and he managed a warm smile for his lover. "Thank you."

"Okay. I'll get this in a towel and go get you food."

"No, no. Get me set up and then order room service." He was not having Montana wandering the streets on his own at this time of night. Not with what was out there lurking, waiting to pounce.

"Okay. Okay, let me help you with your shirt."

"Yeah, okay." He felt like an old man, having Montana undress him, but it was much easier that way.

"Oh, Jesus. Look at that. I did that..." Montana got him moved to the bed, heading over to grab towels.

"Will you stop that? It's not your fault—you didn't do this to me. The man with the gun did."

Montana didn't answer. He was propped up in the bed, pillows all around him, ice on his shoulder. One pain pill was given to him, along with the bottle of water. Then Montana called for room service—ordering a hamburger and a plate of chicken pasta.

"You're pampering me—I just might get used to it."

"Good." Montana smiled at him, handed him the remote control, and checked his makeshift ice pack.

He chuckled but didn't turn on the TV; he was enjoying watching Montana. Montana went to the window, looked out, then made sure his bag was put away, Montana's backpack shoved in a closet. Still smiling, he let his head rest back against the pillows. He dozed off, only waking when Montana put the pasta in front of him, careful not to jostle his shoulder.

"Oh, thanks, love." He patted the bed beside him. "You're going to join me, yes?"

"I got a burger." Tanny perched on the edge of the bed, watching him. "Eat."

"Yes, sir." He gave Montana a wink.

Montana nodded, munching on fries, watching to

make sure he ate. He managed a couple of bites of chicken and a bit of pasta. But he was tired, pretty much ready to sleep.

Montana took the plate away, settled him down on the bed, covered him up. "Rest, love."

"You, too." He'd missed his lover the last week.

"Let me clean up and stuff. You sleep."

"As long as you promise to come to bed soon."

"Sleep." Montana kissed him, pulled the covers over him.

He closed his eyes, letting Montana's care lull him to sleep.

Chapter Twenty-Three

He ended up sleeping on the big, overstuffed chair. He hadn't been sure how to get in the bed without hurting Billy, so he'd put the chair close and propped his feet up on the mattress. It wasn't too bad, really. He'd definitely had worse. He was woken up by moaning, Billy calling out his name in his sleep.

"Billy?" He sat up, eyes wide, heart pounding. "Do you need another pill?"

Billy's good arm flailed, looking for something.

"Hey. Hey." He crawled over onto the bed, still dressed, needing to make it better.

Billy half sat suddenly, eyes popping open, breath coming in harsh pants. "Montana?"

"Uh-huh. Do you hurt? Can I help?"

"I couldn't find you." Billy tried to sit up.

"I was right here. Shh. I'm right here."

"God. Sorry." Billy blinked and rubbed his eyes. "I was dreaming."

"Do you need anything? A drink?" Tanny checked for bleeding, for fever.

"Yeah, thirsty."

"Okay. Hold on." He got some leftover ice and poured Billy a glass of water. He helped Billy drink.

When Billy'd settled back down, his lover held out his arm. "Come lie with me."

"I don't want to hurt you." He stripped off his T-shirt and slid into bed, though.

Billy wrapped his good arm around Tanny, tugging him close. "I'll sleep better with you close."

"Okay." Tanny put his head on Billy's shoulder, sighed. Oh. So good.

"That's better, hmm?"

"Uh-huh." Tanny blinked at him, eyelids heavy. "Love."

Billy nodded, smiled. "God, I've missed this. Missed you."

"Missed you. So bad."

Billy's lips found his, the kiss soft, gentle.

"You should sleep now." He reached up, stroked Billy's hair.

"You, too."

He nodded. He could do that. He could.

Chapter Twenty-Four

B illy groaned as he woke up. His shoulder was throbbing fiercely, and he felt bone tired. He'd pushed himself the last couple of days, he knew that. But he'd had to get Montana. His lover was curled up next to him, head on his good shoulder. That right there made it all worthwhile. It had him smiling and ignoring his aches, his need to go piss. He'd stay right here until Montana woke up or he just couldn't stand it anymore, whichever came first.

The bruises on the hawk-like face made him want to growl. It made him want to go hit Oliver, give the man a very large piece of his mind. As if he could hear Billy's thoughts buzzing around, Montana's hand slipped out, petted his belly. He covered Montana's hand with his own, twining their fingers together.

Montana hummed softly, held on. "You're okay, Billy. You're okay."

He chuckled softly and squeezed Montana's hand. "I know. You're here beside me. I'm just fine."

Those dark eyes opened, long lashes blinking. "'Kay." Someone wasn't really awake yet.

He chuckled and nuzzled his lover. He needed to get well; they needed their lives back. Montana hummed softly, cuddled in, yawning. "How're you doing, love?"

"I'm okay. Worried about you."

"I'm fine, love. I might have pushed it a little yesterday. I wouldn't change a thing, though. I needed you here with me, hmm?"

"I know. I needed to be here, to help."

"You needed to be here because you're mine." He grinned. "The helping part's a bonus."

"Do you want me to call the police? Tell them we're in town? They're looking for me."

"Yeah, I guess we should." He sighed. He wanted to go home. He wanted to be better so they could have their life back.

"I'm sorry." Montana sighed, then smiled at him. "I tell you what, you stay here. I'll just run down there."

"Oh, no. I'm not letting you out of my sight. I don't trust the cops to have your best interests at heart."

"You're hurt, though..." Montana didn't look too disappointed.

Billy snorted. "Not so hurt I can't take care of my boy."

"Your boy." He almost missed the words.

He didn't miss them, though, and he nodded. "Mine."

"Yeah." Montana pinked, nipples hardening, tightening.

He licked his lips, his pain not seeming important at all.

"I should go call them."

"It can wait." He tilted Montana's chin and took a soft kiss. Montana opened to him, the kiss gentle, warming him through. "Mmm... I feel better already."

"Good." Montana rubbed noses with him.

"I suppose we can't put it off forever. Help me get up

and get cleaned up, changed, and then we can call the cops. Find out what's what."

"I really think you should stay here, let me do this."

"No, you don't have to face them alone. They've already done enough to you, thank you very much."

Montana shook his head. "They're going to be nasty. It's going to piss you off."

"You better believe it's going to piss me off." Billy had a thought. "Let me call my lawyer first. I want him here when the cops are called. I want to make sure they don't screw you."

Montana's eyes went wide. "A lawyer? Am I in trouble?"

"No, but if we've got a legal bulldog on our side, we can make sure it stays that way." Billy managed to sit himself up. "You were blackmailed into helping them—I want to make sure that doesn't happen again. I want to make sure you're treated fairly this time."

"Billy, I can't... I can't afford a lawyer."

"But we can. Besides, Watson just might work for free on this one. He's a part of the community."

"He's queer?"

"And kinky."

"Do you know anyone but me who's not kinky?"

"Sure. But most of my friends are members of the Hammer. It's easier, I think, if you share the same interests, hmm? Besides." He gave Montana a warm smile. "You're plenty kinky."

Montana rolled his eyes. "I just love you, huh?"

Poor Montana didn't want to admit what he wanted. What he needed. Hell, the fact that he had the cage on right now only proved just how kinky Montana was.

Montana pulled on a shirt, then looked around. "Do

you want to borrow one of my shirts?"

"I'm not sure it'll close over my chest, love."

"Well, I could go downstairs, see if there's a T-shirt in the gift store thing. Or we could just use yesterday's. It's not stinky."

"Yesterday's is fine, love." He wasn't used to Montana doing for him, but it felt good.

"Okay." Montana helped him get dressed, then disappeared into the bathroom, and he heard water running.

"I'm going to call Watson," he called out.

Montana didn't answer, but he was beginning to understand that that meant Montana didn't know what was appropriate to say.

He dug out the hotel's phone books and looked up the number and then dialed.

"Hi, Andrew, this is William Davern. I need to speak to Watson, please."

"Can I put you on hold, please, sir?"

"Sure thing." It was important, but he wasn't in jail or anything, so not urgent.

It took a few minutes, then the line went live. "William, it's Watson. How are you feeling?"

"A little tired, but I think that's par for the course when you get shot. How are you doing?"

"Fine. We're all worried about you, of course."

"I'm just fine. I need your help, though. Montana and I do."

"Of course, but I must warn you, William, if he's done something illegal, I'll recommend he turn himself in."

"No, he hasn't. In fact, he's been working for the police—acting as an informant somewhat against his will. I'd like to make sure they don't dig him in any deeper."

"Ah. That explains quite a bit. What are your plans?"

"We're staying at a hotel, as obviously the dealer knows where we live. We need to check in with the police—I know they want to talk to Montana, and I'd like to hear what they've done to clear this mess up. But, Watson, I don't want my boy talking to the cops again without you there. Can you meet us at the IHOP on Delouth? We'll arrange to meet the cops there about twenty minutes after you get there." Talk to Watson first, get everything sorted out. It sounded like a plan to him.

"I think that you might be better off coming here to the office, William. I'll talk to you, to Montana, then we'll contact the authorities from here."

"That works for me. We just need to grab a bite to eat. Shall we say in an hour?"

"That's fine, William. Do you need me to send a car for you?"

"Thanks, Watson, but I think we'll grab a cab. I appreciate you fitting us in."

"You got it." The line went dead.

He hung up his cell and headed for the bathroom. "Watson is going to see us, love."

"Is that good?"

"Yeah. He said we should go there, talk to him, and then call the cops from his office." He smiled and moved up behind Montana, pressing close. "He'll keep us safe."

"Okay." Montana looked haunted. He'd been noticing it, but now that he knew why, it was so evident.

"We're going to get this cleared up, love. And we're going to make sure the cops leave you alone from now on." He was keeping his lover safe. Period.

"I hope so. I can't go back now. I've been made."

"That's right. You can't go back. And we need

protection." He began to rub Montana's shoulders, wanting to ease his lover.

"You wouldn't if I hadn't been involved."

"It's done, love, I would rather need protection and have you in my life, than not need it because I never knew you. Okay?"

"If you hadn't known me, you wouldn't know to miss me."

He was going to beat Montana's ass. His eyes narrowed and met Montana's in the mirror. "Stop that, right now. Are you ready to go have breakfast?"

"I'm not hungry. I'm nervous, but I'll drink some juice or something."

"That's a start." It would at least get something into Montana. He needed to fatten his boy up again, get rid of that too-skinny look that being nervous had brought back.

"Do I need my backpack? Or are we staying here tonight?"

"I have no idea—you should bring it." He kissed Montana's neck. "I wish I had more answers. Things'll likely be more settled after we've spoken with Watson and the cops."

"It's okay. I'm cool."

He chuckled. "I'm not sure that's entirely true, but you will be." He gave Montana's ass a soft slap. "Come on, love. Let's do this."

"Right. Breakfast."

"Yes, breakfast. And then the rest of our lives."

He took Montana's hand and led him out.

Chapter Twenty-Five

Tanny wandered the lobby, pacing back and forth. Jesus, this was a fancy-pants fucking place. Too fancy for him. Too... glass and wood and shit.

"Montana." Billy called to him, one hand held out to him. "Come sit with me. Watson will see us as soon as he can."

"I don't want to sit."

"Come sit anyway."

"But..." He headed over, twisting his hands.

One of Billy's hands slid over his, stilling them. "Take a few slow breaths. It'll help your nerves."

"Nothing's going to help."

Billy opened his mouth, but before he could say anything, the guy at desk near the elevators spoke. "He'll see you now, Mr. Davern." Billy squeezed his hand and stood with him.

The whole place was like a TV show. In fact, Tanny sort of expected police to pour in any second. Police or dancing girls or something.

They went up the elevator and it let them out onto a ritzy-looking floor. Billy walked to the end of the hall, seeming to know where he was going. Every step he took, Tanny felt fucking smaller. The door at the end of the hall was ajar and Billy knocked softly. A sharp "Come in" followed the knock.

"I don't want to do this." He belonged on the street, not in here.

"It's going to be fine, love. Watson will make sure it works out our way."

He stood there, stuck for a second, just caught. Then he took a deep, deep breath. He'd been fucking willing to deal with a scary-assed drug dealer to make things solid for them, he could deal with a goddamned lawyer, right? Right.

Tanny reached out and took Billy's hand. Billy squeezed and gave him a warm smile. "We're going to be fine. I promise."

"Then we'd better go in." He reached for the doorknob, pushed the door open, and stepped in.

"Ah, William, there you are. And you must be Montana." The man was neat and well-dressed, but his eyes were warm and he came around his desk to shake both their hands.

"Hey. Thanks for seeing us." See him, see him not be freaky.

Billy's smile looked proud. "Hi, Watson. I'm so glad you could fit us in."

"No problem at all. Now, come in and sit and tell me all about the situation."

It took what seemed like forever, with Watson's face getting harder and harsher as Montana told the story.

"I have one, serious question. Have you, since you moved in with William, purchased or used illegal substances?"

"No." No, he'd kept one Red, once, early on, but he never took it.

"Montana swore to me that he wouldn't do drugs while under my roof, Watson. He's kept that promise. They pulled him in for jaywalking, for Christ's sake, because they couldn't get him for anything else!"

"I had to ask. Let me make some phone calls, see what our options are."

"Of course—you can ask anything you want. We don't have anything to hide." Billy's hand reached for his and squeezed gently.

Watson nodded. "The first order of business is to assure ourselves there aren't any warrants out for Montana. Then, once we've dealt with that, we'll talk about protection."

"Warrants? Why would there be warrants if he's working for them? God damn it, Watson, if they screw him over on this..."

"If they try, then we fight back."

Tanny winced, head ducking. Billy's hand slid up and down along his spine. "You haven't done anything wrong, Montana. Watson's going to make sure you don't get hurt in this."

"I am. You are the victim here, in this. You and William."

Billy frowned and then shook his head. "I just don't like thinking of myself as a victim. Injured party sounds less... helpless."

"Injured party it is."

"Thank you." Billy squeezed Montana's hand again.

The guy started jabbering on the phone about a million miles an hour, and all of a sudden Tanny wished he was racing again, riding his bike, zooming.

"It's going to be all right," Billy murmured quietly to him.

"I want a motorcycle. A fast one. A dangerous one."

Billy blinked. "Seriously?"

"Yeah. I want to go fast."

"Ah." A wicked smile curved the ends of Billy's lips. "I have something just as good as that for you. Maybe better. No. Definitely better."

"You just don't want me to crash."

"Damn right, I don't. Besides, what we do together is more fulfilling than just going fast."

"I like going fast."

"You'll like what I'm going to do to you better." Billy's eyes had gone hot and his voice was low, husky.

"Shh." He stood up, headed for the window. God. God.

Billy's chuckle followed him. He knew his cheeks were burning, but he didn't let himself look back. Damn it. He could feel Billy's eyes on him, though. It was like they were burning into him. Thank God the lawyer dude was busy on the phone and writing stuff down on a large pad. He watched the cars driving past, telling himself not to look.

It didn't go away, though, that sensation of Billy watching him, wanting him. He ducked his head, swallowed hard. Fuck. Fuck, Billy was... No fair. It was as if Billy was willing him to turn around, to look at his... Master. Fuck. Pay attention. No looking. Damn it.

The phone call continued—how long was it going to take, anyway? Too long.

Billy's stare burned a hole in his back, in his ass. His breath came faster, his heart beating in his chest. He thought he heard the faintest sound, like a growl. His toes curled, his nipples went hard. The urge to turn and look to Billy got stronger with each passing second. His foot started tapping, beat-beat-beat. He didn't think he was going to be able to deny it; he would have to turn and look at Billy.

No. No, he was not. He was not. He was not. He was... His eyes met Billy's in the reflection of the glass. Love and heat and something fierce that might have been pride shone in them, even through the reflection.

He wanted to go home. Now. Billy nodded like he'd read it in Tanny's mind, and then patted the chair next to him. Tanny turned and headed over, moving toward him.

Billy smiled, hand taking his as soon as he was in range. "This'll be over soon, love. And we can get our lives back. Start exploring."

"I'm just tired, man."

Watson hung up the phone and Billy looked toward him expectantly.

"They need you both down at the precinct. Internal Affairs would like to speak with you, Tanny, and William, you need to look at a line-up."

"Internal Affairs? You'll stay with him, Watson?"

"Absolutely. After that, we'll arrange for police protection at your home and at Montana's workplace."

Billy took a deep breath and relaxed next to him. "Thank God."

Tanny shook his head. "They won't just stop looking for me."

"They'd be crazy to come after you with the police following you."

Tanny looked at Billy, shocked. "Man, you know that I love you, right? But you can be incredibly fucking naive."

Billy bristled a little. "Watson?"

Watson sighed. "No one can promise his safety, William."

"That's not good enough!"

Sure it was.

Billy growled. "Let's get this police shit over with."

He nodded.

Yeah.

Yeah, let's get it over with, and then he could make plans.

Chapter Twenty-Six

illy paced, waiting for Montana and Watson to come out. He'd picked out the little bugger who'd shot him in the line-up and then been escorted out. Montana had been in there for a long time. When the door opened, a very pale Montana and a very smug-looking lawyer appeared.

He was taking Watson's demeanor as a good sign and Montana's paleness as a sign of his lover simply being exhausted. He opened his arms. Montana hesitated, then came to him, hugged him tight.

"I've got you." He gave Montana his full attention for a moment and then looked over at Watson, his brows raised.

"There was, apparently, an altercation. Mr... Chico was shot and killed. Montana identified the body." He'd started to object when Watson's hand rose. "From photographs. The man who shot you was his right-hand man."

"That's good news, though, right?"

"Yes, yes. There will be an escort for a few days, but there is no apparent danger and you probably won't even notice them."

"Thank God." He gave Montana another hug,

squeezing his lover tight. "So is Montana done here? Can I take him home?"

"Yes. Montana has been cleared of all involvement. He is not wanted on any charges."

Montana was beginning to shudder.

"Thank you, Watson. Thank you so much. And I don't mean to be rude, but I need to get Montana home."

Watson nodded, "I concur. He's had a long day."

He held out his hand and shook with Watson. "Send me the bill, man. You have my undying gratitude."

"Absolutely. You can call anytime." Watson shook Montana's hand, smiled. "You as well, Tanny. You did fine in there."

"Yeah. Thanks."

"Thanks again." He gave Watson a last smile and headed out to look for a cab, his arm around Montana, his lover snugged up against his good side.

"I bet you're ready to get home and rest."

"I bet you are, too. Looking forward to our own bed?" He just wanted things back to normal, wanted to be able to start spending the rest of his life with Montana.

"I think so. I..." Montana shrugged. "There's a cab."

They climbed into the cab, and he kept an eye on his lover. "Are you okay?" he asked quietly as they pulled into traffic.

"Yeah. I'm cool." Montana looked dazed.

"We'll talk when we get home." Or maybe just hold each other in bed for a long, long time.

"Okay." Montana held onto his backpack like it was a security blanket.

It didn't take long before they pulling up in front of the big old house that had been renovated into condos. It had never looked so good as it did right now with Montana at his side. "Home," he said quietly.

"Yeah." Montana nodded, took a deep breath.

He paid the taxi driver and grabbed Montana's hand, leading his lover up to their place. It almost felt like the first time again. Montana's hand was cool, clammy, but they headed in, the place looking normal thanks to Marcus arranging for the blood and stuff to be cleaned up.

"It looks just the same." He didn't know why that seemed strange, but it did.

"Uh-huh. I have to use the bathroom." Montana disappeared toward the bedroom.

He headed that way, too. "Let's shower." It was a place they could always connect, find each other.

"I'm a little freaked out."

"I know. You can tell me what's got you freaked out while we shower." Warm, safe, together.

He had more than a few ideas what might be bothering Montana, but he needed Montana to open up, to tell him. He tugged off his shirt and grimaced. He was going to have to wrap his shoulder in cling wrap or something.

"Careful. Careful. Did they give you waterproof bandages?"

"Oh, they might have." He hadn't been paying much attention when he'd left the hospital. He'd been worrying about where Montana was. "My bag's in the bedroom."

"Okay. Hold on."

Montana hurried out, then came back with the bunch of odds and ends Billy'd come home with. "Give me a second and I'll figure this out."

"Of course you will." Because his boy was a lot smarter than Montana gave himself credit for. Billy parked himself on the toilet lid.

Montana sorted quickly, organizing the wrappings and bandages. "Okay, these great big ones are the waterproof ones."

"Okay. What do you need me to do?" They looked almost like some weird body condom.

"Stand still and I'll put them over your stitches." Montana kissed his shoulder. "They look really good, by the way."

"Yeah? No seeping, that's a good thing, huh?"

"It looks really good. Healthy."

"I'll be back to my old self in no time." He met Montana's eyes. "And it wasn't your fault." Montana blushed a deep, dark red. Yes, he'd been right; Montana was trying to take this whole thing onto himself. "It wasn't."

"I'm still sorry."

"I'm sorry I got hurt, too. I'm even more sorry you were harassed and dragged into this whole thing."

"Yeah. Me, too." Montana nodded, kissed him gently, before pulling back and doctoring him.

"You're good at that." And he was enjoying the pampering. He was enjoying being home and being with his lover. His beautiful boy.

"I was a driver. I doctored a lot of people. Had a lot of stitches."

"Of motorcycles, you mean?" Sometimes he was reminded that getting details from Montana about his life before he'd come here was like pulling teeth. With a spoon.

"Uh-huh."

"So you were pretty good, then, huh?" Another reason to believe Montana might not have been entirely responsible for what happened to his sister.

"I was. I had a sponsor and everything."

"No kidding? You must have been very good."

"Maybe." Montana shrugged. "I liked it."

"Did you only race in good weather?" He asked it casually.

"God, no. I mean, sometimes, if it was vicious bad, then they'd cancel an official race, but normally on the little ones, we'd just go."

"So you knew how to ride in bad weather. You were a good driver, knew what you were doing." How could Montana never once have questioned that the accident that had killed his sister was his fault? He'd just shouldered all the blame his family had heaped on him, accepted it on their say-so.

"Yeah. Come on. Shower."

He got up and followed Montana to the shower, admiring his lover's ass, admiring the scars that marked Montana's back from shoulder to ass.

"Take the cage off," he said quietly.

Montana nodded, slipped the cage, and put it aside. They stepped into the shower together.

"Oh..." He closed his eyes as the hot water hit his skin. He hadn't realized just how much he'd missed showering until this moment.

Montana washed him, hands gentle and careful. "You should rest."

"I think I should stand right here for a while." He grinned, eyes still closed. "Maybe forever."

"The hot water will run out."

That made him laugh, and he reached out, finding Montana's waist and pulling him closer. "My practical sub."

He got a chuckle, soft, husky. "Uh-huh."

"Come here." He brought their mouths together, the kiss long and lingering.

Montana kissed him back, the love evident in the soft attention. They kissed for a long time, not arousing each other, just loving and caring, sharing.

"You should rest, Billy."

"We can go to bed together." He had to make sure Montana wasn't still freaked out before he let himself sleep.

"I... okay. Okay, yeah. That's cool." Montana dried him off, dried himself off, then got the bandages off his shoulder. He let Montana pamper him, still enjoying the attention.

Once they were in bed, he drew the covers up over their heads, making a cocoon and drawing Montana in close on his uninjured side. "I love you."

"Love you. Take a nap. I'll order pizza later or something."

He chuckled. "Are you ordering me around, love?"

"Yep."

Still laughing, he nuzzled, rubbed their noses together. "Soon, love. First, how are you feeling?"

"Like I've taken something."

"Jittery? Out of control?" Before Montana had started taking care of him, his lover'd been freaked out, almost shaking.

"Stunned. Distant. Like nothing's real."

He hugged Montana tight. "Will you sleep with me? And then, after, we'll work together on dealing with all this."

"Yeah. Yeah, I could rest, man. I've never seen a guy shot in the head before, not a real guy. The pictures were weird."

"If you need to talk about it now, we can do that, love." He was tired, but Montana came first.

"Nah. I'm good." Montana kissed his forehead. "Sleep."

He tilted his head, bringing their mouths together in a lingering kiss. "You, too."

Montana nodded, watched him, fingers on him until he fell asleep.

Chapter Twenty-Seven

He didn't sleep; he couldn't. He felt like he'd slept for days and days. Maybe months. Tanny cleaned the apartment, top to bottom, then he started painting the kitchen.

Over. It was over. Things were over with the police and he wasn't dead and he was still home.

"Montana?" Billy appeared in the kitchen doorway, wearing his robe and blinking.

"Go back to bed, Billy. It's early." It was only quarter to seven. Billy'd been asleep all evening, all night.

"What are you doing?"

"Painting."

"I know. I guess I meant why?" Billy wandered over to one of the stools and sat on it, eyes wide as he took in how much Tanny had done.

"I couldn't sleep. I needed to do things." He needed to move, to wander.

"Like paint the whole kitchen?" Billy held open his arms.

"Uh-huh. I cleaned the house, too." He stripped off his dirty shirt. "How's your shoulder?"

"You should have woken me. And I'm fine."

"You were sleeping." He leaned in, checked the

stitches. They looked good.

"You were supposed to be sleeping, too." Billy didn't wait for him to answer. Instead, he got a long good-morning kiss.

"You want..." He blinked, a little dazed. "Uh, breakfast?"

"I'd like something before we start, yes, please."

"Start what? You're not working today, you're hurt. Do you want cereal?" He headed over to grab a bowl.

"Sure, cereal is fine. And I mean start us. Start making things right again."

"I don't understand." Were they not right? Was Billy mad at him? Were they going to break up?

"You were freaked out yesterday. I want to deal with that. And we have a new, deeper relationship to begin exploring."

"Oh." Oh, okay. Okay. Okay. He looked at his hand, at the bowl that was shaking, and he put it down, hard.

Billy grabbed his suddenly free, but still shaking hand and pulled him in close. He was given a hard kiss. "Is that the dealing with yesterday or the deeper relationship that's got you shaking?"

"Neither. Both, I mean. I'm just... It doesn't matter."

"Stop that." Billy snapped the words out. "It matters. You matter."

"Aren't you supposed to be resting?" He needed to pour cereal.

"I just woke up, love. I don't need to rest."

"Let me make your cereal so I can paint above the back door."

"You don't think the painting can wait?" Billy did let him go, though, and his stomach growled loudly.

"Margaret said I don't have to come to work until Monday."

"So the painting can wait. I will take breakfast, though, please. I'm starving!"

He nodded and made Billy a bowl of corn flakes, only spilling the milk twice. He poured himself the biggest glass of juice ever.

"Sit," Billy ordered as soon as he'd put the cereal in front of his lover.

"Huh?" He was tired of feeling like he was in trouble.

Billy's hand slid over his shoulders. "Take a breath, love."

He met Billy's eyes, fingers clenching around the glass. "I'm trying. I'm trying real hard."

"I'm not trying to fight with you, love."

"Me, either. I just don't want you to be pissed."

"I'm not pissed. I'm worried about you, about how you keep trying to deflect me."

"I don't know what that means." He was going to cry. Really. That's what he wanted, to just sit and cry like a baby. Tanny didn't even think he was sad or anything. It was more that he could now.

Billy held out his arms again and gathered him close. "It's okay, love. You're safe now. You're safe here."

"I know." He looked at Billy. "I know. It's a little freaky, really, because it's over."

"And now you can freak out because it's safe to, hmm?"

Tanny went boneless as he nodded, relieved beyond bearing that Billy understood without him searching for the right way to say it.

Billy kissed the top of his head. "Eat if you're hungry. You need to have your strength for what I have planned."

"I'm not. I have my juice."

"Okay." Billy's smile was warm and then he ate

quickly, watching Tanny out of the corner of his eye.

"I need to clean up my brushes and stuff."

"No, you need to come to the bedroom with me."

"But they'll ruin..."

"We can buy new ones."

He blinked again. He was doing that a lot. Billy finished up his cereal and stood, holding a hand out to him.

"But..." He wasn't sure what they were doing, here. Now. Still, his hand fit perfectly into Billy's.

Billy pulled him into the bedroom, pulled him up against the strong body.

"Don't hurt yourself."

"I'm fine, love."

"I just worry. I don't want you sick."

"I'm not sick. Just a little dented." Billy's mouth closed over his.

He let himself lean into the kiss, tongue sliding against his lover's. The kiss quickly grew fierce and he almost didn't notice them moving over to the bed, he was so distracted by it. He moaned and followed, focused completely on the kiss. One-handed, Billy started to fondle his chest, fingers tweaking his nipples and sensitizing the skin around his navel. He moaned, swayed, knees more than a little weak. Billy's kiss went on and on, stealing his breath.

"I... Billy." They moved onto the bed.

"Got it in one." Billy winked and then dove back into more kisses.

Tanny stopped worrying about it and let himself sink into the kisses. Billy pushed him onto the bed, following him down, body solid and good. Tanny hummed, snuggling in, breathing deep of Billy's scent.

"Gonna spank you," Billy murmured, hand going to his ass and squeezing one of his cheeks.

"Why?"

"Because you need it."

Billy was already naked and shifting on the bed, moving to sit with his back against the headboard.

"I don't. I haven't been bad." He stripped quickly, without really even knowing he was going to.

"It's not about punishment; it's about need. You're on edge, you're freaked out about what you saw, what happened. You need a release." Billy tugged him, pulling him over his lover's thighs.

"I am, but..." He wasn't sure that would help.

"Trust me, love." Billy shifted him so his cock was firmly held between Billy's thighs, and then it began, Billy's hand dropping onto his skin, the sound loud in their bedroom.

He tried to pull away, tried to get away from the pressure, but he couldn't. Billy's hand stayed on his ass where it had landed, and then it disappeared and came down again, the sound even louder this time, the smack undeniable.

"Don't..." He didn't want to.

"Just let go, let it all go, love." Twice more Billy's hand came down, smacking one cheek and then the other.

He sobbed once, jerking. Scared. Worried. Mad.

"All of it." Again and again, Billy's hand landed on his ass. Some smacks were hard, others light.

"Stop it." He shook his head over and over.

"You need this." His ass began to push up as Billy's hand came down on it.

"I don't..." Billy wouldn't find a rhythm, wouldn't

settle. "Jesus, will you make your fucking mind up?"

Billy growled at him, hand coming down hard over and over, right in the middle of his ass.

"Fuck. Fuck. Fuck." He jerked, really trying to pull away.

The spanking continued and there was no way he could accuse Billy of not focusing, not settling and finding a rhythm now. It was hard and fast and making him absolutely crazy.

"Stop it! Leave me the fuck alone! I was trying to do the right thing and your fucking friends threw me out! I don't even have keys to my own place!"

"That's it. Tell me everything. Let it all out." The smacks continued, fast and furious.

"Let me go, you prick! I never fucking lied to you! Not once! And I was so fucking scared and this is supposed to be a safe place. You said people like me were safe with people like you and Oliver hit me!" His head was going to explode.

"Yes. Yes. I know. Keep going."

"Motherfucker! Bastard! Let me go! I just want it to be over!" He wanted their lives back.

"It is. Let it all out. All of it. Every last bit."

"I can't keep doing this!" He sobbed, beating on Billy's legs. "I wanted to get high. I wanted to, so bad, and I didn't and no one cared!"

The spanking stopped for a moment, Billy's voice low, but sure, "I cared. I care." Then it started again.

He groaned, telling Billy about how tired he was, how angry. How hard it was to read the signs, how stupid he felt. How he'd just felt like this was home and then he'd thought he'd lost it and now here he was. He told Billy about being so scared and about praying that Billy would ask him what was happening because he didn't lie.

"That's it," Billy said softly. "Tell me everything, love. Everything."

"Stop hurting me. It burns."

If anything, the spanking got harder. "Focus on the burn and keep talking."

"Fuck you!" He didn't like this. Not at all.

Billy's hand continued to come down, moving around his ass now, but with the same strength, the same speed.

"You asshole! Why are you doing this to me?" This wasn't like before. This wasn't hot or sexy or good. This ached.

"Because you need to let everything out."

"What the fuck are you talking about?" He couldn't breathe.

"I'm talking about everything you've already told and everything you have left to tell me. Things you won't otherwise tell me." Billy had stopped spanking him and now was rubbing his burning ass.

He fought to catch his breath. "You're so goddamned nosy. There are things you don't get to know."

"No." Billy started smacking him again. "I'm your Master."

He groaned, arched. "S...says who?"

"Says us. Says me."

"I don't..." Tanny couldn't do this, he couldn't think. "You have to stop. Please. My head hurts. I'm so tired."

"Not yet." The swats were softer now—they didn't need to be hard, his skin was so sensitive. "Tell me why you didn't sleep."

"I couldn't. I needed to be busy. I needed to just breathe. I wanted to do stuff."

"Why?"

"I don't know. I needed to make things clean. I needed to."

"You need to make things ours again, hmm?"

"It's my fucking house, too. I don't have to sleep." He was starting to get mad again.

"You need to take care of yourself, though." Billy had stopped spanking him again.

"I don't want to sleep." What if he woke up and it was all a dream?

"Why not?"

"Because I don't want to."

"There's a reason why you don't want to." Billy squeezed his ass. "And 'because' isn't it."

"I don't have to tell you things. Some things are private."

Billy snorted. "Our lives are entwined."

"So?" He wasn't being ugly. He wasn't. He didn't get it.

"So. If I'm going to help you, if I'm going to be your Master, there isn't any such thing as private."

Tanny sobbed softly. "You don't make sense. My fucking soul hurts, man."

"I'm not trying to hurt you, Montana. Just the opposite."

"What do you want? I can't do the right thing if I don't understand."

"We talked about this. About deepening our relationship, about being all but married. I want all of you. The good bits, the not so good bits. All of it."

"Everybody has secrets. Heart secrets. Stuff they never tell." Everyone.

"I want all of you. There's nothing you can say that will make me change my mind."

He tried to get up. "I want to look at your face."

Billy let him, helping him to sit, to straddle Billy's thighs.

He stared at Billy, slapping the tears from his face. "I'm fucking scared to sleep because this is all I want, to be with you and here and shit and what if it's a motherfucking dream? And yeah, okay, I know it's fucking dumb, and you're an asshole for making me tell you."

"I am not an asshole for making you tell me. Now I know what your fear is, I can help."

"You are, too." Billy didn't think he was dumb?

"Am not." Billy reached over to the bedside drawer and pulled out the heavy cuffs.

"What are you doing?"

"I'm putting the heavy cuffs on you. I'm not attaching them together or to anything, but you need the weight. It'll help you know it's real."

"I'm not crazy. I know it in my head." Just not in his heart.

"It doesn't matter what you know in your head, though, does it?" Billy closed the heavy cuffs around his wrists. "And I can tell you that this is your home, that I'm your lover and nothing is ever going to change that until the cows come home. That doesn't mean you know it deep down. Oliver took what confidence you had in that away."

"He took my keys. I didn't even have anything. My sweater." That sweater he'd earned.

"I know." Billy growled, face angry. "He owes you an apology and a hell of a lot more."

"I just... I'm not a whore. I didn't take advantage of you. I worked." He worked hard. "Do you hear me, Billy? I worked hard for you. I painted and I learned shit.

And I didn't use!"

"I hear you, Montana. I know. I am so proud of you—I have been for a long time. I thought you knew that, and if you don't, then I've failed you as much as Oliver did."

"Good. Good, I want you to hear me. I'm stupid, I know that, but I'm not a liar and I didn't mean to bring them here!" He couldn't breathe anymore, he was so angry, so loud.

"You are not stupid! And I know you never would have done it if you'd thought I'd get hurt." Billy was yelling now, too.

"Good!" He screamed the words out. "I love you, you ASSHOLE."

"I am NOT an ASSHOLE. And I love you, too." Billy grabbed him by the arms and tugged him.

Their mouths slammed together. Tanny moaned, then wrapped around Billy and held on tight. The kiss was deep and hard and then it was over. Billy rested their foreheads together, panting like they'd just been running instead of kissing.

"I'm so tired, sir."

"Then sleep, love. I will hold you, and you have the cuffs heavy on your hands—you'll know it isn't a dream."

"Promise?"

"I promise."

"Okay." Tanny closed his eyes and let himself believe.

Chapter Twenty-Eight

illy watched Montana sleep, holding his lover in his arms. He dozed some, but mostly he looked and he thought. He'd screwed up somewhere along the line and hadn't made sure Montana knew without a doubt that this was his home. Damn Margaret for being right, but he had been playing house and Montana had somehow known.

Well, no more.

Every so often Montana would jerk, almost wake, then he would sink back into sleep. Billy stroked Montana's back. He kissed the top of Montana's head. He thought about the things he had to do to make his boy know that his place was right next to Billy, no matter who or what happened.

Checking to make sure Montana was still asleep, he reached for the phone and dialed Oliver's number.

"Hello?" Oliver sounded ancient, exhausted.

"It's William." He couldn't keep the growl out of his voice.

"How are you feeling?"

"Furious, actually." He could easily tear Oliver to pieces.

"I can understand that."

"You hit him, Oliver. You hit my boy. In anger." It made him shake, just thinking about it.

"I did. I thought one of my best friends was dying, and the police were telling me he'd been involved. I was wrong, but I didn't know that at the time."

"There's no excuse for hitting someone else's boy without permission. Especially in anger. And then you took the keys to his home from him and sent him out into the streets with only the clothes on his back. How dare you, Oliver? How dare you?"

"What exactly do you want, William? I was wrong. You were shot, and the police told us he was involved with the drug dealer. I made a mistake. I can't go back and change it." That was Oliver. No beating around the bush.

"You can apologize to him for a start." Billy wasn't sure what else he needed Oliver to do to earn his forgiveness; he was still so mad.

"I would be happy to."

"At the Hammer." He didn't know how many had been at the hospital to see Montana's treatment at Oliver's hands, but he wanted there to be no doubt in anyone's mind, especially Montana's, that Oliver was truly contrite. "You are sorry, right?"

"William, I'm not a child, and I have never been afraid to admit when I was wrong. If the situation had been reversed, what would you have done?"

"I would never have hit Jack. Never." Billy shook his head. "I'd like to believe I wouldn't have assumed the worst, Oliver. I think that's what hurts the most, that you forgot that this was my boy."

"He is a young man with a dangerous addiction, and I did not forget. You trusted him, and I was told he violated that trust. I interfered where I shouldn't have, but I did have you in my heart."

Billy shook his head. "I am so angry at you right now, Oliver." He heard Oliver's words, but they were just excuses, and he couldn't see past what Oliver had done, the way his friend had violated his trust and his boy and it all buzzed angrily around his head.

"I understand that. I've spoken with Jack and Xavier and have tendered my resignation at the club. I will send Montana a formal written apology."

Billy gasped, surprised – no, shocked—he hadn't expected that. Oliver was one of the founding members of the Hammer. For him to resign meant that perhaps he did understand how deeply what he'd done had hurt not only Billy himself, but Montana as well.

"I can't ask for more than that." His words were tinged with sadness now as well as anger.

"I hope your evening goes well, William."

"Good night."

He hung up the phone, feeling somewhat vindicated, feeling sad, feeling angry, still. At least he had something to give to Montana now, more than just his own words that Oliver had done wrong. Oliver himself was trying to prove it.

Montana was awake, looking at him. "I don't want his apology." His boy's voice was raw, creaky.

"He owes it to you. You deserve it. You don't have to forgive him."

"Everything's messed up for you."

"He's apologized to me as well. And he's resigned from the club—he knows what he did was wrong. He hit you in anger. He hit you without my permission. He took your home from you, which no man has the right to do."

271

The anger began to overtake the other emotions again, and Billy tried to take a few deep breaths.

Montana sighed, stood up, and headed for the bathroom.

He got up and followed. "There are a few things I'd like to do myself, so that you don't feel that anyone can take your place away from you."

"Huh?"

Montana did his business, started brushing his teeth.

"I'm having your name added to the condo papers and I'm drawing up my will—you'll be my beneficiary, of course. I'll have Watson draw up the papers to make you my legal proxy to make medical decisions, should I be unable. Things like that." He wanted everything all legal and transparent so no one would doubt that this was Montana's home as much as his, that it would be clear Montana was his lover, his partner, not some stray he'd picked up off the street.

"Are you sick?" Montana stared at him. "Is the bullet thing worse?"

"What? Oh, no! No, nothing like that. But getting shot's reminded me that shit happens and you're better off if you're prepared for it. I already asked you for forever— I'm just working on the legal angles of that now."

"Oh." Montana looked at him, swayed.

He reached out automatically to steady his lover. "Are you okay?"

"Yeah. Yeah, that scared me."

"I'm sorry." He drew Montana close, hugged him. "That wasn't my intent at all."

"It's okay. You hungry?"

"I am. You slept for a fairly long time. I bet you're hungry, too. We could order pizza." He wasn't in the mood for cooking.

"Okay. You have my money, huh? From before?"

"You know I do." They really needed to get Montana's ID and a bank account. He could hold Montana's card and checks and stuff, but Montana needed an account in his own name.

Billy was never letting something like this happen again. Ever.

"Cool. Then I'll buy pizza."

He stopped his automatic protest—sometimes Montana needed to contribute, Billy knew that. "Okay."

"Okay." Montana looked at him. "I feel like I'm thinking through oatmeal."

"You still need more sleep. And you're protecting yourself still, I think. From what happened. From what you saw at the station."

Montana blinked at him, then shrugged. "I dunno."

"I do."

"Huh?" Montana stepped closer to him.

He grinned. "You said you don't know, and I said that I do."

"Know what?" His poor tired boy. Montana had done well, coping and surviving.

"That you need more sleep. That you need me to help you deal with the last few weeks, and yesterday especially." He stroked Montana's back. "Come back to bed, love."

"I thought you wanted pizza..." Montana stumbled toward the bed.

"I want you well and happy."

"You're the one that's hurt."

"Physically, yes."

Montana slid into the sheets, almost asleep again

already. "You talk in circles."

"No, you just don't want to admit that I'm right." He climbed in with Montana, cuddling, his touches encouraging Montana to relax.

Montana hummed, but didn't argue. In fact, his boy was dozing. Billy closed his own eyes and held Montana close.

Chapter Twenty-Nine

He slept for two days, then, somehow, it was Sunday and he had to go back to work tomorrow and he hadn't finished painting the kitchen. Tanny considered getting out of bed, pulling at the cuffs on his wrist. Shower. He needed a shower.

Billy rolled over and one leg slid over his. Billy's arm wrapped around his waist.

"I need to do stuff." Billy was so warm.

The snuffling noise that came from Billy made him think his lover was mostly still asleep.

"Love you, but I gotta get up." He slid out from under Billy's arm.

That did wake Billy up, grunting and blinking and giving Montana a warm smile.

"Hey. Gonna take a shower." He started working the cuffs off.

"Stop that. I didn't say those could come off."

"Huh? But I need a shower and I need to finish the kitchen and stuff."

"That's not the point. The point is, I didn't say you could take them off."

"I didn't ask, though..." He didn't get Billy sometimes.

"I'm the Master, remember? I put the cuffs on you,

and they stay on until I say they can come off."

"Okay... so say they can?"

Billy shook his head. "No. I don't think you're ready for them to come off yet."

"Why not?"

"Because they're reminding you that this is real, they're grounding you." Billy hauled himself out of bed. "I'll wash you so you don't ruin the leather."

"Careful. How's your shoulder?" It was looking so much better.

"It's not bad, actually. Better." Billy grinned at him. "And not going to distract me."

He chuckled, just a little unnerved. "Uh-huh..."

Billy grabbed one arm and tugged him in close, kissed him lightly. "Good morning."

"Good morning. I've slept forever, huh?" He wrapped his arms around Billy and hugged.

"We both did. I think we needed it." Billy rubbed their noses together and then just held him for a long moment. He listened to Billy's slow, strong heartbeat, jonesing on it. "You feel good."

Tanny nodded. He did. He felt better.

"Good." Billy kissed his throat, mouth warm on his skin. "I'm going to wash you now. And then feed you. After that..." Billy shrugged. "Maybe we talk, maybe we just make out."

"I need to finish the kitchen before I go back to work, too."

"We'll see. It'll still be there tomorrow or next weekend."

"Yeah." It would be messy and he still wanted to do it, but he felt too good to argue.

Billy finally stood up and took his hand, and they

wandered together to the bathroom like they had all the time in the world to get there. He followed, eyes returning to the stitches. They looked like spiders.

"It'll look better once the stitches are out."

"Yeah." He was still sorry, though.

Billy stopped them and kissed him, right there in the hallway. He blinked up, surprised, then pushed into the kiss. Billy pushed him against the wall, good arm around him, keeping his naked skin from pressing against the cold plaster.

"Billy." He moaned, body responding eagerly, immediately.

"Right here. So are you." Billy groaned and rubbed against him, their cocks sliding.

"Yes. Want you." He didn't know if Billy should, but he did.

"Me, too." Billy's mouth covered his again, tongue demanding entry.

He arched, held onto Billy's head, his cock filling and sliding against Billy's belly. Billy's tongue fucked his mouth, slipping in and out between his lips. It was easy to relax, to arch against Billy and fly. Billy's hand slid down to grab his ass, squeeze and tug him in closer. He wanted. He wanted so bad. He pushed back into Billy's touch, his heart pounding.

"Missed this," growled Billy. "Missed you."

"Yes. Yes, I love you."

"Yes." Billy bit at his bottom lip, sucked it into his mouth. That made him grunt, groan, rub a little harder. "No coming until I say so," growled Billy.

He moaned, arched against Billy. So mean. Billy stopped kissing him and began to lick the skin of his jaw, his throat.

"Billy..." He swallowed, their stubble rasping together.

Billy didn't answer, he just kept licking and kissing and nipping at his skin. He reached down, fingers wrapping around Billy's prick. Groaning, Billy bucked up against him.

"I could suck you." Billy loved that.

"You could."

"Is that a yes?" He hated when Billy was confusing.

Billy cupped his cheeks and took a long, hard kiss. "Yes. Yes, suck me."

He nodded, his lips swollen and red. "Uh-huh."

He eased down, focusing on the full, heavy cock. Billy made a noise and rubbed the hot cock against his lips. It was easy to close his eyes, open up, and suck Billy in. Billy's prick was hot and silky and tasted so good, like home. Tanny focused on just that, on how good it was to just love on his best friend, his Billy.

"My sir," his brain whispered to him.

"That's it, Montana. Suck me. Take me in." He looked up, almost startled. Billy looked straight at him, eyes so full of love. "Feels so good."

He ran his hands up Billy's legs, caressing as he took Billy down to the root. This strangled sound came out of Billy's mouth. He sucked harder, swallowing around the tip. "Montana!" Billy's hands slid through his hair, and he could feel the strong thighs trembling.

His fingers nudged Billy's balls, encouraging his lover to come. Billy shouted his name again and then spunk filled his mouth. He swallowed Billy down, humming around the fat cock, pulling hard, taking everything. The hands in his hair slid, Billy stroking his head now.

He pulled off of Billy's cock and kissed Billy's wrist. "Better?"

"Yeah. I needed that." Billy smiled. "Thank you."

He kissed the tip of Billy's prick. "Anytime."

"Your turn." Billy tugged on his arm.

"Careful. Careful of your arm." As he stood, it occurred to him that they were still in the hall.

"I'm fine, love. Certainly not hurting enough I can't take care of you."

"Okay. I worry."

"Good to me." Billy cupped his cheek, thumb sliding across his lower lip.

His eyes dropped closed, his lips wrapping around Billy's thumb. Billy's groan was like the best kind of music. He rested back against the wall, feeling all melted. Billy leaned into him, letting him take Billy's weight. Their lips met softly, Billy parting his. He moaned, breathed into Billy's mouth.

His lover's tongue slipped into his mouth, playing gently with his. His need eased back, letting him breathe. Billy's hand wrapped around his prick, moving slowly and gently to match their kisses. His entire body moved with the touch, riding the pleasure. That had Billy moaning into his mouth, the solid body resting against him.

He could stay right here. Forever. Really. Billy didn't seem to be in a hurry to move things along, either. Each kiss was followed by another, the slow, wonderful strokes continuing. His entire body was warm, he felt fluid, at home. The weight of the cuffs felt good, the leather warm, reminding him he wasn't dreaming. This was real. Real and his and good.

The gentle strokes gave way to fingertips exploring. Billy traced the veins on his cock and the head, circling it, rubbing the tip. Every now and then that hand would leave his cock altogether, Billy tracing his name where it was inked on Montana's belly. Every time Billy did that, Tanny smiled.

"Sexy," Billy muttered against his lips. "Sexy and mine."

"Yours. I promise."

"Good." Billy's fingers slid down to cup his balls. His thighs spread instinctively. "You know..." Billy gave him a sudden, wicked grin. "Promises of forever usually come with rings."

"Huh?" He worked with his hands a lot. Rings really didn't work.

"Yeah, a ring." Billy's fingers slipped behind his balls and rubbed the sensitive skin behind it.

"Mmm..." He sort of lost track of the conversation.

"Right here." Billy pushed against his skin.

"Feels good." He went up on tiptoe.

"Yeah? We should do it. A little gold ring for me to play with. An eternal symbol of my love and commitment." As Billy spoke, his finger drew circles on Montana's skin.

"Wait. What?" He wasn't quite getting it.

"You're going to wear my ring. Right here." Billy pushed against that spot behind his balls again.

"But..." He swallowed hard. "Man, that'll hurt bad."

Billy tilted his head and then shook it. "No, not really. Sure, when it first happens, but no worse than your nipples, and then imagine how it'll feel, something constantly there where you're so sensitive."

"I don't know, man."

Billy chuckled. "I do, though."

His cheeks heated. "Are you laughing at me?"

"No, love. I wouldn't do that to you."

"Okay. Because I'm not smart, but I'm trying to figure shit out and do it right."

"Stop that." Billy growled at him.

"Stop what?"

"Saying you aren't smart." Billy growled again. "I hate it when you do that."

"It's true. I don't lie."

"It is not true. You aren't stupid at all. Not at all."

"I feel that way."

"You don't give yourself enough credit." Billy's hand moved to cup his balls again. He went up on his toes, rocking a little bit. "You're my smart, sexy, beautiful boy."

"I..." How did he answer that? He was Billy's. He was.

Billy kissed him hard. "You are."

"I'm yours."

"That's right." Billy's hand found his cock again, the stroking more intense now.

"Oh. Oh, feels good. Billy..."

"I know. From this side of it, too."

"Does it?"

"Yeah. You're hot and silky and hard. Feels amazing to hold you in my palm."

Tanny felt his cheeks heat. Good. He wanted to be special.

"I love the sounds you make, too. I love knowing you're making them because of what I'm doing." Billy stared into his eyes, the truth of his words shining in them.

"I want you." With all he was.

"Yeah. Yeah, I know that feeling, too."

He didn't know what to say. What did you say?

"Come for me, love. I want to taste you."

"Oh, damn." He jerked, driving harder into Billy's hand.

"Come on, love. Give me what I want." Billy's hand tightened around him.

"I try. I always try." His toes curled.

"You do. You do better than try, too." Billy jerked his prick, hard, demanding that he come, so he did, his spunk splashing on Billy's wrist. Billy groaned like it was him who'd just come.

He shivered, gasping a little. "Damn."

"Good, huh?" Billy grinned, looking smug and pleased.

"Uh-huh. Always." So good.

"Starting to feel real again?"

"Yeah. Yeah, starting to."

"Excellent." Billy took his hand and tugged him along the hall to the bathroom.

"Back to work tomorrow."

"Yeah. How do you feel about that?" Billy switched on the light in the bathroom and moved him to the middle of the room.

"Huh? I like working. It'll be a little weird." He'd been a wreck before.

"I want you to promise me, if that asshole cop shows up and starts hassling you, that the first thing you'll do is call me."

"I'll try, huh?" He needed to save enough to get himself a cell phone.

"You need a cell phone," murmured Billy as he started filling the sink with hot water, almost like he'd been reading Tanny's mind.

"Huh? How do you do that?"

Billy looked at him. "How do we get you a cell phone?"

"No. How do you know what I'm thinking?"

"Do I? I guess we just think alike, hmm?" Billy grabbed

a washcloth and a bar of soap.

"That's pretty cool."

"Yeah, actually, it is." Billy wet the cloth, soaped it up, and began to wash him. "Arms up—cup your head."

"...'Kay..." This was weird.

Billy hummed, sounding happy as he washed Tanny's body.

"You don't think this is a little weird?"

"You can't go in the shower with the leather cuffs on, and I'm not about to give you permission to take them off yet."

"Why not?"

"Because they'll get ruined if they get wet." Billy went to his knees and began to wash his belly.

That wasn't what he'd meant, really... Billy's fingers slid over his cock, and then his balls, dragging the soapy cloth along behind his fingers. "I..." Okay. Weird. Hot, but weird. Really.

"Yeah, love?" That soapy cloth moved behind his balls, rubbed over his hole.

"That's real... personal." Weirdly more personal than making love.

Billy glanced up at him. "Yes, it is."

"It doesn't make you weirded out?"

"No, it doesn't."

"Are you sure?"

"It makes me happy." Billy leaned forward and kissed his hip. "I love you, you know. For me, that means everything."

"Good." At least he thought that was good. Maybe it sucked.

Billy smiled and nodded before washing his legs right down to his feet. There he was, soapy from head to toe.

"Should I get in the tub?"

"No, I'll wash the soap off the same way. And only familiarity will stop you from being wigged out by it."

He didn't know what to say about that. He was wigged.

"What bothers you about it, love?" Billy stood and rinsed the cloth in the sink.

"It's just... close? What's that word that's like personal or private?"

"Either of those work." Billy got up close and held his gaze. "There isn't anything we can't share, love."

"You keep saying that, but..."

"But it's the truth."

"We all have secrets."

Billy grinned up at him. "So you keep saying."

"What?" He was starting to itch, to shift a little.

Billy began to rub away the soap with the cloth. Water dripped down him some, but Billy didn't seem worried. He closed his eyes, breathing sweet and slow, shivering with something not cold. Billy rinsed him everywhere, the touches just as intimate now as they'd been earlier. His breath was coming faster; it was shallow, quick.

Billy finished rinsing him and got a towel, began drying him almost excruciatingly slowly. He couldn't just stand there. It was insane. Crazy-making.

"Shh, just relax, love."

"I'm trying." It was hard. Weird.

Billy kissed his belly, tongue sliding on the tattoo. His belly jerked, twitched. Humming, Billy nuzzled and moved downward.

"Billy..." He was caught, panting.

"Uh-huh." The word was little more than a breath across his cock.

He wasn't hard again, but he was getting there. Billy kept on nuzzling: his belly, his cock, his balls, the touches building one on top of the next. He wasn't sure what to do, what to think. His body knew, though; his hips arched and jerked and begged for more.

"So sexy," murmured Billy, tongue swiping across his slit.

"Yours." He wasn't sure what he'd done to deserve being loved like this.

"That's right. Every inch." Billy took in the head of his cock and began to suck.

Tanny's eyelids got heavy and his hips began to rock steadily, sliding his prick in and out of Billy's lips. Billy's good hand came up, fingers playing with his balls.

"I... Your hands are warm." He could feel Billy trying to smile around his cock.

"That's not all that's warm..." Billy nodded and it did weird, but good, things to his cock.

"Can I put my arms down?"

Billy tilted his head and then shook it, and he swore he saw an evil glint in them.

"Billy..." His cock throbbed.

His lover just sucked his cock harder.

"I. I. Billy..." He was aching.

Billy's fingers tugged sharply on his balls. His eyes flew open and he jerked away, startled. The touch gentled and the sucking continued. Billy was pretty agile with his tongue, moving it all over his cock as Billy sucked. Tanny panted, eyelids going heavy again, heart pounding. The fingers holding his balls started to stroke and roll and pet them, the heat ratcheting up again.

"What do you want me to do?" The question hiccupped out of him, surprising him.

Billy pulled off long enough to tell him, "Feel, enjoy. No coming until I say so or give the signal."

"'Kay. Okay." He nodded, legs starting to shake.

Billy's arm wrapped around them, supporting him. Tanny closed his eyes, lost in the motion and pressure of Billy's mouth sliding on him, tasting him. The heat and wet pressure were almost unbearable. Billy's head bobbed faster and faster, the suction growing even harder, more intense. Harsh little sounds poured out of him from deep in his chest.

Nodding again, Billy's head bobbed over his cock. The hand on his ass pulled him in closer, harder.

"Love you. Love you. Fuck, Billy. Want you so bad..." He was gonna scream.

Billy looked up into his eyes and nodded once. His hands fell and slammed against the wall, hips bucking furiously as he shot, hard. The sucking continued until he just couldn't take it anymore. Billy seemed to know exactly when that was, pulling off slowly. Tanny slumped against the wall, panting, shaken and sated and dazed.

"You'll never look at washcloths the same way again."

He shook his head. No. Never.

Billy grinned up at him, looking very, very smug. And happy and hot, a shiny drop of come on the corner of his mouth. He reached out with trembling fingers and wiped that drop away. Billy turned his head enough to suck Tanny's finger in, pulling on it like Billy'd done with his cock. He shuddered, blinked down at Billy, shaken.

Dragging up along his body, Billy slowly stood and pressed their mouths together. Billy grabbed his hands and held the leather cuffs, warming them. "I have you."

"I love you." He meant it, too, with all he was.

"I know." Billy sounded so serious, was taking him seriously.

"Okay." He leaned into Billy and let his lover hold him.

Chapter Thirty

Billy made his way down the street toward Rainbow Artists. He wanted to hurry and check his watch, but he forced himself not to. He was sure Montana was just fine. Still, he was pretty happy to finally see the place. The bell over the door rang as it always did, and he waved toward the cash register and made his way to the studio at the back of the shop.

Margaret was in her chair, Tanny was kneeling down beside her as they discussed papers, Margaret pointing and talking, Tanny touching each one, smelling it. Billy stopped for a moment, not wanting to break their concentration. It was a treat, too, seeing Montana so focused, learning.

Margaret nodded as Tanny handed her a piece of paper, started talking to her. That Margaret took Montana seriously, loved and cared for him, believed in him—those things made him fiercely glad she was in their lives. Montana needed more people like the two of them.

Her eyes found his and she smiled, touching Montana's shoulder and pointing. Those dark eyes met his and Montana smiled, waved. He grinned and waved back, finally heading over. "So, how was your first day back?"

"Good. We have a big order."

"No, son. You have a big order. I have someone to deal with it. How are you feeling, William?"

Billy chuckled and went over to give her a hug. "I'm feeling pretty good, actually. Almost back to normal. How're your knees?"

"Good today." She patted his back, hugging him. "His stomach's been rumbling for the last half hour. Go feed him."

"Margaret!" Montana's laughter was warm, fond.

"You heard the boss-lady. Let's go eat." He held his arm out for Montana.

Montana nodded, came to him. "I'll see you tomorrow, lady."

"Have a great afternoon, son."

Billy waved at her and slid his arm around Montana's waist. "So, Mr. Growly Stomach, what do you feel like for lunch?"

"Burgers? Ice cream?"

"Ice cream is dessert. We can go to the diner on Oceanfront, though, get both."

"Cool." Montana bumped their hips together. "How are you feeling? Did you do okay driving?"

"I walked, actually. It's such a nice day, you know?" It had nothing to do with the slight ache in his shoulder.

His boy frowned. "Uh-huh... Let's get you home. I'll make sandwiches."

"No, I want to take you out. I'm fine, love."

"I don't know. You should be careful..."

"Walking and eating don't put any strain on it, and when we get home I'll let you check the stitches, change the dressing."

"Are you sure?" Montana's hand was on his back, moving in slow circles.

"I'm sure." He grinned at Montana. "Who knew you'd be such a nurse?"

Those dark eyes shot up at him. "I just worry."

"It wasn't a complaint, love."

"No? Okay. Did you see the new papers? They're made out of grasses."

"No shit?"

"Yeah. They smell really amazing."

Billy chuckled. "Well, as long as you're not smoking them," he teased.

"Dork. I wouldn't."

He laughed and hugged Montana to him.

Montana pressed close for a second, then pulled back. "How was your day?"

"I got two editorials in and dithered with a third. I missed you, though."

"I worried about you all morning."

"I hope I'm not going to have to start doing cartwheels to convince you that I truly am fine."

"No. I just... You were shot. I don't want to hurt you." A police officer drove by and Montana went stiff. The cop didn't slow or look at all.

Billy couldn't blame Montana for it, but he wished it wasn't so. It galled him still, made him so angry that the cops, who were supposed to protect the city's citizens, had deliberately and willfully led Montana into danger. That they'd used him. Billy patted Montana's arm.

"I'm okay." Montana gave him a shaky smile.

"It's okay if you're not."

He got a surprised look. "What?"

"It's okay if you're rattled when you see the cops, or they bring up bad memories. It's okay to not be okay."

Montana shook his head, just a bit.

"It is." He growled a little to show he was serious.

He saw Montana shiver, but noticed that Montana ignored him, as well. They got to the diner and he let it drop. For now. His boy had so much to learn, so many things.

They went to a booth, and he waited until Montana sat first and then took the menu from him. "I'll order today." Some things were better done at home, others could be done in public.

"What?" Montana's head tilted. "Are you okay?"

Billy chuckled and patted Montana's hand. "I'm fine, love. It's all a part of you being my boy."

"I... Can I ask you a question?"

"Of course."

"Has something changed? With us, I mean."

He reached out and took Montana's hand in his. "Yes. We've talked about this, about committing to each other fully, about deepening our Master/sub relationship."

"Yeah, but... I feel like you're following rules I don't know."

"Okay. How can I fix that? Would you like to speak to some of the other subs?" He wasn't sure how exactly to go about this; the men he'd known in the past had all known the score, searched him out because he was a Dom.

"No." That was sure, immediate. "No more people."

"Then talk to me. Ask me questions. Tell me when you're getting tripped up by something."

"I don't even know what I'm getting tripped up by. I just know that I went away and things are different now that I'm back." Montana reached out, took his hand. "I want to stay. I want to do everything right."

"That's what I want, too." He took a deep breath and

thought how to say this. "I realized, when Oliver drove you away, that if I'd done my job properly, if I'd been a proper Master to you and given you what you needed, that you would have had the confidence to tell Oliver he wasn't your Master and couldn't make you leave."

"He's got money, he's got a rep. He could make me. Besides, I was fucked up, scared and shit."

"If you had confidence in the Master/sub relationship, if you understood it fully, it wouldn't have mattered." He squeezed Montana's hand. "Besides, we were just playing house, and what you need is for us not to be playing. You need the lifestyle for real."

"But how do you know?"

"Because I can feel it in my bones. Because I can see it in the way you respond to me, to the things we do."

"Okay, but if we try it and we don't like it, we'll still be together, right?"

"Yes. I'm not going anywhere." Montana was going to like it, though.

"Okay. Me, too. Neither. Whatever. I want to be with you."

"Good. That's the most important thing." Billy smiled at Montana. "I love you."

"I love you, too." He got a grin. "So? What's for lunch? I'm starving."

"That's good to know before I order for you, hmm?" He chuckled and glanced at the menu. "We're having burgers and you're having yours with fries, I'm having mine with rings, and we can share."

"Cool." Montana grinned, stretched. "I want a root beer, too, please."

Billy raised an eyebrow. "You do, do you?"

Montana nodded, looking at him. "Yeah. That's cool, huh?"

"I did say I was going to order for you."

"Okay..."

"I liked it when you called me 'sir.'"

Montana shifted. "Yeah? It was... That's like, just ours."

"You don't like saying it in public?"

"I don't know. I thought... It's sort of in my head all the time. Does that make sense?"

"It does. That's because it's a part of who you are, who I am, and what we are together."

Montana sighed. "I'm trying to make it make sense."

"Sometimes what we feel is just... what we feel, whether it makes sense or not."

That seemed to make an impact, Montana nodding, looking sure. "Yeah. Yeah, I get that. Sometimes your heart knows stuff."

"Exactly."

He smiled and then looked up at the waitress at the counter, nodding to her to come get their order.

"Have you made a decision?" The waitress was a pretty little girl, all smiles at flirting glances at Montana. His lover didn't even seem to notice.

It was silly, but it made Billy glad that his lover was oblivious. "Yes. We'll both have burgers, fully dressed, one with fries, one with onion rings, and two root beers, please."

"You got it. Salads?"

"No, not today. We'll have dessert later, though."

"Good deal."

Montana was folding the napkins, making little animals. Her shoes make clickety-clack noises as she left their table.

"That's neat. Reminds me of the planes you made

from the soda cans."

"I don't miss doing those." Montana winked at him, handing him a napkin giraffe.

Chuckling, he moved it across the table. "The giraffe travels the wild plains of Africa."

Montana laughed, creating a lion and a horse in short order. "There, a zoo."

"You don't see many horses in a zoo, do you? We need a pen—to draw on zebra stripes."

"Yeah. Although I've seen wild horses in a zoo before."

"Now, that just doesn't seem right." Wild horses ought to be, well, wild.

Montana nodded. "It was sad. My uncle and his friends broke in and freed them."

That had him smiling. "Good. Looks like you had some interesting role models."

Montana shrugged. "Growing up on the res is different."

"Yeah?"

Montana didn't talk about his past much—Billy always encouraged any confidences.

Montana nodded. "It's like a different place. We had our own schools, our own law. We didn't have plumbing, even."

"I can't imagine not being able to go to the bathroom, let alone not showering..."

"There was an outhouse with a chemical toilet. We used to sneak into the locker room at the high school to shower."

"Wow." No wonder the street hadn't seemed that bad to Montana. Even at his worst, Billy had always had amenities.

"Yeah. It was okay. It wasn't just us; it was everybody."

"Makes a difference, doesn't it?"

"Yeah. You don't know different, 'cept for the TV." Montana shrugged. "I got out for a while."

"Because of the racing." He was going to pull every detail out of Montana that his lover was willing to share.

"Yeah." He got a quick grin. "I liked it. I could go fucking fast. Made real money there for a while."

"And then your sister..." He let the words fade off, hoping Montana would finish the sentence, that maybe they'd learn something new.

"When she died, all the money got used. All the sponsors went away. I came west."

He nodded and patted Montana's hand. "And it's still a blank—what happened, I mean?"

"Yeah. The doctors say it's gone from banging my head on the pavement—it might never come back. I just got little flashes of that day, maybe. The whole week is gone."

"Are you still beating yourself up over what happened?"

"Huh? Man, I killed my sister, fucked up a whole career. It sorta deserves being sorry."

"I still don't think it's as black and white as that." He didn't trust the secondhand accounts of what had happened, not for a second.

"Yeah, but you love me. You believe I'm better than I am."

"I do love you, but I don't think I believe you're better than you are." He pursed his lips for a moment. "I see the potential in you to be amazing."

"I think that's sort of amazing."

He shook his head. "You're something special." His boy's cheeks went bright red. He squeezed Montana's hand. "It's just the truth, hmm?"

"Thanks, Billy."

The moment was interrupted by their food, the smell of the burgers making both their stomachs growl. They dug in, both of them eating eagerly. They shared the fries and onion rings, though they mock fought for the last few rings, Billy nearly choking as he laughed.

Montana laughed with him, eyes warm, happy, and lit up. God, his boy was beautiful, especially when he was happy. Billy drank the last of his root beer and sat back with a satisfied sigh.

"Did you leave room for ice cream?"

"Always. I love ice cream."

"I've noticed." He considered and then decided. "We'll share a banana split."

"Oh, cool!" Montana looked suddenly young.

He loved being able to make Montana forget everything and return to a happy, simple place.

"Do you like whipped cream on yours?" Montana asked.

"Yep. I'm going to ask her for two cherries, too."

"You like those a lot?"

"No, one for you and one for me."

"Cool. Which flavors do you like best?"

"I'm old fashioned. All vanilla with chocolate, butterscotch, and strawberry sauces. Whipped cream, nuts, and a cherry, all on a split banana." Sometimes the classics were the best.

"No, banana splits are strawberry, pineapple and chocolate."

"Oh, I don't know about that... I suppose I could give up the butterscotch. For you."

"I've never tried butterscotch."

"Oh, it's yummy. We'll save it for some other time when it's not overshadowed by the whole banana split experience."

"Have you ever played truth or dare?" Now that had come out of nowhere.

"When I was a lot younger." Billy tilted his head. "Why do you ask?"

Montana chuckled. "I got dared once to deep throat a banana."

"Oh, I can think of much better things to deep throat than a banana." That earned him a laugh, a nod. "Did you want to play?"

"That could be dangerous with you."

He nodded, grinned. "It could. You did bring it up."

"Okay. You go first. Truth or dare."

He figured Montana wanted to talk, but did he want to lay a dare or two on as well?

"Dare," he decided.

"Uh. I dare you to..." Montana chewed his bottom lip. "This is hard. I dare you to... I don't know, Billy."

Billy chuckled. "All right, I'll choose truth, then."

"Tell me what you want more than anything, right now."

That was easy. "For you to believe in yourself."

Montana ducked his head, blushed dark, dark. He reached out to touch Montana's hand, giving his lover, his boy, that connection. Montana squeezed his finger.

"Do you want to go on?"

"Sure. Sure, we're just going to have dessert."

He waved to the waitress. "I did mean the game."

"Me, too."

"Oh, cool." He smiled at Montana and then at the waitress. "We'd like to share a banana split, please. Two cherries."

"Absolutely. Another root beer?"

"No, we're good, thank you."

"Can I have a glass of water, please?" At his look, Montana shrugged. "Ice cream always makes me thirsty."

"Make it two, then."

Once she'd gone, Billy twined their fingers together again. "So? Truth or dare?"

"Truth."

"What scares you the most?"

Tanny's lips twisted. "Fucking up."

"In general or at something specific?" No wonder his boy worried on everything so hard.

"Everything. Man, I fuck so much up. I get tired, you know?"

"I think you fuck up far less than you think you do." He sat back and regarded Montana seriously. "What's the last thing you fucked up?"

"This whole police deal."

Billy shook his head. "How is that your fuck up?"

"You got shot. I ended up in Oregon. Oliver's life's fucked up..."

"And you shot the gun, handed over your key to Oliver, made the assumptions Oliver did. That was all your doing, was it?"

"Don't be an asshole. It was all my fault because I'm the junkie."

"That's not true." Billy growled. "You've been clean since you moved in with me. That asshole cop forced you to do things for him you didn't want to do. You should have told me, yes, but otherwise, you didn't fuck this one up." Billy hit the table with his fist. He was pissed off at Montana taking on the weight of every single bad thing that happened around him.

Montana jumped, then stared at him. "Calm the fuck down, man. This is a game."

He took a breath, and then another. "I'm sorry. I just. You." He shook his head. "You were used, love. That makes you as much a victim in all this as anyone else, probably even more."

"Well, I don't want to be one no more."

"No, I know. And you don't have to be. You have someone in your corner. It's harder to make a victim of two people who stand together than two who stand alone."

"Was that English?" Montana winked at him.

"It was. We just stand together against the world, okay? You and me, not you all by yourself." Montana needed to understand that meant for everything, not just the good parts.

"You and me." Montana smiled at him, nodded. "I like that."

"Yeah, so do I." His hand slipped off the table as their waitress came back to set an enormous banana split in front of them, along with two spoons. "Oh, man. That's enormous."

"Yeah. Wow." Montana handed him a spoon. "Truth or dare."

"If I say dare, are you going to hem and haw again?"

"Nope. I'm going to make you try and tie a knot in the cherry stem with your tongue."

Laughing, he managed to nod and say, "Dare."

"I dare you to try to tie a knot in the cherry stem with your tongue." Montana was chuckling.

Billy shook his head. "I'll try."

He grabbed the cherry and held it out to Montana. "I want to watch you eat the actual cherry first." Montana reached for the cherry. "No, no. Just open up." He pressed the cherry to Montana's lower lip.

Those dark eyes went hot and his boy opened, tongue wrapping around the cherry. He groaned at the sight, his cock taking a sudden, sure interest. Montana tugged the cherry off the stem and he remembered, suddenly, that Montana was many things, but shy wasn't one of them.

He licked his lips. "Stunning." He could watch Montana do that all day long.

"I like cherries."

"You're very sexy when you eat them."

"You have a dare to do." Montana was beaming.

"You mean try. I've never been able to do this." He put the stem in his mouth and tried to figure out how to even begin.

Those dark eyes watched him, even as Montana took a spoonful of whipped cream and chocolate sauce and licked it off the spoon. That wasn't helping. At all. He groaned and tried to bend the stem between his tongue and the back of his lower teeth. He managed to pop it out of his mouth and it went flying toward Montana, landing on the banana split.

Montana's laughter was soft, gentle. "Good try." The stem was plucked off, put to one side.

"I just can't get the mechanics right."

"It takes practice. Want me to show you again?" At his nod, Montana took the other cherry stem in, then wiggled before sticking his tongue out, stem tied.

He shook his head. "That's amazing!" Billy grinned suddenly. "No wonder you're so good at blowing me."

"Dork." Montana grinned, going beet red.

"No, I don't think so." He was a man in love.

"So, whose turn is it?" Montana scooped up another bite.

"I think it's mine. Truth or dare?"

"Truth."

"Of the things we've done together—what did you like the best?"

"Do you mean sex or everything?"

The question surprised him, but he liked that Montana had made the distinction. "I'd like the answer for everything." He could ask about the sex later.

"I like when we have breakfast together on Sunday."

Smiling, he reached out and took Montana's hand. His lover never failed to surprise him, and the love he felt for Montana felt too big to stay inside him sometimes. Like now.

Montana held his hand, squeezed. "What about you?"

"I like that a lot, too, but I think my favorite is when you're wearing the leather cuffs and we're just together, sharing the peace."

His boy nodded. "I like together."

"Yeah." They sat for a moment or two before he shook himself. "Our ice cream is melting."

They laughed together, then started eating.

"You know you can talk to me anytime." Billy fed a chunk of banana with a dollop of ice cream on it to Montana.

"Mmm."

"And if you aren't comfortable just sitting and talking to me, you can always ask to play truth or dare and I'll know." Those dark eyes met his, and he thought he saw relief in them. He smiled, glad they'd hit on something that might make it easier for Montana.

"You want to finish our game at home? I'm full."

"Yeah, I think home would be more appropriate as we move into more dares, hmm?"

Montana nodded, and he got a grin. "If you feel up to it."

"I'm already up for it." He had been every since the cherry thing.

They paid, then headed out, arm-in-arm. It felt fucking fantastic. Billy figured he was the luckiest man on earth.

Sean Michael

Chapter Thirty-One

By the time they got home, Montana was worried that Billy was hurting. "Are you okay?"

Billy chuckled. "You're not getting out of continuing our game, love."

"I don't want you to hurt, though."

"Give me a couple of those pain pills and I'll be fine."

"Okay." Montana sat him down, found him pills and a drink.

"So good to me." Billy tugged Montana down next to him.

"I love you."

"It's mutual, love." Billy leaned them close together.

He searched Billy's eyes, making sure everything was really okay.

Billy leaned their foreheads together. "I promise, if anything starts hurting, I will let you know."

"Okay." He took a kiss.

Billy deepened it, opening his mouth with a warm tongue. He reached up, touched Billy's temple, stroked his lover's face.

Billy nuzzled into the touches. "Truth or dare, love?"

"Dare." He hummed softly, eyelids getting heavy.

"I dare you to get yourself off while I watch—and I

want lots of nipple action."

"What?" He wasn't even hard, really.

"You didn't hear me?"

"I did. I just... I'm not... you know." He should have picked truth.

"Interested? It shouldn't take much to change that."

He nodded and opened his jeans, a little bit disappointed that Billy would want it all over so fast. Still, Billy was tired and maybe wanted to rest, so he needed to get the game over with. Then, while Billy was napping, he could paint the kitchen.

Billy shifted, turned partly sideways, one fingers sliding on his collarbone. "Take your time, love."

He tried to think about something to make himself hard, but that wasn't doing it, so he just started working his cock, making his body do its thing while his mind wandered.

"You're not into this," murmured Billy.

"Huh? I told you I wasn't yet. I'm trying."

"No, stop." Billy gave him a wry smile. "That thing with the cherry got me all worked up, and I assumed you were, too."

His cheeks heated and he was suddenly embarrassed, ashamed. He tucked himself back up, got up to get Billy more water. "Sorry. I'll get more."

"Montana. Sit."

"You're out of water."

"I don't want any water; I want to have fun with you."

But he'd fucked that up by not getting hard fast enough. "I said I was sorry."

"You don't have to be sorry, Montana. We don't have to do that to have fun. Besides, I might have jumped the gun, I think it was your turn."

"I just... I wasn't. I wasn't ready." He sighed, sat down.

"That's all right. You just need to talk to me, hmm? Tell me things instead of trying to force it."

He shrugged. "I want to do it right."

"You're here, with me. That's right." Billy sighed. "Although I've somehow killed the mood, and I'm not even sure how."

"No. No, man. It's not your fault. I just... We walked and stuff and I wasn't... and then I was trying to..." Fuck. Fuck.

"It's okay, love. Really. We can start over, see if we can't catch it again."

"Okay. Okay." Jesus, he hated being nervous. "Truth or dare."

"Dare."

"Kiss me?" It was a pussy dare, but it would help both of them.

Billy leaned in immediately, lips soft and warm as they pressed against his. He pressed into Billy and kissed the man back, tickled beyond belief to know he'd been right. It did help, the kissing. Billy shifted, sitting back against the couch and bringing him along without breaking the lip and tongue-sucking kisses. Better. So much better.

He moaned into the kiss, letting their bodies rest together. Each kiss flowed into the next, some soft and barely there, most much deeper than that. All of his tension dissolved, his body fit perfectly in the curve of Billy's. The kissing went on and on, Billy not seeming to be in any hurry to stop. His hands explored Billy, first sliding up to caress the poor hurt shoulder, then down to pet Billy's hip. Billy rumbled beneath his touch, the sound happy.

He hummed, Tanny licking at Billy's lips. "Love you."

"Yeah, it makes the kisses better, doesn't it?"

"Don't know. I never kissed somebody I didn't love."

Billy got a goofy look on his face.

He rubbed their noses together. "It's your turn, love."

"Truth or dare, Montana?"

"Truth, this time."

"Hmm... this time we'll go with what's your favorite thing we do sexually."

He cuddled in, thought about it. "I like a lot of it. Most of it. I like making you come, sucking you."

"Oh, I like that, too." Billy kissed him. "But what's your favorite?"

"I don't know if I can answer that. There are things I like to do, there are things I need to do. There are things that blow my mind. There are things I want that scare me. The thing I like every day, though, is the kissing, the holding each other."

Billy's mouth found his, tongue tickling his teeth, then Billy drew back and grinned. "You realize you just gave me fodder for the next six times you say truth?"

"Huh?" He took another kiss. "Truth or dare?"

Billy considered for a moment. "Let's go with truth."

"What's your favorite thing, sex-wise?"

"When I come inside you and then plug you, keeping me inside you."

He groaned, hips jerking instinctively.

"Mmmhmm." Billy's fingers slid from his throat to his belly. He scooted into the touch, body aching.

"Truth or dare?" Billy whispered.

"Dare." He nuzzled into Billy's throat. "Although truth is... hot."

Billy chuckled, the sound throat and sexy. "So is it dare, or is it truth?"

"Yeah..." He found the perfect spot on Billy's throat and started sucking.

That laugh sounded again and Billy tilted his head back. "What... what things blow your mind?"

"When you push me, when you put your hand in me, other times..." He shut himself up by sucking harder.

"What—What other times?"

"I don't... when you..." He groaned, nibbling on Billy's skin.

"When I what?"

"When you..." He shuddered and scooted closer.

"Oh, God. Tell me."

"When you spank me, when you make me." He bit down on Billy's collarbone. "When you're my sir."

Billy jerked and grabbed his head. "I'm always your sir."

"Always?"

"Always."

"Truth or dare." He held on, clinging.

"Truth, my boy."

"Why do you call me your boy?" Why did it make him so hard?

"Because you're my submissive. Because you're mine."

He nodded without thinking. Billy's.

"Truth or dare."

"Truth..." He was beginning to rock, to move against Billy's thigh. This was hot, intense, intimate.

"What things do you want that scare you?" Billy's hand slid around to his ass, encouraging his movements.

"I want to... I want you to... Billy. It's when you make me and I want it."

Billy framed his face. "That's because you're my boy."

He nodded, aching a little. "That makes me ache."

"It's a good ache." It wasn't a question—Billy knew.

"Yes." They were breathing together, moving together.

"No coming until I say so."

Tanny nodded. He wanted, but he wasn't in trouble, wasn't that close. Yet. "Is that a dare?"

"No, it's an order."

Tanny lifted his head, met Billy's eyes. "Oh."

"Yes. Oh." Billy's hand went back to his ass. "Don't stop."

"I want you." Tanny's eyelids felt so heavy.

"Good. That's good."

"Are we still playing?" He stole a kiss.

"Sure." Billy's lips captured his. "Truth or dare."

"Dare." He moaned into the kiss.

"Okay. Um." Billy kept kissing him. "You should, um..."

"Uh-huh..." He unfastened Billy's jeans, fingers searching for the hard cock.

Groaning, Billy pushed into his touch. "Dare you to wear... my ring."

"Your ring?" He licked his lips, fingers wrapping around Billy's cock, stroking.

"My ring. Your perineum. Forever promise." Billy gasped out the words, bucking and pushing into his hand.

He didn't understand exactly, but he nodded, trusting Billy with all he was. "Anything."

"Thank you." Billy closed his eyes, hips moving fast and hard.

"Love you." He wanted Billy to come for him, to feel so good.

"Love!" Billy cried out, face frozen for a long moment as heat poured up over his fingers.

Tanny groaned, brought his hand to his mouth, licked

the bittersalt of Billy's seed.

"God, that's sexy."

He ducked his head, cheeks heated.

"Look at me, Montana."

He slowly brought his eyes up to Billy's, vibrating.

"You are sexy and gorgeous and you turn me on very much." Billy grinned, hand squeezing his ass. "Truth or dare?"

"Truth." Wait? Was it his turn?

"If I tell you to come, right now, without a touch to your cock, will you?"

"I don't know." He pressed closer. "I never have." His balls ached, though.

"Even if you don't today, eventually you will. That's what the cage training is all about." Billy nuzzled his neck. "Doesn't it sound hot? You coming, just because I said so?"

He arched, nodded, and lifted his chin, begging more kisses. Billy gave them, mouth devouring his whole. He reached down, unfastened his jeans to let his cock free.

Billy growled softly. "I didn't say you could do that yet."

"Huh? It aches."

"No touching—you're going to have to wait. It's your turn."

"My turn?" God, he wanted.

"Yes. To ask me 'truth or dare.' The game?"

"Sorry. Sorry, right. Truth or dare?"

Chuckling, looking relaxed and happy, and slightly wicked, Billy answered, "Dare."

"Touch me?"

Billy raised an eyebrow and slid one hand along his neck, fingertips barely dancing along his skin and making him shiver. "My turn—truth or dare?"

He moaned at the simple, perfect touch. "Love your hands... Dare. Dare, Billy."

Sir.

Billy looked into his eyes, grinned. "Take out your cock and stroke yourself at least five times. No coming."

"Mean." He took his cock in hand, stroked it twice, then groaned. So much different than before. So hot. So fine. The third stroke had him grabbing his balls.

"Two more." Billy's voice was thick, aroused. Again. Because of him.

"Love you." He managed the two strokes, panting hard, aching.

"I know." Billy's hand took his, pried it away from his cock. "Well done."

He arched, body wanting the touch, needing it. Billy twisted their fingers together, pressed them against the couch.

"Need you."

Billy simply nodded. "Dare."

"Help me. Help me, sir."

"You're going to have to be more specific."

"Touch me. Fuck me. I need to come."

"Not until I say so. Besides, 'touch me' and 'fuck me' are two different dares. Which one?" Billy was doing it on purpose.

He groaned in pure frustration, then closed his eyes, made himself try to chill out.

"Shh." Billy nuzzled his neck and then blew on his skin, making a shiver go through his body. "Take a deep breath and tell me which one."

"Touch me. Touch me." Then they could fuck after.

Billy's hands let go of his and slid through his hair,

cupping and caressing his scalp. He leaned into the touch, hips still rocking even as he loved the sensations. Soft kisses pressed against his eyelids and Billy's hands came around to stroke his cheeks. He turned his head, sucking in one of Billy's thumbs, pulling rhythmically.

"Sexy lover."

He moaned and sucked harder. More. More, please. Billy's free hand slid down, finding his nipple piercings through his T-shirt. He cried out, working Billy's thumb, hands reaching for his cock.

"No touching," growled Billy, hands leaving him.

"Billy... Billy, please..."

"Truth or dare."

"Dare." Anything.

Billy gave him a single word. "Come."

He jerked, spunk pouring out of him, his entire body convulsing. Groaning, Billy swiped a hand through the come on his cock and brought it up. His lips were painted with it, and then Billy licked it off. He sobbed softly, a little overwhelmed, a lot lost.

"Shh, shh." Billy nuzzled and held him. Tanny curled in, staying close, trusting in Billy's arms. "I love you." Billy kissed the top of his head and held him tight.

"Love." He was starting to blink, to doze. "I can't be sleepy."

Billy laughed. "Why not?"

"'Cause I slept all weekend." He was, though.

"So what? You had an orgasm, now you need a nap. It happens."

"Mmmhmm." He nodded, not really listening anymore.

"Sleep, love. We've got the rest of the day."

He wasn't sure what they needed it for, but they had it and... Before Tanny finished his thought, he was asleep.

Chapter Thirty-Two

Billy arranged to meet Montana at the tattoo parlor after work. Treat had assured him it wouldn't be very busy at that time, and he and Montana could take their time picking out their jewelry and getting Montana's guiche piercing. He glanced at his watch as he waited. He hated waiting, but he'd been early, entirely his own fault.

He saw Montana across the street, looking, then looking at his watch. It was still ten minutes before they were supposed to meet. Montana went into a bookstore, which surprised him. Billy knew Montana's reading ability still wasn't stellar. He was curious as hell, but he didn't follow Montana in; he just needed to wait another ten minutes and he was sure the mystery would be solved.

He did go into the coffee store a few shops down and ordered himself a hot chocolate with whipped cream on it. Montana brought something out, dropped it in the mailbox, then checked his watch again. Billy waited until Montana looked up and then waved.

Montana's eyes went wide, then he was given a huge, warm smile. "You're early!"

"Yeah, I miscalculated," he said as Montana crossed the street and came toward him. "You're early, too."

"Yep. I had a couple things to do. What did you order?"

"Hot chocolate, extra whipped cream. You want a sip or two?" And what went into the mail?

"No, I think I'll get a latte. You want a cookie? Breakfast seems like years ago."

"You should probably wait on food and too much drink until you've had the piercing done."

"You think I'll puke?"

"You were okay with the nipple rings, so no. But I think we shouldn't tempt fate."

"Okay. After, though?" Montana sighed. "You ready??

"Yeah, after." He kissed the top of Montana's head. "Yes, I'm ready. Let's go find the perfect ring."

"Okay." Montana looped their arms together. "Don't forget your drink."

He grabbed it and they headed into the tattoo parlor. He still wanted to know what Montana mailed. "So what were you doing at the bookstore?" He asked it as casually as he could.

"Buying a pretty card and one of those gift card things for Heather, to say thank you for letting me stay and stuff. Margaret said that she'd like that a lot."

"Oh, that was sweet of you. Did Margaret give you an advance on your salary?" He still handled all of Montana's money.

"No." Montana's cheeks went a little red.

Billy frowned. "Then how did you pay for it?"

"I made some airplanes for the shop."

"Ah. And they paid you cash for them." He held the door open for his lover.

"Yeah. I needed some cash that was just mine."

"The cash I bank for you is all yours, love. All of

it." He waved at Treat and headed toward the jewelry counter.

"No, that's for bills and stuff. I need money for things."

"Okay." He was pleased, actually, that Montana felt comfortable having some of his own money.

Montana nodded, relaxing for him.

"Hi, Treat." He held out his hand to the piercer.

"William. So nice to see you again." The lean man smiled, nodded.

"You remember Montana, I'm sure." He pulled Montana in close, hand on his lover's hip.

"Of course I do." Montana's hand was taken, shaken. "You're interested in a guiche?"

Billy nodded, beamed. "Yes. A commitment ring."

"You want plastic? Metal? Gold?"

"Gold, I think. We'd like to look at our options."

"Of course. Peter-love, William would like to look at all our jewelry."

Billy smiled at Treat and Killian's sub and tugged Montana over to see with him. There were dozens of different rings—big ones, tiny ones, colored ones. "Which one appeals to you, love?"

"A little one."

He chuckled. "Not too little. I want to be able to get my tongue into it."

Peter smiled at them, winked. "You might try big enough for chains and fingers. If they're too small, those types of things are really irritating."

"Oh, we definitely want it to be big enough for fingers, don't we, Montana?"

"I..." Montana gave him a wide-eyed look. "Do we?"

He nodded, squeezed Montana's hip. "We do. This isn't just ornamental. I want to be able to play."

Montana gave him that wild-eyed look again, but didn't argue. Poor love. He was going to love it, though.

"I like the plain gold ones, or maybe one with a bead. What do you like?"

"The plain ones, I think. I like the silver ones, but I'll never see it."

"That doesn't matter—you have to wear it, so it's important that you like it."

Montana looked at him, suddenly serious. "Billy, it's our ring. I'll like it."

He cupped Montana's chin. "All right, thank you."

"Oh..." The exclamation was soft, but he looked over and Peter was cuddled into Killian's side, beaming. Treat's attention was split between his lovers and Billy and Montana.

Billy chuckled. "We'll have a plain silver ring, large enough it'll take my fingers."

"Excellent. If you'll take him back, my friend, we'll put him in the stirrups, and the entire area needs to be shaved."

"I can take care of that." He was, in fact, looking forward to it.

"I thought you could. Just press the button by the door when you're ready for me."

"Thanks, Treat."

Billy led Montana to the room in the back. Montana didn't say anything, didn't babble, was just quiet, drawn into himself.

"Are you worried about anything?" Billy led him to the chair with the stirrups.

"I'm okay." Uh-huh.

"Do we need to play truth or dare?"

Those dark eyes met his, and Montana opened his

mouth, then he got a single nod.

"Okay. I'm going to start." He pulled up a chair next to the one Montana was sitting in. "Truth or dare?"

"Truth." Good boy.

"Tell me what you're worried about with the piercing process today."

"I don't want someone touching me there that's not you. That's yours, now. I'm not worried about it hurting, but..." Montana sighed, rolled his eyes. "What if I fart?"

"If this was a doctor's visit, would you have the same qualms?"

"I don't know. Probably."

"Because Treat is a professional. I'll be doing the shaving, then we'll cover everything with one of those hospital sheet type things. The only part exposed will be the skin behind your balls." He squeezed Montana's hand. "Treat has his lovers—there won't be anything sexual about it. And if you fart—say excuse me."

Montana squeezed him back. "It'll be fast, right?"

"It'll be very fast. Treat knows what he's doing." He brought Montana's hand up to his lips and kissed it. "Truth or dare?"

"It's my turn to ask."

He chuckled. "All right, I'll take truth."

"What excites you most about the ring?"

"I think it's a tie between the symbolism of it—our commitment ring—and the way it's going to make you feel when I play with it."

"You think it'll be hot?"

"Oh, yes." He nodded enthusiastically. "Extremely. Truth or dare?"

"Truth."

"Is there anything else you're worried about?"

"I'm hungry and I'm a little wigged about the money thing."

He tilted his head. "You mean that you had control of your own cash?"

"Yeah. I don't know what to think about it."

He nodded. "It's something we can talk about at home, hmm?"

"Maybe, yeah. I don't know."

"Is there anything else about the guiche?" He didn't want to brush Montana's worries aside, but they were here for the piercing, it really needed to take precedence.

"It's going to be weird, inside me."

"It'll be wonderful." He slid his hand over Montana's chest and touched the nipple ring, the barbell.

"Let's just get it over."

He kissed Montana softly and started undoing his jeans. "I brought you some sweatpants. So you had something loose and easy to wear when it's done."

"Okay. Thank you." Montana helped him, the lean hips and belly exposed to him.

He stroked Montana's belly and then helped put his feet in the stirrups. "Very interesting. I wonder if we could get some for the bed..." He waited a beat and then gave Montana a wink.

"Jackass." Montana chuckled, cheeks bright pink.

Grinning, he found the shaving cream and the razor already set out for him, along with a pair of scissors. Montana had squeezed his eyes closed tight, breath coming fast. "I'm going to be very careful." It was going to be intimate and sexy, but not painful.

"You won't hurt me."

The sincere faith in those words made him smile up at Montana and nod. "That's right."

Montana hummed, visibly trying to relax.

Billy had been considering drawing this out, having fun with it, but Montana's nerves were running high enough. He didn't figure making his boy hard and playing with him at this juncture would be helpful. So he simply shaved the area carefully and quickly.

He patted Montana dry, then covered Montana's cock with a towel, put the sheet with the hole over Montana's legs, and pushed the button.

Treat came in a moment later, smiling. "All ready?" He was looking at Montana's face as he asked.

"As ready as I'm going to be, huh?"

Billy smiled and took Montana's hand. "Go ahead, Treat."

"It'll go quickly." Treat settled between Montana's legs and Montana tensed.

"Just relax as much as you can, love. It goes easier if you do." He leaned in to whisper into Montana's ear. "I'm sure a spanking hurts more."

"Do you want a blow-by-blow?" Treat asked.

Montana shook his head. "No, man. Just do your thing."

"With this ring, I thee wed." Billy hadn't realized he was going to say the words, but now that he had, they sounded right.

"Love you, huh?" Montana winked at him, then winced.

He squeezed Montana's hand tight and held his own breath.

It was almost anticlimactic, the way that Treat stood, smiled. "You know to watch for infection, hmm?"

"Yes. And how long for it to heal?" Montana's skin would be sensitive, but he didn't want to cause undue pain.

"To touch? Just be careful. No heavy, heavy play for three or four weeks."

"We can manage that, wouldn't you say, Montana?"

"Yeah. I'll be out in a minute, huh? Let me get dressed."

"I can help you with that, love."

"Whatever. I'm cool."

I'm cool. The universal Montana phrase for being stressed and nervous and out of his comfort zone.

"We'll be out in a moment to pay, Treat."

"Take your time." Treat headed out, closed the door behind him.

"Do you need anything?" He grabbed Montana's sweats.

Montana shook his head. "I'm cool."

He snorted at the repetition of the words, but figured they'd be better off taking care of anything that needed taking care of at home. "Let's go, then." He pushed the sweatpants over Montana's feet and slowly pulled up his lover's legs.

"Okay. I'll be right there."

"Uh-huh." He slid his hand along Montana's shoulders, rubbed. Montana stopped, leaned into his touch. "You're wearing my ring," he said quietly, feeling pride and happiness.

"Uh-huh. I am. I've never been somebody's before."

"You're mine now, though." He brought their mouths together for a long kiss.

Montana moaned into his kiss, leaned back toward his touch. He deepened the kiss. His. His boy. His hand wrapped around Montana's shoulder and held on tight.

"We... we should go home."

"Yeah." He stroked Montana's cheek. "Time to take my boy home." That cheek heated under his touch and he wanted to push, wanted his boy submissive and aching and desperate for him. "We need to get home. Now."

"Okay." Montana nodded, offered him a grin. "No stopping for lunch?"

He supposed he could turn lunch into its own kind of torture. It certainly would be for him. "Hungry?"

"No. I was, but now, I just want to be home."

Smiling, he nodded and slid his finger along Montana's lower lip. "Me, too."

"Okay. I don't know how I'll sit in the car."

"Carefully." He winked.

"Butthead!" Montana's laughter filled the air.

He laughed as well, leading Montana out so he could pay the bill. He had one of those plastic donut things in the car.

Peter was at the counter, all smiles. "All done?"

"We are, thanks. So how much do we owe your Master for his excellent work?"

"Fifty-five."

Billy pulled out his credit card and handed it over. "Is that all? What about the jewelry?"

"Treat says it's a commitment gift from us."

"Oh, thank him for us, Peter."

"Yes, sir. I will." Those lovely eyes met Montana's. "It was nice to meet you."

"Yeah. Cool."

There was that word again. His sweet boy needed some privacy to deal with what they'd just done. He nodded at Peter, took Montana's hand and let him out toward the car. Montana moved carefully, cheeks hot.

"Painful?" He opened the back door first, grabbing the donut and putting it in the passenger seat.

"A little. Sorta."

"Sitting should be okay with that." He helped Montana sit. "When we get home, you won't have to sit. Not at all."

"No?"

"Oh, no. I have plans for you that definitely don't involve sitting."

Montana pinked, sat gingerly.

"Squirming, yes. Pleading and begging, oh yes." He grinned as he sat and did up his seat belt. "Lots of plans. No sitting."

Montana's groan made his cock throb.

"Can you wait 'til we get home?" he teased.

"Yeah. I just need a few minutes alone."

"For what?"

"Stuff. To touch it. To just deal."

"You need a handheld mirror so you can look." He reached out and touched Montana's knee. "You don't have to deal alone."

"I... I don't know what to say to that."

"What you mean is 'I don't like talking about things.'"

"You love talking about things."

"With you, yes." They started the short drive home. "Truth or dare?"

"D...dare." Oh, Montana was really resisting talking about how he was feeling about things.

"I dare you to... get yourself hard."

"In the car?"

"Yes."

Montana nodded but didn't touch himself, just leaned back and closed his eyes.

He glanced over. "Love?"

"Uh-huh?"

"What are you doing?"

"Remembering."

"Oh." He smiled, taking the long way around to get home. "What are you remembering?"

"What I always remember when I need to get excited."

"And what's that?" They'd discussed it before, but things might have changed. Besides, he liked hearing about it.

"What if it's a secret?"

"Why would that be a secret from me?"

Montana turned, smiled at him. "I don't guess it is, really. I'm just used to my thoughts being only mine."

"I like knowing your thoughts. I like knowing everything about you."

"I know. It's weird."

He laughed and shook his head. "No, it isn't. It's romantic. Now tell me what you remember to get turned on."

"Isn't that another dare?" Montana hummed softly. "I remember when you put your hand inside me, about how you felt..."

Billy groaned, his own cock responding immediately. Yes, Montana had mentioned that before. It was hot, sexy to hear his lover saying the words, though.

"Sometimes I think about other things, but it's that a lot."

"It's a very sexy memory." He tightened his hands on the steering wheel. "Is it working?"

"Uh-huh. Truth or dare?"

"I'm driving, so I'd better take truth." He was pretty sure he knew what was coming.

"What do you think about when you want to get hard?"

He grinned. That hadn't changed much since the last

time they'd talked about it, either. "You. The things I want to do with you. Your submission."

"What does that mean? I mean, what do you want?"

"I want you to be happy, Montana. I know that submission will make you happy. Finding that place of peace."

"I don't know if you're right, but I want to be with you anyway. No matter what."

"That trust is part of what tells me that I am." He reached over and squeezed Montana's leg again. "We're almost there, let's save the next 'truth or dare' for when we get home."

"Okay." Montana squeezed his fingers.

He pulled into a spot near the house and turned off the engine. "Home again, home again. Come on. We have a ring to explore, to talk about, to enjoy."

"Is it cool with you if I'm feeling a little wigged out?"

"Yep. Your feelings are always valid, Montana. That's part of why I want to talk about it, hmm?" They headed up the stairs, Billy keeping the pace slow.

"Uh-huh." Montana headed straight for the bathroom when they got in.

He followed, stopping to grab a handheld mirror from the bedroom as he went.

"Truth or dare?" he asked as he got to the bathroom.

"Truth." Montana's hand was on the door. "I think I need a second."

"All right." He handed Montana the mirror and took a step back. "Two minutes, and then I'm coming in."

"Okay." Montana closed the door, then he heard a clink, a soft gasp, and a chuckle, then the water started.

He counted impatiently to a hundred and twenty in his head, and then knocked, just to let Montana know he was coming in, and opened the door. Montana was in the shower—naked, water pouring down around him. Groaning, Billy stood in the doorway and watched for a few moments.

Montana was washing himself, eyes closed, hands moving over his lean muscles in long caresses. His boy was fucking stunning. Amazing. Beautiful. Billy began to strip. Montana was wearing his ring. The thought made him ache.

He went to the shower and stepped in.

"Hey. Sorry. I needed to get my head on. I'm okay now."

He chuckled. "Your head is right there."

"Thanks for noticing."

"That's my job, you know. Noticing you." He reached out, his hands joining Montana's on that fine, slick skin.

"Whose turn is it?"

"Yours. Truth or dare?" He wasn't entirely sure that it was Montana's turn, but it needed to be Montana's turn, so he went with it.

"Truth."

"How are you feeling?"

"Wet. Shivery. A little like..." Montana shrugged, sighed. "I don't know how to say it."

He rubbed Montana's shoulders. "Try."

"I want. I feel like I'm waiting."

"What are you waiting for?"

"I don't know." Those dark eyes met his, a touch desperate. "Have you ever felt like something big was happening, but you don't quite understand it?"

He nodded. "You've got the symbol, now you need the deed."

"Huh?" Jesus, that trust, that curiosity, was perfect.

"The ring is the symbol of our commitment. You're wearing it, and now I need to do something so that you feel it here." He put his hand on Montana's heart.

"I don't know. I just know that I feel... like I'm waiting."

He pulled Montana in close and pressed their lips together, kissing Montana hard. His boy opened up to him, moaned into his lips. He slid his hands over Montana's skin, the soap making everything slick.

It was Friday. He had the weekend, possibly through Monday to keep his boy busy, focused, needing him. He bit at Montana's lips, putting a little sting into the kisses. Montana whimpered, then opened for him. He rubbed his palm over the ringed nipple, his little finger catching in it and tugging. He felt the groan, felt Montana's skin tighten.

He rolled the other nipple beneath his fingers, then played with the barbell, tugging it, pushing it through Montana's nipple and back again. It was only a tiny way, but it was enough to provide a huge sensation. Montana's cock grew, filling against his thigh.

"No coming until I say you can." Hard was good, coming was not allowed. And for now, he wanted Montana to not come just because that's what Billy demanded. Later they'd get out the cage, bind Montana to the bed.

"Why?" Montana rocked, eyes focused on him.

"Because I said so."

His boy rippled, jerked against him. Yeah, Montana liked that. He stroked his lover's belly, fingers lingering as they always did over his name.

"Yours." Yes. Yes, he knew. Now Montana needed to understand.

Wrapping his hand around Montana's prick, he began to stroke.

"Fuck... Billy, easy."

He shook his head. "No, love. That's my call."

"You'll make me come."

"No, you won't come."

"I..." He got a confused look.

"I said you couldn't, so you won't." They'd been working on this. With the cage.

"Okay. I. Why? Why don't you want me to?"

"Because having control over your orgasm is a good thing."

He felt Montana shiver. "I don't understand you. I need you, though. I do."

"That's what's important—that you know what you want. That I give it to you." He played with the slit of Montana's cock, finger pushing against it and moving side to side.

"Fuck!" Montana grunted, pulled away. "Stop..."

"Oh, I don't think so." He tugged Montana in close again, fingers carefully exploring the hard, hot cock.

"Billy..." Montana squeezed his eyes closed, lips open as he panted.

He let go of Montana's cock to grab hold of his lover's balls. He stroked, rolled, fondled.

"My knees are shaking."

"We'll move to the bedroom soon."

"Soon."

Montana pushed closer and took his lips in a fierce kiss. He grabbed hold of Montana's tongue and sucked hard. His boy fought him for control of the kiss, arching into him and rubbing. Growling, he grabbed Montana's hands and tugged them behind his lover's back. Their kiss got wilder, hotter. Montana was right with him, hungry for this.

He tugged on Montana's hands so his lover was bowed back, his tongue pushing hard into Montana's mouth. He had to be careful—the tub was slick and his shoulder was still tricky, but, even arched back, Montana was taking care of him.

He bit the tip of Montana's tongue and growled the order, "Come."

Heat sprayed between them, Montana sobbing softly into his lips.

"I have you, love. I have you."

"Help me."

"I am." He always would.

Montana nodded, breath slowing.

He straightened them both, taking one soft kiss after another. He eased Montana out of the tub, drying them before moving them toward the bedroom. He lay Montana down on the bed and stepped back for a moment to admire. Montana's legs were carefully held apart, the sweet belly bare and tight. Smiling, he grabbed Montana's ankles and slowly pushed them back, exposing that sweet bit of flesh. The skin was bare, a tiny bit swollen around the ring.

"Beautiful." He looked up into Montana's eyes. "Mine."

"Yeah. Yeah, I am. Yours."

"For always, Montana. No matter what happens, no matter what anyone else says." He needed Montana to know that, to believe it.

"I don't want to let you down."

"You won't." There wasn't a test. Montana wasn't going to let him down by pushing, by needing, by loving.

"Promise?"

"I swear it to you, Montana. You are mine and nothing will change that, ever."

"I was scared." Those dark eyes held his. "I was scared because you're my home and I'm happy here, I love you."

"I love you, too. And that will never change." He let Montana's legs go and climbed onto the bed to take Montana's cheeks between his hands. He stared hard into Montana's eyes. He didn't want there to be any mistake about his next words.

"Nothing anyone says to you or about you can take that away. I don't care who tells you that you have to leave—you don't, because this is your home, too, and no one has the right to tell you to leave. I don't care who tells you to leave me alone—that isn't what I want. Not before, not now, not ever. No one speaks for me. No one is your lover, your Master, and your partner but me. Got it?"

Montana nodded. "And no one is yours, either. No one wants you to be happy as much as me. I gave up being high for you."

"I know. And you do make me happy, Montana. More than anything ever has. More than I even thought possible."

"Good." Montana never looked away. "Good, Billy."

"Yes, it is good."

He leaned in and brought their mouths together. The kiss was hard, fierce, as he laid his claim on Montana. The kiss was deep, and he felt it all through himself. He took Montana's wrists in his hands and held them together above his boy's body. Enough playing. He needed Montana to be home, here, his. Now.

He gave Montana a last hard kiss and went over to the

drawers, pulling out silk rope, extra lube, a plug, and a cock ring. Montana looked over at him, eyes curious.

"I know you remember your safeword."

Montana nodded. "Yeah."

"Good. Use it if you need it, but only if you need it."

"Okay. Will I need to?"

"I don't know. I'm going to push you, but you can take a lot, more than you believe, even."

Montana shrugged, looking uncomfortable. "Okay."

"This is what you need, love." He sat next to his lover and brought Montana's wrists together in front of him. His boy had long fingers, beautiful skin, even with the scars. He wrapped the rope around Montana's wrists, careful not to make it too tight, but it wasn't loose enough Montana could slip his hands out, either.

"What are we doing?"

"I'm going to tie you up, put the cock ring on you, and make you scream—for the very best reasons."

"Okay. Is your shoulder up to it?"

He grinned. "I'm fine, love. And I'll be careful."

"Okay. I worry about you."

"Thank you." He touched Montana's cheek and then carefully brought his lover's bound arms up over his head and looped the end of the rope around the headboard. He secured it, making sure nothing was straining. Montana trusted him implicitly, not even tensing under his touch. "I'm not going to do your legs today—I don't want to aggravate the piercing."

He put his finger through the ring on Montana's nipple and tugged it. "When the guiche is healed, I'm going to put a chain between the two rings and then I can tug and pull."

"Sir." Montana didn't give breath to the word, but he

heard it nonetheless.

"Yes, I like the idea, too." Leaning over, he tongue Montana's other nipple, pushing at the barbell.

Montana's breath sped up, coming in quiet, yet harsh little gasps. Billy hummed, his hand roaming over Montana's body. Ribs, belly, hips, and thigh, he explored and stroked. Montana melted into the mattress, seeming almost asleep. Billy's fingers slid between Montana's thighs and encouraged him to spread his legs.

"It aches a little."

"I'm not going to play with it today." He did touch it, though, just briefly. It was hot from Montana's skin, but smooth and foreign. Neat. And when he moved it, his boy moaned. It was going to be so much fun to play with. He moved it one more time, and then let his fingers drift down past it.

Montana's ass cheeks clenched, then relaxed, like they were trying to tempt him. Moaning happily, he slid his fingers along the heat of Montana's crack, his fingers lingering over the wrinkled flesh of Montana's hole. The tiny hole was soft, hot, and he pushed the tip of his finger in, teasing. He loved the way Montana felt inside. Hot and tight and all his.

Montana began to rock, began to move on his finger. He pulled his finger away immediately, moving to cup Montana's balls instead. Montana's low moan was a clear complaint.

Bending carefully, he kissed the very tip of Montana's cock. "I didn't say you could move."

"You didn't say I couldn't." Smart boy.

"That's right. And I'm not punishing you for doing what you weren't told not to." He kissed the tip of that beautiful cock again. "Now I'm telling you, no riding my fingers."

Montana whimpered, the sound soft, deep. This time when he kissed Montana's cock, a bead of pre-come slid from the tip. He licked it away, groaning at the salty flavor.

"I want you." Montana moaned for him, softly.

"Good." He grabbed the cock ring, grinned up at Montana. "I want you, too."

"You want me to what?" Montana teased.

He chuckled and bit at Montana's hip. "I want you to go crazy with need. To lose your mind in all right ways and find your subspace."

"What is that, really? Are you going to help me?"

"It's a place where there's peace, where you feel good. You've been there before. And yes. I'm going to help you." They would go over this until Montana trusted himself, believed in himself enough to believe he had it right.

Billy slid his fingers along Montana's cock, then the ring, teasing the silky flesh.

"Peace." Montana's eyes closed, his boy smiling.

"It's a good place, love."

He kept running his fingers and the cock ring along Montana's prick. The long, thin cock jerked, drops leaking onto Montana's belly. He bent to lick them up, the taste so good across his tongue. He could eat Montana right up. Montana's hips jerked, rolled up toward his mouth. He turned his head enough to take a quick swipe from the head.

"Fuck. Oh, hot."

"Yeah. It is." He took another swipe and then scraped his teeth along the same path.

Montana pulled away, then pushed back, grunting softly. He'd known Montana would like that. He did it again, teasing softly and then scraping roughly. Montana tugged on his ropes a bit, the low cry sweet as hell. He took the cock ring and slid it onto Montana's prick. He wrapped a second one around Montana's ball sac, then connected them with a pretty leather band.

"God, you look amazing." He bent and nuzzled the trussed-up balls. The velvety-soft skin wrinkled, drew up for him.

He breathed in deeply, loving the smell of his lover, the way need strengthened it. So many lessons they could learn together. So many. He spread Montana's legs wider, admiring the glinting gold ring buried in that very private flesh. He was going to make his boy aware of the pleasures that tiny hole could bring him, make his sweet lover feel more than any drug ever could.

He blew on the flesh around the ring. Montana bucked like he'd touched that sweet skin with an electric shock. Oh, fuck, yes. He blew again, his fingers sliding slowly up along the inside of Montana's thigh.

"Fuck..." Montana arched, pulling away from him.

"No, no, you stay right here." He pulled Montana back down and blew some more, his fingers reaching Montana's ass and teasing his hole.

"You make me crazy."

"I try." He pushed one finger inside. Montana's hole clenched, squeezed his finger. He wiggled his finger, pushed it deeper. Montana grunted, tried to pull away. He put his hand on Montana's belly. "You stay right there."

"Billy..."

"I'm here." He fucked Montana with his finger.

"I have to move."

"No, you don't."

"I do, too, damn it." That was a growl.

He slapped Montana's ass. "Do not."

"Fuck." Montana jerked, stared at him, challenging

him. "Ow."

He snorted. "Ow? That didn't sound convincing." He spanked Montana again.

"Fuck you. Let me go, man."

"No." He wasn't going to argue the point with Montana—his lover was just pushing because he could, because he wanted to see what would happen if he did. Billy wasn't stopping, though, or changing his plans.

"Why not?"

"Because I'm the Master and I get to decide what we're doing." He pushed his fingers in deep and hit Montana's gland.

Montana groaned, eyes rolling back in his head. Blowing again on Montana's new piercing, he continued to use his fingers to fuck his lover. He couldn't wait until he could really play with the guiche. Montana tried to not move, Billy could tell, but the sensations won over control. He gave that sweet ass a gentle swat.

"I'm trying." Montana looked down at him, and he could see the utter need in those eyes. "I'm trying, love."

"Try harder." He leaned in to bite at Montana's inner thigh, hard enough to sting, but not to really hurt.

"Fuck you. I do try. Hard."

"Good. Keep it up." He slid his fingers away and slicked them up before pushing three back inside Montana's body. "You can ride them now."

Montana moaned and began to move immediately. His lips were open and damp, and the look on his boy's face was pure bliss. He pushed his fingers deep, making sure to find Montana's gland often. Every time he did, Montana cursed, yanked against the ropes, and moved faster. He slapped the tip of Montana's prick with his tongue.

"Fuck. Fuck. Gonna come. Gonna come, love."

"No, you're not."

"Uh-huh..." Montana twisted, almost throwing him off.

He pulled out his fingers and lay over Montana, holding his lover down.

"Oh. Oh, fuck. Billy." Montana panted, chest heaving under him.

"No coming unless I say you can." He pointed his tongue and licked around Montana's lips.

"You have to be careful, then, huh?" Montana moaned for him.

He shook his head, grinned. "No, you do."

"I can't be more than I am. Can I?"

"You can be more than you think you are." He pressed their lips together again. "Because you are amazing."

"I'm not. One day you'll figure that out."

"You are. And one day you'll figure that out." He rocked down against Montana.

"Hot. You're so hot, Billy."

He bit at Montana's lips. "And you're on fire."

Montana's cock was leaking, dripping against him, between them. Not even the cock ring could stop that. It was sexy, hot as hell, the way Montana needed him. He was going to keep his boy, too. Keep him there and needy, keep him happy and whole. He rolled his hips from side to side. Montana rolled back, nudging up against him.

He nodded. "You can move. You can want. You can need. You can be desperate. But you can't come."

"What happens if I do?"

"Then we do cage training." He paid attention to the effect his words had on his boy.

Montana stopped, looked at him. "And what does

that mean, I mean, exactly?"

"We've already done some. You wear the cage for however long I deem necessary. While I... enjoy your body." Sweet, beautiful torture that Montana had already proven he loved, even if he didn't want to admit it.

"I hate the cage."

"Uh-huh." He looked into Montana's eyes, silently daring his lover to say it and really mean it. He rubbed their bodies together again, that hard, dripping prick not even thinking about going down.

"I do. I don't lie. It makes me crazy, it distracts me all the time. It scares me." Montana's mouth was moving, but so was the long body, rocking up toward him, staying close.

"It also excites you. Just the thought of it makes you hard. You like it when I'm in charge, when I command even your body's reactions."

"I don't know... I... I don't know if I like it." Montana groaned for him, hips moving faster.

"Your body knows." He licked Montana's neck and pressed down hard, stilling Montana's lower body. He was in charge here.

Montana's hips pushed up, demanding that he use more force. His boy had to push, and he had to prove he was strong enough to take it. He slid his knees to either side of Montana's hips and locked his ankles around Montana's shins, holding him still again.

"You're heavy." He could feel Montana's muscles working, feel the strong heart beating.

"Not too heavy." He wasn't crushing Montana.

"No. Not too heavy. I like it. You feel good to me."

He grinned, rolled his hips. "Good." Their cocks slid and leaked between them.

Montana leaned up, hid his face in Billy's throat with a soft, tiny moan. It made him chuckle, but the sound was more arousal than anything else.

"Don't laugh at me." Montana bit him.

"I'm not laughing at you, love. Never at you."

"Okay. Okay, because I don't do that. I try hard, Billy. I try hard to be right."

"I laughed because it made me happy. It feels good, making you moan and hide your face."

"Okay. I like making you happy. I'm learning. I'm learning these things."

"You're a fast learner." He began moving again, rocking. "So smart."

"Smart?" Montana sounded so young, so desperate to believe that.

"I don't lie, either, love."

"No. No, you've never lied to me."

He nodded, kept rolling. "My beautiful, smart boy."

Montana keened a little bit. "Stop saying that..."

"I won't." He humped. "You're beautiful." He humped again. "You're smart." Pressing hard into Montana, he finished with, "You're mine."

"Yours." That was one out of three.

Growling, he bit at Montana's lips, his hips rocking like mad now. He could feel Montana moving with him, tensing, then releasing. "No coming yet," he reminded, biting at Montana's ear this time. Montana's moan was pure need.

He licked his way back to Montana's mouth and pressed his tongue inside. Montana's lips wrapped around his tongue, sucking steadily, firmly. Their hips moved to the same rhythm, their bodies finding just what they needed. He was in danger of getting lost in this, lost in Montana.

He pulled away, pressing kisses over Montana's face as he stilled their movements once again.

"Billy..." His boy moaned, tried to follow him.

"Right here. We need to slow down a little, hmm?"

There was a soft moan, but Montana nodded. "Okay. Okay, I can get that."

"We're going to do this all day long." He licked Montana's lips. "Longer, maybe."

"We'll starve."

"My beautiful, practical lover."

Montana winked at him, took a deep breath. "It's been a long day, Billy. Kind of confusing."

"You don't have to think about anything, love. You don't have to worry or think or do anything but feel and do as I say."

"You say that like it's easy."

"It can be." He started rocking again, so slowly.

Montana didn't answer; he just hummed, the sound soft, satisfied. They moved together, eyes locked, passion and love fusing them. Montana's skin was soft, a touch slick, the fine feel of it fascinating.

"I love you," he said quietly.

"Good." Montana nodded. "I need you, too, huh?"

"I know." He brought their mouths together and breathed into his lover's mouth before kissing him.

Montana's eyes slowly closed. He licked his way into Montana's mouth. So good.

All his.

Chapter Thirty-Three

It was Saturday afternoon and Billy was making him crazy. Crazy. Really crazy. He was frustrated from not knowing what to do and tired from being ramped up and then left hanging. He felt like he was missing something. And it pissed Tanny off.

Billy came into the bedroom, humming and carrying a small bottle of oil. He looked, tugged at the cuffs. He wasn't tied to the headboard anymore, but now the thick cuffs were on.

"You ready for a massage?"

"I need to get up, run around, huh?"

"I think a massage will do."

He closed his eyes and counted to thirty. He'd count to a zillion if he had to before he lost his fucking mind.

"We'll start with your back. Turn over." Billy helped, pushing him around.

Bossy. Billy was being bossy. Pushy. Billy's hands were solid and sure and put him on his belly with little trouble. Then the oil was dripped onto his back, his ass.

"It's slimy..." He wiggled.

"It's oily; it makes my hands move more smoothly over your skin, your muscles." Billy began to massage him, starting at his shoulders.

"Are you mad at me?" The question surprised even him.

"What?" Billy's hands stopped. "Why do you think I'm mad at you?"

"Because..." Tanny sighed, chewed his lip, trying to find the right words. "You feel far away?"

Billy shifted and then flipped him. "I'm right here, love."

"I'm sorry." Jesus, he didn't know when to keep his fucking mouth shut.

Billy shook his head. "No, if something's bothering you I want to know about it. Don't be sorry. I just... I don't know why you feel like that."

"I don't, either, but you're not... you're different and I'm all frustrated and stuff and I'm fucking scared that I'm gonna do something wrong."

"You can't do anything wrong. There is no right and no wrong, just what works for us." Billy kissed his nose. "How am I different?"

He took a deep breath, let himself relax. "You just are. Are you sure you're not mad? About the whole police thing? Because I'd get it."

Billy shook his head. "I'm not mad, love. I swear."

"I would be." Tanny sighed. "Everything just feels weird, Billy. Like I'm off a little."

"We're shifting, love. Moving into deeper submission, domination."

"So do you feel weird, too?"

Billy tilted his head. "Not weird. It is different, but I think I'm settling into it, and you're fighting it a little. You've fought the submission from the start, even though you need it, crave it."

He sighed, tugged at the cuffs. "I don't understand

how to do it right."

"We'll get there, love. And I don't expect you to be perfect."

"What do you expect?" That was what he didn't fucking get.

"I expect you to try. I expect you to be my partner. I want you to find your subspace, to fly more often than not." Billy smiled at him. "I want you to be happy."

"Dork." He caught himself smiling back, leaning up to kiss Billy. "Before, it was different, huh?"

"Before was light and easy and just for fun. And in the end, you didn't trust it. This is strong and good and permanent."

"It hurts inside, that your friends would believe that I'd hurt you. I know it shouldn't. It..." He sighed, shook his head, and let it go. It was over.

"Why shouldn't it hurt? Of course it hurts!"

He shrugged. No, it shouldn't. He deserved it. He was pretending to be real, he was pretending to belong, he was a faker and filthy.

Billy frowned. "What are you thinking?"

"Why?"

"Because your face went funny."

"Funny? Funny how?"

"It just changed. You shrugged and your face changed and I want to know why."

"I... I don't want to tell you." That was honest. He didn't want to say it out loud.

"I think maybe you should."

He shook his head, a ball of... something he didn't know if he understood or not sitting in the pit of his belly. It was a little ashamed, a little needy, a little hot. It was weird.

"You'll tell me." Billy began to massage him again, on the front this time, starting at his shoulders.

That touch felt good, sure, and this time it wasn't irritating at all. This time it was good. "I said I didn't want to, though..."

"You never want to talk. It's important you do, though." Billy's body rolled on his, their balls rubbing.

"You're warm. I like that." See? Talking.

Billy just smiled and continued the massage. Tanny let his eyes close, let himself relax a little bit. The touches slid next to his nipples but didn't touch them. He relaxed more, breathing nice and slow, in time with Billy. The massage moved down his body, thumbs digging into his belly. This low groan pushed out of him, releasing the pressure inside him.

"Mmm, yeah." The massage continued, Billy watching him as the strong fingers moved over his skin.

He kept breathing with Billy, in and out, deep and slow. Every now and then Billy would moan, and he could feel the heat of Billy's cock against his thigh. He wasn't even aroused, just focused on being warm and quiet, only for a minute.

"That's it, my beautiful boy."

"Mmm." He was so good, right there.

Billy's mouth pressed against his, Billy's breath filling his lungs. Another moan left him, the room beginning to spin slowly. Oh... Everything faded together: Billy's touches, his breath, the soft sounds he made. Tanny melted; his breath was Billy's breath, his heartbeat was Billy's. He floated on it, in it. With Billy.

He thought he might have cried a little bit, but he wasn't sure. It didn't matter because it was just salty, not sad. Billy's tongue slid over his cheeks, licking the salt away. Tanny hummed, eyelids heavy, limbs heavier.

"Love you." The whisper filled him, echoed.

He nodded. "Love."

"Yes." More breath filled his lungs, Billy's body solid and strong and hot on top of him.

He hadn't felt so good in... he couldn't remember how long. They rocked slowly together, moving easily. His eyes opened and he stared into Billy's eyes. Billy stared right back and he could see the love there, right there. For him. Tanny took a deep, deep breath, something inside him feeling like it could crack open. Billy's fingers pushed at his skin, rubbing up along his sides. Another one of those sounds left him, scaring him a little bit.

"Shh, shh. You're doing so well, love."

He clung to those words, trusting in them even as Billy kept touching and hurt, raw sounds escaped his throat. Billy nuzzled their cheeks together, licked his lips, licked the tears when they left him.

"What's happening to me?"

"You're finding your subspace. It's a good place."

He nodded. It was a little different, but good. Safe.

Billy kissed him slowly, tongue sliding into his mouth. He opened up, let Billy in. It was so easy to love this man. His sir. The kiss flowed as a part of the flying sensation, so good. They were breathing together again, sensations coming in waves. He had no idea how long it had been going on, but Billy kept them flying, kept him not caring. He could just stay here. Forever.

Billy didn't seem in any hurry to be anywhere else but here, either. He didn't think it could last forever, but Billy sure was making it seem like it could. The kisses and the rocking fused together, became stronger. He began to move along with Billy, pushing just as hard, rolling up into Billy's body.

"Yes, love. Like that."

Tanny nodded, moving faster, loving the praise, the encouragement.

"So good. Make me need so much."

"Yours."

"That's right. You're mine." There was a growl in Billy's voice as he said it.

That made him smile, made the ache in the pit of his belly appear, made him nod.

"All mine. Head to toe."

"Yes." He could agree to that.

"Mmmhmm." Billy bit his lower lip and the easy rhythm sped, their bodies coming together with more force.

Tanny gasped, bucked up, begging for more, needing this. Groaning, Billy gave him what he needed, hips pumping against him.

"S..." His sir. His. He. Oh...

"I want you to come with me."

He nodded, almost sobbing with relief. "Please."

"When I say, love. When I say."

"Anything." He meant it.

"I know. We'll start slow." Billy wasn't moving slowly anymore, though. His hips were coming together with Tanny's in full body slams, moving fast and hard.

"Love. Love. Love." He chanted the word, completely caught up in it.

"Wait for me. Let it build."

Tanny nodded, willing to give Billy anything, hearing nothing but that voice.

"Soon, love. I promise." Billy's cock rubbed against his, so hot and silky.

"I love you."

"Good." That growl was back, Billy's focus on him intense.

"Sir. My sir."

"Yours." Billy's hand pushed between their bodies and grabbed hold of both of their cocks.

"Fuck..." He jerked, tugging and pulling at the cuffs again.

"You wait for me."

"I will. I will. I promise. Please."

Billy nodded, hand working their cocks. Tanny squeezed his eyes shut, fighting to hold on with everything he had. "Good boy. Come now."

His eyes flashed open, not sure if he'd heard right.

"Come."

He cried out, almost screaming as his balls tightened, come shooting from him.

"Yes!" Billy's prick poured out as well, their bodies sliding together with ease.

Soft sobs escaped him, poured from him.

Billy nuzzled his face, raining praise down on him. "So good. I'm so proud of you."

The tears kept coming, but Billy didn't seem worried at all, Billy was right there with him. Billy lay on him, licking the tears from his face, kissing him, touching him.

"Love you." It finally stopped, leaving him melted and empty.

"And I love you." Billy shifted and cleaned them both up before drawing him into the strong arms.

He curled in, resting, so happy. "So good."

"Yeah." Billy kissed the top of his head.

Tanny thought he could just stay, right there.

Forever.

A soft kiss to his nose made him think maybe Billy thought so, too.

Chapter Thirty-Four

Billy made grilled cheese sandwiches with bacon along with tomato soup. Comfort food. Food to keep Montana easy and comfortable. They ate, him feeding Montana. It was slow and lovely and kept the sweet mood between them. Montana's face was relaxed and his boy stayed close, smiling at him, laughing.

It felt good that he'd been able to do that for Montana. Felt good knowing it wasn't the last time, either. His sweet boy had, after two days of fighting, found his subspace. It was a beautiful thing. He fed Montana the final spoonful of soup.

"It's good." Montana hummed over the bite.

"Mmmhmm." He leaned forward and took a kiss, tongue slipping briefly into Montana's mouth. "You are."

Montana pinked for him, smiled. "You spoil me."

"I don't think of it as spoiling. I think of it as taking care of you—making you feel good."

Montana rested one cheek against his shoulder.

"How are you feeling?"

"Safe."

Billy thought that might be the first immediate, honest feeling Montana had ever offered him. "Good. I always want you to be safe." He thought he felt Montana's cheeks heat. "What else do you feel?"

"Happy. Quiet, sorta."

"It's a good place, hmm?"

"Yeah. Yeah, is it okay?"

"It's what we've been working toward. It's a very good place, a good thing."

"Okay." Montana's hand petted his belly.

"We'll do it again. Often."

"It was hard, getting there."

"It'll get easier, love. Until you the day comes that you can get there easily."

Montana nodded against him. "I want to do it right."

"You're doing it very right, love."

"Good." Montana's face lifted for a kiss. "What happens next?"

"We do it again."

The look of desire, confusion, worry, and need warmed his heart.

"How's that plug feel? It's probably time for a bigger one." He'd plugged Montana after they'd finished making love.

"I... It's in me. It's warm."

"Easy and comfortable, too, I'll bet." He stood. "I'll be right back."

He could feel Montana's eyes on him. He grabbed a couple of plugs, one a little larger, one a lot larger, and the lube, then returned. He waggled them obscenely at Montana. One of Montana's eyebrows arched, but his boy grinned. "Plugs. The smaller of the two first, and we'll end the day with the big one." It was almost as big as his cock. They had one that was bigger. He was considering switching to it in the morning.

"Why? Is there a why?"

"To make you feel good."

"Does it make you feel good, too?"

"God, yes." Billy chuckled and looked down at his cock, already more than half-hard.

Montana nodded, and Billy noticed that his boy had pulled the blanket from the back of the sofa and covered up.

"Cold, love?" He could stoke the fire.

"A little. I just... I felt naked."

"Well, you were." He gave Montana a wink and went to the fire, built it up.

"I still am, really. I'm naked under here."

"Yeah." He tugged the blanket away. "I like you naked."

Montana's blush covered his entire belly. Humming, Billy bent and licked the warm, salty skin. Montana's chuckle was soft; it made him smile. He pressed a kiss next to Montana's navel, and another at the start of his name. His. His boy. His love. His Montana.

He kissed his way up to Montana's mouth, tongue dipping in to tease, to taste. Montana curled closer, moaned into his mouth.

"You taste so good." Montana tasted like his.

"Good. I wouldn't want to taste bad to you."

He chuckled. "That would definitely suck."

They smiled at each other, then Montana started laughing for him. God, he loved that sound. Just loved it. They settled together, forehead to forehead, grinning at each other.

"You're something special, you know that?"

Montana rolled his eyes.

"You are. No denying it, there's no point. I know what's true."

"But..." Argumentative boy.

He tapped Montana's lips. "No buts."

Montana's cheeks pinked, but he felt the response in Montana's body.

"You are special. Beautiful. Sexy. Smart. And mine." Montana murmured, but he kept his finger there on his boy's lips. "That's right. Special, beautiful, sexy, smart, and mine. Maybe I should get those words tattooed on you." He'd certainly repeat them until Tanny believed them.

"No... Just yours."

"There's no 'just' about it."

"I'm not smart." Stubborn boy.

He growled, bared his teeth. "You are."

Those dark eyes flashed, challenging him. "Am not." That was hot.

He grabbed Montana's hands and drew them up over his lover's head. He stared into Montana's eyes. "Are, too."

Montana arched against him. "N...not."

He pressed Montana into the rug. "Are."

"No." Montana was right there with him, pushing, watching.

"Yes." He pushed right back, holding Montana's gaze.

"No. I'm stupid. I've always been stupid."

"Nope. I know that's not true—it doesn't matter what you've been told, what you believe. I know."

"I don't read so well. My math is iffy. I took drugs. I killed my sister."

"So you don't have a formal education, most students do drugs at some time or other, and I don't believe you killed her."

"Did you ever use?"

"I smoked a joint or two."

"I don't like marijuana."

He chuckled. "No, I didn't like it much, either."

"No? I like going and going. Speed, racing. Being still is hard."

"I know. It's one of the reasons why I make you do it."

Montana stayed close, kept their eye contact. Billy was going to take this as a win.

"I don't really understand that, I guess."

"I don't think that matters—you don't need to understand it to get to your subspace." Because Montana had been there, in that place, even though he claimed he didn't understand.

"How did someone make that up?" Montana was breathing with him now, completely focused on him.

"Make what up? The whole thing? People needed, people figured out what they needed."

"No, I mean the subspace thing. Someone had to invent it."

"Or find it." He didn't think it was an invention so much as a necessity.

"I don't get it." Montana leaned a little, licked his lips. "Do you have one?"

"Subspace? No, but I can find a place of peace— especially with you."

Billy could see Montana working on the concepts, trying to fit things together and understand, make them things he understood.

"We fly together, hmm?"

"Yeah. Yeah. It's like being high, sorta. Can I ask you something?"

"You can ask me anything you like."

Montana sighed. "How come this is cool but the speed

is bad? I mean, leave out the legal parts. Why is it cool to need you and not the ice?"

"I'm good for you and the drugs aren't." He wasn't going to kill Montana; the speed would have. Possibly sooner than later.

Montana smiled against his lips. "You're sure about that, huh?"

"I am." He had no doubt about that.

"I still feel it sometimes, the need."

"I think you always will."

Montana winced. "That scares me, man. Bad."

"You'll never have to face it alone, love. You come to me when it gets too bad and I'll take care of you. Always."

"Always? No matter what? You swear?"

He reached down and pressed his hand between Montana's legs, touched the little ring. "I do."

"I promise I won't use. No matter how much I need to."

"I believe you."

Tears filled Montana's eyes, but his boy didn't move away. He held that gaze, let Montana see how he felt. One tear escaped, and Montana's breath hitched.

"I love you."

"Love you."

"Good."

He drew his hand along Montana's breastbone, right down all the way to his lover's cock. Montana wasn't hard, not yet. Which was fine—that hadn't been what they were focusing on. At all. He hummed, felt Montana up, enjoying the heat and silk of Montana's cock, the balls loose in their sac. Those long, black eyelashes drooped, Montana's eyelids going heavy. He nodded. Montana could sleep, relax and rejuvenate. He approved.

"Feels so good." Montana took a deep, deep breath.

"You do." He nibbled lightly, giving Montana sensation, but not pushing.

He watched as Montana relaxed, sinking deeper and deeper.

"That's right," he murmured. "Let it all go and float."

His boy. His fine boy just sank into his subspace so well.

Billy closed his eyes, breathed with Montana, and enjoyed the moment.

Chapter Thirty-Five

He glued the end papers, humming under his breath. Once they set, he could brush on the gold metallic ink. The light was changing; there must be a storm coming, but he wanted to get this done now before he looked up, before he worried about it. He was lost in the process—the ink, the glue, the paper, the smells, knowing he was making something beautiful.

"Good afternoon, Margaret. How are you doing today?" Billy's voice rang through the room.

"Not bad, friend. I was just about to make coffee. Your boy's at the work table, creating."

"He looks pretty focused." He could hear the smile in Billy's voice.

"He's brilliant. I'm glad he's home. I missed him." That made him smile.

"You and me both, Maggie."

"I bet. Things seem better, huh?"

"Yeah. We're getting there. No more playing, I promise."

"Good man." He heard Margaret sigh. "Bill, go make this old woman a cup of coffee, please?"

"Oh, you're not old, Margaret. But I'll get you the coffee."

"Old enough. Your boy might need some juice. He sounds a little congested."

"I'm fine, Margaret. Hello, Billy."

"Hey, love." Billy came up and kissed the side of his mouth. "And if Margaret thinks you need juice, then you need juice."

"I'm okay, really."

"He's getting a cold."

"Margaret!" He was fine. He didn't even feel bad.

Billy chuckled and then whispered loudly. "You know she's always right."

"I'm not sick. She's..." He looked over at Margaret and winked. "A crazy old lady."

Margaret's laugh rang out, making him grin. "Don't make me beat you, son."

Billy cut in immediately with, "No, no. That's my job."

Tanny chuckled, but he knew his cheeks heated.

Billy's fingers slid over his shoulder, a brief, warm touch. "Be right back."

"Get back to work, son. You'll lose the rhythm."

"Yes, ma'am."

He heard Margaret's soft chuckle. "Such a good boy. He's got to be so proud of you."

Warmth filled him, and he bent to work harder, to focus.

A little while later, Billy was back, handing Margaret a coffee and putting a bottle of juice next to him, out of range of his elbows.

"Thank you." He still wasn't sick.

"Should I come back in a little while?"

"I've got about five minutes left."

"Oh, I can wait, then." Billy settled on one of the

stools. "How're your knees, Margaret?"

"Okay, for old knees." Margaret chuckled. "I only have to come in a day or two a week, now. He's doing it on his own."

"That's great, Margaret. I'm so proud of how well he's doing."

"I am, too. He's very focused here, now. Not jumpy. Interacting with customers." Margaret was talking loud enough for him to hear, like it was normal to discuss him with Billy. "I'd like to have him take a few business classes, though. Business math, especially."

"I think that's a great idea. We'll look into it. It might be worth it for him to get his GED first."

"Absolutely."

He could feel his shoulders tensing. "I'm not going back to school."

Margaret clucked her teeth. "You need to, son. You have to do this."

"No. I'm finished with this one." Man, he was grumpy.

Billy's hand landed on his shoulder, rubbed it. "We've talked about this, Montana. You finish your GED and you open up a lot of doors for yourself."

"I'm not going back to school where a bunch of fucking assholes can call me retarded. Fuck that."

"See, Bill. I told you. He's coming down with something."

He turned and looked at Margaret. "Because I'm fucking stating an opinion?"

"Montana! Don't swear at Margaret."

"Don't yell at me!"

Margaret didn't say a word.

"I wasn't yelling," Billy told him softly.

He closed his eyes. "Are you ready to go, man?"

"Of course. Goodbye, Margaret, it was nice to see you."

"I'll see you Monday, Tanny."

"No, Margaret. It's Wednesday. I'll be in two more days this week."

Margaret chuckled. "We'll see, son. Take your juice with you."

"Come on, love." Billy's hand was warm.

He grabbed his juice, smiled at Margaret. "Have a good night."

"You, too."

Billy's arm went around his shoulders. "You okay, love?"

"Uh-huh. I'm good."

"You seem a little touchy."

"Do I? I don't mean to be. Margaret was being weird."

"How so?" Billy led him down the block; it looked like they were walking.

"She kept nagging me. You need juice. You need this. You need that. And I just wanted to work and shit."

"Maybe she's starting to feel a little superfluous around there."

"So, I should fuck up?" God, being a real person was fucking complicated.

Billy chuckled. "No, she needs to learn how to let go."

He sighed, rubbed the back of his neck. Jesus, he had a headache.

"Drink your juice, love."

"I'm not sick." He took the bottle and tried to open the cap.

"You're not feeling great, though, are you? You're frowning and rubbing your neck." Billy took the bottle from him and opened it, passed it back.

"I'm not fucking sick." Still, the juice tasted good going down.

Billy frowned as he watched him drink. "What's the big deal if you are?"

"I'm not, though." He was just tired of feeling like everybody knew fucking everything but him.

"You're awfully touchy."

He sighed, rubbed his neck again, and tried to be nice. "How was your day?"

"Not bad. I got a couple articles written, picked up the groceries. There's soup on the stove when we get home."

"Soup? What kind of soup?"

"Beef and barley. From scratch."

"Oh, wow."

"Yeah, I was feeling adventurous. Turned out good, too, if I do say so for myself."

He loved that, and it sounded so good. "Cool."

Billy smiled and took his free hand, walking with him. "I thought we could get busy after we ate."

He chuckled, bumped their shoulders together. "Did you?"

Billy grinned and nodded. "I did. A nice hot meal, not too heavy, and an afternoon of delight."

"Sounds good." He rolled his shoulders, trying to make the last bit of the tension go away.

Billy shot him a look. "You sure you're all right?"

"Stop asking me that. I'm cool." He just was a little... tense.

"Sorry, you just seem kind of edgy." Billy kept saying that.

He sighed. "I am, maybe? Fuck, I don't know, Billy. Maybe it's just a hard day."

"Okay. So we'll go home and make it a better day." They were almost there, just a couple more short blocks.

"Yeah. Maybe I need to run around the block ten times."

Billy chuckled and then tilted his head. "Would you like to go running? Or maybe go to the gym? I mean, as a part of our routine. I used to do the gym fairly regularly myself."

"I used to..." He shrugged. "No, I'm cool." He didn't want to think about what he used to do.

"What did you used to do?" Billy always latched on to every little thing.

"Nothing. I don't want to talk about it."

"You know saying that just makes me want to push until you do."

"I don't know what to say to that, man."

Billy nudged their shoulders. "You could just tell me what you don't want to tell me. Save us the whole song and dance."

"There's nothing to say. I used to do stuff I don't now. I don't like remembering before I came out here."

"Well, then, how about we make our own exercise routine? It can be something we do together."

"I... Okay. I could try."

"Would you like to do something at home, at a gym, go jogging, something else?" Billy grinned. "I'm easy."

"No stupid classes."

"Stupid classes? Like what?"

"Aerobics or stuff. I don't want to look stupid."

"Everyone looks stupid doing aerobics. Yoga and that dance crap, too." Billy grinned at him. "We could run, though, if you wanted. Go jogging a couple times a week."

"Okay." He imagined Billy would forget about it, anyway.

They got home and Billy let them in, hand going to the small of his back to guide him into the kitchen. The place smelled really good. He inhaled, humming softly.

Billy dished up a couple of bowls of soup and two glasses of milk, putting them both on the table.

"Thank you." He sat, spooned up a bite, sniffing it as it cooled.

Billy came to sit next to him, smiling. Billy looked happy. He leaned over a little, resting for a second against Billy.

"Mmm." Billy kissed the top of his head.

God, he was tired, deep down, all of the sudden.

Billy pushed him back into a sitting position. "Are you sure you're okay, love?"

"Yeah. Yeah, no worrying."

"You seem off today." Billy chuckled. "Sorry, I don't mean to keep harping."

"It's cool. I just..." He shrugged. "Let's eat."

"You just what?" Billy asked casually, taking a mouthful.

"I don't know. I'm sorta... it's not tired, it's not feeling bad. My skin doesn't fit."

"Like you're coming down with something, or like you're out of sorts and need your Master to beat you?"

He stopped, really thought about it. This was important to Billy, to be honest. Sure.

"I don't want to be sick."

"No, being sick sucks. If you feel like you might be getting sick, though, there are things we can do to increase your odds for not getting sick."

"We can?" He reached out, took Billy's hand. It felt

good to let Billy help him.

Billy's fingers twined with his. "Sure. Lots of liquids, the soup's good for you. Some folks swear by garlic, but I think that's mostly because no one will go near you, so you don't catch whatever they have."

He chuckled, took another bite of his soup.

"Lots of rest, too."

"I have things to do."

"Taking care of yourself is the most important thing you have to do."

"No, it's not." Taking care of Billy was much more important.

Billy frowned. "What do you mean, it's not?"

"Taking care of you is way bigger."

"Oh." Billy got a goofy smile and leaned in to kiss him softly. He found himself sliding over, pushing into Billy's lap. Billy's arms slid around him, held him close. "Taking care of yourself is part of taking care of me, hmm?"

"We should eat our soup." Billy felt so good.

"We should. Not eating isn't going to keep you from getting sick." Billy reached for his spoon and scooped it through the soup before holding it up to his mouth.

He opened up, humming as he swallowed. "It's so good."

"I'm glad you like it." Billy fed him another spoonful.

"I do." He melted into Billy.

Billy rumbled, the sound happy, and continued to feed him mouthful by mouthful. He found himself dozing by the end, warm and relaxed and surprisingly happy.

Billy pressed the glass of milk to his lips and then whispered, "You want some dessert? It's crème caramel. Well, from a mix."

"What's that?" He drank the milk, licked his lips clean.

"Custard stuff with caramel sauce. It's yummy."

"Like pudding?"

"Thicker than pudding."

"Mmm." He nodded, but he didn't get up. Billy was warm.

Billy chuckled and stood, arms wrapped around his ass so he didn't fall to the ground.

"Billy?" He held on, eyes wide.

"What?" Billy went around to the counter and nodded at the little dessert dishes. "Grab those."

He snatched them up. "Got 'em."

"Let's go eat in the living room." Billy carried him out and half sat, half fell onto the couch.

"Careful!" He chuckled as they bounced.

"It was farther down than I thought." Billy rubbed their noses and then settled him more comfortably.

He sighed and cuddled in. Billy grabbed one of the desserts from him and fed him his first bite of crème caramel. It took him a minute to decide if he liked it. It was so different from anything he'd had before. Billy put the next spoonful into his own mouth, eyes closing, a low moan sounding. Tanny watched, smiled. That was like sex. Billy looked at him from beneath heavy-lidded eyes and offered another spoonful.

"You go ahead." It was way cooler to watch Billy.

"You don't like it?" Billy pouted, but then he took another spoonful and the bliss of the dessert took over.

"I love how you like it."

"It's a favorite." Billy took another spoonful, proving that. The moans were amazing, as was the look on Billy's face.

He reached down, fingers tracing Billy's abs. Billy's moan got deeper. "I want..." He wanted to suck Billy, just to taste and relax, to help make Billy feel good.

"What?" Billy licked his lips.

"I want to... You. I want you."

"You have me, love. I'm all yours."

Tanny nodded, worked open Billy's jeans. "I just... You have your dessert." He'd have his.

Billy chuckled, legs spreading for him. "Are you saying I'm your dessert?"

Tanny's cheeks burned. "Uh-huh."

One warm finger slid over his features. "I like that."

He slid down to kneel on the floor, cheek rubbing over Billy's crotch. Billy groaned, both hands sliding over his head, dessert clearly forgotten. It was easy to fish Billy's cock out, nuzzle and lick and lap at it. Billy moaned and made sweet little noises for him. Billy tasted good—salty and male, and he felt warm and solid.

"Feels good, love."

"Tastes good."

"Good." Billy cupped his cheek, stroked his skin. "Don't stop."

He nodded. "I won't." Tanny let his eyes fall closed as he took Billy in, began to suck and moan.

"Damn. Yes. Montana." Each word sounded like it was being dragged from Billy's throat. No one else called him Montana. Only his Billy. His sir.

Billy's prick grew harder in his mouth, hotter. Tanny sucked harder, lips tight around the shaft and pulling hard. Billy's hips jerked, pushing his cock in deeper. He moaned and sucked, throat working.

"Yes," murmured Billy, hips picking up his rhythm, pushing the hard cock into his mouth over and over.

Billy. Billy. Billy. He loved. He pulled harder, swallowed eagerly.

His sir's fingers wrapped around his head, Billy's hips thrusting, pushing the thick cock deeper and deeper. "Montana. Soon."

Yes... He relaxed his throat, let Billy in deep.

"Yes!" Billy's hips snapped sharply several times, and then heat flooded his mouth and poured down his throat.

Swallowing, he took every single drop.

Billy's fingers slid through his hair. "Love. So good."

He moaned, tongue cleaning Billy off. Billy kept petting him as he did it, sweet sighs coming from his lover. Tanny settled, cheek on Billy's thigh as he stretched out on the sofa.

"You good?"

"Mmmhmm." He was. Really.

"Good." Billy's fingers kept petting him, and it was warm and quiet and so relaxing.

"Love." His eyes were getting heavy.

"Yeah. Love you, too."

"Cool."

Chapter Thirty-Six

Billy let Montana doze at his knees for awhile. It did seem that his lover was coming down with something—be it a cold or a headache, something. Plus, Margaret had an uncanny sixth sense about that kind of thing. Like how she knew when a storm was going to roll in, only not knee-related.

Or maybe it was. Who knew.

At any rate, he figured it couldn't hurt for them to relax and take it easy for a day or two. Montana was such a mixture of peace and fury; it fascinated him.

He figured they were going to have to have a discussion about school. He knew Montana could finish his GED at home, going to school over the Internet. Maybe with that under his belt, he'd feel better about taking business courses. Just the basics, so he had a better handle on that end of the business.

Somewhere in Montana there was a deep-seated belief that he was worthless, stupid, and Billy wasn't going to have any of it. If it took the rest of his life, he'd change that. He stroked Montana's head; he was a determined man and could face his lover's stubbornness head on.

His boy smiled, stretched. There were times already when they were there, when Montana lost everything but the now.

"You okay? Dozed off."

He chuckled and nodded. "You looked very cozy—I didn't want to disturb you."

"Sorry. It was nice."

"No sorry necessary." He tugged Montana up to give his lover a soft kiss.

"Mmm." Montana leaned against him, pressed close.

"You're in a better mood." It was nice when Montana was warm and happy.

"I just needed some rest." Montana sighed.

He kissed the top of Montana's head. "Which you've had now. So we can talk about getting you a piece of ID." Montana was going to need it for his GED, among other things. It was long past time for them to get it.

"Why?"

"Because you need one."

"I don't even know how to start."

"We call the state and find out what we need to do to get you one."

Montana sighed. "Okay."

"What have you got against getting ID?"

"Nothing. It just... It makes things real. Everything keeps getting more and more real."

"Real is good, love. I'm real. What we have between us is real."

"I just... I don't know."

"What don't you know?"

Montana frowned. "Why are you always asking me questions?"

"Because you never volunteer anything."

"What does that mean?"

"Oh, love." He kissed Montana softly. "You keep

everything so tightly inside. So I ask questions because I want to know you. Inside and out."

"What about the ugly parts? The nasty parts?"

"All the parts."

"I need to keep things inside. I need to remember why I have to be good."

"You don't have to be good to make me happy."

"I have to be good to deserve you."

"You deserve me because you are you."

Montana shook his head. "No. I suck."

"Mmm, yes, you do indeed. And you're very good at that, too."

Montana chuckled, swatted him.

"It's true." He gave Montana a wink and pulled him closer. "I think you're great."

"I think you're a little crazy."

"Gee, thanks."

Montana chuckled. "How else could you explain how much you love me?"

"You think I love you because I'm crazy?"

"I think you'd have to be. You could have anyone on earth, and you want me."

He couldn't decide if it was horrifying or wonderful, the way Tanny adored him. "You're the only one who I want."

"I know. It's like... magic."

"I won't argue with you there. You're my magic." He did like the way that sounded.

"No. No, I'm your boy." Montana's cheeks went a dark, harsh red.

He groaned, his cock jerking at the word. "Yes, indeed. You are. My. Boy. Mine."

Montana's eyes were fastened onto his, the air suddenly

charged. "Yeah."

"My boy, to do anything I want with."

"So long as I don't have to go to school."

No. No, there were no qualifiers. He shook his head. "You're my boy no matter what."

"I... I want... I want you to prove it."

"Right here, right now?"

"Yes. I... I..." Montana stopped, took a deep breath. "Yeah."

"I can do that."

He tilted Montana's face again, taking the sweet mouth hard. Montana's eyes rolled, his hands gripping Billy's shoulders. He dragged Montana up into his lap, fingers searching his lover's skin. Montana moaned against his lips, pressed closer.

"You come when I say so." He looked into Montana's eyes, made sure his lover knew he meant it.

"Or what?" Montana was excited, focused, with him.

"Or you wear the cage for a month." It was always the same threat, but then, it was an effective one.

"A month?" Montana's eyes flew open. Billy could eat him alive.

"That's right. So you'd better come when I tell you to. Not a moment before and not after."

"Okay... I'll try."

"No. I know you can do it." He started pulling Montana's clothes off.

"What are you going to do?"

"I'm going to make you fly."

"Okay." Montana nodded. "I want to be yours."

"You already are." And he was going to make sure his boy knew it for a couple of days. Margaret had already given her nod for time off.

He stripped Montana naked. "Stand in front of me."

Montana stood, unashamed, proud, perfect. Groaning, he reached for the ringed nipple, tugging on the little piece of jewelry. Montana went up on tiptoe, rocked toward him.

"Beautiful." He moved to the other nipple and twisted the barbell a little.

"I..." Montana's cock started to fill.

"Yes?"

"I don't think I am."

"I do. I know you're beautiful and special and smart and amazing and all mine."

"I'm all yours."

"That's right." The growl started from his toes and pulled all the way up into his throat.

He cupped Montana's balls. Montana's sac tightened, wrinkled against his palm. Holding Montana's gaze, he slid his fingers in behind the sweet balls, searching for the warm, smooth flesh beyond them. The ring was there, solid, warm, smooth. Groaning, he tugged on it gently. Montana jerked, went up on his tiptoes.

"So beautiful." One day Montana would see himself the way Billy saw him.

Montana moaned, legs spreading wider.

"I'm gonna play you all day long."

"Play me?" Montana shuddered.

"Yes. Wind you up and bring you back down. Make love to you until you can't breathe. Not let you come until you're sure you can't possibly hold back for another second."

"So mean." Montana moaned, leaning closer to him.

"That's me. Cruel and evil. Mr. Meanypants." He winked, bit at Montana's left nipple.

Montana groaned and jerked, arched up toward his lips. "Fuck."

"Eventually." He wrapped his lips around Montana's nipple and sucked, his tongue playing with the ring. Montana's hands tangled in his hair, his lover bucking. "Wanton lover." He loved that Montana had that quality now, that he needed so beautifully.

"Just want you."

"I like the way that sounds." He nibbled Montana's other nipple.

"You like to bite my nipples."

Yes. Yes, he did. "I do." He bit down again to prove it. That sweet, swollen bit of flesh throbbed in his lips. He flicked the tip with his tongue and then slapped at the barbell. Montana's hips began to rock, the scent of pleasure strong in the air. "No coming unless I say so." His reminder was little more than a growl.

"Uh. Uh-huh." Montana stepped away, breathing hard.

"No, no, no." He pulled Montana back. No coming didn't mean no touching, no loving.

"You keep saying no..." Montana pressed close.

"Then maybe I should just shut up." He brought their mouths together, kissing Montana deeply.

Montana moaned for him, opened beautifully, the need and hunger right there. His fingers returned to Montana's nipples as they kissed, pinching and stroking, deluging Montana with sensation. His boy stepped closer, straddling his thighs.

"Cheeky boy."

"Hmm? You like me close."

He chuckled. "I do. But that's not the point." His sweet boy looked confused, curious. "I'm in charge, hmm? You're my boy and I'm the Master. I decide if you should straddle my thighs or bend over them."

"But, you like this..."

"I do. But it's not always about what I like or just getting off. It's about making you fly, about proving you're mine."

"What do you want me to do?"

He gave Montana a soft kiss first. "Stand back up, love. You can move into my lap when I tell you. If I tell you."

"Okay." Montana nodded, head ducked, hiding inside himself.

"No, that's not okay." He raised Montana's chin, made his boy look at him. It took longer than he'd anticipated, but he was patient and those dark eyes met his. "I love you. And I love your enthusiasm, your willingness to please me, to pleasure me."

Montana pinked, eyes searching his.

"You're new to this—just because I correct you or tell you not to do something doesn't mean you are wrong or bad or stupid. It only means I'm moving you in a different direction, teaching you something new, some new way to be my boy."

"It's a little weird, huh?"

"Maybe a little. Mostly it's sexy, wonderful, exciting."

"Exciting." Montana smiled, the look a little shaky.

"You remember that scared feeling in your belly when you were racing? Do you feel it now?"

"I..." Montana nodded, cheeks on fire.

"That's how you knew you were alive, that's the feeling you were chasing when you got high and here it is, right here in our home when I tell you what to do and you obey your sir because you are my boy."

"I... I... I need to..." He could see Montana's heart pounding.

"You need to kneel and put your head on my knee and just be for a moment."

"I'm freaking out." Montana knelt down, beginning to shake, cheek on his knee.

"This is a safe place to do that, Montana." He began to stroke Montana's head. "Safe." Montana's fingers curled around his ankles and his boy held on, trusting him. He stroked his hands through Montana's hair. "Breathe, love. Just close your eyes and let everything go except for the way we smell together."

He watched those amazing, breathtaking scars move as Montana took a deep breath, sighed, then did it again.

"That's it, love. This place is safe. This place is ours."

"Ours." He could see Montana's eyes close.

"That's right. The home that we built." He drew circles and spirals on Montana's scalp.

"That makes my heart ache. Not in a bad way."

"That's a good thing, then." He bent and kissed the top of Montana's head, hand reaching to trace the scars on Montana's back.

Montana tensed, but only for a moment, then his boy let him touch. He traced his way down over the scars, learning them again. His boy was so strong. So fucking strong. If only Montana realized it.

"They're ugly, but they feel good when you touch them."

"I don't find them ugly at all." He continued to map them, pouring himself into the touches.

"I don't want to cry." No, Montana wanted to bury all his strong emotions, especially those he considered negative.

"Crying can be cathartic."

"What does that mean?"

"Healing. You know how bleeding cleans out the cut? Well, crying can do the same thing with emotional dirt. Things that get left inside fester."

"Emotional dirt..." Montana breathed in, the act a little shaky. "Okay, yeah. I get that."

"Good." His love wasn't stupid at all.

He kept touching Montana's scars, fingers exploring every inch, every ridge and bump and smooth spot. His boy. "So beautiful." He could feel the peace right there for them.

"Yours." The tears came after that, silent, steady.

"Mine. Every inch. Inside and out. I'm so lucky you're mine." He kept murmuring, gave Montana his voice to hold onto.

Montana stilled, relaxed and easy, quiet and happy and close. Breathing with him.

If this didn't prove Montana was his boy, he didn't know what would.

Chapter Thirty-Seven

There was something wrong with Billy. He knew it. Knew it. Tanny didn't know what he'd done wrong, but Billy wasn't letting him in during showers, wasn't coming to bed. It had been going on for a couple of weeks, and he didn't know what he'd done, but he was sorry. Real sorry.

He started staying at work, focusing on learning everything he could, being perfect, making money so that... He forced himself not to think 'he'd be okay if Billy threw him out,' changing it to 'he could help Billy more, take the stress off.'

Margaret had left hours ago, but the store was open until nine, so Tanny just stayed.

"Montana! Do you know how worried I've been?" Billy's voice shot across the room, his lover suddenly right there.

He looked up, biting back his immediate snarl. "I was working. You haven't been home."

"No, I've been... working on a project."

"Me, too." He looked back to his book, forced his hands not to shake.

"I was worried when you weren't home."

"I'm okay." He frowned, sighed, then put his blade

down. "You know what? I'm not okay. You're acting weird. You're stressing me out. You're making me scared and you're hiding shit and I'm mad at you!"

"Oh." Billy sighed and sat on Margaret's stool.

"Am I... am I doing it wrong? I'm trying, Billy. I'm trying so hard to do this thing with you, to be right." He took a deep breath, then continued as fast as he could. "If I'm not, and you want to do it with someone else, I'd understand. I just... You're my home, huh? And I want to stay with you, no matter if you need somebody better at the sex stuff, because nobody's going to love you like me, not with their whole heart." God, he was stupid.

"What? No. No." Billy shook his head, took his hands. "I've never been happier than I am with you. All that stuff about commitment, the ring I gave you, did you think I wasn't telling the truth?"

"I know you were. I thought things were going so good and... What did I do wrong, Billy?"

"You haven't done anything wrong, Montana. Nothing. I promise. Everything is fine."

"Then what's wrong? You've been so weird."

"I'm sorry I've worried you." Billy took his hand. "Come home and I'll show you."

"Promise?" He took Billy's hand. "I just want to be right with you."

"You are, I swear you are." Billy brought his hand up and kissed it. "I've been planning a special surprise."

"What surprise?" He didn't know that he liked surprises.

"You'll see when we get home." Billy tugged on his hand. "Come on."

"Okay..." He nodded, following behind.

Billy'd driven and they climbed into the car. It was as

they pulled out into traffic that he noticed how stiffly his lover seemed to be sitting.

"What's wrong with you, Billy? Did you let somebody hurt you? Did something happen?" He was so tired of this, so fucking worried.

"It'll all be explained when we get home. I didn't think... I'm sorry I worried you, love."

"You don't have to lie to me. Whatever it is, I'll help you."

"I'm not—" They pulled up in front of the house, the trip always so quick when they drove. "Come on upstairs."

"Okay." Okay. Whatever it was, it wasn't about him. He could go with it.

They got upstairs, and Billy brought him to the living room and sat him down on the couch. Billy looked... sheepish. "This isn't how this was supposed to go."

"Just talk to me. Please. Please, I'm so worried."

"All right." Billy started taking off his shirt.

He drew his legs up under his chin. Waiting. Whatever it was, he'd be cool.

Billy slid off the shirt and stood facing him. "I wanted to do something for you. Like your guiche for me. A statement of commitment and love that was permanent."

"Okay." He was beginning to shake. What had Billy done?

"I love you." With that, Billy turned around.

Tanny stared. "I... What... What is it? What did you do?"

"It's your scars. Tattooed, of course. Killian finished it this morning." Billy turned again. "Now we match. Now I'm yours just like you're mine."

"My..." He was going to be sick or scream or cry or...

"But you were perfect, Billy. Your poor back."

Billy sat next to him, taking his hand. "My back is fine. I wanted to do this for you—give it to you."

"Why?" He turned Billy around, tears falling as he touched the poor, hot skin. It felt okay—a little scabbed, not horrible. "Do they look like this?"

Billy nodded. "I know them by heart. I drew them for Killian to work from. They represent strength, they represent life, you."

"I was so worried." He touched each one, fingers as gentle as he could make them.

Billy jerked once, but didn't turn away, didn't stop him. "I'm sorry, love. It never occurred to me—I didn't think how keeping it secret would look."

"I love you, Billy. I want to be enough." He reached for the lotion that they used on his hands when they were torn up, started to lube up Billy's skin, ease the pull.

"You are enough, love. So much more than enough. That's why I did it. And that is the best thing I've felt in days."

"You should have told me. I would have helped you." He helped Billy lie on his stomach, straddled the fine ass, then kept working.

Billy looked back at him, eyes warm and smiling. "I wanted to surprise you."

"I think, right now, surprises are a bad idea. Just the truth."

"You don't like it?"

"Your back?" He looked—really looked. It was fascinating, kind of, and it was going to be there forever. "It's stunning."

"So is yours," Billy murmured.

"Shh." He didn't want to talk about his.

"I got them so you would know I was serious about forever."

"I believed you." He'd even offered to share.

"Good. I still wanted to do something special."

"You did." Billy's entire back was glistening, shining.

"I did." Billy bucked a little, moving him. "Come give me a kiss."

"You should relax. Are you hungry?" He leaned down, kissed Billy's ear, Billy's jaw.

"Not particularly." Billy flexed his ass. "Not for food, anyway."

He reached down, started rubbing Billy's ass, fingers digging in.

Billy groaned and pushed up into his massage. His eyes kept watching the scar... ink. Were fascinated by them. It. Whatever. Was this what Billy saw when he looked at Tanny's back? He didn't know what to think about it. He didn't know how to think about it. But... it wasn't ugly.

It was still Billy, and Billy had done it for him.

"Love you, huh?" He kissed Billy's shoulder.

"Yeah, I know." Billy turned onto his side and brought him in for a proper kiss. "I love you, too. So much."

"Okay." He pushed into the kiss, letting his worry and stress and fear out.

Billy's hand wrapped around his skull, tilting his head a little to the left so Billy could take the kiss even deeper. Tanny looked at Billy, whimpering softly, needing this more than anything.

"I'm sorry," Billy murmured softly, lips resting against his. "I never wanted you to worry for even a second."

"It's okay. It's okay. I just... This is all so intense, so important, and..."

"It is." Billy nudged their noses together. "Next time,

you tell me right away if something is bothering you instead of worrying on it."

"I'm just starting to need this..." Tanny breathed the words into Billy's mouth.

Billy shook his head. "You're just starting to realize that you need it. And I promise you—you have it. No one is taking it away from you. No one."

He kissed Billy again, the touch soft, gentle. Billy's tongue tangled with his, not fighting for dominance, just touching, sharing. It relaxed him deep in his bones, easing his worries. Still kissing, Billy began to work his T-shirt up. Those fingers were solid and warm on his skin.

He chuckled; no one needed him like Billy did. His tattoo was traced and then his ring and barbell were touched.

"I was scared." He hid his face next to Billy's so their cheeks were together. "I've never felt like this before. Never. I need it so bad."

"I'm here for you, Montana. All you have to do is ask, whether by word or deed. We need together."

"I know." He did. That's why he'd been so confused.

"Next time, talk to me, love. See? Talking good."

"I was trying to do things right for us."

"How would talking not have been right?"

"I was just working, hard."

"And I was distracted, so busy trying to keep the tattoo a surprise that I didn't see you. I'm sorry."

"Thank you." He smiled. "You're sure you're not hungry? I'm starving. I could order us a pizza."

"Pizza would be nice, actually. And after that I could spank you. Among other things."

"You might have to sleep. You've been busy." Spank him. Like he was supposed to eat after Billy said that.

"You need me. There will be spanking. Binding. Maybe the cage. We'll see."

This low sound started deep inside him, pushing out. Billy smiled, stroked his cheek.

"I. I. Si... Billy."

"Yes, love?"

"What do you want on your pizza?" He was getting so hot.

By the look in Billy's eyes, he thought maybe Billy knew it, too. "Spinach and feta cheese."

"'Kay." He couldn't move, he was caught.

"We could start now and eat later."

"It's late." He nodded, though. There was always Denny's.

Billy smiled and sat up, reaching for him.

"I want you, bad."

"You do, do you?" Billy's fingers slid over him.

"Uh-huh. I want..." He wanted his sir.

"I know what you need." Billy's fingers worked open his pants, pushing them and his underwear down. The next thing he knew, he was wearing a leather cock ring.

"I... How..." His cock swelled, pushing against the leather. So obscene.

"The tattoo was finished today, and I had lots of time to plan while I waited for you to come home."

"Oh." He shivered, hands running down his body.

"Get naked. I'll do the same." Billy started working off his pants.

He stepped out of his pants, pulled his shirt off. His nipples were hard, balls full and heavy. Billy put a towel on the back of the couch and sat back, hand going to his cock as he watched.

"I..." He licked his lips. "That's mine."

"You think so? I think it's only yours if I say it's yours."

"No." He was sure about that. "You are mine, just like I'm yours. All the time."

"Okay. Yes. But you can't have this unless I say so." Billy kept stroking himself, cock hard in his hand.

"Okay." He met Billy's eyes. "I still want it."

"Good. I want you to have it, but not yet. First, I want you. The lube's on the bookcase. Get it."

"'Kay." He went over to the bookcase, found the little bottle hidden in a box.

When he came back, Billy was still touching himself, but softly now, slowly. "Now get yourself ready."

"For you?"

"Oh, yes. You're going to ride me, but not until after I get to watch." Billy's voice had gone husky, it had that throaty note it always did when Billy was aroused.

He blushed dark, slicked his finger up and reached around, slicking his hole.

Billy groaned. "Turn around so I can see, love."

"It's a little weird..." He turned, though.

"It's hot as hell."

Tanny closed his eyes, touched himself gingerly.

"Tell me how it feels."

"Weird. A little shivery."

"A lot different than when it's me doing that, then?"

He nodded. "You make me..." He shrugged. He didn't have words.

All of a sudden, one of Billy's fingers joined his, pushing into his body.

"Oh!" He arched, stumbling back a little.

Billy's other hand grabbed his hips, steadying him. "Whoa, careful."

"Sorry. Sorry, I..." He grinned, chuckled. "You make

me a little crazy."

"That's not a bad thing. Falling over and hitting your head on the coffee table and passing out when we're supposed to be having wild sex, however, would be a bad thing."

"Yeah. That would kind of suck."

Billy chuckled. "Let's try this again. Bend over and hold onto the table with one hand, and open yourself with the other."

"I... I'll try?" He wanted to do it, but it seemed awkward. Still, he bent, trying to do as Billy asked.

Billy's hand stayed on his hip, helping to steady him. God, how embarrassing. How hot. Billy's finger pushed back in alongside his again, and then Billy licked at his hole, at his finger where it went in.

"B...Billy." He went up on tiptoe, arching, moaning.

"God, you're hot. Put in another finger."

He got another finger in, sliding it inside him.

"Make sure you're good and ready for my cock—you're going to ride it."

"I'm ready. You fit inside me."

"Then come on." Billy slapped his ass. "Get over here."

He nodded, stood, turned to straddled Billy's thighs.

"Mmm." Billy helped, holding onto his waist and guiding him into place.

"This is okay on your back?"

"My back is fine."

"Okay. You want in me now?"

"Take your time, love. Work your way onto me."

"You mean, up and down, huh? Easy?" He wanted to do it right.

"Yeah. Do that." Groaning, Billy tightened his grip

around Tanny's hips. That was good, so he did it again. "Yeah, slow like that. God, it's going to kill me."

"You're a strong guy." He almost grinned. That made him feel really hot.

Billy laughed, the sound husky, needy. He carefully pushed back and took the tip of Billy's cock in, letting it open his hole. Licking his lips, Billy groaned again, and then held his breath. He pulled up, then pushed back again, taking more. Billy's eyes met his, full of love and heat; he could tell Billy was really turned on.

Up. Down. In. Out. He found a slow, steady rhythm. Billy started moving with him, hands pulling his hip, rolling him forward. Soft sounds bubbled up out of him, deep and rich and purely necessary.

"Good." The word floated between them until Billy leaned in and kissed him.

His body opened at the touch, and he sank down, took Billy in. A low, needy moan filled his mouth, Billy's hands tightening even more on his hips. His thighs squeezed as he drove himself up and down. Billy's got into the action, his lover finding his rhythm, starting to drive it. Tanny let his head fall back, feeling every inch of Billy's cock filling him up.

One of Billy's hands slid away from his waist, fingers flicking at his ringed nipple. He arched away, the move pure instinct. Billy's hands caught him and kept him from falling backward. The muscles in Billy's arms stood out as he kept Tanny upright.

"S...sorry."

"S'okay." Billy tugged him close, lips wrapping around the barbell in his other nipple.

His body clenched, squeezing around Billy's cock.

"Fuck, you're tight." The words were barely groaned,

Billy's face full of passion.

"Feels so good." He bucked again, then slammed down.

"Yes! Damn." Billy half growled, half groaned, gaze meeting his. "Keep going."

"Yes..." He did it again, then again.

Billy was soon panting, gasping, and groaning. The strong hands wrapped around his waist again and began to help drag him down over the thick cock.

"So good. So good. Harder. Please."

Billy's hips pushed up, slamming into him now.

"Oh." He nodded, bucking faster, harder, taking more and more.

"No coming," growled Billy.

"Billy..." Oh, fuck.

"No. No coming." Billy kept pushing up into him, though, and he could feel the thick cock get harder. Billy was close.

"Oh. Oh, fuck. Fuck..." He twisted, grabbed his cock.

"No coming." Billy bucked three more times and then filled him with heat.

"Love..." He was going to have a screaming fit. So good.

Billy leaned their foreheads together and panted.

"Fuck. Fuck, I need you."

"I'm right here." Billy slid his hand beneath the cushions and tugged something out from under them.

"Billy..." He moaned, ass working Billy's cock.

"Mmm. That feels so good, love. But are you going to work the plug as hard as you're working my cock?" He sobbed, shaking a little, ass gripping tight. Billy brought the plug up between them. It was thinner than usual, but longer. "See this rounded end? That's going to hit your gland every time you move."

"Billy. Sir." Oh, God. Oh, fuck.

"Yeah, it's going to be amazing. Every time you move." Billy licked the sweat from his upper lip. He whimpered, leaned forward for a kiss. Please. "You beg so prettily." Billy murmured the words against his mouth and then gave him the kiss he wanted so badly.

Tanny's body kept working Billy's cock, his need too big to ignore.

"You need to stop a moment, love. I need to come out, get this in." Billy rubbed the plug along his thigh.

"I ache for you..." He tried to stop, tried to make his body stop moving.

"I'm going to make you ache even harder." Billy's fingers dug into his hips, holding him still.

Panting through open lips, Tanny tried to relax, tried to catch his breath. Billy's hands slid beneath his ass and slowly lifted him up. His body fought, trying to keep the fine cock in. Billy growled at him.

"Let me do this."

"I'm trying. I am."

"Breathe, love. In and out and relax your body." Tanny met Billy's eyes, trying so hard to focus. Those eyes were fastened on him, and he took a deep breath. "There's my boy."

He nodded, the praise making it easier, and he took another breath. Billy kept holding his gaze, kept easing him off the thick cock. It was easier to let Billy help him, move him. The thick cock popped out of him, and Billy was right there, sliding the long plug right in. Tanny cried out, his body jerking, panicking a little, pushing toward Billy, then pulling away.

Billy's lips crashed down on his, the kiss stealing his

breath, his attention. His arms wrapped around Billy's shoulders and he held on, squeezing. Billy kept pushing in the plug, all the way until it nudged his gland.

"S...sir." He gave in. He needed to.

"Beautiful love." Billy jiggled the plug, moved it inside him.

"Please... I can't think. I can't..."

"You don't need to think."

"I..." He twisted, almost pulling away, body overloading.

Billy's hands kept hold of him, though, pulling him against the solid body as Billy's mouth once again closed over his. This time, it was Billy's breath that pushed between his lips. That made him stop, still, his lungs taking Billy in. Billy's tongue tiptoed in on the next breath. He pressed close, arms and legs wrapping around Billy as he shuddered and sobbed.

"I have you." Billy breathed into him and kissed him and held him.

He began to relax, to be able to breathe again. And then Billy shifted him, which made the plug knock hard against his gland.

"Fuck. Fuck. Fuck. Don't. Oh, fuck."

"Hold on, love. You can do it."

A breath sobbed out of him, and the only reason he didn't run screaming was Billy's hands. Billy licked at his lips, placed soft kisses all over his face.

"I can't do this, man. I'm going crazy."

"You can do it. You are doing it." Billy took his hands tugged them behind his back.

He looked at Billy, incredulous, and let himself fight it, let himself test Billy's strength. Billy held his gaze and held onto his wrists as well, not letting go. The struggles just wriggled his ass and made that wand bump into that spot inside him over and over again.

"It's okay? This?" He tugged at Billy's hands. He needed to fight.

"Go for it—I've got you."

Tanny groaned and struggled, letting himself pull and moan. Through it all, Billy held him.

"More," Billy demanded. "I'm not letting go."

"Fuck. Fuck, I..." He growled. "You have to. You will."

Billy shook his head. "Never. I made you promises. I gave you my ring. I wear your scars. I gave you my heart."

He sobbed and nodded. Three things. Just like when he was a kid. Three promises. "I need."

"I know what you need, love."

"Yes." Tanny knew that. Tanny believed it.

Billy looked into his eyes, looked into him. Smiled.

Tanny relaxed, eyes closing, and he let Billy have him.

Chapter Thirty-Eight

God, Montana was beautiful. Absolutely stunning as he submitted, as he gave himself over to Billy's will. Beautiful and sexy and absolutely fucking arousing. Billy was getting it up again already, his cock rallying.

"You're stunning," he murmured.

Montana moaned, but didn't argue. It was time to take another step. His beautiful boy.

"Time to go over my lap now, love."

The plug was in place, Montana's prick was bound—spanking that beautiful ass was next on his list. He saw the full-body shudder, heard Montana moan, but his boy moved. He knew each movement Montana made jostled that plug inside his lover's body. This spanking was going to be something else.

"Fuck. Fuck..." Montana was shuddering, shaking for him.

He ran his hands over Montana's back, tracing the scars. He had the same pattern on his own back now. That seemed kind of amazing.

"I don't... I don't know what to do."

"All you have to do is lie there and not come." He knew it was a tall order.

Montana whimpered. "I don't know if I can."

"You're going to do your best."

"Yes."

"Yes, you are." He rubbed Montana's ass; it was pale and lovely.

"I do, for you. Always."

"I know. Such a good boy." He let his hand fly.

Montana gasped, hips rolling and driving the hard cock against his thigh. God, it was better than he'd hoped. Billy set up a light, even rhythm, smacking Montana's ass. Montana keened softly, hands gripping the couch cushions.

"Hold onto it, love. Hold onto it."

"Trying... So hard."

"I know." He rubbed Montana's ass. "And I'm so proud of you."

"I want you to be. More than anything."

"I am. You're such a good boy. I can see how hard you're trying." He began to spank Montana again, a little harder now, intent on turning the lovely skin a darker rose. Montana whimpered, but the sound wasn't distressed, more needy. "Mmm." He kept spanking, moving his hits down to the tops of Montana's thighs.

"I... It burns."

He knew. "A good burn." It wasn't a question.

Montana moaned, but nodded. His sweet, honest boy.

"I'm not stopping." He made sure to hit the base of the plug now, jostling it inside Montana. That made his boy jerk, slide up against his legs. He kept hitting, alternating between strong and soft hits. Montana started struggling, started trying to pull away. "No, not until I'm done, love."

"I...I can't fucking breathe, man, huh?"

He brought Montana up immediately, shifting his lover into his lap. Montana's cheeks were dark red, eyes watering, the thin chest shuddering.

He growled. "Montana. What's your safe word?"

"I...I... Is that the armpit thing?"

"It is. Do you remember when you're supposed to use it?" They should have gone over this again before now.

"I..." He got a completely blank look. "No..."

"If you need me to stop at any time, for any reason, you use it. You can't breathe? Just say armpit."

"Okay. Okay. I'm sorry, huh?"

"You don't have to be sorry, but you do need to remember to use the word, love. I can't stress how important it is for me to know that you'll take care of yourself and use that word when you need to."

Montana leaned into him, breath easing a little bit. "Because sometimes I say no when I need you not to stop, huh?"

"That's right. And sometimes you tell me you can't take any more when you can. Sometimes you say I'm mean or evil, but what you really mean is please don't stop. So. Armpit."

"Okay. Okay. Armpit. I got it."

"Good." He kissed the top of Montana's head. "Because it's important."

Montana kissed his jaw, nodding. "I promise."

"Okay." He shifted his legs, knowing it had to be moving that plug inside of Montana. He watched Montana's eyes go heavy-lidded. Yes. He shifted again, this time twisting the barbell in Montana's nipple at the same time.

"Oh." Montana jerked, cock bouncing against his belly.

"Oh, yes." He did it again, ready to get back into their space. This time he got a deep, needy moan. "That's right." He took Montana's mouth, his hand wrapping around Montana's bound cock.

Montana's fingers dug into his shoulders, his boy jerking, crying out into his lips. He tapped the slit with his finger. He loved how responsive Montana was, how hungry. He opened Montana's mouth with his own, tongue invading. His finger slipped over the slit in that thick, heavy cock, pressing in. He had a cock ring with a sound built in. Montana would love it. After he'd freaked out over it.

The metal sound was nice-sized—not big enough to hurt, but big enough that Montana wouldn't forget it, would feel every inch. He wrapped his hands around Montana's waist and lifted him. "There's something I need you to get for me."

Montana blinked at him. "Okay?"

"In the blue box on the second shelf."

"Which shelf?"

"DVD shelf by the fireplace. You're looking for the cock ring with the rod attached to it."

"Rod?" He got a curious look, but his boy went, trusting him.

He nodded as Montana held up the right one. "Yeah, that's the one."

"Okay." Montana didn't look.

Billy chuckled. His boy would look when that hot ass was in his lap again. Montana was taking careful, mincing steps, trying not to jostle the plug. It was beautiful. Montana was beautiful. He might have purred like some great happy cat. Montana blushed dark, head ducking.

"No, don't hide from me, love."

Those dark eyes met his, Montana visibly trembling. He patted his thighs. "Come sit."

Montana took a few more of those tiny steps. He reached out and tugged Montana right into his lap.

"It's big." He could feel Montana's heart beating.

"The sensations?" He slid his hand beneath Montana's ass, threatening that sweet ass again.

Montana nodded, rising up a bit to avoid his hand. Chuckling, he chased Montana's ass, pushing at the plug. Montana groaned, stretching as far as he could, belly so tight it rippled for him. He stroked over the lovely muscles with one hand and kept pushing at the base of the plug with the other. The box rattled onto the sofa beside him, Montana's hands landing on his shoulder. He kept playing with the plug, twisting it and bumping it up against that little spot.

"I. I don't... I don't know what to do."

"What makes you think you have to do anything?" Montana just needed to be here, to be with him.

"Don't I?"

Billy shook his head. "You lie back and enjoy it, love. Every second of it."

"Spoil me." Montana leaned in, stole a kiss.

"That's my job."

"You've given me so much." Montana gave him another kiss.

"I have. All of me. Just like you've given me all of you."

"Yes." Those dark eyes met his. "I got the better deal."

"Not from where I'm sitting." He pushed hard on the base of the plug.

"Sir!" Montana almost crawled over the top of him.

He grabbed hold of Montana's hips and tugged him

down hard. "Still think you got the better deal?"

"Y...yes." Stubborn.

"You didn't." He gave Montana a hard kiss and then reached over for the box, pulled out the cock ring with the sound attached.

Montana looked down at it, tilted his head. "Giles had one of those at Oliver's Christmas party."

"Did he? So you know what it is, then?"

"You said... You said it went on his cock."

"On and in." He watched Montana's face.

Montana shook his head, but Billy wasn't sure he knew he was doing it.

"You've never felt anything like it."

"No. No, it will... No."

"Yes. Yes, it will be wonderful. An amazing experience. Yes."

"No." Montana took his wrist in shaking hands. "It'll hurt."

He turned his hand around and twined their fingers together. "So does the spanking."

"I can't." Montana held on. Tight.

"Look at me, love. Right here in my eyes." He waited until Montana's gaze was fixed on his. "I have never really hurt you, have I?"

"No. It scares me. I don't want to."

"All the more reason to do it." He loved that mixture of curiosity and confusion. "Pushing boundaries. That's my job, too."

"I... I'm scared."

"I'm right here and I'll be right here the whole time. It's going to be okay."

"Promise?" He had to love that trust.

"I promise. I will not damage you, Montana."

Montana nodded, arms wrapping around the lean chest. He raised Montana's chin, taking a kiss. Montana's kiss was shaky, tentative, his boy holding himself tight.

"I have you," he murmured, licking his way into Montana's mouth.

"I'm sorry."

"For what? Being honest about your reaction?"

"Well, I sorta meant for being a wiener."

"No, no, I'm sticking the sound in your wiener," he teased gently.

"Is it going to hurt?"

"It'll be uncomfortable, but it shouldn't hurt. Some men love it."

"Do you think I will?"

He smiled and nodded. "Oh, yes. I think you will. I do." He slid his hand on Montana's prick, teasing the slit with his fingertips.

"I..." Montana's belly went tight, the firm ass sliding on his thighs.

He slowly worked the ring Montana was currently wearing off, not worrying too much about being gentle.

"I'm going to freak out a little bit."

"I've never said you're not allowed to freak out a little." He stroked Montana's freed prick.

"Okay." Montana's ass left his legs. "Oh."

"You stay here, hmm? On my lap, close. You can hold on if you need to."

"Yes, sir." Those dark eyes bored into his. "Can I call you sir?"

"Always."

Montana took a breath, nodded, then relaxed onto his lap. He pressed several kisses on Montana's face and then took the sound cock ring in one hand and Montana's cock in the other.

"It's going to tear me inside."

"No. No, it won't." He dipped the sound in the tube of lube and then placed the bottom ring over the top of Montana's cock. "Easy now."

Montana tensed, fingers digging into his shoulders.

He nuzzled their cheeks together. "Easy, love. Easy."

"I'm scared." Montana looked at him.

He held Montana's gaze. "I am not going to let anything bad happen to you, Montana. You know that. Trust me. Trust yourself."

"No. I'm your boy." Montana took a deep, deep breath, relaxing a little.

"That's right. My boy." He put the tip of the sound into Montana's cock. The soft keening noise from Montana made his cock throb. "I have you, love. I have you, my boy." He pushed it in a little farther.

His boy gasped, fingers digging into his shoulders, but Montana didn't move away.

"That's it. So good. Such a good boy."

Montana moaned for him, chin dipping once.

He pressed a kiss to Montana's forehead and then watched as he continued to push the slim, silver rod into Montana's cock. Montana moaned, balls tight, drawn up as his boy fought to cope.

"I have you, boy."

"Promise?"

"Promise."

Epilogue

It took about two weeks before Billy's back healed completely, the soreness and tightness completely gone. He kept Montana busy during those two weeks, filling their afternoons and evenings with lovemaking and pushing. The sounds, his fist, the flat of his hand; Billy explored all sorts of ways to make Montana scream, to send him into a place of focus and peace.

He cuddled closer to Montana and gently traced his scars. Montana sighed, kissed his chin, then leaned in and held on. He smiled and kept touching, stroking. He loved finding this quiet place with Montana.

His cell phone started ringing, the sound irritating, bothering him. He tried to ignore it, but finally rolled over and picked it up, flipped it open. "Hello?"

"M...M...Master Billy?" Someone was crying.

He sat up, pressing the phone to his ear. "Yes? Hello? It's Billy."

"I... I... Help me? Please?"

"Jack? Is that you?" He reached out, fingers finding Montana, touching his lover, his boy.

"Yes. Yes, Master Billy. I... He's gone."

"Who's gone? What's the matter, Jack?"

"M...my Master. O...Oliver. He... he... he's gone."

Snared

CPSIA information can be obtained at www.ICGtesting.com
Printed in the USA
BVOW081357050112

279906BV00008B/1/P